Walter Allen was born in Aston, Birmingham, in 1911. The youngest of four sons of a silversmith, he grew up in a working-class community and won a scholarship to King Edward's Grammar School, Aston (although he felt his real education took place in the city's Public Reference Library). In 1929 he went to Birmingham University to read English, where he made friends with Louis MacNeice and Henry Reed, the latter having been at the same school. On graduating he worked as a freelance journalist and broadcaster, for the *Birmingham Post*, the *Gazette* and BBC Midland, and later for the London weeklies. His literary acquaintance ranged from W. H. Auden and E. M. Forster to the regional writers John Hampson, Walter Brierley, Peter Chamberlain and Leslie Halward, with whom he was linked in the so-called Birmingham Group in the mid-Thirties. Allen's first two novels, *Innocence is Drowned* and *Dead Men Over All*, appeared in 1938 and 1940, and in 1938 he moved to London to read scripts for MGM, where one of his co-readers was Olivia Manning.

After the war, Walter Allen and his wife Peggy (whom he married in 1944) lived in Edgbaston, before settling in London. He contributed to *Time and Tide* and *Penguin New Writing* and reviewed widely, notably for the *New Statesman*, where he later became literary editor. In the Fifties he was also well known for his weekly radio programme 'Talking of Books', his highly influential study *The English Novel* (1952) and the acclaimed *All in a Lifetime* (1959). *Tradition and Dream*, also in Hogarth, was published in 1966, and in 1967 Allen gave up literary journalism to become the first Professor of English Studies at the New University of Ulster. Between 1955 and 1975 he also spent several periods as a visiting professor to American universities. His own account of this full literary life is given in *As I Walked Down New Grub Street* (1981). He is now retired and lives in London.

ALL IN A LIFETIME

Walter Allen

New Introduction by
Alan Sillitoe

THE HOGARTH PRESS
LONDON

To Peggy

Published in 1986 by
The Hogarth Press
Chatto & Windus Ltd
40 William IV Street, London WC2N 4DF

First published in Great Britain by Michael Joseph Ltd 1959
Hogarth edition offset from the original British edition
Copyright © Walter Allen 1959
Introduction copyright © Alan Sillitoe 1986

British Library Cataloguing in Publication Data

Allen, Walter
All in a lifetime.
I. Title
823'.912[F]   PR6001.L6724

ISBN 0 7012 0672 1

Printed in Great Britain by
Cox & Wyman Ltd
Reading, Berkshire

INTRODUCTION

The common man, so called, is rarely able to tell his own life story. Each person has one, but any attempt to tell it, at least in writing, is likely to result in the distortion of the tale and the impatience of the reader. The novelist who attempts the task for him has a harder job than if dealing with the uncommon man, because however much he may be acquainted with the reality of the common man's condition, and even though he may once have been a common man himself, he needs more than the emotional sympathy and dash of sociological reality which is often regarded as sufficient basis for such novels. Inspiration, imagination, and a certain distance are necessary to turn the material into a story which may be read with complete faith in its veracity. Many people may be writers, but few are artists.

When I read *All in a Lifetime* on first publication it was obvious that here was a real story, common though the hero was. Re-reading the novel twenty years later confirms my opinion that it is also the chronicle of an age that has gone and of values that no longer seem to apply. Having induced Walter Allen to let him tell his own story, as it were, Billy Ashted makes a work of art out of his life's journey, which began about 1870 and covered the period – no accident I'm sure – in which Winston Churchill lived and flourished. During that time three wars were fought, and social conditions changed absolutely.

Talking about the book, Walter Allen explained in an interview that '. . . what I had in mind was doing three things; I wanted to write a life of my father, who was dead, and had been dead a few years; I also wanted to write a kind of novel about the rise of the Labour Party; and I also wanted to write a novel about the development of Birmingham. I was conscious of trying to do three things at once. I think I did one thing, but the other things are there, to some extent.'

This is no simple tale which travels from A to Z, however. At the beginning of the novel Ashted, a man of seventy-six, is being looked after by his son Will, who is a production engineer running a factory, and Will's wife Beryl. He flees from their cloying solicitude, and finds his way to the house of his favourite sister. He wants to stay there, but she is unable to look after him, and informs Will, who comes to reclaim him. Ashted discovers late in life that the old in their weakness have no escape from the coils of the family, whether they want it or not, and he is unable to make up his mind as to its virtue.

Sitting back in his son's opulent motor car, like an absconded prisoner recaptured, he recalls how, as a young father keen to teach his son music, he had struck Will across the knuckles with the violin bow because the boy was unable to keep time. He notices the angry red neck of his son, and knows that he too must be thinking about the incident. Will has never forgiven him, because what happened forty years ago seems like yesterday. Only happy times assume their due distance.

As he reflects on the difference between their lives, and on his own early existence, Billy also ponders the life of *his* father. Back in his son's house he begins to write his memoirs, to show that he still has his faculties, and, incidentally, to prove that he can act in a responsible manner (though his family thinks it merely a game to keep himself happy). He sets out to give his life the kind of pattern which defines him as not such a common man after all.

In one sense, these memoirs offer a pattern for an age as well as a single life. In page after page of vivid yet seemingly effortless narrative we are funnelled back through the layer-cake of social and historical conditions. Although England, separated from Europe by the Channel, has had no foreign armies rampaging upon its soil, it has not lacked an exciting history, most of which has taken place overseas. England has also been the balcony from which people watched violent revolutions, and worse, acted out on the mainland. But changes have taken place here none the less.

Ashted was one of fifteen children, and his father, a metalworker much in demand because of the artistic quality of his work, died before the age of forty. Although illiterate, he was no simple person, and Billy inherited his complexities but, because of qualities derived from the mother, not his unhappiness. He is too busy, and intellectually curious, for that. In understanding him, we are never allowed to underrate him. Being a complicated person described in deceptively simple terms, and left with his fundamental mysteries intact so that he remains as solid as someone you once knew, makes Ashted one of the most memorable characters of twentieth-century English fiction.

Musically gifted, he has no ambition to use his talent. He is a bit of a drifter, cultured, amiable, and democratic, a Renaissance artisan of the Black Country. In middle age he takes up the hobby of lens grinding, and likens himself to the great Jewish philosopher Spinoza because, tedious though it is, such work gives time for the gathering of thoughts. In the Second World War he shelters during air raids under the stairs with his wife, and loses his fear when, at the noise of one explosion, he recognises the sound of breaking glass. He will only have to walk on to the street and pick up all he needs for grinding his precious, sanity-saving lenses.

By writing, the secrets of Ashted's life are similarly revealed. He polishes his mind, and recalls what has been of importance, eventually achieving an object through which he can see the truth of what happened – where he went wrong and where the country also went wrong, as far as he is concerned. The tribulations of his family and friends are put more or less into proportion and set to the right scale. Understanding comes to him at last, or as much as can come to anyone in a single lifetime.

George Eliot wrote in *Adam Bede*, 'All passion becomes strength when it has an outlet from the narrow limits of our personal lot in the labour of our right arm, the cunning of our right hand, or the still, creative activity of our thought.' Walter Allen was a great admirer of George Eliot and wrote a book about her. And George Eliot translated Spinoza. It is intriguing to wonder if Allen is calling attention to this connection, and easy to conclude that he was nourished by it.

When Phil, another of Ashted's sons, who becomes an atomic scientist, hears that his father is writing an 'auto-biography' – a word which makes Ashted wince – he says to him, 'You have seen in your lifetime a whole social revolution. You have lived through it. In fact, it's not too much to say that you are in yourself a cross-section of that revolution.'

His father realises what he means: 'There *has* been a shift of power; for the poor the conditions of life *have* changed completely since the days when you and I were children . . .'

Ashted and his life-long friend George Thompson as young men talk passionately about what benefits socialism may bring to the poor. They discuss the ideas of John Stuart Mill, Ruskin and the Webbs, but Ashted decides that the facts 'don't seem so important to me as the emotions they stir up'. If they had been as important, he would now produce only a sociological and political work. This is what his son Phil wants, something which will be a 'footnote to History'. But Ashted is too much of a man – or maybe too much of an Englishman (and a working-class Englishman, one may add) – to dabble in stuff like that. Instead, he works his way inexorably into the centre of his personal experience, which nevertheless mirrors the changing world.

In this he is contrasted to his alter ego Thompson, who believes in propaganda rather than art to influence people's views. The only good 'art' is that which is 'the jam covering the pill of Socialism,' he says. With such a blinkered but all too comprehensible attitude he 'gets on' in a way which Ashted never will. But the reflective craftsman is able to explore himself and his world more thoroughly than the ambitious politician ever could. At the age when his family too readily assume that he is becoming senile, he has little more to look forward to in physical terms. But his mind is collected wonderfully in all its experience and wisdom.

By allowing Ashted to tell his story with such apparent inconsequentiality, Walter Allen also says much about the art of writing fiction, as well as the difficulties and realities of existence. His method reminds me of those litter-collecting men who used to be seen in public parks with needle-tipped sticks stabbing up pieces of paper – in Ashted's case, raking among the detritus of his past and turning what he finds into gold. In the activity of writing he begins to understand himself and others, and goes on honing his life as he once polished his lenses, until by the end of the book we are sorry he cannot continue and that, like everyone else, he is mortal. If one definition of the hero is someone not easy to forget, this certainly applies to Ashted.

The bombing which took place during the war anticipated by some decades another blitz on English cities – that of the planners – whose only merit was that it caused no immediate casualties. A few years ago much of Nottingham was being demolished, and I stood entranced by the mechanism of a ball-and-chain vehicle advancing from house to house, destroying walls and chimney stacks in a mindless but dramatic fashion. Lorries took the rubble away.

Walter Allen grew up in a similar neighbourhood. 'It was purely a working class street, you know. Tenement houses, long lines of terraced houses, not tenement houses, terraced houses.' And much of Ashted's and his parents' lives were spent in such streets, whose plan was being wiped off the face of the earth. People were moved to 'high-rise hencoops' as they came to be called. A great many of these old houses were demolished before their time, and what were thought of as slums are now remembered differently. Some high-rise buildings are already being pulled down. Maybe the name of Progress was taken too much in vain. Everything has its price. To know what it was like to live in such houses and the reasons for their disappearance one must turn to those who set their stories there, and for that one can't do better than read Walter Allen's classic tale of Billy Ashted.

Alan Sillitoe, Wittersham, Kent 1985

1

'My God, what giants!' From her four-feet-ten mother looked up at five-feet-three of Horace and five-feet-two of me, and oh, the awe and astonishment in her voice. She had suddenly realised we were grown up. That was sixty years ago, in 1890, a Sunday morning in the kitchen; Easter it must have been, for Horace and I were wearing new clothes and brand-new curly-brimmed billy-cock hats. Off to church I suppose.

I have never forgotten mother's cry, and it came back to me all over again when I burst in on you last Wednesday week. I don't think it was because of any real likeness in you to mother, but you were always big sister to me and I was surprised to see you so small. You stood in the hall, your hands wrapped in your apron, and 'Billy!' you said, 'Whatever's the matter?' And well you might ask, for there I was with the tears rolling down my face, blarting like a baby. 'Billy! Whatever's the matter?' And I said: 'I can't stand it any more, Lizzie. I can't stand it. I won't go back. I won't go back whatever you say.' But I did of course. You made me; and though I was very angry with you then, now I see that you were right. We sat in the kitchen, and I wouldn't take my overcoat off but just sat there with my bag at the side of my chair. 'You were always the stubborn one, Billy,' you said; 'you were always the one for changing the world, you and your socialism and your free thought. And I bet you haven't eaten a scrap since last night.' And first you made me drink a big cup of Oxo with pieces of bread in it and then you put some cold potato and cabbage in the frying-pan and we had bubble-and-squeak and sausages. I felt much better then, and ashamed of my performances, crying and all that like a child. But still, I won't go back, I thought.

We sat each side of the hearth drinking brandy and hot water. 'Now you tell me what it's all about, Billy,' you said.

And I did, as well as I could. You didn't understand, but that didn't matter. Your life has been much harder than mine, but you have always known your duty and I have never known mine. I say this with all respect, for there is no one, Lizzie, I respect more than you. Well, even if you didn't understand me, you heard me out; and how could you understand me? What I had to say was full of self-pity, but all the same I see now that I was really arraigning the universe. And really you knew that too, for you said, when I'd done: 'Tut-tut! Kicking against the pricks like you've always done!' And then you gave it me good and strong; you were big sister all right—and how, when we were children and you were pushing us out in the mail-cart, Tom and Florrie and me (I never remember being in the mail-cart with Horace or Edwin), you used to clout us and fuss over us and wipe our snotty noses for us!

'Well, you can stay here tonight,' you said. 'You can have Johnny's bed and Johnny shall sleep on the floor, it won't hurt him for once, and when he comes off the late shift he shall telephone Will because I can't, I've never learned how to use the thing, and he'll tell Will where you are, and Will will come and fetch you tomorrow.' Then you said: 'Putting Will to all that trouble and him so busy and important and all; not to speak of all the worry and anxiety for him and Beryl. You ought to be ashamed, Billy, I do declare.' 'But I'm not going back,' I said. 'Oh, yes you are'; and you said it with such spirit that I knew for the first time just how and why you had triumphed over life and all the host of tribulations that had borne down on you throughout your life one after another. Poor old Paul, I thought; he never stood a chance against Lizzie. But I swear I thought it in admiration, Lizzie, for after all you made a man of him where there was scarcely a man at all.

But then, having given me a good clout, you leaned forward and wiped my nose for me. To be exact, you leaned forward and put your hand on my knee. 'You and your Karl Marx,' you said, though why you said it I don't know because I haven't been a Marxist for close on forty years; the first war finished that for me, when I saw how the German comrades behaved, though even so I still think there's much more to old Marx than you'd guess from the newspapers. 'You and me, Billy,' you said, 'we're the last of the old uns. Edwin and Florrie

8

have gone, and Horace—you and Horace were the most alike, but he went after religion while you went after politics and what you called a full life—and Harold and Frank and Bessie of the young ones, and we're almost all there are left, and we are very old, Billy. And when you are very old like we are you become as a little child again. You can't look after yourself any more; other people have to look after you for your own good.'

That made me angry again. 'You're on their side,' I said. 'That's exactly what they want me to think. But I'm not a child, and I won't be made into one. I've got a mind of my own still.'

And that made you angry again. 'Then I don't think much of it,' you said. 'You should have seen yourself; standing on the doorstep bellocking like a great big bull-calf that's lost his titty. I'd be ashamed.' But the nose-wiping followed the box on the ears as usual. 'Don't you see, Billy? It's all in the Prayer Book. Man that is born of woman hath but a short time to live, and is full of misery. He cometh up, and is cut down, like a flower. Any time now, Billy, we'll be cut down. Our mothers and fathers looked after us when we were little, as we looked after our little ones in our turn. Now that we are old and little ones again, it is right and proper our children should look after us. And believe me, Billy, they know best what's good for us.'

I didn't know what to say to this. Put in the Prayer Book terms, translate human life into the natural rhythm of plant life, and I don't know what to say. Though I did notice that when Johnny came home from the late shift it wasn't he who gave any signs of knowing best but you, Lizzie. You weren't standing any more nonsense from him than you were from me. But there it was. When Johnny came home everything went as you'd decided it would. And if you think I bear you any malice you're wrong, dead wrong.

Well, Will arrived in his motor car next afternoon to take me back. If he was any more pleased to see me than I was to see him, he didn't show it. It was very inconsiderate of me, he said; I might at least have thought; God knew they did their best; he didn't so much mind for himself but it was the strain on Beryl, what with the children and all. There was nothing I could say, and the odd thing is, he made me feel guilty. He made me feel like a naughty boy. So did you, Lizzie. But as ever you wiped the tears away. As we were leaving you said: 'Now Billy, you promise to behave yourself.' And I promised, sincerely; if only because I'd realised I was too old for all these capers. And then you said: 'And you write to me every now and then and tell me how you're getting on. Us old uns must stick together.'

That's exactly what I'm doing, Lizzie. Only it will be a thicker letter by a long chalk than any you've ever had in your life before. Because before I'm cut down, if there's time, I'm going to go through it all, Lizzie. I'm going to find out where things went wrong; if they did. I'm going to come to terms with myself and with life. At least I'm going to try.

2

But when I read through what I've put down I see what non-sense it is. Coming to terms with life! As though I'm any more likely to succeed now in doing what I've failed to do throughout my seventy-six years. The truth is, Lizzie, when I wrote that about coming to terms with life I'd worked myself up into a state. By thinking of you I'd taken on something of your strength. But that was yesterday and today's today, and I can see now that though I was trying to be truthful I was projecting something of the feeling of strength I had then into my account of riding home with Will.

Oh, I set out stout-heartedly enough, and all through the drive I felt you near to me, very near, as though you were holding my hand. Will was in the driver's seat of course; I sat in the back. It was where he'd put me and where I wanted to be. Talk was the last thing either of us wished for. He sat driving that machine, the master of it, and I stared at the back of his neck. It was red, I thought, with anger, and I could imagine the set of his jaw and the thin line of his angry compressed lips. And I thought—it struck me suddenly as it had never done before—'Will is a boss!' A master was what we called them when we were young. I felt very small and frightened at that, not at all a giant. He wasn't my boss of course, but still he was a boss, and it made me sad, for the knowledge seemed to get in the way between us: you know, Lizzie, I've been against bosses all my life. Yes, I know what you will say; but good or bad, Lizzie, bosses are always bosses.

It wasn't anything Will himself would be aware of. Being a boss is a natural thing to him. If you mentioned it to him he'd only laugh and say, 'Well, I've got my bosses too,' and start talking about the managing director and the chairman of the board. All bosses together. But sitting there in that luxurious motor, vaguely pondering over the strangeness of life that it should have made me of all men the father of sons who were bosses and drove about in motor cars, I had a sudden intuition. Perhaps I was hypnotised by the red angry back of Will's neck; but I suddenly knew what he was feeling. Oh, I can't say I knew exactly what it was but the image that came into my mind out of the blue as they say stood, I am sure, for his feelings then. And this is very shameful, Lizzie; it's something I'm deeply ashamed of; so much so that if there's a Day of Judgment, as you think there will be and I don't, I know it will be one of the first things God courteously calls my attention to; for I do not see how God, if there is a God and He goes to the trouble of holding Judgment Day, can be anything less than courteous.

Perhaps I was dozing, I don't know; but I found myself suddenly transplanted back to the front room at Harland Street. You remember the house: it was the one dear Rose loved best. She loved the long garden behind it and the little one with the privet hedge in front. It was the only house we ever had with an indoor lavatory, and we had the landlord put a bath in too. The rent was twenty shillings a week, which was a lot of money in those days, more than we could afford; but we managed to stay there eighteen years. Well, there I was in the front room, or the parlour as Rose liked to call it, back forty years, with fiddle tucked under my chin and Will, a boy of ten or eleven, at the piano. You know how I always loved my fiddle, and from the beginning it was always my ambition to have one of the children able to play the Beethoven sonatas with me. All began to learn an instrument some time. Poor Harry tried hard, as he always did, but he never did more than play a passable fife in the boy scout band. Phil was not much better. Tom I set to learn the fiddle; but when I found that his idea of practising was to lie on his back on the hearth-rug in the front room with one leg thrown over the other and to saw away at his violin in that position, I gave him up in anger and disgust. Of course, I have often laughed over this since, it was so typical of Tom, who was always the most carefree of the boys; but at the time I was very angry indeed.

So I am afraid it was Will who had to bear the brunt of my passion for making music. He was by far the most promising of them, and I can thank God that however misguided my attempts to teach him were I did not kill the love of music in him, for as you know, he still plays. But the most curious thing in my musical life is this, Lizzie, that of all the numbers of people I've played with, I on my fiddle and they on their pianos, I've never found any who kept time properly or even understood the supreme importance of time. That is, except for a handful who didn't even know I was playing with them. You'll think that odd; but during the war, when I could find no one to play with me, it struck me one evening while I was listening to Campoli playing with the B.B.C. Symphony Orchestra on the wireless, why shouldn't I join in? So I took down my fiddle and I did; and we played the Brahms Violin Concerto very well together. After that, whenever there was a concert with a violinist on the wireless playing something I knew, I would play with them. So I can honestly say I have played with the B.B.C. Orchestra, the London Philharmonic, the Hallé and the London Symphony, as well as with Campoli, Heifetz, Menuhin, Primrose, Alan Loveday and Ginette Neveu. They were wonderful evenings.

But there was no wireless in the days I am talking about, and having searched in vain for a pianist who knew the meaning of time, I decided to make one for myself who did, and I chose poor Will. In recent years he has been good enough to say to me: 'Well, at any rate, Dad, you did teach me the importance of paying proper attention to time.' But in doing so, I fear I showed myself a terrible task-master; and as we were driving back in Will's car, it all came home to me. As I say, we were in the front room at Harland Street, playing a sonata together. The boy was doing his best, but he had absolutely no notion of time. 'No, no, no,' I kept on saying, 'go back. Try it again.' And back and back and back we went until in the end it really did seem that he'd mastered the passage. I was overjoyed and felt proud of the boy. 'Now,' I said, 'we'll just take it straight through once more from the beginning.' One, two, three, off we went—and the same thing happened as before. 'Time, dammit boy, time!' I shouted, fiddling away like mad. And then I saw the boy's lips puckering; but I wasn't to be put off. 'Time!' And the tears began to stream down his cheeks and then he'd lost the time altogether, and that made me so angry after I had thought we'd at last achieved something that I cried out in a passion, 'No, no, no!' and in my fury brought my fiddle-bow down across his hand.

That was shameful, Lizzie. But the curious thing is this, that as I relived it in the back of the car, I felt all over again my rage at Will's not being able to keep time. I was full of righteous indignation, and it wasn't until I'd quite woken up and was staring at Will's neck again that shame swept over me. And more than shame: a kind of pity, for Will, for myself, and for the human plight, that incidents trivial in themselves fix two human beings into seemingly unalterable positions of fear and hatred and distrust.

I am morally certain, Lizzie, that as he was driving his motor, with his neck flushed with anger at what he calls my lack of consideration for himself and Beryl, it was that episode Will was brooding upon. Emotionally for him I am still the monster of cantankery, the demon for an unreasonable perfection, who rapped him over the knuckles with a fiddle-bow because he was too young to understand the importance of time. I am still his symbol of injustice.

It is a terrible thing, Lizzie. I could protest that it isn't fair, that one ought not to have to pay such retribution for a moment's lack of self-control; but if I am haunted by the unfairness, I'm haunted too by the knowledge that for years and years I have harboured a similar grudge against my own father. I realise now that for years and years I have been unfair to him. Our father, we have all of us always agreed, was a brute, and I think the real drive behind at any rate Edwin and Horace and Tom and myself was to be as different from him as possible. But nowadays, Lizzie, as I come to think about father more and more, I realise that though he often behaved brutally he wasn't a brute. He was simply a very ignorant man who because he was ignorant was cheated right and left. Naturally, when we were boys it was mother's side we took; rightly, for mother had to be protected. We have always been properly indignant for her that she should have had to bear fifteen children in rapid succession on a husband's wage which, though good for the time, because of the demands on it compelled us to live in a slum. No need to remind you, Lizzie, about all that: it was your job for years, as the eldest, to take all our Sunday clothes in the mail-cart to the pawn-shop every Monday morning. I remember you saying, Lizzie—it was before you married, and you were thinking of mother—'Not for me, Billy! Nothing like that for me!' and I have sometimes thought that was why you married Paul, for no one could have been less like father.

Father was an ogre to us. Throughout my life I have had a recurring dream which, unlike most dreams, was simply a transcript of reality. I am a boy of sixteen again, it is Saturday night, and Edwin, Horace and I are waiting in the bedroom at Fussell Street, waiting for father to stagger in, waiting for the worst, waiting for the crash and the blows and the cry, waiting to dash downstairs to protect mother. In my dream I hear the crash and then I wake up sweating, terrified. We were terrified of father; but we felt ourselves called upon to be men and we were ready to act like men. Mother had to be defended. I called this dream a transcript of reality. So it is. And yet you know, Lizzie, reality was never as we feared it would be. In actual fact, father hit mother once, when we were far too young to intervene. It was a dreadful thing to do: we heard it, and it was horrible: it stamped something on our minds indelibly and for ever. But he did it only once, and I have no doubt at all now that he was thoroughly, deeply ashamed of himself. In a sense, though we were right to behave as we did, Edwin and Horace and I took too much upon ourselves. We judged and condemned him with a terrifying certainty. We didn't see—and Horace never did see, even at the end of his life—that father was more to be pitied than blamed; and yet Horace was more like father than any of us, except that whereas father took to drink Horace took to religion. Because of a single unwitting act of father's, we were fixed in one unrelenting attitude towards him.

How he must have suffered. Oh, I know he was obstinate, that he wouldn't listen to us even when we really were in a position to advise him. But think how ignorant he was. I can see him still—and you have to remember he died almost forty years before he reached the age you and I are now—sitting by the hearth of an evening struggling with the evening paper. He wouldn't be beholden to us: we could read, he practically couldn't; and that must have made it worse for him. I can see him still, spelling out the words in the headlines through his magnifying glass. He never got past the headlines. And how ashamed we were of his ignorance; we felt his illiteracy as a slur on ourselves. It was so unnecessary, too: that's what we all said. Horace was the most censorious of us. 'If he was too lazy to go to Sunday Early Morning School to learn to read when he was younger,' he'd say, 'that's no reason why he shouldn't learn from us now.' But father was too proud; I've only ever known one other man as proud: that was Horace. You know what Horace was like. Once when Smithers'—and after all they were the largest firm in the trade and his biggest customer—went to him with a job and said, 'We must have it by Monday week,' he said to their messenger, 'Must? Must? No one says "must" to me, young man; and Mr Smithers may have his work back.' And Mr Smithers had his work back and had to keep it until he sent Horace a note of apology and said 'may we' instead of 'we must.'

That was Horace all over. It was also father, as I see now, when I remember how so often he refused to go to work on Mondays until the boss sent a boy round to beg him to come.

He was proud and stubborn and I think he felt everyone was against him. His own fault? Perhaps. But I can't throw stones any longer, Lizzie, for I see him a sort of shorn Samson, a giant—he was almost exactly the same height as myself!— who was robbed of everything but his pride. That was why he drank. I say nothing against our dear mother, but every one of us as we were born and grew up turned against him. Yet he loved children, and my earliest memories are of how he would laugh when he dandled me on his knee and I tugged at his beard. You say his drunkenness kept us in needless poverty. I know. For years I was bitter because it meant I was never able to finish the schooling I began. And yet I am sure we only encouraged him in his drinking: do you remember how, as soon as we were old enough to write our names mother had each one of us sign the pledge and wear the blue ribbon on our jackets? She was brandishing us in his face. It was enough to drive any man to drink.

You will not agree, Lizzie. You have forgiven him no more than Horace did. But I believe he was an ill-used man, and I believe this because my happy memories of him are all overlaid by that recurring dream. The dream was true to fact. Edwin and Horace and I did wait up Saturday night after Saturday night to defend our mother against something that had happened once, when we were children, and that we were not allowed to forget. We waited for the blows and the cries and the crash; and they never came. Or rather, they did once; the cries, I mean. And we dashed down the stairs, Edwin and Horace and I, with a sort of horrible shrinking courage. It was the moment we had lived for, the moment of our justification, and we knew exactly what we would do. And then at the open door we paused. Mother was crying, 'Don't, Bill! Don't!' and father was cursing and shouting 'Shut your gob, mother!' for, as you remember, he never called her anything but mother. And what was he doing that there should be cries and cursing? He was standing on a chair, swaying, holding up a picture he had bought at the pub, trying to hang it on a nail. And suddenly he so swayed in his drunkenness that he lost his balance and capsized, himself, chair, picture and all. Down he went to the floor, but the providence that looks after drunks was kind to him, for it was as though he were merely falling on to a bed. He hit the floor and immediately, it seemed, he was asleep and snoring. Mother said: 'Let him stay there, drunken pig.' And we all trooped upstairs again, as full of righteousness and moral indignation as he was of beer.

Oh, I grant you, Lizzie: he was a bad father. I, in my resolution to be as little like him as possible, determined to be a good father. So, in the world's eyes, I have been. Yet my son is as firmly fixed in his attitude of revolt against me as I have been in my attitude of repudiation of my father. What is the difference between us? We both of us failed. Or is that self-pity again? Is it that there can be no such thing as success?

3

I AM in favour again! And do you know why? Because they
have discovered I have taken to writing—writing this long
letter to you and to myself, for you, Lizzie, will probably never
see it. The first two days I was back I was very much in disgrace. Nothing was said; everything was to be as it was before.
But oh! the atmosphere. I was like a little kid that had played
truant, and I was never so heavily forgiven in my life. You can
always tell when there's crisis in Will's house because they
start telephoning at all hours of the day and night. The
evening I got back there was telephoning to Phil in Cambridge,
long conversations ticking the pennies away, and grave faces
when the telephoning stopped. Short of stuffing my ears with
cotton-wool, there is nothing I can do to prevent myself
hearing. The telephone is in the hall; but the pretence is that
no one can hear it when it is being used. The telephoning went
on throughout the next day and then, as it always does, it died
a natural death. The sad fact is, Lizzie, that Will and Beryl
have to put up with me. But yesterday the atmosphere
miraculously changed. I couldn't understand it. What do they
mean to do? I thought: kill me with kindness? They were
smiling on me, and calling me 'father' in exactly the same
tones as you call a small child 'dear'; and I felt very angry. I
assured myself I was too old a bird to be caught with that sort
of chaff. And then last evening I overheard Beryl talking again
on that telephone. 'Such a good thing,' I heard her say, 'it
takes his mind off things and gives him something to do. Like
the lens-grinding he used to do.' And then she said: 'They're
just like children: the secret is to keep them occupied.' I
took no notice of this; indeed, if it hadn't been for the
reference to lens-grinding it probably would have made no
impression on me at all. I couldn't understand what Beryl

was talking about. But this morning everything was made wondrously clear.

I was sitting in my room after breakfast, smoking my pipe and reading the *News Chronicle*. Will had driven off to the works and the children had left for school. There was a knock on the door and Beryl came in. I couldn't understand it: it was more than an hour before the time when they pack me off for my morning walk so that my room can be cleaned. Then I noticed she had her hands behind her back and it seemed to me she was actually timid and confused. 'Father,' she said, 'I've brought you some paper,' and she held out a ream of the most beautiful foolscap in the one hand and in the other a new pen and a box of nibs. I pretended to be stupid. 'That is very kind of you, Beryl,' I said, 'and I see that it is very nice paper; but what do I want paper for?' (You must understand that so far I have been writing on any old scrap, to be accurate on the blank pages of one of Timmy's old school exercise books; elementary French: *Où est la plume de ma tante?* on one side of the page, me on the other.) 'For your writing,' she said; and she busied herself clearing my table and arranging a virgin folio of foolscap on my blotter with the new pen at its side: invitation to write! 'My writing, Beryl?' I asked, still stupid. Her back was towards me, but I could see she was confused. 'The writing you've been doing since—since you got back.' 'Oh that,' I said, 'a trifle. Just a little nonsense I've been indulging myself in.' 'I'm sure it's not nonsense, father,' she said; 'and you must have something better than that dirty old exercise book of Timmy's to write in.' I was determined to be sullen. I said coldly: 'I don't suppose I'll have occasion to use the paper. All the same, it's very kind of you.'

It wasn't until Beryl had left the room that I remembered her reference to lens-grinding on the telephone the night before. I was staring at the blank sheet of foolscap on the table. Or perhaps it was staring at me. Anyway, it was a facer. I must admit I was a bit angry. It seemed to me they were trying to force my hand. I'd half a mind to stop this writing altogether. And then Beryl's words came back to me: 'They're just like children.' It was almost the same as you'd said to me, when we were drinking our brandy and hot water by your fire. And it struck me, there I was, behaving just like a child.

And I thought: After all, what does it matter? Beryl's was an action kindly meant if a little transparent. And besides, I've always loved virgin writing paper. Now it lay on my table like a challenge I couldn't refuse.

Staring at it, I realised suddenly how I must seem to these children of mine: like an unpredictable untameable animal that must be kept somehow under control, and since it cannot be cowed must be placated. Poke a ream of foolscap through the bars! Then I remembered the lens-grinding. I was grinding one of my lenses the afternoon Will and Beryl turned up in their car, out of the blue as they say, a month after dear Rose died. They rang the bell but I didn't hear them; and they walked into the house. In fact, the bell was out of order, and why should I bother to have it repaired? A needless expense. If anyone wanted me they could bang or tap the window. They walked in and I didn't hear them: there I was grinding away, the world forgetting, by the world forgot; happy as a sandboy.

'Father!' Will said. His voice, so unexpected, gave me quite a turn; but I congratulate myself I showed nothing. 'Well, my boy?' I said, as though his appearance at my elbow was the most ordinary thing in the world. 'Father,' he said, and the pitch of his voice was just a little too high, so that I knew that whatever he'd come to do or say he was having to brace himself up to it, 'Father, Beryl and I have come to take you home.' 'But my boy, this is my home,' I said.

I remember now they were standing close together, as though huddled for mutual protection. They stood some little distance from me, looking down at me as though I were an animal that might bite.

'But father,' said Beryl. 'You can't stay here all alone, with no one to look after you.'

'I can look after myself,' I said mildly; 'in fact, I do look after myself, though I have to struggle for the right to do so. The neighbours are very kind,' I said, perhaps a trifle bitterly. 'I'm sure you don't get enough to eat,' Beryl said. 'My dear, throughout the war your mother-in-law and I never took up all our rations. Food doesn't mean much when you're my age.' And indeed it did seem a trivial subject to have come a hundred miles to discuss. And it was rather a sore point with me. Left to myself, I did very nicely, thank you, with a rasher of bacon or an egg or a chop occasionally, and fish and chips from the fish-and-chip shop two or three times a week. In fact, I was much put out by the kind attentions of my neighbours: the women were always running in and out with little delicacies for me, dishes of stew and bowls of soup and cuts off the Sunday joint and slices of fruit cake, which I had to pretend to be grateful for, though as often as not I put them down the w.c. and pulled the chain on them as soon as the women had gone.

'I'm sure,' she said, 'you'd be much more comfortable with us.'

I did not answer. I knew I would not be more comfortable with them; I was too old a dog to learn new tricks. 'It's not only that,' said Will, 'I've talked to Phil and we're both agreed you can't live here alone.' 'Suppose something happened to you,' Beryl said; 'say you were taken ill or anything.' 'Then I should knock on the wall for Mrs Jones next door,' I answered. 'I have a stick in the corner there for that very purpose, and one next my bed in my bedroom. The good woman insisted upon it.'

'You can't stay, father,' Will said very decisively. I went on being mulish; it was all very disagreeable to me; Rose and I had valued our independence more than anything. 'I can stay as long as I can pay the rent,' I said. 'People would think it so odd if they knew we let our father live all by himself uncared for hundreds of miles away,' Beryl said. 'It isn't that, father,' said Will; and he suddenly sat down beside me; and in that moment I think I knew, though I wouldn't admit it, that the game was up. 'Don't misunderstand us, father,' he began; 'we all tremendously admire the way you looked after mother and the way you are determined to keep your independence. But—and here you must bear with me—the plain fact is, you really aren't up to it any more. It would be a miracle if you were. You can't keep the place clean,' and he rubbed his finger along the front of a bookshelf and stared at the dust thick upon it. 'Clean!' I said scornfully; 'a lot of silly fuss! What does a bit of dust matter?' And I'm bound to say, Lizzie, I felt, as I still do, that that too was a trivial subject to motor a hundred miles to discuss.

Will drew his chair closer to mine. He was embarrassed, and

he was being very kind: I honoured him for it. 'Don't think Phil and I don't sympathise, father,' he said. 'We do. If we were in your shoes we'd feel exactly the same; and we're proud of you. But the truth of the matter is, you're too old. It's not fair on you, and you're not being fair to us. We've had letters.'

Then I understood it all. Those interfering women running in and out with their cups of tea and plates of stew and shepherd's pie and apple tart: spying, that's what they were doing, and writing letters. 'God damn and blast the women for a pack of interfering bitches!' I cried in my rage. 'They think it very odd,' Beryl said, 'seeing we're in the position we are.' Beryl is very proud of her position. 'They behaved quite rightly, father,' Will said very gently.

I knew I was beaten. And besides, I suddenly felt very tired, as though everything had become too much effort. The traitor within me whispered: You *are* too old. You might as well admit it. They saw I'd weakened. 'It isn't as though you'll be with strangers,' Beryl said. 'Your own flesh-and-blood: that's different; and you know how Timmy and Susan adore you. And you can see just as much or as little of us as you like. You can have your own room and you can bring your own furniture, have your books and wireless and play your violin.'

'I don't play the fiddle any more,' I said. 'I gave it away; to a very promising little boy.' And then I realised that it was probably this same very promising little boy's mother who'd written to Will, and I said: 'I grind lenses instead,' and I looked meaningly at the work on the table in front of me. It was a horrid filthy mess. 'Will you let me grind my lenses?' I asked maliciously. She flinched from the spectacle of my worktable as though from dog-mess and I saw her lips quiver. 'Well . . .' she began uncertainly. 'No more grinding of lenses!' I said; and I jumped up and impetuously swept lenses and everything off the table. It was a very stupid action on my part, for it merely made them believe I was odder than I really was. I can't understand now what came over me, for almost in the same gesture as my sweeping the contents of the table on to the floor I was shaking hands enthusiastically with them both, exclaiming, 'A new life! I start a new life!' Beryl gave me an old-fashioned look, but Will held my hand in his and said, 'I can't tell, father, what a relief this is to me.' My heart warmed to him and I muttered: 'God bless you, son!' and started blubbering like an old fool. Feminine consternation forthwith. I could have kicked myself. Dainty hankies dabbing my eyes, cups of tea brewed and consumed at a great rate.

Now, why did I behave like that? It was no relief for me to be taken away from the house I'd lived in with dear Rose for so long, especially since I had little faith that Will's proposal would work. I'd tried something like it before, more than forty years ago, when it was suddenly borne upon George Thompson and me that we could forward the Socialist State by behaving as far as possible as though Socialism had already been achieved.

Still, that was the way I behaved, and now I know why. There's a saying I had from Phil years ago. It comes from a book I've not read. It intoxicated Phil—he was a student at the time and was constantly repeating it. It attracted me enormously, and I added it to my store of talismanic sayings. It goes like this: 'To the destructive element submit yourself, and with the exertions of your hands and feet in the water make the deep, deep sea keep you up.' Sink or swim, in fact; but it's more than that: a counsel of great desperation. I remembered it then, but I couldn't say it because I feared Beryl might think it impolite towards her. So I made a ridiculous spectacle of myself instead.

I knew I had done wrong as soon as I'd committed myself. But there was no turning back. I had placed myself in Will's hands, and very efficient he was. Dealers arrived to buy my furniture; the landlord was given notice; and the room that was to be mine at Will's was specially done up for me: I was solemnly called upon to judge between various samples of wall-paper. Triviality upon triviality! And Beryl was as happy as I've ever seen her: it was exactly as though she was preparing for the arrival of a new baby. In a way, that was what I was; only I was to be a very old baby. She had everything planned for me. I realised this fully when we were in the motor driving down to Will's. She had an ideal conception of me; not of me as me, for she has known me long enough to know the kind of man I am, but of me as a grandfather, a sweet old gentleman, a pink-and-white seventy-five-year-old baby with a pipe in his mouth instead of a dummy. It was foolish of her to try to

23

pin this ideal conception on to me, but I am sure she found my complete inability to conform to it unforgiveable. The first occasion Will had to rebuke me after my installation in his home was for cursing and blinding in front of the children. I have forgotten the reason. The truth is, Lizzie, in the last few years I have become a great swearer, indeed you could say foul-mouthed, I, who throughout my life have been fastidious to the point of squeamishness about such things. You will not approve. For me it is merely another triviality which I note with mild interest as a sign of oncoming senility, like this much more humiliating weakness of being unable to control the working of my tear-ducts.

Driving down, she was describing to me, with palpable and touching enthusiasm, the delights of her home. 'And only ten minutes' walk away, father,' she said, 'there's a really pretty little park. The Sons of Rest meet there every morning and afternoon, in a little pavilion the Council has specially built for them!' The Sons of Rest! I was struck dumb. Me a Son of Rest! Obscenities rose to my lips; but I checked them. I was silent. 'They are such nice old gentlemen, and some of them are very interesting, too.' There was a park near my old home, and there were Sons of Rest there. I've no doubt there are Sons of Rest in every park in England. I'm afraid, Lizzie, almost the last time I saw your Paul I was cross with him because he wanted to take me to the Sons of Rest: I remember I spoke very sharply to him. And now, more than five years after that, here were Will and Beryl throwing me to the Sons of Rest. I ignored it. I said, instead, very soberly I think: 'I shall miss my lens-grinding'; and as soon as I'd said it a desperate hope welled up in me, which was foolish because I marked how Beryl's mouth set in a rigid line as I spoke. 'If I could grind just a few weeks longer,' I said, 'I could make Timmy a telescope.' I thought: If Will speaks it will be all right, for here he must be on my side. But weakly he said nothing; and Beryl said: 'If Timmy wants a telescope we can always buy him one. There's no need for you to go to all that trouble, father.' Beryl is a house-proud woman: there is no female so formidable as a house-proud woman.

Here I fear you will be at one with Beryl, Lizzie, and I must say straight out, it does you less than credit. You would have been kinder. You would have indulged me in my harmless but messy game of lens-grinding; but you would have felt exactly the same. No one honours womankind more than I, yet nothing makes me wilder than women's attitude to men, that at bottom they are great big boys who must be allowed—or forbidden— their naïve boyish enthusiasms. I couldn't for the life of me have explained to Beryl what lens-grinding meant to me, just as I despair of making you understand. Will understood all right, which is why it was cowardly of him to keep silent as he did.

Lens-grinding was a late discovery of mine. I took it up during the war when I stopped working. There was dear Rose to look after, but that wasn't enough; and playing the fiddle and reading weren't enough either. After more than fifty years of work I was lost without something to do with my hands. It was the black-out that directed my mind towards making lenses. For when the black-out settled down on us I realised that I was seeing the stars for the first time. I needed a telescope, but one of the size I wanted was much too expensive for me. So why not, thought I, make a telescope? Everyone said it was impossible. How will you make the lenses, they asked. Lens-grinding is a highly skilled craft, etc. Well, I could but try; and try I did. Very soon I'd forgotten all about telescopes; or, rather, they'd become merely the excuse I needed for busying myself with lens-grinding. It is very slow work, and that was part of the pleasure; it needs infinite patience and care, and that, too, was satisfying. It was also, in a quiet unexpected way, fortifying; as I discovered during the first blitz. We were in the sitting-room when the sirens sounded the warning, and even I could tell, within the first minutes, that we were in for something very different from the raids we'd had before. The sky seemed full of aeroplanes, buzzing like so many bees trapped in an inverted glass bowl. Mr Trent, the air raid warden, poked his head round the door, for whenever the alarms went I opened it so that he could reassure himself about us: it was a kindness to do so, for he was a well-intentioned man and worried for us. 'Jerry again!' he said; 'on his way to Liverpool, if you ask me.' But he beckoned me with his finger and I followed him out into the hall. 'Don't want to alarm you, Mr Ashted,' he said, 'but tonight I do think you and the old lady ought to stay under the stairs if you won't come to the shelter.'

Now, until then I had refused either to go to the shelter or to seek refuge in the cupboard beneath the stairs. I'd taken a high line: 'If the buggers are going to kill me,' I said, 'I'll meet my death standing up'; and Rose agreed with me. But this time I said immediately, 'Very well, Mr Trent. We'll go under the stairs.' He shook my hand, he was so relieved; and began to tell me what good shelter stairs provided, how very often when a whole house was bombed to rubble the stairs still survived and the wise ones who sheltered beneath them were rescued unscathed. Into the tiny space beneath them we put an armchair for Rose, and blankets, and I sat on cushions at her feet. So we sat in the dark together, or rather, I sat in the dark, for Rose had been in the dark some time; and we held hands. And then the attack began in earnest and we knew that Liverpool was not the target. Dear Rose was as patient and as brave as she always was: I was the coward. As the bombs fell nearer I couldn't avoid feeling that it was I those German boys twenty thousand feet above were aiming at; I felt—such curious shapes egoism takes—that it was me they'd come all that way to kill. I was never so frightened in my life. And then, suddenly, I was frightened no longer. The nearest bomb of all came down: it rushed towards us like an express train tearing into a tunnel; and then, as the din gradually lessened, I heard the tinkle of breaking glass, and I thought: I'll be able to get all the glass I need for my grinding in the morning just by going out and picking it up. It was a wonderful thought: I'd be able to pick and choose, judge and reject. And the prospect of doing so buoyed me up throughout the eight hours of that raid and throughout all the others. The treasure-trove I found during those months of the blitz! By the time it was over I'd got enough pieces of glass, of assorted sizes and thicknesses, to keep me grinding twenty years I should think.

And how soothing it was, the process of grinding! Of course I made many false starts; I had to learn by experience. But I was in no hurry. 'I'll see the war through, grinding,' I said; and I was never one of those who believed the war would be over soon. In a strange way, I thought of it as my war work. Certainly it kept up my morale. God knows I am not a patient

26

man, but it gave me a store of patience to set against the seeming unending length of the war. And the day I achieved for the first time a tolerably accurate lens was as proud as any in my life.

Of course, there was vanity in it too. It hadn't escaped my attention that Spinoza had earned his bread as a lens-grinder, and the very fact of following his craft seemed to enable me to capture something of the inwardness of that divine spirit. Vanity, indeed! Yet I am compelled in honesty to say that some of my best thoughts, some of those that have pleased me most, have come to me in the process of grinding. For the mere manual part of it, and the concentration essential to it, seemed to leave my mind wonderfully free. In fact, although throughout those years I was never more tied, by the war, by increasing old age and by the necessity to look after Rose, with all the attendant irksomenesses of housework and cooking and shopping, yet, making my lenses, I attained to a condition of real freedom.

So you will see, Lizzie, what I forfeited when I agreed to give up my little home and go and live with Will and Beryl. It wasn't only independence in the ordinary sense, though that is much, as no one knows better than yourself: it was also freedom of a much rarer kind. Well, I lost it, and I blame no one but myself. Beryl and Will have done the best they could according to their lights, and no one can do more. It is the human state that each one of us sees by a different light— hence all the tears. But now it seems, if only I am cunning and forbearing and utter only words that turn away wrath, that perhaps I shall be allowed a substitute for lens-making. Perhaps I am even now making a lens, a magnifying glass through which I shall see myself and my life more clearly.

4

PHIL has been here for the week-end and so for three days I have written nothing. Now that I take up my pen again I realise this writing is more difficult than lens-grinding, though fraught with just as much danger and perhaps more. But of the danger more anon.

Lizzie, these have been three delectable days. It only wanted Tom with us, but everything one wants one can't have. Looking back, I see I basked in the presence of my sons. All was easy and sympathetic; and I was discreet. But that is being unfair to them. I was just natural, myself, as I feel I haven't been all the time I've been with Will and Beryl. It was as though Phil, coming in from the outside, saw me as no different from the way I have always been. His presence seemed to restore the natural order, and as we sat round the fire on Saturday evening all together I felt very proud of my children. Not that I pretend to understand them, Lizzie, for when I am actually with them I find them disconcertingly different from the way I imagine them, which is, I suppose, always as they were as children. I feel, in fact, that startled realisation of having produced beings entirely separate from and other than oneself that mother must have felt when she suddenly looked up at Horace and myself and said, 'My God! What giants!'

The strangeness of it! No man could have been more ambitious for his children than I, but how vague my ambitions for them were. The furthest flight I was capable of was to see them as schoolteachers, living, apart from that, in circumstances very much like my own. How wrong I was! They live in entirely different worlds, worlds I never envisaged. Yet when they were boys what I was conscious of was their extraordinary likeness to me. They seemed miniature editions of myself, and I often worried about this, for it seemed to me they had all my weaknesses and faults writ larger even than they were in me. And here they are today, men on their own, assured. They seem to me even self-made. I often find it difficult to realise I had any part in their making: Will a production engineer—we didn't have such things in my day—and a boss, running a factory, and Phil an atomic physicist.

In recent years I have felt that Phil was the nearest to me. During the last ten years, because he has been in America so much, I have seen less of him than of Will, and now I find him in some ways more remote from me than his brothers. I cannot easily explain this, for I don't really understand it, but watching him and listening to him at the week-end, I thought that if George Thompson had had a son he would have been exactly like Phil. Now, George and I were as close as two men may be, but no two men were less alike. Phil is decisive as George was; he knows his mind as George did; he is as contemptuous of what he thinks nonsense as George was, and it's as difficult when one's with him to indulge in nonsense as it was with George. I always felt of George's mind that it was a very powerful disinfectant or perhaps even a surgeon's knife. Sometimes it intimidated me, as Phil's does now.

There was no beating about the bush with him. We were sitting round the fire on Saturday evening. He and Will had been talking about possible developments in industrial techniques as a result of the harnessing of atomic energy, and I had been silent, listening with respect and, indeed, between ourselves, purring inside me like a cat at the spectacle of my brilliant sons. I was feeling, in fact, that in the eyes of the world they had done well by me, so that it seemed to follow that I must have done well by them, however unwittingly. And then Phil suddenly turned to me and said: 'Father, I hear you are writing?'

'Yes, Phil, I am writing,' I replied gravely, for the fact that he took my writing seriously made me take it seriously, too.

'But what are you writing, father?' he asked. I could see Will and Beryl listening, all ears as they say; but I ignored them. I addressed myself solely to Phil, who had asked the question seriously and deserved a serious answer. I thought for a moment, for the question itself was a challenge to me. What precisely was I writing? Until then, I had thought of it simply

29

as a long letter to you, Lizzie, a way of keeping myself occupied. But I realised when Phil spoke that it was more than that.

I said, and not at all in a self-deprecating way, as I might have answered Will: 'I am writing my autobiography,' for that, it had suddenly dawned upon me, was exactly what I was doing, and I might as well say so.

Phil nodded his head several times, very emphatically. 'Good,' he said, 'good. Now, that is excellent.' I was struck again by his resemblance to George and I felt twice the man for his vigorous approval.

'Now, that is a really sensible thing to do,' he went on—and how old he sounded and how young he made me feel. He leaned forward, and the light caught his spectacles in such a way that I could not see his eyes, and for some reason that made me stand in even greater awe of him. 'You know, father,' he said, 'you have a great opportunity. A great opportunity— so long as you don't aim at frills or fine writing.' He jabbed the stem of his pipe towards me as he said this. 'Avoid fine writing, or for that matter, fine sentiments, like the devil. That way lies literature.' It was the first time in my life I've ever heard the word literature used as a term of contempt and I confess I do not really understand what Phil meant. 'Put down everything as simply as possible,' he said; 'as though you were writing a report. Just say what happened and when, without any emotion of any kind. A bald recital of facts, that's what's wanted; as though you were giving evidence before a royal commission.'

'Yes, Phil,' I said. 'I see.' But I didn't.

'There's no reason,' he said, 'why, if you go about it in the right way, you shouldn't write something of real sociological interest. For look'—and he again pointed the stem of his pipe at me—'you have seen in your lifetime a whole social revolution. You have lived through it. In fact, it's not too much to say that you are in yourself a cross-section of that revolution. You were one of the first members of the Labour Party, a pioneer even, and you have watched it change from being regarded as a tiny body of cranks to one of the two permanent parties of the state. And that means you have watched and been active yourself in a whole shift of power. You, father, have remained working-class and I dare say you still call yourself a Socialist. I don't know what Will and I are. Not working-class, I suppose, though for that matter I've never been able to think of myself as middle-class; and I've no notion at all of how Will votes. If he's like me, I fancy he doesn't find a deal of difference between either party. But here we are, in our way emblems of the English revolution, of the shift of power: a production engineer and a nuclear physicist, the real rulers of England, of the world for that matter, capitalist or Communist. Whatever we call ourselves, we come from the working-class; no question of that; and we're part of your story, father. You made us, and I don't mean only in a physical sense. Well, that's only part of it—of your book, I mean, your autobiography. But you see the value of it?'

Phil looked first at me and then at Will and Beryl. It was, if I may say so, Lizzie, a solemn moment. I saw myself through Phil's eyes: I was a kind of king-maker. There *has* been a shift of power; for the poor the conditions of life *have* changed completely since the days when you and I were children: and I saw that I, taken as a representative man, was in part responsible for the change. And I saw, too, that Phil and Will realised this and respected me for it.

'But mind you, father'—and once more the warning jab of the pipe-stem—'no fine writing, no fine sentiments. Curb your flights of fancy and your philosophical speculations. Otherwise, it will all end in literary guff.'

'Yes, Phil,' I said mildly; 'of course. But this objection of yours to literature: I don't quite understand it.' And remembering the boy's passion for poetry, the names he used to flash out in conversation like swords or banners to rally armies and challenge foes—Eliot, Conrad, Lawrence, Gide are some I recall—I really did not understand, though of course I have seen little of the boy these last few years.

'Oh, literature,' he said. 'I do assure you, father, literature's dead. It died with the conviction of personal immortality. The only literary immortality that matters now is to survive as material for a footnote to a work of history. That's what you must strive to make your book, father: material for a footnote to a serious work of history.'

I still don't understand; and on reflection I can see that in much of his advice Phil was merely engaged in the time-honoured pastime of the young of teaching their grandmothers

31

to suck eggs; that, and behaving like George, who never had any difficulty in planning other people's lives. But I was grateful to him: he had heartened me. I am not just writing a letter to Lizzie, I told myself: I am writing something of real sociological interest. 'Real sociological interest': it was as good as a new hat to a woman. It gave me a fresh notion of myself, and I went to bed that night and the next, for Phil talked on and off about my book, as he called it, throughout the whole of Sunday, with strengthened determination.

Now, alas, I feel that if ever Phil reads this he's going to be very disappointed. What he wants from me is a Blue Book— and how like George that is. I remember George Thompson arguing with brother Horace once and suddenly smacking the Webbs' Minority Report of the Royal Commission on the Poor Law and shouting, so aggrieved was he by what he called Horace's romantic nonsense, 'I tell you, Ashted, this thing of the Webbs is worth all the works of Ruskin put together.' The facts are what Phil wants. But what are the facts? As I sit and stare at Beryl's beautiful white foolscap and occasionally write a sentence, I relive my life. Sometimes I see myself as through the eyes of a compassionate god, sometimes, as though through the wrong end of a telescope, in tiny, exquisite clarity. I'm fascinated by what I see, and moved by it. But, Lizzie, I don't know how to put it down on paper. The facts? Despite Phil, they don't seem so important to me as the emotions they stir in me. And even if I try to confine myself to facts, irrelevancies pour from my pen. Or are they irrelevancies? I don't know. All I know is that the I of today must make his comment on the I of sixty and seventy years ago, and the I of today carries with him the whole burden of the present, so that what happens in the present creeps into the story of what happened in the past. Indeed, I find it more and more difficult to distinguish between past and present.

Which brings me to the reason why I said that this writing was just as much fraught with danger as lens-grinding. Since it was discovered I was writing I have been as good as gold; and sitting in my room, I have felt myself sunned by the approval of Will and Beryl, poor souls, who want me only to be quiet: the old ought to be quiet. This morning, though, the goodness was exposed as a sham, and the gold as the thinnest film of gilt, all too easily rubbed off. I was good, really, because I was living in the past; at times it was more real to me than now. And this morning, still in this ecstasy of memory which Phil's encouragement had further impelled me into (ecstasy is the right word, Lizzie, for it's a Greek word meaning being out of oneself), I went for a walk and, not noticing where I was going, walked to that cursed park where the Council has built the little shelter for those damnable Sons of Rest. Whether they were there this morning I don't know; I simply did not see, for my eyes were turned elsewhere, turned inwards. But as I was walking back, Beryl drew up in the car and stopped for me to get in. I did not want to get in at all, but what could I do? She had seen me come through the park gates and she said, archly, 'I do believe, father, you've been to the Sons of Rest'; and I, not thinking, still in ecstasy, took the question at its face value and answered honestly, 'No, Beryl, my dear,' I said, 'I have been to Wolverhampton with Horace.'

Lizzie, you could hear the silence that followed. I did not understand it. I had told the truth, but I could feel something was wrong; and before we were quite home I ventured to ask: 'Beryl, is there anything the matter?' She shook her head hastily and I noticed she blinked back a tear; and then she turned the car into the drive. Women! I thought, women! for I had still not related this strange behaviour to myself; and I went up to my room to stare at the paper and perhaps write. Then I heard Beryl talking on the telephone. She was talking to Will. 'He,' I heard her say, and I had to listen, because I know that 'he' is always me. 'Will,' she said, 'he said he'd been to Wolverhampton with Horace. What could he have meant? Will, you don't think he's going a bit . . . funny, do you?'

At first I misunderstood and was furious. I thought she was complaining to Will that I had, as they say, been 'trying to be funny,' and what is more obnoxious than that? I thought: The woman must positively be looking for slights if she thinks an old man of seventy-five would go to the trouble of trying to take a rise out of her, etc. And then it struck me what she really meant: that perhaps I was becoming deranged mentally. It pulled me up short, and I could be angry no longer, only sad. It seemed that communication between two human beings was impossible, that misconstruction was a necessary sequel to the use of speech; and I wondered what I could say to clear up the misunderstanding. In the end I decided I could say nothing, that whatever I said would only make things worse. But I tell you privately, Lizzie, I cursed this young woman's literal-mindedness, for I know that once she has an idea fixed in her head she does not willingly let it go. I see the consequences: the telephone will ring tonight; I shall be watched all the time, etc. The guns will be kept loaded lest the old animal turn dangerous.

For I *had* been to Wolverhampton with Horace; and how explain this, how explain that I'd spent the morning talking to Horace, whom nowadays I often do talk to? Should I have to say that I know Horace isn't really present but that I'm only talking to myself? For that matter, hasn't talking to yourself always been suspect as a sign of insanity? I had, in fact, been reliving a trip Horace and I took to Wolverhampton one Boxing Day more than sixty years ago, in order to see the Wanderers play. We walked there and back, over the Rowley Hills, and by the time we got to the ground it was snowing, and we watched the game in a blizzard, so that the players were visible only when they were on our side of the pitch. Whom the Wolves were playing I no longer remember but I know they won. I do recall that after the match we ate hot peas and faggots in a coffee-house, and never did food taste so good. That was the last of our money, and we began the long walk home.

But what I remember really is simply Horace. Horace was a man who never changed. Even at the age of sixteen, he had the clearest conviction of the truth, and conviction remained his unto the end. Myself, I have never had a clear conviction of the truth, though I have spent my life looking for it. This constant uncertainty on my part Horace regarded as weak and probably wilful, but in those days I was Horace's disciple and his truth was mine. He was in fine rousing form that morning more than sixty years ago; as indeed he was this morning before Beryl picked me up. (Incidentally, how I would like to have heard Horace on the Sons of Rest! 'Rest?' I can hear him say in his thin tenor voice; 'and since when was man born to rest?' Horace knew that man was born to trouble as the sparks fly upwards, and what's more, he thought it right and proper.)

Horace, I am afraid, was in many ways not a likeable person, except to those of us who loved him. People who will not compromise cannot be, and Horace never did compromise. He had an exceedingly rigid notion of himself, one that remained constant through the years; and as the years passed he came to seem more rigid, more angular, so that he seemed a walking protest against the ways of the world and its sins that lay all about him. I say 'walking' because Horace travelled in practically no other way; he only took a train in order to reach a point where he could start walking. Every day, as you know, he walked the three miles there and the three miles back between his home and his workshop, and the only difference between him at thirty and at sixty was that at the latter age he allowed himself the luxury of reaching the shop at 9.30 in the morning instead of 8.30, and he considered it unpardonably weak in himself.

Once I had the experience of seeing Horace as it were for the first time, as though he were not my elder and much-loved brother but a stranger. I was going to my workshop, for it was in the days when I had my own little business, and gazing idly out of the window from the top of the tramcar, thinking of subjects miles remote from Horace, I saw this small figure, very upright, striding daintily along (yes, Horace could stride daintily: he was the only man I ever knew who could), a figure plainly out of the past, looking, with his black velour hat and his very dark grey broadcloth suit, like an intensely old-fashioned preacher of some sect far gone in dissent. As you know, Horace was always being taken for a clergyman; he would rebuke the error and explain he wasn't worthy, but I don't think he minded it very much. Certainly, he managed to look far more like the essence of a clergyman than many a priest in a dog collar. Of course, I realised the tiny clerical figure was Horace in a second, but I managed—deliberately— to prolong the moment of detachment and, turning in my seat as the tram passed him, I glimpsed his face. I have to admit it, Lizzie: in its thinness, boniness, and especially in the tightness of the supercilious lips, it was a fanatic's face, the face of a man in whose presence the rest of the world was bound to feel uncomfortable.

The funny thing, I was always being taken for him. This I

didn't understand then, and I don't now. Of course I can see we had the same family face, but the difference between our two versions of it: surely they existed in the most glaring contrast. Mine—or so I have always felt—shrieked out with weakness, Horace's with strength and determination. I compromised: I hid myself behind a moustache. Horace never did. And I have long cherished an image of Horace and myself that sums up the difference between us. We were walking together in Wales; the last time I was ever there, twelve years ago. It was the August Bank Holiday Monday and as hot as I have ever known it. As we walked the road between Llanerfyl and Dinas Mawddwy the sun beat down upon us mercilessly, and there was no spot of shade anywhere. When Horace walked there were no concessions to dress: he walked in Wales as he walked each day to his workshop. I draped my handkerchief over the back of my neck, fixing it between my hat and my head. Then I discarded in turn, as the heat grew more fierce, my jacket, my waistcoat, then my collar and tie. I have no doubt I looked deplorably slovenly. Horace made no comment; he merely hastened his step and walked on ahead. By the time we reached Dinas there was a quarter of a mile between us. He wanted nothing to do with me. He was repudiating my weakness, for the flesh was something to be conquered, not cravenly surrendered to.

Then there was the interior difference between us. I had thoughts Horace never had. His mind was not so much narrow as closed, sealed by certainty; and as he grew older he admitted less and less. I believed in justice: Horace didn't. The very mention of justice made Horace snarl. He hated the notion of it. He saw it as the most powerful and therefore the most damnable will-o'-the-wisp, calculated—and this deliberately, by design of the Devil—to lead men away from their one duty of humbly adoring God. Horace believed in a God of absolute sovereign power Who did not have to justify His ways to man but Who would save or damn him at His own arbitrary will. Just as I spent my life trying to find a church or sect liberal enough for me, so Horace spent his seeking for one that was rigorous enough for him. Neither of us was successful in our search. The straitest, extremest Calvinists always proved too loose for Horace. The odd thing is that we got on together as well as we did. Horace knew that God would not bother to save many but was certain that he would be one of them. He was equally certain that I would not be saved, but he was very nice about it; and the sign was—it was a kind of tact: he did not want to rub my predestined fate into me—he always talked to me as though his views were mine. And of course he had his contradictions, which he was never aware of. Against all the bases of his faith, he remained to the end a good Liberal, even though the Liberal Party had almost disappeared. And he was a good father, a much better one than I ever was. Where his children were concerned, he did not build himself up in God's image, which I fear is just what I, who do not believe in God, or not much anyway, did.

I admired Horace all my life, and I admire him still. He was a heroic being, and never more so than in the way he met his death. He was sixty-six, I was sixty-four. He lay in the General Hospital dying for weeks of cancer. 'This,' I said to myself, 'this is what it is to be old!' It seemed to me an outrage, for at that time I still hadn't reconciled myself to the fact that I too was old. Old age, I now know from bitter experience, *is* an outrage, whatever you may say, Lizzie. Seeing poor Horace, if I'd believed in a God it would have killed any regard I had for Him, for I would want nothing to do with a God Who inflicts such indignities on the beings He has created. If I did believe in God, old age alone would make me believe in Satan and applaud him for his virtuous rebellion against an unfeeling Lord. But Horace—Horace never lost his faith: he was in God's hands, and God could do as he wished with His own. I would hurry away from Horace's bedside in an angry nausea. But Horace was a better man than I: his sufferings he accepted as I could not.

Lizzie, this isn't what I meant to write at all. You see how difficult it is. I am supposed to be walking to and from Wolverhampton, a boy of fifteen and a half with his elder brother; and instead, I am contemplating Horace as I knew him as a man. At fifteen, that Boxing Day we walked to Wolverhampton to see the Wolves play, I had no reservations at all about him. I uncritically adored. What a fine fellow he was at seventeen! That day, I remember, was the first time I ever heard the word 'Utilitarian.' I thrilled to the word as to the name of a race of wicked sorcerers. The Utilitarians: they were, as I was soon to know, Horace's King Charles' Head; and for years I dreaded their appearance in Horace's conversation. I can assure you, Lizzie, it is really very difficult indeed to equate John Stuart Mill with Satan, but Horace could do it, and throughout his life he never stopped doing it. Had he ever read John Stuart Mill? He would have as soon supped with the devil. George Thompson, who was always contemptuous of Horace (though in fairness I must say no more than Horace was of him), once challenged my brother on the subject of Mill. 'But look, Ashted, have you ever *read* Mill? Have you read *Liberty*, *The Subjection of Women*, *Representative Government*, *Utilitarianism?*' Mill, of course, was one of our gods, George's and mine. Horace hadn't; and it made no difference. He had read Carlyle, and that was enough. In any case, Horace was a man who *knew*. He was impervious to argument, and George was the incarnation of argument. They looked at each other and sniffed in mutual contempt. Neither felt the other was worth arguing with. After that, I did my best to keep them apart, for I suffered in the presence of their antagonism. 'I *know*,' Horace said. 'But how can you know?' George retorted; and invoked logic and science and Mill and Marx. Logic! Science! Mill! Marx! Horace merely smiled his maddeningly supercilious smile. 'You're impossible,' George barked. Horace *was* impossible; and after that, George never referred to him as Horace: he called him Savonarola or Calvin or Knox. 'Well, Billy, and how's John Knox getting on these days?'

Well, I loved them both, Horace and George Thompson. They were the best men I ever knew, and they were incompatibles.

5

I WENT to sleep last night very depressed, for I did not see how
I could possibly meet Phil's requirements; and if I couldn't,
what was the point of going on with this? I realised he'd
changed my whole notion of what I was doing. But knowing
myself, I knew I was bound to fall into what he called literary
guff; and that would be no good at all. I saw exactly what he
meant, and I could recognise the justice of the implied criticism.
Though the words were different, it was George's complaint
about me. 'Billy,' he'd say, 'when, O when, will you learn
there's no room for sentiment and fancy in the Socialist Movement? One agitator is worth a hundred dreamers, and there'll
come a time when one planner will be worth a hundred
agitators.' I'd mention Morris and Walter Crane and Edward
Bellamy. George was always very patient with me. He'd
compel his fine mobile lips not to sneer and say, 'Well, yes, I
grant you Morris and Bellamy. There's always a place for
propaganda.' Propaganda! He would never admit that Morris
was more than propaganda; and if mildly I said 'Poetry?'
he'd dismiss it with 'Jam on the pill.' Our ideas of socialism
were really very different; because we were such close friends
and because we agreed on our immediate aim we did not
discuss them or let them divide us. But while he was fired by
Marx's Theory of Labour Value I was in a dream of an ideal
world based on *News from Nowhere* and Carlyle's Abbot Samson.
I see now it was literary guff.

It wasn't that George had no poetry in him or that he
knew nothing about it. He knew far more than I about it,
as he knew far more about everything. He was the most
methodical man I ever saw, and he had a prodigious memory.
It was the combination that made him so formidable in argument, that and his decisive manner. Just as he could quote you

statistics about the infant mortality rate in Salford as contrasted with that of Bournemouth or give you the figures for the national income for the past century along with wage rates for a multitude of industries over the same period, so he could quote you Shakespeare and Wordsworth and Thomas Gray and Tennyson by the yard. He knew all about it; he had felt its power and taken its measure; and deliberately he had put it aside. It was a weakness he couldn't allow himself to indulge in, one the more insidious because so attractive to him naturally. It had to be propaganda, the jam covering the pill, to justify itself. Otherwise it was just self-indulgence. Once, when he was very exasperated with me, he said, 'I tell you, Billy, Blatchford is more use to the Movement than all your Morrises, and the *Clarion* has had a greater effect than *News from Nowhere* ever had.' And I remember him saying more than once: 'There are far more varieties of people's opium than religion alone, and they are just as enervating, Billy.' For George there was a world to be changed, and everything that impeded the work immediately to hand was weakness. Poetry, literature, he allowed when, so to speak, they were practical things. He always encouraged Phil, gave him books he thought he should read, and discussed them with him. But the end was a practical one. It was necessary to pass examinations, and if literature was a subject for examination, then it must be mastered. Its value beyond this was irrelevant.

That, of course, was when he was in his most militant phase. In the last years of his life he mellowed, and I have often thought his mellowness was a by-product of his tragic fall. He accepted the consequences of his fall with nobility and calmness of spirit. You never knew him well, Lizzie, and I think it impossible that you could have liked him. He was so strong in himself, seemingly so self-sufficient, that he was bound to appear lacking in human sympathy to those who did not know him intimately. When it was suddenly made public, in the crudest and most sensational way, that he too was human, with all that implies, the general reaction was a mean pleasure, however hypocritically it was masked, that the colossus had feet of clay. Pride goeth before a fall—and how people in their littleness rejoice when the proud fall! George bore the ignominy of that stoically. But think of what it must have been like for him. He had done everything himself; he owed nothing to any-one; more than any man I have known, he was self-made. He had achieved much, but even so, he was still only on the foot-hills of power, and he had no reason to believe that he would not climb far higher. And overnight, everything was at an end. Those who had been his friends abandoned him, and worse than that, accused him of treachery. Ironically, it was his enemies who stood by him and helped him. But he had to leave politics, for though his former friends had rejected him he refused steadfastly to align himself with their foes. And, as I say, he seemed to become mellow.

It was as though he suddenly found himself in reduced circumstances and living in a house too big for him; so he shut off one wing of it, locked it, and threw away the key. It was like that. He was as wide awake and as vigorous as ever, but relaxed. For the first time for many years he had leisure to stretch himself. I remember he bought a gramophone and spent hours listening to records; to Bach and Beethoven and Wagner's operas and Gracie Fields. 'I believe I like Miss Gracie as well as any of them,' he'd say. He took to reading novels as well, and he read them as though seeking for reflec-tions of his own life experience and for light upon it.

This semi-retirement did not in fact last for long. After three or four years it was as though his former friends and colleagues were suddenly ashamed of the way they had treated him; and then, too, it must have become plain to everyone what a waste it was that such a man must live in seclusion. He was made a magistrate, and once again, as he walked from the tram terminus to the police court, he was one of the best-known figures in the city; short, broad, very erect. To me, his closest friend, for whom he was always almost beyond criticism, his head and countenance grew nobler with the years; that great brow became more domed, the bone structure more pro-nounced, the eagle nose thinner and stronger, the lips beneath the heavy drooping moustache more set; and the chin faced the world even more proudly than before. His voice was as brusque as ever; he did not so much talk to you as command; yet the tone had in it now a new, unaccustomed gentleness. There was a change. In his political days his passion for justice had sometimes seemed abstract and doctrinaire; he was, as he admitted to me in this last phase of his life, often contemptuous of the weakness of his fellow-men, of their silliness and in particular of their need for the comfort of what he called illusions. But now this passion for justice was humanised because it was concentrated on the individual suffering men or women in the dock in front of him. He discovered a well of pity within him. His comments from the bench were constantly being quoted in the newspapers, for he never minded disagreeing with other magistrates—'Most of them don't know and cannot know,' he'd say to me, 'because they haven't experienced the harshness of life as we have, Billy'—or criticising what he considered cruel or stupid laws. It *was* a change in him, Lizzie, and if you had seen him in those days you'd have loved him, not feared and disliked him, as I'm sure you did.

He had always dismissed what is called social work as trifling or at the best palliative. I remember his scorn for me when I helped Father Andrews at his boys' club at All Saints. 'Little Sir Billy Bountiful, taking the equivalent of a bowl of soup and a text to the deserving poor.' George hated charity; he believed it was a way of buying off the poor, throwing them a sop so that they should not claim their rights. In theory, I agreed with him, and do so still; but I was sentimental, as he said; the revolution seemed to be taking so long to arrive that you had to do something in the meantime, however trivial, to help the dispossessed. And George, barred from politics, found himself taking a similar line. From his duties as a justice of the peace he branched out into other social work. He went on the boards of several hospitals; he became a governor of the University, and that gave him an especial personal satisfaction.

All this furthered the change in him. It brought him out, as it were. He was moving among representatives of the people we used to call the class enemy, industrialists, professional men, gentlemen of leisure, retired officers. He had met their like before, of course, and even mixed with them, but always under some constraint, as soldiers of opposed armies might fraternise during an armistice. He did not need telling that capitalists are not wicked; he knew they are just as much the victims of the historical process as the workers. They are not to be blamed for fulfilling their class destiny. Propaganda is one thing, truth another. But in some degree we are all deceived by our own propaganda, and I think in this instance there was more to it than that. I cannot see how any working man, brought up in the kind of society in which I was reared, could fail to be class-conscious. It is as plain to me now as it was fifty years ago that my boss—any man who employs me, whom I am dependent on—is my enemy: he stands in my way; his power curbs me and robs me of freedom of choice. So my ambition was always to escape his domination. I wanted to be my own boss. I mean just that: I did not want to be anyone else's. George was never class-conscious in quite that way, perhaps because he lacked any feeling of inferiority. My rebellion, at any rate in some of its manifestations, was often absurd. I refused to call any man 'sir'; I won't now, for that matter, but the refusal is habit rather than principle. But I see it was silly of me to refuse to raise my hat to ladies. Women, the argument ran, were as good as men, therefore one insulted them by discriminating in this way. That was stupid. In these matters, I was more doctrinaire than George, who told me time and again that I wasn't really a Marxist at all but an Anarchist. 'Anarchist' was a Marxist term of contempt. I now believe that most of the time I was only rationalising, as they call it, finding specious reasons in which to dress up an attitude I had inherited from my father. Father would not raise his hat or say 'sir' to anyone, though I think he would have made an exception if he had met Mr Gladstone. But for no one else.

Less extreme in this respect than I, George was still surprised when he found capitalists human beings with generous impulses to which on occasion they gave rein. If he had still had a political future he would have suspected their intentions towards him. But he knew he was not being bought because he had nothing to sell. These men—or some of them: there was a retired general among them, who sat with him on the bench, two or three industrialists, a lawyer, the Vice-Chancellor of the University—approached him as a man, and George responded to them as a man.

When I read this through, Lizzie, it seems I have all the time been emphasising change in George; but that is not what I feel about him at all. His convictions did not change; he held to them as strongly at the end of his life as at the beginning. But when he was driven out of politics he had to become somehow different if he was to survive at all; the difference made him more human—but that is wrong: he was always human. I mean rather something like tender—because the scale in which he could work was limited to individual human beings. I know that his critics have said he began his career warped, warped by the circumstances in which he was born and over which he had no control. I don't believe this. He was a straight tree from the beginning. But even if that were not so, how wonderful that a man who began his life warped could, by the end of it, straighten out and blossom like a tree that had been perfect from the start.

But George has led me astray. I began this chapter, Lizzie, to show you how I'd found the way to write the kind of book young Phil wants; how, when I woke up in the morning after that depressed night, miraculously I had the pattern. The mystery of sleep had revealed it to me in the book I loved above all others in my boyhood, *Robinson Crusoe*. I read it then for its reality; I see now it is really an allegory of life, perhaps of every man's life. I set out to tell you about that and then intended to begin my own book accordingly. And see where it's got me: Phil led me to George and to what George would have called sentiment and Phil calls literary guff. But I don't care. I know now that this is my book; not Phil's. And remembering George and writing about him has warmed me, Lizzie, as nothing else could have done, warmed me and given me fresh courage. He was a good man and the nearest I have known to a great one; and he was my friend. He is with me still, and what a comfort that is.

All the same, partly for his sake, partly for Phil's, when I take up my pen in the morning I will be objective. Back to the facts! Let fact be supreme! And as a sign, I now copy out the first words of the book that shall be my model no matter how far on occasion I may drift from it. 'I was born in the year 1632, in the city of York, of a good family . . .'

6

BUT it was in 1875 that I was born, and I cannot say that my family was good, for I trace it back no further than my grandfather, who was born, of parents unknown, in the workhouse at Tipton, Staffordshire, in what is called the Black Country. So I must suppose I have not even any real right to the name of Ashted, which was no doubt bestowed arbitrarily upon him by the workhouse master in place of any known name. I never knew my grandfather, for he was a miner and was killed in a pit accident before I was born. Nor have I ever seen so much as a picture of him, and since my father referred to him only when he threatened us with the chastisements he had received as a boy from *his* father, I cannot be said to know anything about him at all.

Not even a respectable family, I am afraid, much less a good one. But things are rather better on my mother's side. Her maiden name was Brooks, and her parents had come from I think Shipston-on-Stour, which they had left, as farm labourers, to better themselves in the new factories. My grandfather Brooks, whom I vaguely remember as a ruddy-faced old man who still spoke with the slow speech of a countryman, bettered himself to the extent of becoming a labourer in a brass foundry. I have no doubt that the parish register at Shipston would unfold a long and honourable line of Brooks, but I have never bothered to go there and see; partly because I have never cared for the lush, soft countryside of that part of the Midlands, and partly because I have never been interested enough: no doubt if I went back far enough I'd find a lord among us somewhere, for that is true of us all.

I was the third of fifteen children, of whom three did not survive infancy and one died at twenty, and was christened William Ewart after Mr Gladstone, who embodied for my father, a William too, all that was noble, wise and great.

My father was a metal-worker, mainly in silver and brass; a craftsman so skilful and ingenious that he never lacked for work even when times were at their worst; and this despite an independence and obstinacy that amounted almost to sullenness. He could scarcely read or write and was bitterly ashamed of this, becoming more so as his children grew up and went to school. But he was a very proud man, and his pride was a prison: to have learnt to read or write, once his children could do so, would have been to admit that he was not self-sufficient, and this he could not bring himself to do. He made his deficiency a virtue and pooh-poohed the value of what he called book-learning; though he must have known that his own want of it had led to his being cheated of his rights a score of times. When I was a young man I often wondered how it was, considering his intractability, his surliness, his habit, which he erected into a principle, of going to work only when it pleased him, that his master continued to employ him, for though Mr Bagshawe often sacked him he always summoned him back by telegram next day. This pleased father: it made him feel indispensable: 'See,' he'd say, 'they can't get on without me, and the buggers know it!' But I understand now. Apart from his manual dexterity, which was great, my father was naturally and ceaselessly inventive; but the patents that were taken out for my father's ingenious devices were taken out in his master's name, and to him was thrown a payment of perhaps five pounds as one would throw a bone to a clever dog. He was indispensable all right, but not for the reasons he thought.

I said his pride was a prison. Ignorance and frustration were the bricks that built it, and I am afraid we children—so many of us, and coming at such inconvenient times—were the bars. Because there were so many of us he could not help being poor, at least while we were too young to work. Our poverty was certainly aggravated by his bouts of drinking, which in those days were much more common among working men than now because the pubs were open all day. I am not disposed, though, as I was when young, to blame him for this drinking. I see now that he had to escape from himself and his carking condition somehow, and, as they say, drink was the shortest way out of

Manchester. His was the common fate of the working-class father of his day. Mr Forster's Education Act of 1870 lay like a gulf between him and his sons. As they grew up, the simple fact that they had been to school drew them away from him: it was their mother who became the centre of their existence. When fear of him had died down, he became almost an object of contempt, someone at any rate to be ashamed of; she an object of pity, to be reverenced and cherished.

We did not live on the lowest level of poverty; there were always neighbours and children at school much poorer than we. Still, we were very poor, just because there were so many of us young and helpless at the same time. I suppose now the symbol of our poverty would be the house we dwelt in for the first ten years of my life; as soon as Lizzie, my eldest sister, and Edwin and Horace, my elder brothers, were all old enough to work, we moved. So you see I have to guard against exaggerating the duration of our poverty; and I mustn't write, either, as though the twelve of us children were all helpless infants at the same time: I was twenty when my youngest sister was born, and by then so many of us were earning that Lucy was brought up like a princess, or so it seemed to us elder ones.

That first house was in a court off Fussell Street, behind a row of terrace houses. In the court there were two rows of ten houses facing each other. Each house had four rooms and a scullery; and between the two rows of houses was a line of water-closets. It was not the worst kind of court: the houses had tap-water, though only cold of course; in some courts there was nothing more than a communal tap at the entrance. It was filthy, but we no more noticed that than pigs notice the squalor of their sties. It stank, but since we had been born in it the stink was not thought remarkable or even offensive: it was, I am sure I believed as a child, just the normal, natural odour of air. I remember that when I was a man, and an ardent and bitter socialist, I once went back to Fussell Street to look at the place where I had spent the first ten years of my life; and then the stink—it was of ordure and urine—hit me in the face physically, like the blast from a furnace, and for a moment I thought I might vomit. I was outraged to think that I had been brought up in such nauseating conditions, and my bitterness was naturally intensified. But, as I say, while I was actually living there it was all normal enough. After all, nearly all the children I knew lived in a similar state, and for me now the symbol of those early years is not the dirt and the filth, the sheer physical offensiveness of it all, but my eldest sister Lizzie's weekly Monday morning trip to the pawnbroker's on the corner of Fussell Street and Whiteway Street. Lizzie was the eldest of us, five years older than I, and she was a second mother to us all. All of us in turn when we were very young went to the pawnbroker's with her, clutching the side of the mail-cart she was pushing, piled high as it was with the family's best clothes. How absurd it was! It would have been unthinkable not to have worn special clothes for Sunday; and then money was raised on them on Monday, which had to be repaid, with interest, on Saturday so that the decencies could be observed on Sunday again. Week by week, the amount of money the pawnbroker advanced on the clothes diminished. And even at the beginning, when they were new, the sum couldn't have been much; for though they were new to us, they were not new in any other way: they had been bought for us by our mother either from a jumble sale or from this very pawnbroker's as unredeemed pledges. Never once did our mother fail to redeem our clothes on a Saturday night, at any rate the outer vestments, for sometimes the money would not stretch to underclothes. But it was the outer vestments, what the neighbours saw, that mattered, and we had only contempt for neighbours who were forced to appear in the same clothes on Sunday as those worn on weekdays.

We were, you see, very respectable, and since everyone else behaved in the same way, we saw nothing strange in this weekly ritual visit to the pawnbroker's. We stood in the queue outside the shop with all our neighbours, though there were two schools of thought on this. One believed that to be first in the queue was dangerous because then, so early in the morning, fresh to business, the pawnbroker was sharper-eyed, examined the goods more closely, could the less easily be imposed upon. The other school, while conceding the possibility of this, maintained that by the time the end of the queue reached him, the pawnbroker had become less willing to pay out money and so was the more prepared to cavil at the quality of the wares

48

offered. This was a favourite theme for argument in the queue itself, and Lizzie always tried to be at the half-way point. My own belief now is that the pawnbroker was guided entirely by his knowledge of his customer's reliability and that the articles themselves were little more than tokens, of ritual value only.

Though we were poor and knew it in a theoretical way, so far as our immediate social environment was concerned we stood high in the social scale. As I say, we *always* had best clothes for Sunday; and then our father was in regular work and, besides, was a craftsman. The social gulf was between craftsmen and skilled artisans on the one hand and labourers on the other. My father was very much aware of his dignity and status as a craftsman. Our social rank manifested itself in other ways, too. It was made plain at elections. My father naturally voted for the Liberal candidate and took good care that the candidate's portrait appeared in the front window. We all wore his favours at election times. Nearly all craftsmen and artisans were Liberal; but labourers usually voted Tory. This puzzled me as a boy and it puzzles me still, but I see it now as a kind of universal law, for in the days when I was politically active, the early days of the I.L.P. and the Labour Party, I soon discovered that it was from the superior working man, the skilled man, one got a respectful hearing while canvassing, whereas the unskilled were reactionary almost to the last degree. I believe this is still true.

Then the difference of status showed itself in such things as food. I remember—perhaps I was eight at the time—discussing the Christmas dinner with another boy. 'We had goose,' he boasted. 'We had goose, too,' I said. 'Was yours,' he asked, 'a green-bummed 'un? Ours was.' It was not a term I knew, but since it seemed to argue distinction in a goose I maintained that ours indeed was. Later, I asked my mother what the adjective meant, and after she had rebuked me for using such a common expression, she explained. A green-bummed 'un was a goose that could be bought very cheaply towards mid-night on Christmas Eve because putrefaction had begun to set in. When I asked her, in all innocence, whether our goose had been of such a kind she was aghast with horror and shame that I could think of such a thing. Tears came into her eyes, and 'Pray God we never sink so low as green-bummed 'uns,' she said.

49

It was mother, of course, who kept us respectable, who fought, one might almost say, to maintain our status. She had no help from father, who, though stiff with pride, cared nothing for respectability. I see now that she handled him badly, perhaps as badly as it was possible to do. People talk of women's wiles: I do not think they existed in the working-class women of my childhood. My mother certainly had none where my father was concerned, and I think she would have scorned them. With more tact, she might have managed him better, but tact was not a quality she recognised. The result was often comic, even if it didn't appear so at the time. Every Saturday night my father came home drunk, and what followed never varied. My father was generally happy in his cups, at least at the moment of entering the house. He would be singing, it might be a hymn—'Let us with a gladsome mind' was a favourite—or a music hall song, at the top of his voice. 'Bill,' my mother would say, for she always waited up for him, though there was no need to, 'Bill, remember the neighbours.' It was a fatal remark. Father stopped singing. He swung drunkenly round. 'Bugger the bloody neighbours,' he shouted at the top of his voice; 'I mind my business. Let the bloody neighbours mind theirs!' I suppose every Saturday night for twenty years my mother uttered those disastrous words to my father. But had she not done so, she would have felt, I think, that she was somehow condoning his behaviour. She was full of rectitude, stiff-necked, as I see now; and her character was shown by the phrases that were constantly on her tongue. She would have as little to do with her neighbours as possible. This was a principle, expressed in the phrases 'I believe in keeping myself to myself' and the corollary 'I won't be beholden to them.' As I see it now, she must have lived an intensely lonely life, for she had no companionship with her husband and scorned friends. It was also an intensely busy life. It was bound to be, from the nature of her state, with small children always about her; yet I suspect she made it busier than it need have been. She had to be on the go the whole time, and when nothing else remained to be done she would start cleaning the house again, scrubbing floors on hands and knees, raddling the front door step, whatever the hour, even though floors had been scrubbed or step raddled only the day before. It was as though she was engaged incessantly in fighting an unseen enemy. She was father's opposite in every way and, admirable as she was, she could be no comfort to him. But that was not how I saw things then.

Throughout my life I have been extremely class-conscious. It came upon me suddenly, like a physical blow. I was eight years old and the time was the August Bank Holiday. It was the late afternoon and very hot, and we were tired and bedraggled. We were in the country, making our way back to the point where the steam tram would take us back home. We must have looked an odd lot. There were, I suppose, seven of us children, and father and mother. We were dirty and sticky in our Sunday best, because in those days when you went into the country on Bank Holiday you wore your Sunday clothes. We were all small, stunted. None of us has ever grown above five feet five, and father, the biggest of us then, couldn't have been more than five feet two. We must have looked like a family of midgets trailing along the field path, pushing with us the inevitable mail-cart in which sat a child of one and a child of two, their mouths firmly bunged with comforters. Father, I remember, had a bottle of beer in each jacket pocket, and from time to time would stop and take a swig from one of them. We were walking very slowly, it was almost too hot to move; and fatigue and the heat had worn down our pleasure to a sullen irritability. But we were doing nothing wrong; we were not trespassing; merely walking along a public footpath that cut across some gentleman's estate. And then we saw the gentleman. He was on horseback, with two boys also on horseback, perhaps no older than I was, but at least four inches taller. They were a noble sight. When I saw them I felt myself light up in an enthusiasm that had no envy in it. They were like gods to me, so ruddy they were and handsome, so full of the pride of life. We dragged our way towards them, and they looked at us steadily as we approached, watching us from the height of their horses. As we straggled abreast of them they drew back to let us pass; but not generously, so that we had barely room to pass and had to flinch to avoid the horses' heads. And as we passed, I heard the gentleman say to his sons, 'Gutter rats!' He spoke quite dispassionately; he did not bother to lower his voice; it was as though he was pointing out to his children a species they had not seen before, one so remote from them as to be incapable of sharing the one language. We trudged on, saying nothing, as though we had heard nothing. Indeed, I cannot be sure that the others did, because I could never bring myself to mention it to any of them, even to Horace. When we came to the stile at the main road father took another swig from his bottle while Tom and Horace struggled to lift the mail-cart over. I looked back, and the gentleman and his sons were still watching us.

Years later, I read or was told, though whether true I do not know, that in India and Africa fine English ladies thought nothing of undressing and bathing in front of their native men servants, the notion being that the natives were so far removed from them in every way that they were not human. When I read or heard this I remembered instantly that episode on the field path. It was exactly like that.

As I say, I did not mention this occurrence to any of the others. It was as though I was struck dumb. I did not understand it. I could not see how the expression 'gutter rats' could apply to us. But I knew it was somehow shameful and I knew also that if I asked my mother about it tears would come into her eyes. It became a secret wound, an ulcer that festered; and what especially carked me was the realisation that when I had first seen the gentleman and his sons it was with a pure enthusiasm; I might even say a pure adoration, as in the presence of the beautiful. When, years later, I read *The Tempest*, my sympathy was instantly with the much-wronged Caliban.

After that, my education in consciousness of class was swift and progressive. When I was eleven I won a scholarship from the board school to the King Edward's Grammar School at Barnfield, and in a way I was luckier than I knew. The school at Barnfield had not yet been built, and the teaching was carried on at the High School in the centre of the town. These grammar schools, which in a way were branches of the old High School, were new institutions. The High School had been founded for the poor boys of the town, but after three hundred years it had become the school for the middle-class. I suppose the grammar schools were established in order to make good, at least in some degree, the wishes of the founder. I would have been proud to go to the Barnfield building, had it existed, but

I am sure my feelings of awe would have been nothing compared to those I had on going to the High School. It was in what is now called Victorian Gothic—Pugin was the architect —but for me Gothic and Victorian Gothic were one and the same, and Pugin's school, with its pinnacles, its fretted windows, great oak beams and leaded lights, was venerability itself. It was as awesome as a cathedral (and almost as dark), and I responded to it ardently. My spirit soared each morning as I entered: I saw it, as it were, as the nursery of greatness, and I too would be great. And none of this was dimmed at all by the fact that we were not of the High School and Pugin's building (they've built a cinema and a Marks & Spencers where it used to stand) and that we were ignored by the High School boys proper. They left us coldly alone as often as they saw us, for in fact we were taught separately by different masters and attended at different hours. This crude manifestation of class I was young enough to take for granted without rancour. I knew that the boys of the High School were the sons of the town's industrialists and professional men; I had nothing in common with them. The one thing I envied them was that they learned both Greek and Latin, whereas Latin was deemed enough for us. Nor was I bothered at all by the class differences between myself and the other boys of the Barnfield School. At the board school, I had been in the highest rank of the social hierarchy; here, I was certainly in the lowest, indeed so lowly as to comprise a rank all of my own. Yet I did not care and was not seriously aware of it. In a way, I was lucky, as I see now. I knew very well how great the odds were against my being there at all. True, I had my scholarship, but there were still books to be bought, and there had had to be new clothes. Indeed, the only reason I was able to go was that Lizzie and Edwin and Horace were now at work, so that, for the time being at any rate, we were not so straitened in means as we had been. At the same time, there were no compulsory games and no special clothes for games. Had there been, that alone might well have prevented my going; nor indeed was there any uniform at all, save for the mortar-board that I wore with such pride. I was the first boy from Fussell Street ever to go to any school higher than a board school and I was proud of it.

While I was at the Barnfield School I was in a dream, a

dream of glory. I was moved not only by the building but by the romantic quality of it all, it was so different from my real world. I was moved, for instance, by the fact that the masters taught in gowns and that we learned exotic subjects like Latin and French and algebra. It was as though I had my being in a dedicated place, and I felt at home there; as I must have been because I was top of the form in all subjects at the end of each term.

At Barnfield I became my mother's son: I kept myself to myself and would not be beholden to anyone. I made no friends, partly no doubt because a great part of schoolboy friendships springs from the boys walking the same way home, and none of my classmates lived anywhere near Fussell Street. But perhaps I did make one friend, of a sort. He was a boy named Whipple, the son of a draper in a small way of business. He wooed me in his own currency, which was doughnuts. His wooing was not disinterested. He was fat and stupid but he had the grace to know it, and he fed me with doughnuts in return for tuition with his algebra and Latin. He must have told his parents about me, for, to my surprise, he came one day armed with messages inviting me to visit them on Saturday afternoon to help him with his work. I did so, and after that went every Saturday afternoon. The Whipples lived in what seemed to me enormous opulence: when we worked together on Saturday afternoons the two of us had nothing less than a room to ourselves, a room in which you could have put the whole ground floor of our house. I realise now that they had only just come into this opulence and that they were impressed by it almost as much as I was; for every Saturday, before lessons began, young Whipple would take me upstairs to see the bathroom, a thing which, needless to say, I had never seen before, and solemnly point out to me its grandeur, turning on the taps, both hot and cold, of the wash-hand basin and the bath and flushing the closet to prove to me that it worked.

After our lessons I was regaled with tea, such a tea as I never had at home. A kind of ceremony was made of it, with the parents, who were both fat and red, hovering over me and plying me with good things: steaming pork sausages, muffins, fruit cake, scones and strawberry jam. They obviously believed I did not get enough to eat at home; and always, when the meal was ended and it was time for me to go home, Mr Whipple would say, as though striking a fair balance of qualities, 'You may be poor but you're clever!' and then give me a sixpenny bit.

I am bound to say that I took easily to this patronage. Alas, it was not to last: when I had been at the school four terms I had suddenly to leave: my parents could no longer afford to keep me there. There was a new baby, and it was time I worked for my living.

This seemed to me so reasonable that though I left the school with sadness I did so without repining. Indeed, it was not until comparatively recently, that is within the past thirty years, that I suddenly realised how odd it was that the masters themselves should have made no effort to keep me there. I had after all been consistently at the head of my class. It was my son Phil who pointed out the strangeness of this. I can only think it was not strange then. Yet it was a wonderful experience for me, going to the Grammar School, one that changed my life. Or so I feel, for I cannot prove it. It opened my eyes to horizons I would not have glimpsed from Fussell Street alone. It was rich and strange. Those masters in their gowns were transfigured men, built, or so it seemed to me, on a vaster scale than ordinary humanity. They were Gothic like the building they inhabited, and their ferocity and eccentricity matched the gargoyles that looked down on us as we entered and left the school. I remember the headmaster, The Rev. Mr Simmons, M.A. (Cantab.). How formidable I found him. I believe now that all schoolmasters cultivate some pet foible, some special branch of knowledge to which they attach transcendent importance. Mr Simmons's was mental arithmetic; but the problems he propounded were based on curious knowledge in which each boy, as he came to the school, had to be instructed. This was the length of the human intestines. I can see him now, at prayers in Big School, a giant in his black gown and black beard that completely hid his clerical collar. He reads the General Confession with enormous dignity, in organ tones, we repeating the words with him, and then the Prayer for the Founder and the Lord's Prayer. And no sooner is the last amen said than, in one prodigious leap it seems, he has come from behind the lectern, is at the edge of the dais pointing an enormous hairy hand at a small boy and shouting, 'You, boy! The price of your tripes at threepence three-farthings a foot? Quick! Next. Next. Next.' And so, if the sum was at all difficult, in the end, 'Ashted!' I am afraid I was never wrong. 'Humph!' he would say, and then, 'Dismiss!'

I was there for fifteen months. There wasn't time for me to learn much more than that in any right-angle triangle the square on the hypotenuse is equal to the sum of the squares on the other two sides, *mensa mensam mensae mensae mensa mensae mensas mensarum mensis mensis* and *amo amas amat amamus amatis amant*. Yet even that was something, and indeed I found even so small an amount of Latin as I have invaluable in my work. As an engraver and die-sinker I was always having to cut Latin mottoes on medals and cups. Our customers were often men of much better education than ourselves, but that did not prevent me on numerous occasions from being able to correct their Latin grammar by inserting the correct case ending or the proper form of the verb. Indeed, on my smattering of Latin I have been regarded as a prodigy of learning in every work-shop where I was employed.

7

I LEFT school, as I say, without repining. I was neither outraged nor rebellious. I was thirteen: it was time to start being
a man. The truth is, being at the Grammar School had nothing
to do with actual life, life as lived in time. I don't mean to
imply that it was not real; it was intensely real, but it was
purely private to myself, to an interior life outside time. I
scarcely related it to actuality at all. Perhaps I was not there
long enough. I had always known I should be a silversmith
like my father and my elder brothers, and being at the
Grammar School did not change that. I had no sudden
thoughts of becoming a doctor or a clergyman or a school-
master; I never for a moment thought of school as a possible
bridge to a superior station. Was it that I was without ambition?
Perhaps so: I don't think I have ever been ambitious for
myself, except in a very modest way; I am sure George would
have said, in a too modest way, and so would Phil. There was
a time, many years later, when I thought it might be possible for
me to make my living playing the fiddle; but I did not dream of
anything more grand than playing in the quartet at the Rialto
Cinema a quarter of a mile away from where we lived. Yet I
feel it was not as simple as lack of ambition. Though I scarcely
saw any of my classmates at the Grammar School once I had
left I have from time to time heard of their activities or seen
them reported in the newspapers. They were the sons of shopkeepers and small manufacturers, lowly enough certainly, but
to me as a boy proud sprigs of the upper class. And what did
they do with themselves? They became shopkeepers and manufacturers and, as by-products, aldermen and magistrates. And
one, it is true, became a millionaire. George knew him—they
were on a hospital board together—and scorned him; and
that was in George's mellower days. George called him the

57

'Poor White', because, with all the money in the world, he was completely lacking in resources within himself. For George, the symbol of this was the gold bath the millionaire had had installed in his great house. 'A precious lot of good that school you went to did *him*,' George would say. Still, he became a millionaire, and what could be more successful than that? Yet I think the success was almost automatic; I think he could not help himself. I realise now that his parents were probably well off by our standards when I knew him as a boy, though there was little to show it. His father had a little press shop, in a very small way, as *his* father had done before him; and when the Poor-White-to-be left school he went to work in it, too, and did his stint on the presses himself. I suppose it was the Boer War, with its sudden enormous demand for regimental badges, that first put them on the path to a future; and the 1914-1918 War, with its millions of conscripts all of whom had to wear regimental badges, that took them the rest of the way.

My classmate became a millionaire, but it was not talent which made him one, nor ambition. If he thought about it at all, and I question whether he had imagination enough for that, he was probably the most surprised man in the world. I think, in fact, that none of us had ambition in the usual sense, the Samuel Smiles sense, for, as I see it now—and I think this is as true of my lower middle-class schoolfellows as of myself—we were too submerged for ambition to be possible. Our horizons were too narrow. Only genius or some overmastering talent could have rescued us. George himself is a witness to this. He was a man of inordinate ambition, and in certain fields there was nothing he could not conceive of himself doing. Yet for all his innate ambition he was in his twenties before he discovered the forms which his ambition might take. He had to find it out for himself, and by the time he did he was already committed to ways of life that tended inevitably to frustrate it. He had to make the best of a bad job.

Within six months of starting work I did, in fact, acquire an ambition. But more of that later: all I say now is that it had nothing to do with my work. I had been put to learning the silversmith's craft and I went to work at Darnley's. Those were barbarous days for boys beginning in factories and workshops, and the first months of a boy's working life were often hell, a hell of persecution, petty tyranny and sometimes even of obscene degradation at the hands of his fellow-workers. I was spared this; Darnley's was a more respectable shop than most. But a few years later, when I was grown up, I was so outraged by the spectacle of the continuous stupid bullying that went on almost as a ritual—indeed, I see now, at this moment of writing, that ritual was precisely what it was—that I joined the local Athletic Club and took lessons in boxing, the more effectively to intervene in the protection of boys; for I had learnt from observation that, given reasonably fair conditions, the man who knew something of the art of boxing could generally prevail against any opponent, however much stronger, who was ignorant of it.

As a boy at Darnley's, though, I was privileged. I was spared not only the grosser indignities of initiation ceremonies, but also such time-honoured jokes as being sent out to buy a pint of pigeon's milk, a pound of elbow grease or a rubber-headed hammer. There were two reasons. One was my father's prestige. He did not work at Darnley's, but he was famous in the trade, famous in several ways. His drinking exploits were spoken of with great respect. Then there was his ferocious independence: 'Cocky Ashted,' I heard a man say once, 'don't give a damn for nobody.' Yet neither his feats as a drinker nor his habit of sacking the boss would have been significant had he not been also a superlative craftsman. That was the foundation of his fame and the respect in which he was held; for workmen have a reverence almost for superlative craftsmanship. I was accepted as his son.

The other reason was the presence in the shop of my brother Horace. He was only two years older than I. No doubt he, too, when he had first gone to Darnley's, had been protected, however much he must have resented it, by the invisible influence of my father. By the time I came to Darnley's he was almost aggressively not the man our father was; except in one respect, his workmanship. It was still, of course, of promise rather than achievement, but the deference paid to him was that to a prodigy; and I was his protégé. He had imposed himself upon the rough men in the shop by the sheer force of his character. Even I, who loved him, can see it was not always an endearing character. His work apart, he had nothing in common with his mates. He was, in the shop phrase, 'sanctimonious,' excessively so, as uncomfortable a presence to have in their midst as a parson in a dog-collar. He didn't bother to hide his pitying contempt for them, or rather for their talk and behaviour, for he would never have admitted contempt for them as immortal souls. I can see him now, and I can fix the occasion in my memory. The time was towards the end of the day; work had slackened off, except of course for Horace, with whom it was a point of honour to work right up to the moment of knocking-off time: it was what he had contracted to do in return for his wage. The talk, in the relaxed early evening atmosphere, was of monstrous births, of women who had borne litters of rabbits or puppies, the superstitions of the very ignorant. I was pretending to work but listening with guilty fascination; and suddenly I looked up and saw my conscience made visible: Horace at his board, bent over his work with the graver poised above the die, in his eye the watchmaker's glass, and below, the thin lips twisted in a sneer of unutterable disdain. In memory, his pride and scorn were nothing less than satanic. Hastily, I closed my ears and busied myself with my work.

The strange thing is, he was accepted. Or perhaps it is not strange: men respond to power, and Horace had power. In a curious way, his mates were proud of him; they recognised indomitableness. The first day I went to work at Darnley's a boy a little older than myself, a sawney possessed of a sudden enthusiasm for grown-up life and therefore the sounding board for all the received opinions of the shop, told me a story about Horace. 'Your big kid's a rum bugger,' he said, and he recounted the instance of Horace's rumness that had him goggle-eyed. A new hand had come to work at Darnley's who was particularly foul-mouthed. He spoke to Horace, asking him for some information, in speech interlarded with the dirtiest oaths. Horace ignored him. The man repeated his question and his obscenities. Horace took no notice. The fellow jumped up, brandishing his buff-stick, a weapon commonly used for rapping boys' knuckles or striking them across the head. 'Yo' heard!' he bawled. 'Answer me, you young bleeder.' Very deliberately, Horace placed his graver on the bench at the side of the die he was working on and removed the glass from his eye. Then he looked up at the man. 'Are you speaking to me?'

he mildly asked. 'You bloody well know I am.' 'Then kindly wash your mouth out before doing so again'; and he inserted the glass in his eye once more, picked up his graver and dug it again into the metal of the die. All was still in the shop as the workmen watched and waited, staring at the new man looming with his buff-stick in hand above Horace and Horace quietly working as though ignorant of everything else. 'Yo' could have heard a pin drop,' the boy told me. They waited. Horace went on working. Slowly the stick wavered in the man's raised hand; he seemed to sag and draw back. Then he turned to the watching shop and mumbled, 'Some of these nippers is too big for their boots.' He was defeated, and they stared him out without saying a word. He sat down at his bench and took up his work. At the end of the week he left.

No wonder Horace was my hero and I his disciple. I worshipped him, yet, urge myself on as I did, I was never more than a half-hearted disciple. I felt guilty about this, taking it as evidence of a lack in myself. Horace was already set, fixed and self-contained. Where he got his notion of Divine Election from I don't know, for we had been brought up in the broad Church of England and bundled off as children to St Barnabas' every Sunday morning; the Vicar was a very pleasant gentleman who preached an unreflecting feudalism. But Horace, without at that time knowing it, was already a dyed-in-the-wool Calvinist; and there, though I pretended passionately to agree with him, I couldn't follow him for more than five minutes at a time. I was predisposed, perhaps, to worry at the spectacle of human suffering, especially when it seemed remediable and preventable, the suffering that comes from poverty in particular. Horace brushed all this aside. He wasn't unsympathetic; he was in fact a very charitable man; but whereas I saw unfairness he saw God's justice. It was too deep for me. I might have been convinced if I had been as convinced that I was one of the saved as Horace was of himself; but I felt salvation must have something to do with merit or at least with effort. Horace assured me this was not so. I couldn't understand this capricious God of Horace's whose whimsical behaviour seemed to me much like my father's when drunk: sometimes He cursed and cuffed, sometimes kissed and cast pennies in all directions, and you could never tell which

He would do, from one half-hour to another. Of course Horace was a Radical, and often a fierce one, but only because he had persuaded himself that the rich and powerful were more likely to be damned than the poor. There was Scriptural warrant for the assumption. But social reform seemed to him a meddling in God's province. Man's lot on earth for him was largely an irrelevance, though he did admit that an unpropitious lot might be a means by which a man could acquire merit, which God might—though no one could presume to know—find worthy of notice. That 'might' wasn't good enough for me.

No; my debt to Horace lay in his very unlikeness to the world in which we lived. He showed me, simply by being the youth he was, that other values were possible. He pointed the way to a different world, indeed to many different worlds, some of which he himself was not at home in and had no sympathy for. In our billycock hats and with our stiff dickies under our waistcoats we became great walkers. He introduced me to the country, and week-end after week-end we roamed the country-side that was near us. We revelled in it, though in our different ways. Horace saw nature as God's vestment; it was to be adored as an aspect of God: he flatly opposed it to sinful man and his works. For my part, it ministered both to my sense of wonder and to my desire for knowledge. I was overjoyed by the spectacle of natural life, by the ceaselessness and prodigality of it; and not only by natural life but by country life generally. It was a pageant of magic pictures. I remember once—it was winter and it may well have been a Boxing Day, for it had become a tradition with us to walk in the country that day—looking over a still and silent landscape, in which it seemed all life had withdrawn into itself and lay shrivelled up in hiding. Suddenly we heard a clamour and saw straight away below us the long line of hounds and the riders following, men in red coats and ladies in black with silk hats and bowler hats. It was the first fox-hunt I had ever seen and it was like a frieze come to life. It is fixed in my mind still like something out of heraldry, so sharp is the fusion between the violence of the movement on the one hand and the formal order of it on the other. It was all so fast: one moment the hounds and riders stretched out before us in sudden barbaric noise, and then all was gone, the landscape as still and silent as before and untouched. I was entranced; my heart was lifted up, exultant. I was not envious; I did not want to be in the hunt; I spontaneously rejoiced at the colour and richness and the splendour, the magical expression, it seemed, of sheer animal exuberance and high spirits. How long I held the mood I don't know; not more than a few moments in actual time I expect; for Horace said: 'Barbarous!' and dismissed it thus, his lips tight in contempt and disgust. 'Barbarous!' I agreed. I was too much in awe of him to admit that for me beauty had suddenly been and as suddenly vanished.

As a youth in the country I was like a small child suddenly set free; it was as though I had been turned loose in Tom Tiddler's Ground, with all its store of gold and silver waiting to be picked up. And the country has always had this effect on me. I have never been able willingly to turn and retrace my steps while there was a corner visible ahead or the brow of a hill to be surmounted, for round every corner, beyond each hill, wonders were waiting. Horace was mildly indulgent of me: curiosity was normally a sin, but curiosity in the country was, so to speak, an innocent sin. Birds delighted me. At home we had sparrows and starlings, and there were blackbirds and thrushes, robins, chaffinches, tits and rooks, in the parks and the suburbs; but here in the country there were so many I did not know, whose gay plumage and neat motions mocked my ignorance. Nothing would satisfy me until I knew them. I got books from the free library and in the course of time learned to identify some of them at any rate. I remember the first goldcrest I ever recognised. It was in a small pine wood that flanked the side of the road. So tiny a bird I had not seen before. What could it be? And then—for I had the information laid out scientifically in my mind, habitat, plumage, characteristic movement and so on—it came to me what it must be. In my excitement, I ran after Horace, calling, 'Horace, a goldcrest! I've seen a goldcrest!' And Horace nodded his head and smiled benignly. He wasn't surprised at all. It merely made no difference to his pleasure in nature not to know one bird from another, unless it were small, in which case it was probably a wren, or very big, in which case it might be a buzzard, or a herring gull, in which case it was a seagull. It was enough that it was one of God's creatures.

Horace also led me to education. As I have said, what I had learnt at the grammar school had no relation to anything in my everyday life: it was gloriously useless, like the fascinating pebbles a child hoards. But Horace told me that if I wished to be a good craftsman I must go with him to the evening classes at the School of Art. I did so, and almost before I knew it I was going to evening classes every night of the week except Saturday and Sunday. The Art School was not enough for me; or rather, it led to other things. I was to spend my life working in gold and silver. I felt the need to know all about them, and this the Art School could not tell me. My curiosity was such that I could not be happy until I had discovered why gold was gold and in what consisted the silverness of silver. So I added classes at the Mechanics' Institute to those at the School of Art and began to learn chemistry and physics and metallurgy; and so I discovered yet another world, a world of precise measurement, a world, it seemed to me then, of fundamentals. I learned why gold was gold and not silver.

It was at the Mechanics' Institute that I met George Thompson, a very young moulder, three years older than I, and he impressed me as soon as I saw him. Most of the students were artisans bent on improving themselves. We were a very humble lot, content, even grateful to take what the lecturers told us as gospel; and the lecturers were pretty perfunctory. There was a minimum of practical work, and the demonstrations of experiments that the lecturers staged for us were often sketchy. Sometimes they didn't work, and then the lecturer would say, 'Well, you see the idea, anyway.' For the most part, the instruction consisted of the lecturer dictating to us while we, always a sentence behind, laboriously wrote down the lecturer's words as faithfully as we could remember them.

Naturally, I saw nothing wrong with this method of teaching at all: the lecturers knew, and they were telling us. I was ready to venerate them as men of knowledge: they were, in fact, board-school teachers whose fate it was to teach during evenings in the same horribly dark, dingy, overcrowded classrooms they taught in during the day. They were a depressed set of men. George was merciless towards them, but they had to put up with him: he was, after all, by far the best student they had, and examination results were important to them.

The rest of the class hated him: he broke up the even flow of dictation. As one man grumbled to me: 'How can the teachers get through the syllabus if that Thompson keeps on interrupting?' For George would jump up amid the lecturer's droning and say, 'Sir, I don't see that'; or—it might have been about the laws of heat—'The experiment quoted doesn't prove the law.' Once, even, at the end of one demonstration: 'I did not understand that. Could you please repeat the experiment?' and then it was perfectly plain that the lecturer had made a botch of his demonstration, knew he had, and was trying to fob us off with a faulty display. George would have none of it; and I watched him with wonder as he rose from his desk, short, though not as short as I, but with very broad shoulders and his great domed head and rock-like jaw. I watched him, as I say, with fear and trembling, for to me the teachers represented not only knowledge but also authority; they were little gods, and George was a Prometheus defying them.

But that is to be subjective, as Phil would say. George stood out in those classes as Horace would have done, for his qualities of decision and certainty, the sense he gave of belonging to himself, of owing nothing to anyone, of being in a way self-created, a law unto himself. *He* didn't see the teachers as gods. He saw them as men who, very often, were not doing their jobs, whether through laziness or ignorance, and who yet were at that moment essential to him; and he wouldn't be fobbed off. He was not prepared to take things on trust, and if the proof offered did not seem to him adequate he was going to say so, in order to obtain one that was. He was serious in a way that no one else, teachers or students, was.

I had been attending these evening classes four weeks before he spoke to me. He kept himself to himself; indeed, he walked and talked in a manner so brusque that he seemed to be brushing people aside. When he did speak to me it was in characteristic fashion. At the end of the class he walked across the room to me and said: 'Ashted, join me in a pie at Boswell's.' I was taken aback. Here was no tentative fumbling towards acquaintanceship, but something that was half-way between an order and a challenge. And there was something else. In those days, we working men were sticklers for the formalities; we mistered one another like mad. You could work at the next bench to a man for years, spend a third of your life with him for years, yes and be intimate with him, and neither of you would ever be anything else but Mister to the other. Christian names were reserved almost exclusively for use by members of the family and by relations; while to be called starkly by your surname was insulting; it was to be treated as an inferior. Horace was very firm on that: nobody ever addressed him as Ashted twice, or called him Horace without his permission; except, of course, George, who disregarded such considerations as frivolities.

So I ought to have been affronted by George's curt demand. Instead, I found myself following him out of the classroom in a state of bewilderment. 'Me?' I had asked, and George nodded impatiently. I felt flattered: George had chosen me, why or for what I did not know.

He led the way to Boswell's. I had not been there before, for I was still boy enough to regard it as grand and sophisticated beyond me. It stood almost at the top of Lorimer Street, just round the corner from Council Street, in the centre of the town: a few steps, and you looked across to the small Cathedral, which was and is still what is called a pro-cathedral, a church built at the beginning of the eighteenth century by a disciple of Wren: I have always loved it for its beauty, though Horace, who believed churches should be either Gothic or huts of corrugated iron, hated it, calling it a gewgaw and, sometimes even, a Pagan bauble. Boswell's was one of those coffee-houses which sprang up half-way through the last century, backed by philanthropic business men, in order to wean the working-classes from public houses and gin-palaces. It was famous for its hot meat pies, as I appreciated when, timidly, I followed George to a zinc-topped table in the far corner. One sat marooned as it were in mingled odours that had the density and palpability of fog. Steam, through which loomed vaguely the great copper coffee and tea urns on the counter and the figures of men at other tables, was the solvent in which these odours were borne, and the odours were those of tobacco pipes, wet macintoshes and bubbling hot meat pies. It was a pleasing blend of smells that titillated the nostrils and made the mouth water, for dominant all the time was the savour of the pies. It promised richness and succulence, a tenderness of meat, a

66

consistency of gravy-soaked pastry, unsurpassed. I sat down
with George and knew I wanted one of those pies more at that
moment than anything in the world.

The waitress came over and washed our table-top down with
a wet rag. 'Two pies and two coffees,' commanded George,
without consulting me; and then, having taken a pipe and
pouch from his pocket, he began furiously to load the pipe and
almost instantly as furiously to puff out huge clouds of blue
smoke with evident relish; but not before he had pushed the
pouch across the table towards me. 'I don't smoke,' I said.
'Pity,' he grunted, and nothing more was said by either of us
until the coffee and pies arrived. We fell on them as though
starving. Too soon they were gone, and peremptorily, again
without consulting me, George commanded two more. And
those we lingered over, sipping, as it were, the richness of the
gravy on the taste-buds of the tongue, testing the firmness of
the meat on our teeth. Then, when they were finished—and
George did not scruple to mop up the gravy on the plate with
half a piece of bread—he said: 'Boswell's pies are *good*,' and
then he quite confounded me by adding: 'If a man write a
better book, preach a better sermon, or make a better mouse-
trap than his neighbour, though he build his house in the
woods, the world will make a beaten path to his door.' He
stared at me. 'Who said that?' he demanded. I did not know.
'Emerson. Ralph Waldo Emerson. You must read him. There
are great truths there. What do you think of this? "History is
but the lengthened shadow of a man." Eh?'

It was a notion entirely new to me. I did not know what it
meant but I saw straight away that Horace would never agree.
I said lamely, 'I've never thought of that before.'

George looked at me sardonically. 'No doubt there are a lot
of things you've never thought of before, Ashted. That night
school: I wonder if it's ever struck you how very shoddy it is,
how incompetent the teaching. You may take my word for it,
Ashted: what we are given there is a parody of knowledge. And
why? Because our betters still believe that anything is good
enough for working people, the likes of you and me. Yet even
that is progress, Ashted, because only a few years ago nothing,
not anything, was good enough for us. So we mustn't be
indignant, or rather we must keep our indignation for more

67

serious things and try and use the third-best that's thrown to us in such a way as to give us an inkling of the first-best. It can be done.'

He got up. 'I've got to be up at five,' he said, 'and must go now. Come and see me on Saturday evening at seven o'clock. I live on the corner of Barwell Street and Heathcote Street West—it's a shop. I've got things to show you and I'll lend you Emerson.' He got into his overcoat.

I stood up. 'But I owe you for the pies and coffee,' I said. He waved my words aside with his hand and, without saying anything else, turned away, paid at the counter and was out through the door. When it was closed behind him I too got up and went.

I might have run after him and caught him and accompanied him on his way, which was also mine; but I was shy. I felt he wanted to be alone now. I was shy for another reason too: *I* wanted to be alone; not to think, but to feel, to indulge in the luxury of rejoicing. I had a friend. For the first time in my life, I had a friend.

I walked out of Boswell's and without realising it into Council Street. I was lost to all about me, rapt in the revelation of friendship, so that I walked into a passer-by whose surly 'Look where you're going, can't you' shocked me into a dazed awakening. And as when one is suddenly jarred out of a deep sleep one doesn't know where one is, so it was then: I stared across the street without understanding. It had been raining and was now fine, the deep blue sky lit with brilliant stars that flashed. Silhouetted against the splendid sky was the cathedral church, and I saw it as though for the first time, as though I did not know it was a church, as though it had no name. And what I saw was its strange beauty, or the beauty of its strangeness. Did I know then that this church and the whole school of architecture it belonged to were derived from a remote Mediterranean world centuries old? I do not think so. All I saw was that this church, which was not old as churches go, somehow rebuked by the grace and elegance of its proportions the sprawling industrial ugliness, the narrow streets, the shops, the factories, the rotting tenements in which it was set. It rebuked them and yet it was enhanced by them. And—why, I still do not know—this sudden realisation of a rebuking, austere, ennobling beauty seemed to reflect the equally sudden realisation of my friendship with George.

No wonder I felt mazed or drunk. Something new had come into my life. I had never had a friend before. I'd not been aware of the deprivation. I'd not been a lonely child: when you're one of a family of children that increases every year loneliness isn't possible. In a way, I think I was lonely then, at that moment of perception, for the first time in my life; as though friendship had brought loneliness with it. Of course there had always been Horace, but a brother, however much loved and however close to you, is not a friend, for he is part of you; and perhaps even then I had dimly realised that if Horace had not been my brother we could never have been friends. Outside the blood-relationship, I could have as well hated him as loved him. Whatever it was I felt for Horace I knew that what I already felt for George was utterly different. And I walked home willing Saturday evening to come straight-away; I couldn't wait.

When it came, however, I was full of fear: had I been build-ing a huge fabric of illusion on foundations that were not there? Almost I did not go. I was impressed, too, by George's parents' keeping a corner shop. It was, as I saw while I hesitated outside, just like any other corner shop, behind its windows a jumble of goods, a ham, packets of Lipton's tea, tins of Cadbury's cocoa, bottles of boiled sweets, iced cakes, a coiled washing line, a few oranges, a basket of monkey nuts, bottles of hair oil and cough mixtures and patent medicines; as though everything that was in stock must be represented in the shop window. And high in either window a fly-paper hope-fully dangled, though it was not the season for flies: one was supposed to assume a concern for hygiene. Still, corner shops were corner shops; none of us who did not own one was ever convinced that they were not, to use the common phrase, 'little goldmines.' To enter, to go behind the counter into the living-quarters beyond, was to climb a rung in the ladder of class and power.

As I opened the door, the inevitable bell tinkled, and did so again as I closed the door. Within, it was cavernous and shadowy, for the gas light was turned low. There was that curious, warm smell of all corner shops, frowsty, but neither quite repellent nor wholly enticing; an atmosphere of its own, a compound of vegetable smells, apples, new bread, Indian corn and lamp oil. From within came a man's shout of 'shop!' answered by a girl's voice, 'Coming!' And the girl appeared, pausing to turn up the gas light before facing me behind the counter, a girl who could only be George's younger sister, perhaps two years my junior; but all I noticed then was her flowing mass of chestnut-brown hair, the longest I had ever seen; it hung right down her back, cascading from a great bow of red ribbon at the nape of her neck. She stared at me solemnly. 'Please,' I said, 'is George in?'

For answer, she lifted up the flap of the counter so that I could pass, and shouted, 'George! There's a young man!' A moment of waiting, and George emerged from the interior. 'Ah, Ashted! This way.' He led me through the living-room, not bothering to introduce me to his family but almost ignoring them in the sense of purpose that mastered him, through the kitchen and scullery into the backyard. He flung the door of the wash-house open with a flourish. 'There!' he said.

I was entranced, for here was what every young man of my cast of mind wanted at that time and despaired of getting: a room of his own. It was lit by an oil lamp, and the light was good because the brick walls had been newly whitewashed, and heated by a small, obviously home-made coke brazier. The disadvantages were plain; when George closed the door the room filled with bitter fumes, but since he did not seem to mind I did not, either; and when the smoke became too heavy we merely opened the door slightly for a few minutes and appreciated the fug the more after the blast of cold. But what particularly excited me was what George had done with his mother's wash-house. Boards had been laid across the top of the copper to make a large table; he had converted the room into a small laboratory. 'Of course,' he explained, 'most of the experiments I can't repeat at all. I haven't got a balance, or a supply of gas for a bunsen. But there are a few things I can do, and those I can't we can always compare notes about and discuss and read up. What I think we should do tonight is start going through the course on Light from the beginning.'

George didn't ask for my consent; he took my agreement for granted. He was right, of course; but how, I wondered, had he come to pick me out as his partner from the fifty or sixty young men in the class? It was unimportant; what mattered was that we spent an enjoyable and profitable hour squinting at the images of pins in mirrors and prisms, testing for ourselves the first laws of optics; and much that had before been dark and obscure to me became clear as George questioned and expounded. We went on until George's sister called us to supper.

As we crossed the yard George said to me: 'You'll find a deal of nonsense is spoken and believed in this house.' It was said as a flat statement brooking no contradiction: George was dissociating himself from his family. In fact, I recall nothing very nonsensical being said at the supper table. I was not in any case in a mood to be critical. I had had very little experience of visiting other people or of being entertained in their homes. I was made welcome, and it seemed that the prestige George enjoyed in his family was automatically shared by me as his friend. So in a quite unostentatious way I was made much of, and I for my part was prepared to fall in love with the Thompsons as a family. They were very different from my own, so different they seemed odd. It was extraordinary to me that George's father should be sitting down with his wife and children to supper on Saturday night; I could not remember my father doing anything so unnatural in his life. But there was Mr Thompson carving the boiled ham at the top of the table as though the celebrant of a religious rite. At his elbow was a jug of beer that Rose had fetched from the off-licence round the corner: a jug of beer on Saturday night—it was as good as total abstinence. And then the smallness of our numbers gave an air of spaciousness to the meal: there were only George's parents, his younger brother Hugh, perhaps the same age as myself, his sister Rose, who had held up the flap of the counter for me when I first came, and George himself. I gathered there was an elder brother, Morgan, who was out, where I did not know but certainly on some errand disapproved of by George. And it was a very much better meal than we ever had at home on Saturday night; cold boiled ham and brisket, with piccalilli and pickled onions and cheese and cocoa: it was almost up to the Whipple standard.

It was, I felt, a happier, certainly a more harmonious family than mine, and one living on an altogether grander scale. Mrs

71

Thompson questioned me in the conventional way. Where did I live? I was conscious that in her eyes the address was inferior to theirs. How many brothers and sisters had I? And when I answered 'nine' she tut-tutted and said, 'Your poor mother!' What job of work did I do? I said I was to be a silversmith, and she nodded approvingly, saying, 'There's nothing like a steady trade.' George sat apart from all this; perhaps it was what he meant by nonsense. And the questions came to an end with Mr Thompson saying heartily: 'That's enough now, mother. Don't pester the lad any more.'

The scene was perhaps not very different from anything I had met before, but I couldn't escape realising that the assumptions governing it were very different indeed. Like my father and every other working man I had ever seen at table, Mr Thompson was collarless in waistcoat and shirt-sleeves, but apart from that he did not resemble them at all. Even I, who knew nothing about such things, could see his table manners were something special: he was scrupulous to leave a fragment of ham and brisket, a sliver of onion on the side of his plate at the end of the meal, 'for etiquette.' I had heard of this but not seen it practised before and was much impressed. And once, when he broke wind, he redeemed the grossness and made it humorous by affecting astonishment and saying: 'Rose, my dear, drive that little dog out of the room.' His face was, as it were, a weaker edition of George's, soft and ingenuous and rubicond where his son's was hard and stern and decisive. It shone with a wide-eyed, naïve hope which was expressed, too, in the sentiments that seemed to fall naturally from his lips. He poured beer from the jug into a tumbler, which he courteously raised in my honour. 'May you ever climb the hill of prosperity,' he said ceremoniously, 'and never meet a brother coming down.' That, he explained, was the toast of the Royal and Ancient Order of Buffaloes, of which he had the privilege and honour of being Worthy Primo at the Star and Anchor lodge. 'The pater,' he said—and the piety and pride were unmistakable—'of course was a Mason.'

Now, no one had referred to his father as 'pater' in my hearing before; it was a word that belonged exclusively to boys' tales of upper-class school life, and it seemed to me so ludicrously la-di-da that I could scarcely restrain a giggle. I was saved by George: looking wildly about me, I was suddenly aware that his apparently impassive face turned to mine was creased by a wink. This, I guessed, was the nonsense.

Mr Thompson said no more at the moment. I had time to realise that the use of the word 'pater' was not necessarily affectation, for despite his clothes, he did not look like any working man I knew and his accent was certainly not working-class. There was a Welsh lilt in it, but apart from that, his voice was more like the vicar's than my father's. By the end of the meal I knew what the nonsense was about, for Mr and Mrs Thompson addressed themselves to me with a snobbery so innocent that it was scarcely snobbery at all: they merely wished it to be understood that they were not as others were. To me, it was all hugely romantic. They had not, Mr Thompson let me know, always kept a shop; it merely served to pass away the time until his ship came home, like the job he had as an assistant in a draper's shop in the town. For Mr Thompson was the son of a younger son of a Welsh baronet who owned vast acres of North Welsh mountains: when the present baronet died, and he was so old his death could be expected hourly, then they would come into their own. Mr Thompson had been assured, by the baronet himself, who was a gentleman of the old school, that he would not be forgotten; and this seemed the more certain because only five years ago he had inherited one hundred guineas from Sir Morgan's sister. Until they came into their heritage, however, they must hide their light under a bushel. They had been given to expect, or thought they had been given to expect, at least a thousand pounds. What could not be done with a thousand pounds? His eyes afire with visions of commercial grandeur, Mr Thompson added to the thousand the sum he would infallibly get from the sale of the shop. Then we should see. His long years in a subordinate capacity at the draper's would prove not to have been wasted, years that had given him, he dared say, as intimate a knowledge of Manchester goods as any man outside Manchester. Rapidly, as from long brooding upon it, he sketched for me the emporium of his dreams, the draper's shop to revolutionise all draper's shops. Of course it would not come at once; the beginnings were bound to be small; but it was a fact well known in commerce that the hardest thousand to make was the first; that obtained, every thousand after was progressively easier. 'Did you realise, Billy, that money breeds money?' He smiled at me in pure benevolence, in angelic innocence. 'And should you feel like a change from silversmithing, Billy, there'll always be a place for you, and for any friends of my sons.'

I could not see myself behind a counter in a draper's shop; privately, I thought it no life for a male human being; but I listened much impressed. And so did Hugh, though he must have heard it a thousand times. George brought it to an end by getting up and saying with grim humour, 'When you have your emporium I'll cast the door-knobs for you. Come, Ashted.'

We returned to the wash-house. 'Money breeds money,' George repeated. 'Do you know the next subject we ought to study, Ashted? Political economy. In a year's time we must start political economy. Meanwhile, there's Heat, Light and Sound, and chemistry and metallurgy—and Emerson. This is what Emerson says.' And like the born teacher he was, he began to expound Emerson to me.

It was half-past eleven when we left the wash-house. George tucked the volume of Emerson's essays beneath my arm. 'I'll walk back with you,' he said. As we went through the shop to the street we met Morgan coming in. He was two years older than George, taller, gaunter, very much a masher, and not quite sober. George nodded to him briefly. The meeting had made him grave. As we walked back, he analysed, with a dispassionateness I was incapable of where my family was concerned, the foolishness of his father's illusions and the danger they threatened to his brothers and sister. 'We live in this world, Ashted,' he said; 'we have only ourselves, our own brains and our own efforts. We must not deceive ourselves. My father is a child. He thinks a thousand pounds is a fortune. And if it came, he would not keep it a year. Simply by being his, it would transfer itself into the pockets of false friends who he would swear were saints from heaven. But he will not listen to me; and he is ashamed that I am a moulder.'

Years later, when he had made his own place in the world, George presented himself at the ancestral home in North Wales: he derived a grim satisfaction from not being admitted. But Morgan Thompson was ruined by his father's dreams.

I SPENT the whole of the next afternoon with George, in the wash-house, where we went through the subject of Light like men with scythes advancing through a meadow; and in the evening I accompanied the Thompsons, Morgan alone being absent, to the service at Boulter's Lane Chapel, to hear the Rev. Claud Higgins preach. The *Journal* always referred to Boulter's Lane, for street and chapel had become synonymous, as 'the cathedral of Nonconformity,' and Mr Higgins was famous as a fearless Radical, both in religion and in politics. He was accustomed to speaking of Darwinism as a new revelation and he gloried in the Higher Criticism. In his black gown he made a fine figure in the pulpit, tall, rather plump, with a curly brown beard and astonishing eyes that seemed, even in that vast building, to pierce into yours. He was a great orator and used a wealth of florid gestures: at dramatic moments in his sermons he would fling out his arm and point accusingly at us, denouncing not us but some wretched representative of Popery or High Anglicanism or Toryism he conceived to be in the congregation. He addressed him in scathing terms. Horace called Mr Higgins a 'humbugging actor,' and perhaps he was. One of the events of our year in those days was to hear him read 'A Christmas Carol' in the Town Hall at Christmas; those who had heard both said he was the equal of Dickens himself.

But that Sunday evening it was all new to me. After the Church of England, I found it scarcely like being in church at all; it was more like a concert, it seemed to me, or a lecture; at any rate an entertainment. The chapel itself was huge and bare, with plain glass windows, pitch-pine pews, and walls that were painted green until half-way up and were then white. It held a thousand people and was full, as St Barnabas, or even the Cathedral never was. There was no feeling, I found, of taking part in a service; one was in an audience; and the peak point of the proceedings was Mr Higgins' sermon, which lasted an hour, though one wasn't aware of that, the display of eloquence was so artful and glittering.

We sat, as befitted our station, in the gallery. Below us were the rich, whose carriages lined the streets in the neighbourhood during every service. For ours was essentially a Nonconformist town, as Mr Higgins reminded us proudly each Sunday, and Boulter's Lane was its fashionable church. I can see now that much of the pleasure George's parents derived from attending there came from its intense respectability; by merely sitting in the gallery they were in touch with the wealth and power and rectitude of the established order. You had only to peep over the gallery railings to see the leaders of our community: aldermen, industrialists, eminent surgeons and lawyers, the editor of the *Journal* and the local artists who exhibited at the Royal Academy. George's mother had 'belonged,' as she called it, to Boulter's Lane since girlhood, and her teacher in the Young Women's Bible Class had been no less a lady than Miss Amy Forster herself, and for three generations the Forsters had been among the leading industrialists in the town, with the prestige that in more ancient boroughs clung to dukes or earls. A curious church, it seems, looking back on it, for George and me to have worshipped in; and only two or three years later we were to react furiously against Mr Higgins. For George in particular he became emblematic of the lackey of the ruling class, a Mr Facing-Both-Ways who hoodwinked the workers with flattery while his employers sandbagged them from behind. Horace's description of him as a 'humbugging actor' was right, really; he was a man intoxicated by his own fluency of speech, his immediate power to move. Yet both George and I were in his debt. He was a great populariser; he talked of new ideas and movements of ideas in such a way that your curiosity was stimulated to find out about them at first hand. George had discovered Emerson through Mr Higgins. Of course he made it all seem much easier than it really was, with his confident 'Modern science tells us' and 'We have it on the authority of the new science of psychology itself.'

That was the first of many Sunday evenings I spent with the Thompsons in the gallery at Boulter's Lane Chapel. Soon my mother was grumbling, 'You spend more time at them Thompsons than you do with your own flesh and blood.' It was largely true, and my mother resented it. She thought of the family as a unit closely knit against the world, a world that was always hostile; she wanted to have nothing to do with the world outside the family, and she wanted us to have nothing to do with it, either. So I was guilty of a great betrayal. She disliked George intensely. In my first enthusiasm, I had taken George home, and no one had liked him. They said of him all the things other people said of Horace, that he gave himself airs, that he was too big for his boots, that he was 'stuck-up.' And I must admit George, when I took him home, didn't behave well. His refusal to compromise, which in those days was a refusal to adapt himself, caused him to be brutal when it was quite unnecessary. My mother was a devoted reader of the *Christian Herald*; she doted on the interminable serial stories dealing with the loves of governesses for curates. There was a copy lying on a chair when George visited us. He picked it up, flicked through its pages, threw it down with a single word: 'Trash!' My mother never forgave him that.

And then, whenever they met, George and Horace argued. Mother loathed arguments; perhaps with reason, for in her experience arguments led to fights. Having been duly intoxicated by Emerson myself, I had lent his essays to Horace; who read them and returned them to me, saying: 'This man can do you nothing but harm. He is a dangerous thinker. He comes near to setting man on a level with God.' I reported this to George, who immediately wanted to see with his own eyes the man who could think so strangely. And I, who wished to bring together those whom I loved so that they could love one another, brought George home. It was a memorable occasion. As I interpret it now, both George and Horace were fighting for possession of me. It was a week-day evening, and barely had the common courtesies been exchanged and George made his comment on the nature of the *Christian Herald* than the fight began. It had a curiously formal quality. Father was at home, and all my brothers and sisters. We composed an audience, grouped, as I remember, about the combatants, who sat facing each other across the green plush tablecloth. George began: 'Billy tells me you disagree with Emerson. Why?'

77

Here I should say that George, who was the least transcendental of men, also disagreed with Emerson, or a great deal of him; but it was not his habit in argument to state his own beliefs, merely to expose the hollowness of the beliefs of others.

Horace answered with deceptive mildness. 'That is a large question,' he said. 'Do you really wish me to explain why? It will take a long time.' That was precisely what George did wish him to do. Horace smiled in his superior way. They were each busy pitying the ignorance, superficiality and folly of the other. 'I'm waiting,' George said; and Horace began. George listened with astonishment and delight. He knew all the stock arguments about free will and predestination; he was sure he had Horace. He listened gravely, and when Horace had finished recapitulated his statement. Did Horace agree? Horace did. And did Horace agree that if that were so, this necessarily followed? Horace nodded. And this? Horace nodded again. And this? Again Horace nodded. Horace agreed, in fact, with conclusions George believed no sane man could possibly accept; the *reductio ad absurdum* into which he was striving to drive Horace was for Horace no absurdity at all. George was more astonished than ever, but no longer delighted; he was as baffled as a zoologist would be if confronted with an animal that conformed to no recognisable species. 'You really mean to say you believe that every single action, every single thought, of every single human being that has ever lived or ever will live on this earth is foreknown to God and cannot be other than what it is?' Horace nodded. 'That this discussion we are having has been foreseen and fixed from time immemorial?' Horace again inclined his head. 'Look,' George said in desperation, 'I raise my hand, so. You tell me that that raising of my hand was foreknown to God and preordained by Him from the beginning of things? That it was impossible I should not have raised my hand at the moment I did, 9.57 p.m., March 19, 1892?'

Horace smiled a beautiful smile. 'I do,' he said. 'I mean just that.'

George tried again. Sarcasm came into his voice. 'And man's aspirations, his altruism, his striving for justice, these are of no avail and worthless? The delusions of man's pride?'

Horace smiled again. 'Exactly. The delusions of man's pride. Quite, quite worthless, and of no avail.'

'And an individual man's acts of goodness, his efforts to lead a virtuous life, mean nothing, redound not at all to his credit, and allow him no confident hope of salvation?'

'They mean nothing,' Horace said; 'and that is why I disagree with your Mr Emerson, why I believe Billy is wasting his time heeding him. Self-reliance, indeed! Pathetic! Snares to catch the wind!'

When I heard, years later, how Dr Johnson 'refuted' Bishop Berkeley by kicking the stone, I thought of George. He had been reduced to a similarly intolerable position from which he could only escape by violent contradiction. 'Preposterous nonsense!' he exploded. 'Sheer superstition!'

Horace only smiled maddeningly. And the curious thing was that everyone watching and listening, myself apart, though they did not understand the argument at all, clearly believed George had been routed and made to look absurd. It was as though Horace was their champion and had won a great victory. My brothers' and sisters' faces were sparkling with glee; my father slapped his thigh in delight and exclaimed, 'I'll have a tanner on that predestination any time you like, Horace'; and my mother wagged her head in a simple pride and pleasure in her son's cleverness. It was as though George had been exposed as a charlatan. Horace himself, of course, knew otherwise: he warned me later that night, after I had got home from walking back with George, that he was a dangerous man who would do me no good. I retorted that since no behaviour of mine on earth could possibly affect my future state, whatever that might be, it could not matter what I did. Horace shook his head and said sadly: 'I told you so.' George's evil influence was already at work on me.

Friendship with George, then, meant a breach with Horace and with my family. There was nothing dramatic about it; it was no more than a natural loosening of ties. There were ten of us children now, and we all assumed, wrongly, there would be no more, and half of our number was working. Lizzie, whose fingers were nimble, was at the cardboard box factory; Edwin was a carpenter, and Tom was learning the same trade; Florrie would join Lizzie at the box factory in a month or two.

Our lot had become much easier. We had moved into a larger house. It had a tiny square of front garden and no less than four bedrooms: mother was inordinately proud of it. But there were still too many of us for comfort. Privacy was impossible, and we all pined for it. I shared a room, with two beds in it, with Horace and Edwin and Tom, but though we all got on pretty well together it was impossible for us not to be in one another's way most of the time. When you are a child your brothers and sisters seem almost part of yourself; what you have in common with them is much greater and more important than the differences between them and you. But now it was the differences that were looming. I was realising that if Edwin and Tom and even Horace had not been my brothers I would have had nothing in common with them. We were becoming strangers to one another, and it seemed to me that I was the only one among them that realised it. We elder boys resembled one another very closely in appearance, so that I was constantly being greeted by people I did not know as Edwin or Horace or Tom. It was the more galling because I at any rate knew how different I was from them. Horace's individuality had always been accepted, but mine had become apparent only recently, both to myself and to others, and was still something to be remarked upon. I felt myself isolated from my kin by my own unlikeness to them.

But really, as I say, it was nothing more than a natural loosening of ties. Groups, however, the group that is the family perhaps especially, fight against loosening of ties, for, if a group is to exist, conformity is essential. More and more consciously I was a rebel. But I was not the only rebel. In her own way, Lizzie, of all people, was rebelling too; and the fact that automatically I write 'of all people' indicates the sense of outrage her rebellion, which was only the natural desire to make her own life, aroused in us all, myself included. Because she was the oldest and a girl, Lizzie had always existed in a special relation to the rest of us, or at least to myself and the children younger than me. Even to me, who was only five years younger, she had been a second mother. I can't remember her as a child but only as a miniature woman. She had washed us, dressed us, cared for us, rocked us to sleep, scolded us, protected us, fought for us, ruled us with a rod of iron. Our existence without her would have seemed impossible, and one would have said that she had no life apart from us. And suddenly she announces her intention of getting married. She did so with the maximum dramatic effect, at the one time of the week when all the family was normally gathered together, at Sunday dinner-time. Oh, the indignation and dismay! She had not even said whom she was marrying before the storm burst. She was rock-like. She stood there, four feet eleven inches of her facing my father and mother through her thick pebble spectacles, giving better than she got.

'I'll have no such talk,' my father banged his fist on the table. 'You'll stay here and help your mother.'

The thick spectacles flashed defiantly. 'I've slaved long enough in this house. If I've got to slave, I'll slave in my own home for a change.'

'There's gratitude!' my mother said bitterly.

'You don't get spliced without my consent, my gel,' my father said; 'and that you won't get.'

'I can do without it. I'm twenty-three.'

Father jumped up in a fury. 'Talk to your father like that, would you, Miss Impudence! Any more of your lip, and I'll give you a belting, old as you are.'

'Lay a finger on me and I'll go to the police station, for all you're my dad.'

'But the little 'uns, who'll look after the little 'uns?' my mother asked.

'Florrie can look after them for a change. Or Edie. Time they took a turn.'

We were stunned into silence. We had taken Lizzie for granted all our lives; it was as though a pillar of the house had snapped. Then the baby, Alice, began to cry, and mother snatched her into her arms, saying, 'There! Now see what you've done, our Lizzie!' And Lizzie sat there, her lips pressed tight together.

'Who's the fellow, then?' father demanded. 'Why don't he come and see me, like a man?'

'You can save your breath because I know what you're going to say, and it won't make no difference,' Lizzie said. 'It's Paul Hunter.'

Consternation again. 'Paul Hunter! You must be mad, girl.

I'll not allow it!' Father banged the table with his fist once more.

'Lizzie,' my mother said, greatly troubled, 'you don't know what you're doing.'

The thick glasses flashed ominously again. 'Any of you say a word against Paul Hunter and I'll go straight out and not come back.'

We knew she would and were miserably silent. It was worse than anything we could have imagined, for now our pride was involved. To have to own Paul Hunter as a brother-in-law: it was scarcely thinkable. Father lifted himself from his wooden armchair. 'You bring children into the world,' he said, 'you toil and moil to feed and clothe 'em, and that's all the thanks you get. Gimme my paper.' Edie handed him *Reynolds Weekly News*, and he lumbered upstairs to puzzle out the headlines before he fell into his after-Sunday-dinner sleep.

Paul Hunter was commonly believed to be feeble-minded. His legs were grotesquely twisted, and he hauled himself along in a corkscrew motion on two sticks. I realise now that he was spastic, but in those days the word was unknown to me. He was scarcely any taller than Lizzie herself, and he seemed incapable of being still; even when seated he shivered and shuddered. He was not frightening in any way; he was indeed the most amiable of men; but he seemed quite unable to prevent himself from rolling his eyes, which were unnaturally large and of a remarkable lustrous egg-white. One was especially aware of his eyes because of the trick he had when in ecstasy, and he was often in ecstasy, of making the pupils disappear altogether.

'You've made your bed, my girl; you've got to lie on it,' my mother said; and I don't know which was uppermost in her mind, bitterness or despair. Certainly no marriage could have seemed less auspicious in its beginnings, and we grieved for Lizzie not out of selfishness alone. Without her spectacles, she was next to blind, and it was plain that Paul would never in any normal sense be able to work for his living. We saw the marriage as a desperate act, a kind of suicide, on Lizzie's part; all of us, that is, except Horace. He supported her from the beginning, and he must have been a tower of strength for his word carried more weight in the family than any of the rest of us children's. I suppose if you're as thorough-going a Calvinist as Horace was you must believe marriages are made either in Heaven or not, and that in any case nothing can be done about them. But Horace was not consistent. He said of Paul: 'He tries,' forgetting that according to his own beliefs trying could be of no avail. And Paul did try. In his way, he tried harder and more often than any man I ever met.

And though the match was hateful to us, the Hunters rejoiced in it. We hated it because we feared that, collectively, we might have a new burden to support: they rejoiced because they had lost one, or at any rate partly so. Paul, it was taken for granted, could never work; when we were first aware of him he made a little something by selling the *Journal* at the street-corner. But his family in our eyes was well off. That meant nothing more, of course, than that they were in a small way of business; they had a coal-yard, where you could go with a wheelbarrow or a sack or a bucket and buy as little as twenty-eight pounds, which was a common way of buying coal in those days. That, at least, was something to be thankful for: we knew that so long as Paul's parents were alive, Lizzie and Paul would never be absolutely destitute.

Paul disgraced himself at the wedding breakfast. He got drunk. Paul had the weakest head for liquor, but he couldn't resist it; and since he was even less co-ordinated and more wild in his movements when drunk than when sober, there were always stupid and unkind men ready to help him get drunk. After the wedding breakfast, mother wept and wept, and they were not the tears mothers are generally happy to weep at their daughters' weddings. She was not to be consoled. And yet, if one had had the slightest perception, it should have been obvious even at that disastrous wedding breakfast that Lizzie would be the one to wear the breeches, as they say. For, before Paul had become quite as silly as he might have been, she had cuffed him publicly over the head, just as though he was a child, and said sharply: 'You behave yourself, you great sawney!' and then got up and lugged him to his feet and led him away before the toasts were all over.

From then on, she treated him as a child, though rarely in public. He was an entirely amiable child; there was no vice in him; but he was very weak, I think because he had been brought up to see himself as feeble-minded, a natural butt and a buffoon. Being a butt and a buffoon were, indeed, the only defences he possessed against the world. But as Horace said, he tried. The Hunters set them up in the business they knew best, a small coal and salt yard. That didn't last long, mainly because Lizzie was too busy having babies to learn the business herself. She did learn something, though: Paul wasn't to be trusted with money. With the best will in the world he couldn't prevent himself from turning the contents of the till into whisky. He was always full of remorse afterwards. It expressed itself in his attending revivalist meetings. He never missed them and he was always the first at the penitents' bench. He was, in fact, the most frequently converted man I have ever met; and he had an almost æsthetic appreciation of the points of the evangelists he had heard. He thought Gipsy Smith the greatest of them all; Gipsy Smith converted him several times. Conversion transfigured him; but then the effects would wear off, and in contrast with the drama and glory of salvation he found the light of common day unbearable. It was then he found in drink an equivalent for the sense of glory. I don't mean that he was a continuous drinker. He was on guard against it as his besetting sin, and after each outbreak of drinking he was truly repentant. His great safeguard for years was the Salvation Army; you could see him in the band on Sunday evenings corkscrewing crab-wise in his blue and red uniform playing his concertina. He played the concertina with gusto.

After the coal and salt yard Lizzie and Paul had a succession of tiny shops, little drapers', usually near a large factory in order to attract the custom of the factory girls. But the trouble for years was that Paul had nothing to do. And then Lizzie had an inspiration: she got hold of a wicker basket carriage that Paul could push and stocked it with brushes and pots and pans and the like. Soon he had a regular round of customers in all parts of the town. He became one of the best-known sights in the town. He was always cheerful, and the only thing that really bothered him was the increase in motor traffic on the roads. Motor cars confused him, but he had his way of coping with them. When they were small, the children were always coming home and reporting how they had seen Uncle

Paul lying on his back in the middle of the road waving his walking-stick in the air in front of an oncoming vehicle.

They reported other things, too. I remember Phil coming home from school, I think it was in 1916, and saying to his mother in all innocence: 'Mum, I saw Uncle Paul this morning. He was singing "Lead Kindly Light" in the Barnfield Road. He was singing it very nicely.' And my mother, who was living with us then, said: 'And well he might, God help him!' And again, more than ten years later—it was when King George V was ill—I remember Will coming home late one night from a dance and saying: 'I saw old Tishy tonight. He was coining money singing "God Save the King" outside the dog track.' Tishy was a race-horse with twisted legs that used to appear in Tom Webster's cartoons in the *Daily Mail*.

Whether Lizzie knew of these additional sources of Paul's income I don't know. We never mentioned them to her. She was a loyal wife. The only remark she ever made to me about her husband was to say once: 'I dread it when he gets converted.'

Well, there was a marriage which on the face of it had everything against it and one the eugenists would not have allowed. Yet, however arduous it was, it was successful. The five children Lizzie and Paul had could not have been healthier or turned out better: the girls have married well and the boys are skilled workmen. Paul lived till he was eighty and Lizzie is alive still.

But all this was in the future at the time I am writing about. The family was falling apart; naturally, though it appeared catastrophic then. But it was of my own rebellion that I was mainly aware. I adopted the Thompsons like a second family. I loved them all, except Morgan. Even then he stood out in my mind as the example of what happens to the working man who does not learn a trade. Old Mr Thompson's dreams of family grandeur, of wealth to come and the drapery emporium just round the corner of time were innocent. George scorned them openly, and I scorned them intellectually; though at the same time I found them romantic. I had a wild wish and sometimes even a hope that they might be true; and besides that, I had a dim realisation even then that such innocent illusions are essential to many men. Destroy them, and you destroy the man himself. In fact, none of the children, apart from Morgan, took them seriously. They were no more than the equivalent, rather highly elaborated it is true, of many a perfectly sensible man's jocular 'When my ship comes home.' But Morgan took them deadly seriously and believed in them implicitly. He had learnt no trade because none was necessary to him; when he came into his own he would be a manager at least. And, when I first knew him, half the time he behaved as though he had already come into his own. As I have said, he was a masher, as we called them then. He was handsome and had a well-bred air, and spent his time and his money in the company of young men who had much more than himself; boasting, said George, who had no patience with him, of how he would repay them when he had come into his heritage. He was known in all the music halls, billiard rooms and hotel bars of the town. Later, he was to be a sore trial to George, for, as hope of the inheritance receded, so he became the more bitter. He became a man who had been done out of his rights, the complete tap-room cynic who sees all success, however moderate, in terms of conspiracy, of a mysterious thing called influence which comes from knowing people. And as an unskilled labourer, for that was what he was, he was at the mercy of every economic breeze that blew, and the more at its mercy because he was so surly, his temper so bad, that no foreman would willingly keep him on a day longer than was called for. Then Morgan had to exploit his own sources of influence, use the people he knew; and the one man he knew who had any influence was George. George was always finding him jobs. He loathed it; he would not ask favours for himself and hated having to do so for his family. 'I know now,' he would say, 'the full irony of father's toast, May you ever climb the hill of prosperity and never meet a brother coming down!'

In those days, though, I saw little of Morgan. When we did meet he would patronise me from his height and say, 'Well, young Ashted!' and offer me a finger. But Hugh, the youngest brother, I liked greatly. He had nothing of the character or strength of mind of George; rather, he was a second edition of his father, but without his illusions. More precisely, in his case, the illusions were diluted. They had been watered down into a universal optimism and benevolence. Hugh believed ill of no

86

man; he shone with good faith and goodwill. His generosity was proverbial among all who knew him. Morgan once said of him: 'One of these days, our Hugh will give his arse away, and then what'll he use to shit?' And it is true that in the end Hugh's trust in human goodness became gullibility: he went into partnership with a rogue who absconded with the money and left him to pay the debts. So his last years were clouded; he was a bewildered man.

I owe Hugh one thing specifically. He had a fiddle, which he had taught himself to play. One day, seeing it on the table, I picked it up, tucked it under my chin as I had seen Hugh do, and drew the bow across the strings. I appreciated the noise, much more, I must say, than any I had heard Hugh produce with it. Hearing me, he came into the room, and I began to apologise for the liberty I had taken; but he stopped me, saying, 'Would you like to learn, Billy? I'll teach you if you like.' And as much as he knew himself, which was almost nil, he taught me. I was and am grateful. For Hugh, the fiddle was simply something on which you reproduced acceptable versions of sentimental ballads or hymns, 'Home Sweet Home' or 'Silver Threads among the Gold' or 'Eternal Father Strong to Save.' For me, it was straightaway immeasurably more than that; it was a magic box, and the bow the key by which you could unlock awe and wonder and delight. Nothing would satisfy me but to buy a fiddle of my own. Having learnt what Hugh had taught me, I thought in my innocence I could play it; and I went to a music shop in the town to buy a piece of music, for you must understand that I knew nothing about music; none of us did. I could read the score of a sentimental ballad—Hugh had taught me that—and I believed that was music. I wanted, I told the shopman, a piece of music for the violin, and since he told me that Beethoven was well thought of as a composer for that instrument, I took his word and bought the first violin sonata, with a confused notion in my head that the first was the one you had to start with. Naturally, I could make nothing of it. I couldn't read it. What on earth could it possibly sound like? I had to know. I went to George with my problem. He looked at me quizzically. 'Heat, Light and Sound, Chemistry and Metallurgy this year, and next year we've decided to do political economy; there's your trade; and now you want to learn the violin as well. Billy, you run a grave risk of becoming a dilettant'—for so in those days he pronounced 'dilettante,' with the accent on the second syllable, never having heard it spoken. 'Do you know what a dilettant is?' I didn't. 'Jack of all trades and master of none.' I saw the force of the argument, but how explain to George the intensity of my desire to know, as it were, along my nerves what those mysterious black marks on the music paper sounded like? He stared at me and then, as if admitting defeat, shrugged his shoulders and said: 'Billy, you're incorrigible. But if you must learn to fiddle, for God's sake do it properly. Go to the best man.' But who was he, and where should I find him? George knew everything. He said patiently: 'The Borough Music School: go there.' And I did, and joined the class for beginners, and as soon as I set eyes on the fierce old German who taught us as though he hated us I put away all hope of playing Beethoven's First for years. But every so often, of course, not daring to tell Herr Schmidt, I got it out and had a try at it in my own way and by degrees, dimly behind the caterwauling I made, began to hear the divine noise that Beethoven had heard and set down.

Having fallen in love with the Thompsons as a family, I suppose it was natural I should fall in love with Rose. Just when it happened I don't know. If you had asked me then, I would have said, in all honesty and some bewilderment, that I had no time for girls. How could I have? Heat, Light and Sound, Chemistry, Metallurgy, the fiddle, my job, the list was endless; a girl would have to come after all those. Rose, I would have said, was just another girl. I have lived with girls all my life; our house was full of them. I noticed that she was changing from a child into a young woman, but the gentleness, sweetness and silence that she radiated I attributed as much to the family circle of the Thompsons as to her. Perhaps I would not permit my feeling for her to become conscious. I was genuinely surprised when one night, in the wash-house, as George and I were poring at polished specimens of brass through a cheap microscope he had bought in a junk-shop, he suddenly said—and I can see it now, for he had his right eye to the eye-piece as he spoke and was turning the screw to bring the object into focus: 'Billy, mother says you come here

88

now to see Rose, not me.' I was taken completely by surprise and confusedly denied it. It wasn't true; and yet in that very moment of denying it I realised that in one way it was true. Rose was the first person I wanted to see when I arrived, and the sessions in the wash-house had become passages of time in parenthesis, as it were, between being in her presence. George looked up from the microscope. He was smiling with pure pleasure. 'But it's wonderful, Billy,' he cried, and he got up and clapped me on the back, saying: 'It's the jolliest thing that ever has happened.'

From that moment, George took it for granted that I should marry Rose, so did I, so, I think, did Rose herself, and so did everyone else. From then on, too, the routine of my visits to the Thompsons changed. Without anything being said by any-one, the kitchen was always left empty for us for at least an hour each evening. Yet I did not seem to do any less work: 'Your old Heat, Light and Sound!' Rose used to say; and I remember now that when George and I were in the wash-house Rose would be there as well, like a presence of comfort and grace. I close my eyes and see her sitting there, her head with its mass of chestnut hair rippling down her back bent over the metallurgical specimen she is polishing for us with 'Glitto.' I say her name and I see her, but I see her, as I always did, in a double-image which somehow becomes one; as at once the girl and the flower she was named after. In the same way, whenever I see a rose I see my Rose.

I lived in a new atmosphere, so pervasive, so subtly all-embracing that it was as though I was transformed or had come into an inheritance of such scope as to change my circum-stances completely. It was a miracle and the better a miracle because it seemed everyone rejoiced in it as well as myself. I don't think we talked much of marriage, though almost auto-matically we began to prepare for it, I to save money more consciously than I had done before, Rose to make ready her bottom drawer, in which, in a way quite mysterious to me, articles like sheets and tablecloths and pillow-cases began to mount up.

As it happened, the money I was saving for our marriage was used for another purpose, for, before marrying Rose, I had my great adventure, sometimes, I think, the only one I have had in my life, and one that, though fruitless as it turned out, I have never regretted.

George and I were very dissatisfied with our lot. In one way, the dissatisfaction was an abstract one: no two young men could have been more absorbed in life than we were, we were in work and we had jobs that, in the limited circles in which we had our being, were good jobs. I already knew that as a craftsman I was better than most, even if not as good as Horace, and that short of a large-scale trade depression I need never want for employment. Yet, when we measured the potentialities that we knew were ours against the opportunities open to us we could hardly fail to be dissatisfied. We might have been less dissatisfied if our talents had been other than they were and our ambitions, which were large and generalised, more restricted. We were not interested in making our fortunes; we despised business; and though we both of us enjoyed our work and regarded it as a point of honour to do it to the best of our capacity, the work we did was valuable to us only because it made possible the pursuits of our leisure. Those were where our hearts lay. We had no thought of turning them to material advantage; we were absolutely disinterested, and we were still, in a haphazard, blundering way, finding out what our true interests were. When I took up the fiddle, George had accused me of being in danger of becoming a dilettante. He was in like danger, for no sooner had I taken up the violin than he was off on an entirely new tack. It did not displace his earlier interests, any more than fiddling did mine; it was something added, to be fitted in to the rest by George's knocking another half an hour off his allowance of sleep, by cutting his dinner-time by a further fifteen minutes.

George was a great rummager through the penny boxes of second-hand bookshops, and any book that contained knowledge that he thought one day could conceivably interest him, he'd buy, whether it was astronomy or algebra or biology or metaphysics. He wanted all knowledge and merely by possessing books he felt that he was on the way to conquering knowledge. Well, one evening, he stopped to look through a penny-box outside a second-hand furniture shop. He picked up a book, glanced within, and what he saw excited him so much he bought it. He showed it me that evening in the wash-house. 'I

must find out more about this, Billy,' he said, and he pointed
out the object of his curiosity:

> *Whan that Aprille with his schowres swoote*
> *The drought of Marche hath perced to the roote,*
> *And bathud every veyne in swich licour . . .*

It was Volume II of The Poetical Works of Geoffrey Chaucer,
edited by Richard Morris, LL.D. What had roused him was
not the poetry but the words; they differed from their modern
forms, and some had disappeared altogether. He wanted to
know why; he wanted to understand the reasons for the
changes in language; and straightaway he was off in pursuit of
philology, and within a few years he was doing work for the
Early English Text Society.

It was not a field in which I followed him; but the point is,
it was becoming more and more clear to us, as we learned more
and learned to know our capabilities better, that our relative
poverty and the barriers of class and privilege were high walls
barring us from the world of learning that should be ours. As
ever, George was more articulate than I, and more bitter. He
was agonisingly conscious of the waste of time our methods of
learning and of finding out what we wanted to learn meant.
'We're being wasted, Billy,' he'd say; 'wasted. They're wasting
us. And there must be thousands like us. Why aren't we at
Oxford University, instead of feeling our way, hit or miss,
teaching ourselves?'

To George and me there seemed no hope for us in England;
we were condemned to stay as we were for the rest of our lives.
'We're like children staring at the sweets through the plate-
glass,' George cried. 'D'you realise the work we're doing now,
which we find so difficult, rich boys years younger than we are
doing in their schools? The waste, Billy, the waste!'

We saw ourselves deprived, deprived of our rights. We discussed it endlessly. We were not at that time Socialists; there
seemed no way out. We lay under the curse of class; we were
poor and therefore had been robbed of our birthright. But
there was a conceivable escape, and one evening I said:
'George, do you know what? Why don't we go to America?'

9

So began my great adventure. I wrote earlier that within six months of starting work I had acquired an ambition. It was to go to America; just that. In its beginning, it was very naïve, a mere boyish day-dream. To me as a child America was as remote as fairyland; it had none of this world's reality. It was immeasurably far away. I know now that precisely at that time the immigrants were pouring into the United States in their hundreds of thousands; but no one ever went from our street, and I never heard of any one of my relations doing so. America was prairie; buffaloes; cowboys and Indians. That was the America I fell in love with at the age of ten or eleven. I met it first in Fenimore Cooper's novels, which I devoured with delighted wonder, following the career of Natty Bumppo in all its transformations from *The Last of the Mohicans* to *The Deerslayer*. What I savoured, as I see now, was the sense of space, the prairies vast as oceans, the freedom vast space gives, and also the high chivalry of Natty and his friends and foes. They were inhabitants, as I say, of a world as remote as fairyland.

That was America. I suppose I could have told you, if you had asked me, that America and the United States were one and the same place. But I do not think I thought of them as such. The United States, that was much more familiar. One saw pictures of New York in the papers: in those days it looked like any other city, and the men and women in its streets like any other men and women; it was, one felt, a kind of England overseas. And then, one day not long after I had started work, the two places fused in my mind. 'America's the country,' one of my mates in the shop said, 'for the working man'; and he began to tell of a friend in New York, or of the friend of a friend, and the fabulous wages he earned, the freedom that was his, the limitless opportunity. 'The United States is the country of the future,' he announced.

'Why don't you go, then?' I asked, in all innocence. He looked at me in amazement. 'Go to America?' he said. 'Go to New York? All that way? It's much too far. I know where I am here.' I realised he had merely been mouthing the platitudes of leading articles and the advertisements of shipping companies. But in that moment also I realised that America and the United States were one and that one could go there; and I said to myself: 'Sometime, I'll go.'

From then on America and the United States became interchangeable terms. But behind those ordinary-looking men in the pictures of New York I saw so many Natty Bumppos; and if I could have formulated the sense of the difference I felt between those New York citizens and their counterparts in Council Street or in Boulter's Lane Chapel, I would have said that the former had it in them to be Natty Bumppos, the latter not. So, secretly—for I told no one of my ambition, not even George, until I made my momentous proposal to him—I began to read everything that came my way about America. I didn't read systematically, but the newspapers, especially the cheap ones, were full of stories of American derring-do and of American enterprise. In those days, the general English attitude towards the United States was a mixture of condescension and amazement. The United States and Americans were at once funny and fabulous; a land of unutterable lawlessness in which braggart vulgarians metaphorically shot their way to becoming millionaires overnight. It was at the same time something of a credit to Britain, for the British had made it; and one day it would grow up, become civilised and then be more like Britain than ever and an even greater credit to it.

Yet, perhaps because of my reading of Cooper's novels, even at that time I read something else between the lines of these sensational articles, something quite different from anything they said on the surface. I saw that the United States was not at all like England, at any rate the England I knew, and I felt indeed that in some mysterious way it existed in opposition to England and the things we took for granted in England. The full revelation had come when George lent me Emerson's essays. There, as I'd never seen it before, I found the idea of

93

America, the idea that made it entirely other than England. This idea, of which I could see no sign at all at home, intoxicated me. Almost involuntarily, I got passages of it by heart, which I remember still. Here is one: 'We will walk on our own feet; we will work with our own hands; we will speak our own minds. . . . A nation of men will for the first time exist, because each believes himself inspired by the Divine Soul which also inspires all men.' 'A nation of men will *for the first time exist* . . .' That was it: the sense of a country based on an utterly new conception of man in his relation to man, a country founded by men who had deliberately left Europe in order to escape the old relationship; who had deliberately begun again, as it were, from the beginning; men who wanted nothing to do with the old world and its kings and hierarchies of rank and authoritarian systems and religions.

How did I reconcile this with the sensational accounts of life in America in the newspapers, with the exposures of crime and scandals and vice? I didn't at all; because I was reading other things too. I read a life of President Lincoln, for example, and a popular pious biography of the time about President Garfield called *From Log Cabin to White House*; and in both I found recorded careers of a kind that would have been impossible in England. I discovered—where, I have forgotten—that in America a young fellow like myself, a workman, could put himself through college, given determination—and that I was sure I didn't lack. There was freedom, there was opportunity without which freedom cannot exist, and there was equality. The cursed burden of class was absent altogether.

So, on a November evening I said to George in the washhouse: 'Why don't we go to America?' It burst out of me, and when I'd said it I was trembling with excitement. George took his pipe out of his mouth and considered. 'It's an idea,' he said at last; 'an idea we must sleep on.'

I'd been afraid of that as soon as I spoke, afraid of his reasonableness. My idea, of course, was that George and I should go together; and I wanted to start at once, that very night if possible. But George was more cautious and less sanguine than I. I tried to fire him with my enthusiasm, clumsily and only half-articulately. I recall he said: 'Natty Bumppo, Billy, is quite irrelevant.' He began a methodical investigation of how one went to the United States, what it would cost, what one could expect. He investigated the prospects in Canada and Australia as well. Canada and Australia meant nothing to me: I was in the grip of a romantic passion; and meanwhile I chafed. At last he reported his conclusions: they were as packed with sense as a sound nut is with kernel, and inevitably, therefore, I found them chilling. Yes, emigration to the United States might be the answer; to see it as a completely classless society was, of course, to be absurdly naïve, yet it was true that young men in our position there had much greater opportunities in all ways than we had at home. *If* we were Americans. But we were not Americans; and as prospective immigrants we were faced with problems that did not exist for the native American, problems largely of ignorance. 'You, Billy, are a craftsman, with your own special skill. That skill is your sole asset in the labour-market, the source of whatever bargaining power you possess. Without that, you are reduced to the level of the unskilled labourer, and there you are at a disadvantage, for in a labourer what counts is brawn, which you do not possess. But how do you know that your special skill is in demand in the United States? How do you know that the supply does not exceed the demand? Do you, in fact, know the centres in America where your special skill is practised? In England, it is confined largely to relatively small areas, not more than a few streets, here and in Clerkenwell. There are other factors. There may well be no native tradition of your skill in the United States; but how do you know that the craft is not in the hands of men of other nationalities, the French or the Germans or the Swiss, who might resent an Englishman as an intruder in a closely-guarded preserve?'

I had no answer to such questions. They were eminently sensible; they could arouse in me only a dumb bewildered resentment. George saw this. 'I don't want to discourage you, Billy, but emigration is a gamble, and we must reduce the odds against you. You must find out more, and more particularly about the circumstances and state of your trade.' But how? George had the answer of course: 'There must be trade papers in America as here. They will indicate the regional distribution of the trade. Write to *The Jeweller and Metal-Worker* for their names and addresses and then write to them for copies.

95

And there's one thing just as important, even more important. It is no use thinking of going without money. I see clearly that to go to a new country without money enough to enable you to live if necessary for months before finding the job you can do is to be defeated at the start.'

I didn't write to *The Jeweller and Metal-Worker* and, having first made my suggestion to George in the November, I sailed from Liverpool on the second Wednesday of the following April. Needless to say I had not got a lot of money. I had £20 of my own saved, my mother gave me £10, Horace organised a whip-round for me among my brothers and sisters which brought me another £10, and George, having shaken his head at my impetuosity, presented me with all his savings—£15—telling me I could repay him at 5 per cent when I was a millionaire in dollars; £55 in all: I had never seen so much money in my life before; it seemed a fortune. I could, I calculated, live on it in reasonable comfort for half a year, and long before the end of that time I would have a job. Rose, George, Horace and my father came to Liverpool with me to see me off. I, who had never before been even so far away from home as Liverpool, was blithely setting off across 3,000 miles of ocean to a new land. Everyone was solemn except me, and Rose wept; but I, I was triumphant, already in spirit 3,000 miles away, or rather a million miles away, in a fairyland called the United States. The lure of America, the excitement I felt, had turned me into a monster of egoism, and I bade Rose wipe her eyes and weep no more, for within a year, within eighteen months at the most, I would be sending her the money for her passage out; and already, before I had descended into the ship's bowels, I had vowed to myself that she should not cross the Atlantic by steerage.

I stood against the rail, the pier swung away from the ship, the four waving figures grew smaller and smaller. I waved till they were out of sight. And it was then the tears stung my eyes. I saw as vividly as though she were still before me Rose as I had left her, the face mute and wet with misery, the shoulders bowed as under too great a burden. My own selfishness struck me to the heart, and, in the moment that I was aware of my selfishness, I was aware, too, of appalling loneliness. In that moment, if it had been possible, I would have had

96

the ship turned about or have jumped overboard and swum for the shore. I was all by myself, and I had never been that in my whole life before.

I was conscious, in this crowded second of apprehension, of other things, too. I was aware of my fellow-passengers. They lined the rails like me, but unlike me, they had not been waving. Instead, they stared at the shore of the Mersey with stolid incuriosity. What they saw on that shore was meaningless to them, was without associations. And then I heard their voices; they spoke in languages unknown to me. They were foreigners to a man, it seemed; but it was I who in that moment felt alien, among the women in the black peasant dresses, the men in garbs of a kind I had not seen before. I was, as it were, alone by myself in more ways than one. I felt myself not only alone but a stranger among strangers with whom no communication was possible; and I looked about me desperately for a face that might be English and saw not one.

There was something else, too. I had merely an inkling of it then and scarcely allowed it to come to consciousness, but in the days of the voyage I had to face its truth. I had expected my fellow passengers to be I don't quite know what. I knew they would be poor or poorly dressed and from all over Europe, but obscurely I had expected men and women more in keeping with the brave new world they were going to. They should have been radiant with hope, stepping with gladness. Instead, I saw the defeated.

No doubt I was wrong, though when I met the few English and Scots and Irish who were steerage passengers with me, I could not think so, for a more discouraged, disgruntled lot I never met; and in their company, though I dodged it after a time, preferring to be by myself or with foreigners whose tongues I did not understand, I had an uneasy sense that courage and the desire for adventure were not what were driving me to my brave new world but failure, the overwhelming lust to escape from responsibilities at home. That was nonsense also, and it belongs to a later stage of the voyage; but the realisation that hit me of the gap between what I had hoped for and what actually was, was dreadful.

All my possessions lay at my feet beside the rail: a small tin trunk containing all my clothes and a few books, my fiddle in its case, and an old canvas shopping bag of my mother's. This last was filled with all the fruit my mother had been able to get for me at that time of year: some apples, oranges, two tins of pineapple chunks and a two-pound pot of strawberry jam; for the man at the shipping office where I had bought my ticket had warned me that, as he delicately put it, the food on immigrant ships was not always what could be desired, and had advised me to supplement the ship's fare with supplies of my own. Asked for suggestions, he was vague and talked about such things as hams. It seemed to me, possibly because of what I had read years before of scurvy in boys' adventure stories about eighteenth-century voyaging, that fruit would be more satisfactory than a ham, besides being less expensive.

Sadly, I picked up my possessions. I was not only lonely but now I wanted to be alone, and I made my way to my berth. The ship, still in the river, seemed almost motionless, and I had no difficulty, laden though I was, in climbing down the narrow, steep companion-ways leading to my steerage. I was amazed at how deeply I had to descend, and as I descended I seemed to pass through layer after layer of smell. First it was the heavy, nose-pricking smell of fresh paint; then the smell of engine oil; then that of cooking. All these remained and mingled, but as I climbed down into what must surely be the very bottom of the ship I was struck by a stench that made me almost retch. I stopped on the stair, to shield my nose for a moment. I knew that smell: it was the court in Fussell Street, but worse: the smell of excrement and urine and unwashed bodies, of too many human beings packed into too little room.

At the bottom of the companion-way I followed the directions painted on the wall and, walking further and further into that appalling stench, saw before me my steerage and realised that the stench was its stench. I was in Steerage No. 1. It proved to be a triangular space, cavernous because of its scarcely illuminated gloom; at night it was cavernous in another, more romantic way, because lit by two lanterns. Its walls were lined with what I can only describe as pens or open cabins. There were eight of them, and each contained sixteen bunks, eight in two tiers on either side. In the centre of the space were two tables, on which the lanterns stood.

I found my bunk and stowed away my baggage as best I

could. My courage was at its lowest ebb. So far as I could see, Steerage No. 1 was deserted except for myself and half a dozen snorers stretched on their bunks. Well it might have been. I had my privacy but how could I enjoy it, even tolerate it, in this hot, fetid atmosphere? Even worse, how was I to endure it at night, when the steerage was full? Wretched, I climbed back on deck.

Six pounds was the price of the ticket in the steerage from Liverpool to New York. For two or three pounds more you could transfer to second cabin. I was greatly tempted to do so, and then, for some reason, it seemed an act of cowardice. Pride or obstinacy made me stay where I was. The ship was filled to capacity. Fourteen days we were on the Atlantic. I lived through them in what I can only think of as a state of unreality; it was like one of those dreams in which one tells oneself, 'It's only a dream: I shall wake up soon.' How could it be I who was living in that ship? It was all as remote as possible from anything I had experienced or imagined. I do not mean that it was all unpleasant: it was a dream, not a nightmare; and increased familiarity with it hardened one to the more unpleasant aspects of it. The utter lack of privacy and the overcrowding I soon took for granted. I discovered that where privacy is impossible curiosity, both in oneself and in others, dies. The stench was another matter. And a new and even more nauseating element was added to it as more and more passengers fell to sea-sickness. God knows I felt sick enough myself on the second and third days, yet I wasn't sick; and I really believe a kind of pride in me inhibited sickness. It seemed to me, as I watched my companions, that they gave way to it unresistingly, lay down and waited for it, and were then as helpless as I have seen kittens when ill. I knew I would feel an angry contempt for myself if I succumbed as easily as they, and I told myself I came of an island race whereas they were land animals from the broad plains of central Europe— I, who had not seen the sea at all until I went on board ship at Liverpool! And then, when the great wave of sickness died down, by the end of the first week, I found I accepted the stench. Indeed, one could scarcely escape it anywhere on that ship. Even on deck at night one felt it in one's nostrils, tasted it in one's mouth. Perhaps it was a subjective stink; but it was not until I had been three days in New York that I realised I had lost it.

It was the nights that were worst, yet, paradoxically, it was the nights that justified the whole adventure and made it glorious. Sleep in the steerage I found almost impossible. The heat was intolerable; the air choked one. Then there were the noises, not only the ship's noises but the all-too-human noises. I was abandoned in a huddle of mad snorers; and apart from the snorers, it seemed that all around me men, women and children were acting out their dreams and nightmares, crying for help in anguished languages I did not understand. One night, there was a long, horrifying scream of pure agony from the other side of the steerage. I jumped up from my bunk, expecting murder at least and expecting everyone else to leap up too. But no one did. It was nothing; only a miserable wretch suffering the tortures of the damned in his dreams. And particularly I was haunted by the noises made by my fellow-passengers in what I have called my pen. They writhed above me, opposite me, and on either side of me; they grunted and roared and ground their teeth, sighed, twitched, rolled over groaning. It was then that I understood that whatever death may be like it is not like sleep, for sleep is never still, never tranquil; with consciousness in abeyance, body and soul are the passive victims of angry passions the waking mind can scarcely know. Almost I could have repudiated my fellow-passengers as they slept; they had become in sleep loathsome parodies of human beings; and almost I could have wished not to sleep myself lest I become like them. Still, night after night, as though conforming to a convention that must not be broken, I tried to sleep. And then, after an hour, I picked up my blanket and groped my way up the long flights of the companion to the deck.

That first night, it was an act of despair. I was suffocating and had to have air. I felt like the hero in the Greek story who put on the poisoned shirt: I had to tear it off; and evading as best I could the pools of vomit that were everywhere, I stumbled and staggered up to the deck. I found a space between the hatches and lay there wrapped in my blanket. But still I did not sleep and did not want to sleep, and after a time got up and stood at the rail. And so night after night, sleeping perhaps three or four hours but no more.

At first I thought I was the only person, besides the sailors going about their duties, on those decks. Gradually I realised I wasn't; on the second night I found my place between the hatches had been taken by a man and woman in copulation; as stealthily as I could I moved away to find another place. Yet I was not conscious of others. It was an easy solitude. Everything was purified in that immensity of sky and sea. It was wonderful to me; I knew I was in the presence of true mystery. Of course I saw the ship in its solitary voyaging through the night and through the vastness of the ocean as a symbol of man. I know it is a cliché; it was no cliché for me then but something apprehended passionately, felt, as it were, on the pulses and in the blood. At times, it was the voyage itself, the ship alone as though the only ship in the world in that vast alien universe, that awed and exhilarated me, the very daring of it in that vastness. At others, as I leaned over the side of the vessel, it was the detail about me that delighted me, the ship's lights reflected on the oiled blackness of the water, the delicate fretted tracery of the white sea foam in the ship's wake, the whorled water itself in its constant movement. But always it was awe that held me, and I could not forbear seeing the visible majesty of the universe we were in as a symbol of something both within it and above it. I will not call it God, for it had nothing in common with any God I had been taught about at St Barnabas' or at Boulter's Lane Chapel. It seemed to me to rebuke that God, for whatever else it might be it plainly had nothing to do with man. I have said that for me the voyage in the steerage was like living in a state of unreality. It was not so of these nights on deck. Then I seemed to approach and at times be almost at one with an intenser reality than I had known before or have known after. And since then, the memory of those nights has been a touchstone of reality for me. I have caught glimpses of that reality elsewhere, in the mountains of North Wales, Cader Idris and Snowdon, especially, but fainter by far; and I might have missed them altogether but for my voyage to America fifty-five years ago.

But by day I lived in a different world; it could not have been more fantastic to me if I had found myself living in a circus or had made my bed, as it were, at a fair in full swing. That was how it seemed to me. At first I had sought out those who spoke my own language; then, disliking them so much, I shunned them. Perhaps I was in a kind of panic, but I saw that they were not at all the kind of men I would willingly consort with at home; and I was uneasily aware of my loneliness and inexperience, aware, too, of my £50, and these seemed the sort of men who might very well try to take it from me. I decided they were better avoided; and fortunately it was not difficult. None of them was in Steerage No. 1. There I was the only Englishman, and I somehow sensed that my fellows there—Germans, Bohemians, Hungarians, Russian Jews, Poles, Latvians and the rest—were as bewildered and inexperienced, as helpless, as myself; indeed, more so, because the ship was British and I at least spoke English. What made me marvel, though, was the way in which, in this triangular Tower of Babel that was Steerage No. 1, friendships sprang up within the first day or two that endured for the whole voyage, and a sea-voyage of fourteen days has a timeless quality. It may seem that friendship is not the right word. At any rate, I found myself choosing to associate with some of my fellows rather than with others, and this though we did not know one another's language; though by the end of the fourteen days we could in a manner communicate. By that time, I must have known three hundred common nouns in German, Czech, Magyar and even in languages whose names I never heard. And my friends, for so I must call them, since at the time I thought of them as such, knew as many words of English. Because I was English I was in demand, if only because we were bound for an English-speaking country whose tongue they must somehow acquire; and at the end of the voyage, when the time came to fill in official forms and meet immigration officers, they turned to me with a pathetic trust, ignoring whenever possible the ship's interpreters; simply because they thought of me as a friend.

But the friendships had to be made first. I think they grew out of some material basis, a feeling of common interest that showed itself by accident. I remember that on the second or third day—we were out of Belfast and steaming past the shores of Northern Ireland—having realised that crowded though we were everyone else was ignoring the lack of privacy and making himself at home, I plucked up courage to take out my fiddle and play softly to myself. I was in fact murdering Beethoven's first violin sonata as usual. I was sitting on my bunk, which was in the bottom tier, as I played, and I was suddenly aware of a man standing above me gesticulating furiously. I had already marked him down as a fellow to be avoided, for his aspect seemed to me villainous. He was a huge man, whose face, except for his tiny eyes and red bulbous nose that looked as though it had been shoved on as an afterthought, was almost wholly obscured by a shaggy beard. He was dressed in the most outlandish garments, in a Russian peasant blouse, his feet and legs bound up in rags. He was a man I shrank from, and there he was, seemingly about to snatch my fiddle from me by its neck and then standing back and playing an imaginary violin in pantomime and, that done, jerking his thumb furiously at his chest. It took me a little time to gather what he meant, and then, so enormously did he loom above me and so ferocious did he appear, there seemed nothing for it but to hand him the instrument. He stared at it with delight. In those great hairy hands it looked like a toy fiddle. I was in agony lest he should break it, for to tell the truth, I no more regarded the fellow as human than if he had been a gorilla. But his face was lit up with joy, and with two strides he was in the middle of the steerage, the fiddle tucked beneath his worn doormat of a beard, and the bow on the strings was making music of a kind I had never heard before. It was wild, passionate and melancholy; I found it almost physically frightening for it seemed to pluck at a nerve in my stomach. It was most decidedly not Beethoven's first sonata; it was not to my mind civilised at all but an expression of primitive and intense melancholy. As he played, quietness fell on the steerage. Everyone was listening, and after a time some of the passengers began to dance, and again it was a dance the like of which I have not seen before or since. For years I was haunted by this music my friend, for the loan of the instrument made him my friend, conjured from my fiddle; I knew that however well I learnt to play, I would never be able to play that music, nor, I suspected, would Herr Schmidt at the School of Music. It was not until quite recent years, with the coming of wireless, that I heard anything like it again, and then I realised it was Tzigane music, the music of the Hungarian gipsies, but played by my friend with a barbaric pathos and splendour beyond anything I ever heard on the B.B.C.

He was my first friend. When he returned the fiddle to me I gave him to understand that he could use it whenever he liked. To my embarrassment, he embraced me. But thereafter we spent much of the day together. We could converse only by smile and gesture, for his language was beyond me entirely, and though he told me what I assumed was his name I could not pronounce it. He on his side managed 'Billy' very satisfactorily, and no sooner was I under his protection than I was 'Billy' to all the members of his national group, whatever it was, and they made me richly welcome. For my part, I felt both proud and safe with this uncouth giant, who was the slave of gratitude, at my side. But judge my surprise when I saw him on the morning of our arrival at New York: in rags no longer but dressed in broadcloth, and with beard trimmed and tamed almost out of recognition. A very respectable Tzigane giant indeed.

I made another friend by being able to play draughts. This man, a Pole, I saw walking the length of the steerage with a draughts board in one hand, while with the other he tapped it with a draught, looking about him appealingly the while. I nodded enthusiastically, and we went up on deck together. For a time we were puzzled because it was plain we were playing by different rules; but we worked out an acceptable compromise and from then on played for at least an hour a day and sometimes for much longer. He was by far the better player but was tolerant of my incompetence, perhaps because he was always so innocently pleased with his own skill.

Meals brought other friends. The other Englishmen travelling steerage grumbled interminably about the food the ship provided. It was certainly monotonous, but I did not find it so much bad as strange. At breakfast there was the choice of tea or coffee, though I never succeeded in discovering which was which; and with the tea or coffee, there was, after porridge, sometimes Irish stew, sometimes rissoles, sometimes fish. The fish I found uneatable, I had been taught by my mother never to eat rissoles except at home, and I was so conventional as to believe Irish stew an impossible breakfast dish. But for me porridge was enough. At midday there was always soup, which

I thought very good indeed, either roast beef or boiled salt pork, which I did not like, and boiled potatoes, followed by plum-duff. The evening meal was much the worst. The other Englishmen swore that we were served with the scraps from the first-class tables, and I believe they were right. Either it was rissoles again or fish-cakes, or practically meatless chicken bones or odd bits of fish tentatively warmed up. In the evenings I largely made do with bread and the food I had brought with me. This was a godsend in more ways than one. We ate our meals on tin plates at the tables in the steerage, and I remember vividly the shock of surprise that went round our table the first time I peeled an orange. I remember, too, how delicious, how wholesomely pungent, its smell was. All round me eyes were wide in envy. I had to resist the impulse to hand everyone at the table an orange, but to all my nearest neighbours I gave a segment. These were people for whom an orange was one of the rarest luxuries in the world. They must have thought me a prince in disguise lapsing into his princely habits. And as I gave them every evening segments of orange so they gave me slices of sausages of a variety of kinds I had never eaten before, highly spiced, strong with garlic, sometimes of the consistency of wafers of leather. If my mother had ever suspected their existence she would surely have warned me against them, but I ate them all with relish; and so my store of apples and oranges brought me by exchange a wealth of strange foods to supplement or take the place of the ship's diet. Because of my store I was often invited to join select groups at mealtimes. I doled out my two-pound pot of strawberry jam like a rare cordial. At my friend the fiddle-player's group I believe I would have been welcome in any case, but whenever I visited them I took something with which to repay hospitality. It was with them that I shared one of my two tins of pineapple chunks. We hacked it open with a huge knife, and oh, the delight on their faces as they tasted pineapple for the first time! My other tin I am afraid I ate all by myself one night on deck. But after that first evening meal I never consumed a whole orange in the public view. It would have been too ostentatious.

So, one way and another, I found myself a privileged person in Steerage No. 1. I had powerful friends, as I discovered one day when a drunken Englishman from Steerage No. 3

suddenly appeared and roughly demanded oranges. There at my side immediately was the giant fiddle-player and behind him his retinue. My compatriot slunk away. I was, almost before knowing it, a member of a community or, more precisely, of a federal union of communities, for that is what our steerage became. The national groups did not exactly mix; it seemed to me that the further east of Europe they came from the more firmly they cohered, like a herd of cattle in the face of the unknown. The Germans and the handful of Dutch and Scandinavians were much less rigid in their allegiances. Yet all were content to exist side by side, and the sense of the larger community they belonged to came out in the evenings on deck after supper, when each group in turn would dance and sing according to its own mode. For mine, of course, was not the only musical instrument in the steerage; there were other fiddles, though not in Steerage No. 1, and there were accordions, concertinas, zithers, mouth-organs, a flute or two and guitars. I suppose in that fortnight I must have heard the folk music of half Europe: it was all new to me. I had no feeling of hearing it as at a concert. These gatherings were not concerts; the players and dancers and singers were not performing; they were expressing themselves, or expressing the continuity and identity of their group, spontaneously. In a way, I envied them.

It was idyllic; but the idyll was not perfect. Our simple self-made entertainments attracted the attention of the first-class passengers. One would suddenly see them, the ladies in their gowns, the gentlemen in the shining shirt-fronts of their evening clothes, thronged on the gangways leading down from the first-class decks. They could come down to us; we might not go up to them. They stood there listening, and I could understand what they said. We were the poor, the great unwashed, the mob, the feared: our present saving grace was that we were picturesque. I wonder now whether anyone else among my fellow-passengers felt towards them as I did: to me their very presence was an insult, and I could imagine bitterly the comments they made on us when they were back in their staterooms. We were a passing show, and after a time they turned away; but before doing so they would fling coins down among us. I hated them.

10

WHAT a strange thing memory is! It is never to be trusted. There is always the discrepancy between the moment as actually lived and the experience as assessed in the mind afterwards, and the two can be utterly different. My visit to New York was the great adventure of my life; but when I think of the city now it is the modern city I see, a city I never in fact saw because it was not there. Images from films and photographs have superimposed themselves upon my mind. I know this, yet I have the greatest difficulty in realising that I have not walked beneath those steel-and-concrete towers and in the canyons between them. The loftiest building in the New York I knew was the American Surety Company, on Broadway opposite Trinity Church. It was twenty storeys high and the wonder of the world: it made me dizzy even to look up at it. And there you have it: the gulf between a four-storey building, the largest I had known at home, and a twenty-storey one is immeasurably vaster than that between a twenty-storey and a hundred-storey. And because they were new, not only to me but to everybody else, those modest skyscrapers were more impressive, more terrifying even, than the much greater ones of today.

I look back to my months in New York with pleasure and delight. But I have to admit that most of the time I was there I was frightened and appallingly lonely. Frightened is not quite the right word, for in the very sensation of fear there was an exhilaration. I felt, I suppose, much as I would have done had I been alone in the African jungle, rackingly aware of unknown and monstrous dangers all about me, so that I had to be on the alert the whole time, keyed up to meet ambush, to sidestep the snake poised to strike. I was utterly unprepared for what I found. At home, I had thought I lived in a great city because I was one of a quarter of a million people. I realised as soon as I stepped ashore at the 8th Street pier that mine was just an overgrown small town. I had not even any experience of London to prepare me, and I was baffled and dismayed by the foreignness of it all. So far as the people around me were concerned, it seemed to be an extension of life in the steerage: foreign tongues on all sides and people of other colours than white everywhere; and when I heard English it was spoken in accents scarcely recognisable—in those days we had not been made familiar by films and wireless with American speech. And it was not foreignness only; there was also a ferocity, a ruthlessness, that I sensed as an almost palpable thing. This was not entirely subjective. It was as though one were confronted for the first time with the naked facts of the Darwinian struggle for existence, of nature red in tooth and claw; and here nature was only just below the surface of society, scarcely bothering to disguise itself. Hitherto, I had met the struggle for existence as the evolutionists saw it only in the sermons of the Rev. Mr Higgins at Boulter's Lane Chapel: he had enthusiastically reconciled it with the Christian ethic, but here one saw the truth.

I remember, for instance, on my second day in the city walking along Fifth Avenue, gaping like a sawney at the sights; when suddenly I saw, beside a waiting cab, four men, two facing two and looking into a doorway, drawn across the pavement. They were armed! Each held a rifle in his hands and had a pistol at his side. I had never seen firearms before except in gunsmiths' windows. I realised they were standing at the entrance of a bank and in my innocence I went and stood next to one of them, just to see what was happening. I was suddenly jerked forward, so that I nearly went sprawling, by the pressure of a rifle barrel poked into my back. 'Beat it, pardner!' the man said, and beat it I did, at any rate for fifty yards or so, and then I turned and saw men carrying bags of money from the bank into the cab under the eyes of the men with their guns. A perfectly normal everyday occurrence: money being taken from a bank; but a very visibly armed guard was necessary.

I could not have been more astonished. No doubt I was very innocent to think it a spectacle to linger over. There were other instances more complex. I was just as astonished at the contrast between extreme poverty and extreme riches that was evident everywhere. No doubt what I saw was the extreme situation always to be found in a great city and to that extent not typical. I realised that even then. You had only to walk up to Harlem, which was then inhabited mainly by Germans and not at all by Negroes, to step into a world of lower middle-class respectability; but in Manhattan you were in the presence all the time of garish opposites, of a sharpness of contrasts I had never before thought possible.

But I anticipate; I am writing as though my discovery of New York was immediate and instantaneous, and of course it was nothing of the kind. I see now that my great protector in that huge impersonal amoral city was my own innocence, that and my temperate habits: I have never been able to take alcohol; more than the smallest amount makes me feel sick, and I don't doubt there is something psychological at work here, the symbol of an extreme revulsion against my father's excesses. Once upon a time, I considered this physical inability to drink intoxicants highly creditable to me, a sign, as it were, of inherent and unassailable virtue. I know now that that is silly. All the same, I am pretty sure that this incurable abstemiousness of mine was a powerful aid to my innocence: it kept me away from the settings of the temptations and dangers that can accompany drinking. Even so, my innocence took me to many places and parts of the city I probably would not have entered had I been more experienced. It wasn't that I lacked caution. I was perhaps over-suspicious. I remember that as soon as I had landed I left the neighbourhood of the docks as quickly as possible, seeing in everybody who hung around them a shark who would try to fleece me of my money; for I had been warned of the crooks who preyed on immigrants.

I marched as it were inland, though I had no notion in what direction I should go; behaving very much as I would have done in an English town when I knew no one there and must seek work. The first essential was a lodging, and I was searching for the equivalent of a respectable working-class district. I was looking, that is, for streets of six-roomed terrace-houses set among which would be little general shops, with pubs at the corners. Of course I found nothing like this. I found street after street of brown-stone houses that had plainly once been the homes of the wealthy and were now tenements, each swarming with families. There were no known landmarks at all. The further I penetrated into the island the more I panicked, for the further I was from anything even remotely like home. I recall walking down Sixth Avenue, bewildered by the over-head railway that ran above one side of the street, deafened by it too, and then crossing Fourteenth Street and finding myself in a succession of small but quite separate foreign countries. I remember that journey now, burdened as I was with my possessions, as a nightmare. I might have been in a fever, so kaleidoscopic were the scenes I passed through. At one point it seemed that all the men were garbed in black and had long beards and hooked noses, and the signs above shops were in a script I did not understand. And then quite suddenly the cooking smells from eating-houses changed, and the men were swarthier and moustachio'd, and I was in Italy. All the ordinary routines of life were carried on in the open air, on the pavements, women with washing-tubs, tradesmen at their work; and the shops were rows of pedlars' carts in the middle of the road. I turned off at an angle into another street, and all was different again. Now everyone was black. I was among whole streets of Negroes, and I felt conspicuous because of my white face and frightened because conspicuous. I turned again, into narrower streets, and the silence was uncanny, and I was again frightened. Everyone here was Chinese, the older men dressed still in faded blue Chinese clothes and with pigtails. Street names apart, the English language had disappeared altogether; the walls of the houses were placarded with posters bearing Chinese characters printed in orange and blue. More strongly than ever I felt that this was no place for me.

How far I walked I don't know. It could not, in fact, have been a very great distance: these separate, self-contained worlds were packed into what must have been a relatively tiny space. And in the end I emerged into streets that were at least no longer exotic in their foreignness but instead, nondescript or neutral, and the more welcome for that. They were shabby to the point of being poverty-stricken; all the same, it was like coming home. I was hungry and had a meal in a small restaurant; and as I paid my bill I asked the proprietor if he could tell me where I might obtain a night's lodging. He jerked his thumb: 'Try three doors down,' he said.

When I saw the room that was offered me my heart sank. It was a tiny back room on the third floor, overshadowed by the blank wall of a taller building, so that sunlight never entered. It was furnished as barely almost as a monastic cell but was a good deal dirtier. But weary as I was from lugging my traps round this vast city, I thought, 'It will do for tonight, and tomorrow I can find somewhere better.' In fact, I lived there for my whole stay in New York and was indeed not unhappy in it. I was by myself, and by myself I was never lonely; I was only lonely when surrounded by other people. Now, I count finding that room one of my luckier strokes in New York City, for I had only to shut my door to shut the world out, and that was a privilege I had not known before. Not that the house was silent. It was never that. It was a tenement, and every room except mine seemed occupied by at least two people; and a more gregarious house I cannot well imagine. Life overflowed into the landings and on to the stairs and was lived perpetually at the shouting level. That house— at one time it must have been nothing less than a mansion —rang day and night with laughter and with screams, and it was not always easy to tell one from the other. That first night as I lay in bed I was very frightened indeed; I lay, as it seemed to me, surrounded by murderers and maniacs who must at any moment break down my door and burst into my room. But nothing happened, of course, and in all the months I was there I don't think I exchanged more than a dozen words, and they were monosyllables, with anyone in the house except with the surly janitor to whom I paid my rent. So long as I did that no one was interested in me at all. It was all absolutely impersonal; lack of curiosity could not have been carried further; at times I would say to myself: 'I could die here, and nobody would care.' The realisation gave me a mournful pleasure as I imagined them at last breaking down the door in my room, not because they were concerned for me but out of impatience because the rent was overdue.

But I had to find a job, and I soon discovered that George had been right and that I would have been better off had I followed his advice. New York was so vast that it offered work of every conceivable kind, but it was not in any real way a centre of the silversmith's trade. Philadelphia, I learned, was the place for that; it was to Philadelphia I should have gone. If I had had any sense I should have caught the next train as soon as I discovered this; but I didn't, and why I didn't is something I have puzzled over for years. I could get work of a kind in New York, but it was of a quality much below that I was accustomed to, and though I soon got together a connection of a sort it was plain that there was no prospect of earning steady money. All the same, I managed, for the first few months at any rate, to make enough to keep me. Yet I knew all the time that if I went to Philly, as everyone called it, I could get regular work at a good wage. Everyone told me so, all the small jobbing jewellers I worked for: 'Kid, you're wasting your time in this man's town. Get the hell out of it to Philly?' Why didn't I? Wasn't I in America to make my fortune, or at least to do better than I could at home?

The answer, when all the rationalisations, the pretexts I made in my letters home, are shorn away, is that I didn't want to. I had found freedom and I was like a spendthrift who has come into a fortune. My wants were small, I had a roof over my head and a bed to sleep in, and without working hard or long I could pay for them. It left me all the time in the world. To do what? Nothing, I am afraid, or nothing that could easily be justified. To roam the streets of New York, to be myself, in the cant phrase. At the time, of course, I persuaded myself otherwise. I read and was delighted by *Walden* in the New York Public Library and easily saw myself as a new and highly original version of Thoreau, one whose Walden Ponds was a street between Second and Third Avenues and whose hut was a dark, damp room in a tenement. I thought that if it ever became necessary I could live as cheaply as Thoreau did.

And what about my dreams of education? Alas, the story is much the same. I read in a haphazard way in the Public Library and I made the pilgrimage to Forty-ninth Street to gaze at Columbia University, but I never crossed its threshold. To live in freedom was like living in a timeless present. Lack of obvious obligations made me irresponsible as I had never been before. But not, as I have to confess, as I have never been since, for I experienced a similar time years later. This was when, in 1920, I set up my own little business. I put all my savings into it, and I could not have chosen a worse time. I had seen so many of my friends, workmen like myself, set themselves up in their own businesses during the war, with great profit to themselves. Of my brothers, Edwin and Tom and Horace, though he was a special case, had all done so; and Jimmy Sillitoe had become it seemed to me very rich indeed: he had stopped being a Socialist and joined the Unionist Party and when he was in London on business stayed at the Constitutional Club. But I was too late: my war service, ludicrous as it was, had kept me out of the harvest, and when I rented my two rooms in Queen Caroline Street the post-war depression had already begun.

Well, I failed. I survived two years and then had to quit, with no profit made and all my savings gone. It might have been worse but it need not have been so bad. It was my own fault. The truth is, freedom from a boss and from the restraint of being employed went to my head. I made the fatal mistake of taking my fiddle with me to the workshop, intending to practise in my dinner-hour, but before I knew where I was I was spending whole mornings or afternoons scraping away when I ought to have been out looking for work, going the rounds of the big silversmiths. For there was work about, of a kind, though of so poor a quality that I could scarcely bring myself to touch it. Yet how could I refuse it, with a wife and family to support? What happened, how I behaved, I can show in a little incident that I still recall with shame.

Jimmy Sillitoe had kindly put some work in my way. More accurately, though I do not wish to minimise his kindness in doing so, he had sub-contracted it to me. While we liked him well enough as a man George and I had always rather despised him. He was a competent enough workman but he had no feeling for his craft. Then, from our point of view he was a renegade. He had left the I.L.P. and gone over to the Tories and in doing so had acquired a new and to me odious self-confidence. 'Of course I still believe in Socialism as an ideal, Billy,' he'd tell me; 'a beautiful ideal. But it won't work, Billy. Not until you've changed human nature.' He also used to say, 'I go where the money is,' and the money at that time was in making the cheapest kind of badges and brooches for

Woolworth's Store. So though it was well-meaning of him to let me into a corner of his Tom Tiddler's Ground it was to me ignominy.

Try as hard as I might, I could not bring myself to begin the work. The more I contemplated it the more difficult it was to begin, and the more pointless it seemed. I hadn't become a master-man, as we still called them, to do that kind of work. It was freedom I was after, and almost in defiance I picked up my fiddle and began to fiddle like mad. The sight of all that trash and trumpery spread out on my bench seemed to compel me to fiddle, and there I stood hour after hour, legs apart, with the weight of my body on the balls of my feet, head thrown back, a proper Albert Sammons.

And Jimmy caught me. I was gloriously happy, lost in the music I was making—it was a Bach Partita I was murdering—and, if it had been possible, I would have sung out loud at the same time. I was so rapt that I simply didn't hear the bell ring. I was unconscious of anything until Jimmy's shattering cry, 'Billy! What do you think you're up to?' He stared at me with horror and then at the work on my bench. 'Nothing done!' he cried. 'You haven't even started!' He was outraged, morally outraged; I don't think he could have been more so if he had caught me slumped over a whisky bottle or with a woman in my arms. 'Billy,' he said, 'you're impossible.' I could not meet his eyes, and without saying a word, I sat down at the bench and began to work. I was bitterly ashamed.

11

IT's no good, Lizzie: the world is now and not in memory, and I've had a rude awakening to the world. Reliving and recording my life as a boy with George and my experiences on the immigrant ship and in New York have been a glorious escape, but I became so immersed in it that I have scarcely noticed what was going on about me. I did notice vaguely that a deal of telephoning was taking place and that everyone was quieter and more subdued than usual, but for days I have dwelt in such a state of benign abstraction that I could well have believed the surrounding quietness was an attribute of it. So one makes the world in one's own image. I know now it hasn't been that kind of quietness at all.

I was in this mood of serene absence at supper last evening, while eating I don't know what; for I was still contemplating the New York I had been writing about earlier, savouring my memories of it, thinking how good it had all been, how right it was that I had made the venture, if only because of the unadulterated joy it gave me in remembering it so many years later. And then suddenly I heard Will shout. 'Father! I'm talking to you!' It exploded on my ears like the bark of an angry dog, a very large angry dog; and when I looked up and saw how red he was about the neck I realised he must have addressed me more than once before.

He was glaring at me across the table, and observing how Beryl looked at him as though in silent pleading and how the children sat with their eyes almost ostentatiously staring at their plates, I realised that this was a family crisis.

'Yes, Will?' I said mildly, for I felt mild.

'Father, I've got something to say to you. Please join me in my room after supper.'

'Yes, Will,' I said. He was speaking to me exactly as he

speaks to Timmy when he is angry with him. Now what had I done, I wondered, for though I was aware of no recent sin either of omission or commission, I am afraid I took it for granted that I was the guilty person, and indeed I found myself feeling guilty. Whatever it was, it was undoubtedly my fault, though, as I told myself, it was just as undoubtedly a complete misconstruction of something I had done or failed to do. How incalculable other people are, and most of all those nearest and dearest to us! That is what I thought. But as covertly I observed the flushed neck, the red face stretched and framed in lines of anxiety, I was determined to remain mild and reasonable.

Having toyed with whatever it was on the plate before me, I excused myself and left the room, and went to Will's to wait for him there. The fact is, I was suddenly weary of it all. Will and Beryl, Timmy and Susan, had to endure that explosive silence; I didn't; and I had no wish to be part of it, however passive. So I sat in Will's room. It is not a room I go into often, for a great deal of fuss is made of it. It's a holy-of-holies; one doesn't enter without permission. It is, if you understand me, a very masculine room, the shrine where the man of the family performs his mysterious rites. Women and children not admitted. Cheques are signed there, and household accounts scrutinised, and school reports angrily discussed with disappointing offspring. All this part of it I can scarcely take seriously, I am too old; and between ourselves, I think Will makes too much of a mumbo-jumbo out of being a husband and a father and the head of a family. But as a room where work is done I have nothing but respect for it. It is an austere, functional room, and it shows the side of Will that I regard most highly, indeed that I reverence, as one should reverence another's special knowledge and talents. On one side, under the window, is the long draughtsman's desk with the high stool below it, and neatly arranged and near to hand for the utmost convenience in using the draughtsman's tools, the geometrical instruments, the pens and pencils, the reference books, the thick *Machinery Handbook*, the bound volumes of the *Proceedings* of the Institute of Production Engineers, the stacked copies of *Engineering* and *Machinery*. On the walls are framed photographs of the factory in its various stages of erection and of its various departments. Here, I thought, is the real Will, and I revelled in the evidences of his existence, even though I had to admit that I had seldom made contact with it. And as I counselled myself to remain serene and mild I rehearsed the formal words. I would not argue; I would not deny; I was not interested in whatever my sins of omission or commission might be. On my side at any rate, there would be no expostulation, no bitterness. I would say, simply but firmly and with dignity, 'My boy, you have all been very kind to me, and I am grateful. The faults are mine and no one else's. For everyone's sake it is best that I move on. You need not worry about me or fret. You have done your best.'

No sooner had the door opened than I began. 'My boy,' I said, standing in front of the fire grate, 'you have all been very kind to me, and I am grateful.' But Will did not seem to hear me and he said, 'I am truly sorry to have kept you waiting, father. There was something I had to say to Beryl and the children. And I'm afraid I shouted at you at supper. I didn't mean to, it was quite involuntary. But I seem to fly off the handle at the slightest thing these days. Worry, I suppose. But it was unpardonable all the same.'

He stood in the doorway, this son of mine who, when I saw him face to face, was always so different from the son as he existed in my imagination. How could this great bull-necked sixteen stone of bald-headed adult male of forty-nine, with his enormous red face decomposed with worry, be of any begetting of mine? What had he to do with me, or I with him? Embarrassed, I said quickly: 'Say no more about it, son. I understand. I know what a worry the factory must be to you; all that responsibility.' And I went on, 'The faults are mine and no one else's. For everyone's sake——'

But he did not seem to understand what I was saying. 'Faults?' he said vaguely; 'what faults? I'm not aware of any.' And then: 'But what am I thinking of? Father, please do sit down.' And as I did so, he crumpled into the other armchair.

He said no more, and I was bewildered; and as the silence continued my bewilderment grew. What was it all about?

At last, 'I'm afraid,' he said, 'you'll have been thinking Beryl and I have been very churlish and inhospitable these last few days, dad. It hasn't been our intention. We'd hoped to keep it from you till it had passed over, but—well, it hasn't, and I think you'd better know about it. I've warned the children; and naturally, that was pretty unpleasant, but it's impossible to guess what he may do, and they're old enough to know.'

I was suddenly fearful. 'Will,' I said sharply, 'what are you trying to tell me?'

He stared at the wall and said: 'It's Tom again.'

'Tom!' I cried, and perhaps there was too much eagerness in my voice, for he turned and seemed to stare at me oddly. 'What's this about Tom?'

'He's about again, and up to his tricks.'

'But, Will——'

'I tried to kid myself, but I knew we were living in a fool's paradise. I tried to tell Beryl it was too good to last, but women are content to live in the moment. Well, I knew it was all over ten days ago, when Phil telephoned from Cambridge. Tom had had the damned impertinence to present himself at the porter's lodge at the college. It seems he'd been hanging around for the best part of a week, and I've heard since that Phil's discovered he'd introduced himself to various people in the University Arms and the Blue Boar as Phil's brother and touched them for the odd quid or so. In the end, it cost Phil twenty quid to get rid of him. I suppose I'll be lucky to get off as lightly.'

'But, Will——'

'He's in town. He rang me up at the factory this morning. Of course I told him I'd break every bone in his body if he tried his nonsense on me, but he laughed at me: he knew I was bluffing just as well as I did. Said the poste restante would always find him and that he'd be around for a week or so, after which time, if he hadn't heard from me, he'd phone again. After which time!' Will laughed bitterly. 'It's sheer bloody blackmail, father, but it's a very peculiar form of blackmail all the same. No one who didn't know Tom would believe it. It isn't the money he's after; he's always had ways of getting that without working for it. No, it's the crack of the whip he wants us to feel. That's what's so damned humiliating.'

'But——'

'Oh, I know we let ourselves in for it. We ought to have been tough at the beginning. You ought to have been tough, dad. I've always said so. I was swayed by Phil, I don't mind admitting it. Phil said Tom couldn't help himself, that it wasn't his fault or anybody else's, that it was something that cropped up in some form or another in all families, and we just had to make the best of it. It was weak of me to give in. But this time I'm going to make it plain to Master Tom that it's the last time. After this, he can stew in his juice. I'm sitting tight.' He wiped his forehead with his handkerchief. 'He has his fun and we pay him to stop, and as long as we go on paying him he'll go on having his fun at our expense. Well, this is the last time. After this, I sit tight and sweat it out. Beryl agrees with me. I shall write to him tomorrow and give him a plain ultimatum. Thus far and no further. At first, he won't believe it, I know, and then he won't like it. There may well be a deal of unpleasantness. I'm prepared for that. I suppose for the next six months I must expect all sorts of chaps I don't usually care to have much to do with, chaps one meets in business because one can't avoid it, coming up to me and wanting me to pay Tom's debts to them, money they lent him because he was my brother. So far as I'm concerned, they'll have to whistle for it. No, dad, my real worry is what he may do when he turns nasty. I wouldn't put it past the little swine to start getting at you or the children. I've made it plain to Timmy and Susan—they've never met him, of course—that they're to have nothing to do with him and that if he should approach them they're to tell me at once. Now, dad, I want you to do the same. If Tom should try and get in touch with you, either by letter or by waiting for you when you're out walking, I want you to let me know at once. God, when I think of what you and mother have had to put up with from him!'

'But, Will,' I cried, 'what are you asking me? Tom is my son!'

'And I'm trying to protect you from him, trying to protect us all.'

I jumped out of my chair in my agitation and began to walk up and down the room. 'Protection,' I said; 'I don't need protection from my own son.'

Will sat in his chair, immovable; but he was gripping the chair-arms. I could see he was striving to be patient with me.

'Look, father,' he said; 'you can't deny it: Tom's a bad lot. I hate to say it about my own brother, but there it is. You've done as much for him as any father could. But facts have to be faced, and there comes a time when there's nothing for it but to cut one's losses. I think the time has come.'

'Losses!' I shouted. 'Bad lot, good lot—what does it all mean? It's just words. What difference does it make to me? Tom's still my son, isn't he? As much as you or Phil. I'm too old to bother about bad lots and good lots. There's nothing you can tell me about Tom I don't know, or couldn't guess if I wanted to; and I tell you it's all the same. To you Tom's just a nuisance, an inconvenience; but he's my son.'

I was trembling with passion. I was quite beyond reason, and knew it, for I was in a realm of feeling in which reason was absolutely irrelevant. Even in the moment I was astonished and frightened at the intensity of my emotion: it was as though I had been suddenly stripped down to depths in me which I had not known existed before. All I knew was that here was something, my feeling for Tom, in a sense my obligation to Tom, that had to be defended against the whole world if necessary.

And in his way Will understood: my passion was as surprising to him as it was to me, but all the same it was a blow to him. How could it not be? He was thinking in terms of conduct, of morals, of right and wrong; but I was far away, in a world of feeling beyond questions of conduct or even right and wrong. 'Look, dad,' he said very patiently, 'you'll agree Phil and I have been good sons to you——'

'Stop!' I cried. 'Don't say any more.' My heart bled for him, for the wound he was about to inflict upon himself and force me to inflict on him, too. Whether he knew it or not, I was pleading with him. 'No man ever had two better sons,' I said, 'but don't you see——?' And then I couldn't continue. What I wanted to say, Lizzie, was that it was just because Phil and Will were the best sons a man could have, and just because they existed in their own right and in the eyes of the world as men of probity and achievement, that my debt to Tom, who was none of these things and who was a bad son, was so great. But how could I say it? Will's notion of the world is based on the sense of justice: what I would have said denied the existence of justice. I said instead: 'You know the parable of the prodigal son.'

I saw he took my meaning. He shrugged and said: 'At least the prodigal son repented. I don't see any sign of Tom repenting. He doesn't even bother any longer to go through the motions.'

There was no answer I could make to that. I sat down again for I felt very, very tired. 'You and Phil,' I said, 'have everything. Tom has nothing, except me, for what that's worth.'

Night had fallen and we sat in the darkness. At last I said quietly, for I was weary of it all, 'You think I'm a foolish, sentimental old man'; and perhaps bitterness came into my voice as I added: 'What good's money to me at my age? Tom's welcome to everything I've got, and I don't care what he does with it, however sordid, if it gives him some comfort.'

'It's my belief,' Will burst out, 'the young swine's been bleeding you for years!'

It wasn't like that at all; but how could I explain? 'No, no, Will. "Bleeding" doesn't come into it. Over the years, whenever I've been able to, I've sent Tom a little something from time to time.'

'You mean to say you've been in touch with him all these years, known his whereabouts?'

'Alas, Will, I can't say "in touch." I've often not heard from him for months on end, and then I can only fear the worst, but I know that care of the Poste Restante, Charing Cross Road Post Office, W.C.2, will always find him.'

'My God, he *has* been bleeding you. A running sore.'

I did not attempt to argue. 'So you see, Will,' I said as gently as possible, 'if Tom is in this town and seeks me out, I cannot possibly deny him. All I can promise is that I won't seek him out of my own accord.'

'Ah, well . . .' He heaved himself out of his armchair and before I could stop him switched on the light. He stared at me and then 'God damn and blast everything!' he cried, and hurried from the room. I suppose he had seen the tears in my eyes. I went up to my room and heard the telephoning begin again.

*   *   *

That was last evening, and now it is evening again. All day I have resisted the temptation to indulge my dearest wish, which is to see Tom. But if I did, what would I do, what would I say, and would I break through the barrier that divides us and, I believe, divides not only us from him but everyone else from him? There is a magic word, I sometimes think, that once I knew and know no longer. But the truth is, I never did know it. The animals are wiser than us, Lizzie, who drive their offspring from the den as soon as they can fend for themselves and then know them no more, recognising them, when they meet again, not as their kittens or puppies but simply as other cats or dogs. But at least they see them as other cats or dogs, as creatures of their own kind existing in their own right; and do we ever see our children as men and women in their own right? Just because they are our children, our sons pander to our weaknesses, our deepest fears and our snobbish ambitions. We demand that they should be idealised versions of ourselves. We project upon them intolerable burdens. We will not let them be themselves. They have always to be miniatures of us, explicable in mind and character in terms of us and the heritage of family we bear. Will seems to live in a state of perpetual anger with Timmy. No need to tell me the anger is an expression of the agony of love: I know all that. Perhaps the love is too great, or disproportionate. Timmy is an amiable boy of seventeen, not much good at anything, always in the bottom half of his form at school. Obviously, being Will's son, he should always be top! I have seen enough of life to know that he will do perfectly satisfactorily in any minor capacity. But what Will demands of him is that, at the age of seventeen, he should think and act like a portly, responsible production engineer and family man of forty-nine, in other words that he should be his father's *alter ego* living with him in permanent and perfect agreement.

Will is behaving merely as I did, though naturally it seems to me he is doing so in an exaggerated manner. Asking for nothing less than paragons, we grieve when our children show in themselves our failings; we are hurt when they prove different from us. How often, when the children were young and behaved in some unwonted way, have not Rose or I, bewildered, said to each other: 'Well, it isn't from *my* side of the family he gets it!' It was a joke of course, but also something more. It was as if to say: Your genes are responsible for this aberration, not mine.

It is Tom I have in mind. Of all my sons, I have always felt Phil nearest to me, no doubt because I see in him myself fulfilled. In him certain sides of myself are developed far beyond anything I could have achieved, and in him, of course, they are unaccompanied by my weaknesses. He is an idealised version of myself. With Will it is rather different. In him I see that part of myself that was akin to and responded to Horace. He has my self-doubt, my nagging irrational worries. They don't show on the surface; on the surface he is a successful business man; but I can guess at their existence. Often he surprises me with his resemblances to brother Horace—and I have to remember that Horace and I were always being taken for each other: the difference between us, plain to me, was anything but obvious to the rest of the world. Will has a comparable integrity, especially where his work is concerned, and also a similar absolute assurance of knowledge of right and wrong. The great abstractions are real to him: duty, responsibility, justice, he feels them in his blood. For him, as for Horace and George too, and Jimmy Sillitoe, and all I have felt closest to, work is a moral imperative. All this I understand.

But Tom—Tom was enigmatic from the beginning. Or so it has always seemed. Now, having written the words 'duty,' 'responsibility,' 'justice,' 'work as a moral imperative', I am not so sure. No one has ever been more devoted to them than I; they have governed my conscious life—and I can admit now that all my life I have hated them. Perhaps we all did secretly, but they enclosed us as in the stone walls and bars of a prison cell. George alone escaped, in his way. I never did, and when I had the chance I refused it, precisely in the name of duty. I talked and dreamt of freedom continually, but when it was offered me I was terrified of it, partly because though it is man's dearest possession it can also be the most destructive. I feared it would destroy me.

So, when I had it in my hand, I threw it away. In New York, I could earn enough for my simple needs with comparatively little effort. Of course, the kind of work I had to do was not pleasant; it was distasteful to my sense of craftsmanship. I see that now as merely one aspect of the prison we had made for ourselves, or inherited. At least, the work, cheap and nasty though it was, gave me the chance of freedom. Why didn't I take it? I am rationalising after the event, but I think it was because I saw myself faced with two contrasted possibilities. One was represented by the Central European and Russian exiles at whose feet I occasionally very humbly sat in cafés and whom I saw in the reading-rooms of the New York Public Library: passionate bearded men who made no effort to adjust themselves to life in America but who regarded themselves as exiles biding their time. One day they would go home. At least, that was the theory, and perhaps some of them did years later. They were revolutionaries, anarchists mainly, though I've no doubt some were Marxists and were later Communists. America they mostly ignored, and when they noticed it generally despised it. They went about their business, which was to live for the future in Europe, taking no notice of it. The only Americans they had any real communication with were men of a similar faith to their own. I suppose Marx lived in much the same way in London. I admired them enormously —they were romantic figures; and I learned much from them. But I could not become one of them. They treated me with a kindly contempt: I was an *Englander* and as such not a serious person. They were right of course, from their point of view. They held nothing sacred except the revolution, and I held too many things sacred and was horrified when they took political murder for granted, or free love. They led me to abysses over which I dared not look.

The other possibility was represented by the bums one saw in the Bowery and the 'Hell's Kitchen' district, bundles of stinking rags at night stretched out on the sidewalks, dope-addicts and methylated-spirit fiends; begging by day and ransacking the garbage-cans in the twilight. Not that I ever feared I would take either to drugs or drink; but I did fear what I can only speak of as a caving-in of my character, a descent into a state of being in which self-respect was no more. I was aware of the danger on all sides. Not all the ardent readers in the New York Public Library were dedicated anarchists and Socialists preparing for the Day: some were bums, and though they might be educated men they were still bums. And I saw the danger, too, in the restaurants I sometimes frequented. There was one—it was famous in its way, for it was first recommended to me while I was still on the immigrant ship—in Orchard Street, near East Broadway. I went there not because I had to but out of curiosity, and it also made me feel thrifty. For thirteen cents you got a dinner consisting of soup, meat stew, bread, pickles, tart and a glass of beer. I went there not more than half a dozen times, in order, I think, to know the worst. It wasn't, of course, the worst: 'Hell's Kitchen' was that, and it was a rung or two above 'Hell's Kitchen' and the doss-houses of the Bowery, but no more. There I saw real poverty, poverty the more dreadful because it was at once hopeless and respectable; the poverty of Jews who had fled the pogroms of Poland to find, if they were lucky, a hazardous security in the sweat-shops of the New York clothing trade. Below them was only the fall into the disintegration of the Bowery. The gulf was still enormous, for it was the difference between the preservation and the loss of self-respect. When I visited that restaurant I was, I suppose, consciously slumming, but the awful thing, Lizzie, was this: by comparison with the respectable poverty of that restaurant I found degradation, the destruction of self and of all the values I accepted that the Bowery and 'Hell's Kitchen' represented, infinitely attractive. If I was to fall, I knew that I would fall the whole way, and with a kind of gladness and relief. And the knowledge terrified me.

It would have been different, of course, if I could have found work in which I could take a craftsman's pride, as I undoubtedly could have done had I moved to Philadelphia. Then I could have sent for Rose and settled down to being an American working man. It would have been different, too, if I had been George. Then I could have used for positive ends my casual employment and the leisure it gave me ; I would have gone to Columbia University or the City College of New York. But as it was, when I at last realised the truth about myself, I was terrified, and I came home. I fled home to safety. I resumed the burden of the great abstractions because I was too weak to do anything else.

I told no one of my escape. I embodied my dream of freedom in my dream of Socialism: it was something that my children would realise. Well, this is just what Tom in his way has done—and how differently it has worked out! I said that for Will, as for myself and my friends, work was the moral imperative. For Tom, not-to-work is an equally strong moral imperative, and he has put as much energy and labour into obeying it as Will has in obeying his. It has taken me years to realise this, and I think it is only in this last day or so that I have fully understood. It is as though in him the strain of duty, of responsibility, that has characterised us had worn itself out; or as though he was born already in revolt against the burden that would be imposed upon him simply by virtue of being one of us. He was always the different one, so that at times I have thought of him as a changeling. You will remember him as a small child, Lizzie, how gay he was, and pretty, and delightful. What in another child would have been rudeness or impertinence in him was a disarmingly spontaneous wit. When he was in the push-chair people turned round to look at him; old ladies patted his curly head; he melted all hearts. His very presence seemed to excite benevolence in all about him. In those days, I rejoiced in his unlikeness to the rest of us; I remember thinking once, 'With Tom the burden is lifted!' though I could not have told you then what the burden was and, indeed, scarcely knew, until the child's freedom and spontaneity made me aware of it, that there was a burden at all. He was an *enfant terrible*, of course, but that was merely an aspect of his innocence: I remember thinking, and saying to Rose afterwards, 'The child in the Hans Anderson story who blurted out that the emperor was naked was Tom.'

Everything came easy to him, or rather, those things that did not seriously engage his attention he made easy by refusing to take seriously. I writhe with shame even now to recall the tortures I inflicted upon my children in trying to teach them music; it was almost as though I saw the learning of a musical instrument, in order that they could play with me, as an initiation-rite into manhood and the responsibilities of life. Alone of my children, Tom would have none of it. There came the day—he was nine or ten—when I bought and presented him with a small fiddle. Now, the other boys had learned the piano, an instrument I count as nothing compared with the violin. So for me it was a solemn occasion. As I gave him the fiddle I made the speech I did on such occasions: pointing out how deep and never-failing was the joy to be had from great music, how added pleasure and insight into it came from the kind of knowledge that could be obtained only from playing oneself, and how the secret of learning to play was practice, practice, practice. He heard me, it seemed, with open-eyed admiration; and I then instructed him in the holding of the instrument and the bow. He was delighted with it, and so for a few days our lessons continued. No child of mine had been so quick; he seemed entirely captivated by it. And then, as rapidly as it had been aroused, his interest dropped; not his interest in the fiddle as an object but in learning to play it. It had become simply a toy. I surprised him one day holding the fiddle at arm's length by the belly with one hand while the fingers of the other tugged at the strings. It was, he explained as violently I protested, a cross-bow; and so I saw it was, for there was the fiddle-bow in the position of an arrow. How indignant I was! I settled down resolutely to give him his lesson. In vain: he seemed to have forgotten everything I had taught him. I lost my temper and shouted and raved in a way that would have made my other sons weep. He simply smiled. It was a smile I could not combat for in it I felt vast amusement and tolerant pity as for someone who fusses enormously over nothing. 'Don't fret,' the smile seemed to say; 'you take this fiddling much too seriously. It isn't important.'

I made no further attempt to teach him the fiddle or, for that matter, anything else. No doubt Will would say I was weak: he did even then. The fact is, I took great delight in the boy, he was so sunny always; and though he went his own way and was, as they say, self-willed, there seemed no harm in him. He did well enough at school, though not as well as I knew he could have done. Perhaps I was blind because I didn't want to see. Will would have told me enough had I allowed him, but I said: 'I won't listen to tales,' thinking the lad's distrust and suspicion of his brother the product of incompatibility of temperament or even jealousy. Will finds all things hard; Tom found all things easy.

When the revelation came the shock was the greater. He was nineteen, a student at a training college for teachers. He came home five days before the end of term, announcing that there was an epidemic of some kind in the college and that, examinations being over, the students had been dismissed to their homes forthwith. It seemed reasonable. Two days after, I had a letter from the principal. Tom had been expelled for cheating in the examinations, and it was hinted that, apart from this, he had proved a most unsatisfactory student, a bad influence in the college. My first impulse was to denounce the man who had written to me in such terms as a liar. I showed the boy the letter. He seemed, and I believe he genuinely was, quite unperturbed. 'Skinny Higginbotham,' he said, meaning the principal, 'certainly writes a powerful letter'; and he added: 'He never did like me.'

'But,' I wanted to know, 'is it true?' If he had denied it I would, against all the evidence, have taken his word.

He smiled delightfully, shrugged his shoulders and spread out his hands in a Gallic gesture. 'I never did care for that college,' he said.

I was outraged. Had the boy no moral sense? 'But to cheat in an examination,' I said. 'Aren't you ashamed of yourself?'

'I admit I don't much like being found out, especially by an old fool like Higginbotham, if that's what you mean. It makes one feel an awful ass.'

It was as though the moral issue didn't exist for him. 'But what about the disgrace?' I urged. 'You must feel that.'

'It doesn't make any difference,' he said. 'Sooner or later I'd have got out under my own steam even if this hadn't happened. I couldn't stand the place anyway. And I can think of easier ways of making a living than being a schoolteacher.'

'That's not the point,' I shouted. 'It's the dishonesty of it, the mean sneaking dishonesty; and you admit it without a blush. That's what I can't understand.'

He shrugged again and smiled wonderfully. 'Honesty, dishonesty,' he said. And then: 'Look, dad. You've been honest all your life, haven't you, and worked hard all your life and done all those things you ought to have done and left undone all those things you ought not to have done. Well,' looking round the room slowly before turning his amused smile again on me, 'you can't say it's got you very far, can you?'

What could I say? What could I do; except be very frightened for him and for us all?

*   *   *

Tom is not as other men are. There is an ugly word for him: psychopath. The act of remembering and recording my first realisation of this affected me strangely, so that for the past eight days I have done nothing, not written a word. For the first five days I existed in a kind of stupor, sitting at my table with the white foolscap in front of me, but not really thinking at all; just in a daze. All I could do was mutter to myself 'Tom': the name alone seemed to fill my mind. But on the sixth day I roused myself. Why shouldn't I find Tom out and see him? I asked myself. Followed a long argument within me. I had led Will to understand that I would make no effort to see him. On the other hand, a man had a right to see his son. Will had no right to extract such a promise from me; some things are sacred. And so on. Then, as I awoke from sleep yesterday morning, I knew I must see him, it would be mean and cowardly not to do so. I would say to Will, if he took exception to my behaviour: 'You must do what you think, but so must I. The deprived need our love just because they are deprived. It is all we can give them in recompense. And Tom is one of the deprived.'

But I was determined to say nothing unless challenged; and after breakfast, when I left for my usual morning walk, I caught the bus into the town. I go there rarely and scarcely know it; and of course I had no knowledge of Tom's movements or whereabouts. But the town is small and compact, and its centre is very conveniently arranged for watching the world go by. In the main square are the post office and the two hotels —large pubs are what they really are. In the middle of the square there is a little ornamental garden with benches round it, and there I sat myself down at half-past ten to wait for Tom; knowing that he was not an early riser and guessing that he would almost certainly call in at the post office to see if there were letters for him at the poste restante and that soon after opening-time he would even more certainly go into a pub for a drink; and The White Hart and The Dennis Arms, the smartest places in the town, where the business men congregate at lunch-time, seemed to me the kind of pubs he would frequent.

The time passed pleasantly enough. The day was mild and sunny, and though I knew there was no guarantee that I would see him, I was quite calm. I had a thought that perhaps he was staying at one of the pubs, so just after noon I went into The White Hart and asked for him. But he was not staying there, or at The Dennis Arms, and I went back to my bench in the square. Once I saw him, or the back of him, and my heart bumped like a boy's as he glimpses the girl he is in love with. He was on the other side of the square, walking away from it; and I darted across the road after him, breathing painfully for he was walking quickly. But I gained on him, calling, 'Tom! Tom!' oblivious of the passers-by who must have wondered at the sight of an old man running and calling after a smartly-dressed young man. But 'Tom!' I went on gasping, for I was quite out of breath. And at last he heard and turned. I almost fell against him and he put out his hand to steady me. 'I'm not Tom,' he said pleasantly, and then I saw he wasn't and I shook my head and said stupidly, 'No, you're not Tom,' and I had to lean against a shop-window I felt so suddenly weak. Tom, I realised, would be almost twenty years older than this young man; and I realised, too, that the Tom I had carried in my mind's eye, the Tom I had gone out to look for, was Tom as a youth. In a spasm of despair I wondered whether I would even recognise today's Tom if I saw him. Perhaps he had walked past me a dozen times while I had been sitting on the bench, and I hadn't known him!

The young man was very concerned for me. 'Are you all right, sir?' he wanted to know, as I crumpled against the plate-glass, behind which stood dummies wearing Mr Montagu Burton's suits. For the moment I couldn't speak so I nodded as fiercely as I could. I was beginning to feel embarrassed, for I felt people were pausing to watch, and no end of a fool, and all the more a fool because I feared that if this kind young man who wasn't Tom persisted in being kind I should start to cry and plunge us both into further depths of embarrassment. But the young man was as capable as he was kind. 'I'm sure a glass of brandy would do you no harm, sir,' he said, for he was respectful as well as kind and capable. 'No, no, no,' I said, I am afraid rather testily, 'I never take the stuff.' He smiled down at me, and for answer took my arm and conducted me to The White Hart, where I found myself in the saloon bar with a glass of brandy. 'I think,' he said, 'you'll find it's what the doctor ordered, sir'; and he was right: it did me a power of good. 'It was the shock,' I explained; 'I thought you were someone else.'

But he was still concerned for me, wanting to know where I lived, wanting to see me home. He was an admirable young man, and my heart warmed to him. The trouble was, he wasn't Tom. 'No, no,' I said; 'you have been very kind and I am being a nuisance. I will sit in the sun on the bench over there,' pointing to the square, 'and when I'm rested I'll catch the bus.'

And that is what I did, except that I sat there for another two hours. I knew I wouldn't see Tom now but all the same I felt at peace with myself; it was as though in that young man I had met a kind of Tom.

It was after five when I got back to Will's. I expected ructions, or rather the rebuke of hurt silence, for I had not told Beryl I would not be in for the midday meal. I had, I acknowledged, been what they call 'thoughtless,' but that was something I could not help; and I saw no way of explaining. My anticipations were quite wrong. 'Ah, there you are,' Beryl said, as though my behaviour was the most normal in the world. 'Have you had a nice day, father?' And without waiting for an answer: 'I bet you didn't have a proper lunch, so I'll give you a boiled egg with your tea.' And a boiled egg I had, not because I particularly wanted it but because to accept it was at least a way to make amends.

There was a different feeling in the house. At first I put it down to the change in my own mood, to the warming effect of my encounter with the kind young man. But when Will came home from the factory, humming to himself as he entered the house and laughing with the children, I knew it was not as simple as that. After supper, standing in front of the hearth flexing his arms in great good humour, he told me. His face had lost its strained tautness and seemed as innocent and chubby as a child's. 'Well, father,' he said, 'he's gone, Tom's gone, for the time being anyway, touch wood. I realise now I've been making pretty heavy weather of things. It came home to me three days ago. What the hell, I thought; I don't have to put up with this sort of thing. So I got on the phone and talked to half a dozen chaps I thought Tom would probably try and touch, if he hadn't already done so, and told them straight that if they were fools enough to lend him money they needn't expect me to make it good, for I wouldn't. Then I wrote out a cheque for twenty quid and put in a letter to master Tom, telling him precisely what I'd done and warning him that was precisely what I intended to do in future and that next time, if there were a next time, everyone would know about him beforehand. He phoned me at the works just after nine this morning. He had the damned impertinence to say he was sorry he couldn't see me but had an important date in London which necessitated him catching the 9.15 train. I have every reason to believe he caught it.' Will was very complacent. 'Of course there will be a next time,' he said, 'but being firm this time will make it much easier to face. The thing is, and I know it now, it's much better to bring these things into the open. No one's going to think any the worse of me because one of my brothers is a rotter, so they may as well know about it in advance. I'm only sorry you've been worried with all this, dad.'

I didn't say anything, but I thought: Yes, there will be a next time; Tom will be back again, and then nothing shall stop me seeing him.

12

I FLED from America home to safety. Then began the years
when nothing happened. That is nonsense, of course. Nothing
happened only in the sense that is implied in the saying 'Happy
is the country that has no history.' They were years of routine,
but I see now they were happy years, and prosperous ones too,
for the routine was packed and running over with purpose,
activity and achievement as a honeycomb is with honey.

I went back to work at Darnley's, but not to my old job. I
had left a boy and returned a man: others saw this if I didn't
myself, and though I knew I had failed in New York, no one
else did, and I came home with the prestige of the man who
has been in foreign parts. Besides, brother Horace had left
Darnley's, and it must have seemed in the order of things that
I should inherit his place. At any rate, I returned to find Mr
Darnley treating me with a deference I had not sought and
myself regarded by all as the principal workman in the shop.
So indeed I remained for more than twenty years. I had no
title to single me out from the others, but Mr Darnley took
on no orders without first consulting me. I suppose chief
designer was really what I was, but I was more than that.
Because of my skill in the craft Mr Darnley was able to contract
for work which otherwise would have been beyond his scope,
masonic jewels, civic medals and caskets and the like: anyone
who is interested may see specimens of my work in the City
Art Gallery. For even then, the number of first-rate craftsmen
was diminishing; the leading firms, and there were never many
of them, depended each on a single key workman, or put out
the orders that brought them prestige to an independent
craftsman such as Horace had become.

I enjoyed my work, and Mr Darnley paid me well. Indeed,
he treated me generously and would have made me his friend

had I accepted his overtures. But we had nothing in common; he was a bluff, hearty, whisky-drinking man who spent all the time he could at the Conservative Club, which suited both his inclinations and his business interests. Besides, though I did not believe employers should be on distant terms with employees, I did think employees should be on distant terms with employers. If I had allowed myself to become his friend I should have considered I was betraying my workmates and putting my independence in jeopardy too. I believe now that if I had got rid of my cranky notions, as he called them, he might have made me his partner. As it was, he treated me with much forbearance, even to the point of recognising the union and allowing his workmen to join it. I had made it plain to him that if he did not do so I would leave his employ, and I suppose he balanced the advantages against the disadvantages and estimated where his interests lay. I'm bound to admit that our union never amounted to much, for as a whole silversmiths retained the mentality of small craftsmen working at home. When trade was bad there were always plenty of out-workers, as they were called, ready and eager to undercut.

Eighteen months after I returned from America, Rose and I were married. By this time, Lizzie, Edwin and Horace were already married, and the family was breaking up. George Thompson had wed Fanny Stevenson a month before. Because my wages were good and my security seemed assured, Rose and I were able to begin our life together in circumstances that for young people in our station of life were almost luxurious. I was able to rent a five-roomed terrace house in a very respect-able working-class neighbourhood. The house had a tiny garden at the front, behind spiked railings, and a longer strip of garden at the back; since there were but the two of us we both had more space and privacy than we had ever had in our lives before; and I rejoiced to see Rose's pleasure in it and in the business of making a home. And believe it or not, we were both proud of the evident superiority of the street we lived in: the women of Menai Street did not go shopping, polish their front-door steps or clean their windows in their husbands' old cloth caps; and people who drank beer did not go out for it with jug in hand but had it delivered in bottles by the brewer's dray. We were most respectable.

I see my life in those days as purposeful activity subdued to the normal rhythms of family life. Rose and I went out to tea or supper or both on Sundays at our parents' or at one of our brothers' or sisters'; or they would come to us. But it was always George and Fanny we saw the most of; in fact, looking back, it seems that George and I were together all the time. That wasn't so, because apart from the vast difference in the trades we followed, we each had interests from which the other was excluded by temperament. George's passion for philology meant nothing to me, and though after I'd played my fiddle, which I was by custom invited to do at any social gathering, he always said, 'Very nice, Billy!' my music was just as meaningless to him. For I had gone back to Herr Schmidt at the School of Music and practised assiduously, an hour every morning before breakfast as well as in the dinner-hour at the shop. Nevertheless, George and I were together a great deal. Oxford University had started extension lectures in the town, and soon there was to be the Workers' Educational Association as well. George and I rushed to join. Naturally enough, we plumped for the economics course and we went, I am afraid, in no great spirit of humility. George had already thoroughly read, and I had at least dipped into, *The Wealth of Nations* and Mill's *Principles of Political Economy* and we were very critical of economics. It was not merely the dismal science; it seemed to us, as presented by the economists, very complacent, and also irrelevant to conditions of trade and so on as working men themselves experienced them. For besides Adam Smith and Mill we knew our Carlyle and Ruskin, especially *Unto This Last*, and they were the men for our money. We knew they knew what they were talking about, for they were talking of the things we talked about ourselves. We didn't believe any university economist could possibly understand these things, which were, of course, all those that together make social justice; and so we set off for the first meeting of the University Extension course with the set intention first of exposing the lecturer and secondly of converting him, if possible.

We could not have had a greater shock. There was no complacency about our lecturer, Mr Glover, M.A., and he was even more passionate for social justice than we were. After the class that first night George and I went as usual to Boswell's

Pie Shop. We were both disturbed, abashed and a little ashamed. George smote his forehead and cried: 'My God, what fools we are! We're so narrow, we behave as though we're the only people on earth who know anything or have good intentions.' And then: 'You know, I never realised.' I knew what he meant, because I had never realised either, never realised that men of another class, a higher class, could feel and think as we did. Then George said: 'You know, we could bring Glover here. He'd come.'

And come he did; after the next meeting of the class George had him in tow; and ever after that we adjourned to Boswell's for coffee and pies after our meetings. I thought, and still think, Mr Glover was nearly a saint, but what fascinates me is to reflect on the difference between my reaction to him and George's. He influenced us both, and he influenced George much more, and on the face of it this is strange. I was ready almost to adore him, as George wasn't. He seemed to me physically beautiful—there is no other word. Very tall, athletic in build, very blond, he had the most sensitive, saddest face in repose that I have ever seen in a man. Yet the intense brooding blue eyes could leap into sudden astonished merriment, and the whole countenance seemed to respond, as at the merest touch, to the mood of the moment. He had, it seemed to me, a child's spontaneity. He was almost ten years older than I, but he looked younger and was certainly younger in spirit: this, George explained, was an attribute of his class. He had already done things that were admirable in my eyes. He had a first at Balliol; he was a rowing Blue. He had sailed before the mast to Australia. He had lived for three years among the Durham miners. He knew his Carlyle and Ruskin much better than we did, and much else besides, for he knew Plato and had read Marx. He was haunted by a vision of social justice and was no more satisfied with traditional economics than we were. He was in fact a Christian Communist and as he lectured to us was formulating the theories he later put into his book, which in my view has never received its just recognition.

He was far more radical than we were, especially in our sessions in Boswell's. 'You ask for justice,' he'd say, 'but do you realise what it entails? And if you do, do you then really want it? Justice for you involves justice for untold millions all over the world; for black men in Africa and Chinamen and the Untouchables of India. Justice won't mean more for you, it will mean less, for compared with black men and Chinamen and Untouchables you already live like princes. And it's all or nothing. If what you want is justice for yourselves and the devil take Chinamen, then you're as selfish as—as Joe Chamberlain.' And at that he burst into a splutter of laughter.

It was typical of him that in later years he should join Mr Gandhi in India. He was a completely disinterested man, the first I had come across, and my admiration for him was immense. But I never knew how to express it. I wanted to respond to him as spontaneously as he did to all about him; and I couldn't: I felt myself become cold and mute and rigid. It was that cursed business of class again: I was imprisoned in it. That was the difference, where Mr Glover was concerned, between George and me. I always called him Mr Glover and he called me Mr Ashted. But from the start George called him plainly Glover, and Mr Glover called him Thompson. They communicated with each other intimately and directly, as between equals, and this although George appeared to react as strongly against him as I towards him. 'Don't delude yourself, Billy,' he'd say; 'Glover's a crank, a simple-lifer.' He'd tell him so to his face, and once he even cried out in his exasperation, 'Glover, you're little better than a curate!' and Mr Glover roared with laughter.

Mr Glover changed the whole course of George's life. The decisive words were spoken in that curious amalgam of smells—coffee, wet rubber macintoshes, hot meat gravy, tobacco smoke—that was Boswell's. 'Look, Glover,' George said, 'let us not range the world. I am not Christ, and though I sympathise with your black men and Chinamen there is nothing I can do for them and therefore I will not sentimentalise over them. Billy and I are concerned with the here and now. Something can be done about the here and now. Let us be practical.' Mr Glover was silent for a few moments, and then he removed his meerschaum pipe from his lips. 'Thompson,' he said, 'there *are* things to be done about the here and now. I can't do them but you can. I can only show you the world, show you the moral issues, so that men like you can act, but act with some degree of knowledge of the consequences of your actions. For you won't for ever be able to escape from my black men and Chinamen. There'll come a day when you'll have to take them into account in your calculations, just as you do the skill and industry of the Germans now. All the same, Thompson, you're right, right to take the short view, as I am to take the long. But I don't think you yet know where your duty lies. You think it is in self-education. You are in love with learning and believe that wisdom comes with learning. It isn't so. Already you have all the learning and all the wisdom you need. Your place is with the work that lies nearest to hand.'

'And that is?'

'Politics. And first, your trade union. You are a moulder: you could be a leader in your union. You ought to be, a man like you. That's where your work lies.'

'You are advising me to plunge into the very activities that you yourself have taught us to distrust.'

'I am.'

'Very well, then.' George thought for a moment. 'I shan't come to your class any more, but we'll meet here afterwards just the same.'

And so George entered politics, through his work in the Foundry-workers Union first of all. Before then, he had paid his dues and little more, though even that was more than it sounds, when merely to belong to a union was in some shops to be a marked man. Very soon, he was the secretary of his branch and within two years the district organiser, a paid official, though his wage was less than he had earned working on the floor. It was all inevitable. He was articulate as none of his mates were; his brain was as keen as that of the best of the bosses; he was a born advocate; and, as a base to it all, he was a first-rate workman. And weekly we met Mr Glover in Boswell's. 'Glover, your material is ideas, mine is men, and men are less tractable. I have to contend with human stupidity and human fear, and I don't know which is the worse or whether, indeed, they're not the same thing.' He became hard and practical, a strategist of the class-war. He seemed to delight in taunting Mr Glover with sentimentality. He had tasted the pleasures of power and found them exhilarating. But he would add, after he had girded at Mr Glover for his wishy-washy idealism, his namby-pamby scruples: 'All the

138

same, Glover, you're a good fellow!' And Mr Glover once said to me, as we walked towards Boswell's after a class to meet George: 'Mr Ashted, your friend Thompson is a good man, as good as he's able, and he's as able as any man I ever knew.'

More than ever, I tagged along behind George; not altogether single-mindedly. Too many things interested me. My fiddle remained chief among these, and more and more I seemed to glimpse in the music I struggled to play evidence of a transcendental unity and order which made everything of this world unreal and shabby by comparison. George thought this dangerous, and so it was, for if it could have been shown to me that this transcendental unity was conditional on the misery of Mr Glover's black men and Chinamen I know that in some moods I would have accepted the necessity of their misery and felt it justified. But besides my fiddle, I was beginning at this time to dabble in painting. It grew out of my daily work. As a designer of medals, cups and caskets, I had to have some small proficiency with pencil and pen-and-ink. To that extent, to sketch was natural. But what really fired me were the paintings of the English water-colour school in the City Art Gallery. Not that I had any serious ambitions of rivalling them, I was not so silly as that; but they suggested a way of recording sights and moments that had given me especial pleasure. I still three or four times a year walked in the country with Horace, and on occasion spent a week-end with him walking in North Wales. I valued this contact with him the more because there were now so many subjects we could not talk about, they being near-blasphemy to him, that for the most part we walked in silence. Certain scenes, combinations of hill, water, colour and light, gave me great delight, and I took to carrying with me a block of drawing paper and a tiny paint-box, so that I could stop and pause and rapidly sketch and paint what I saw. I had no illusions about what I was doing; I did not think I was making works of art. Whenever I set out consciously to attempt that I failed miserably, producing a picture that was stiff and lifeless and conventional, something, in fact, that looked like a copy of a painting of nature. No; I was after something much more humble, on a level, it seemed to me, with the action of a boy who knots his handkerchief in order to preserve a moment that is memorable. I was, I suppose, trying to put a spell on memory, so that the short-hand of my sketch would bring back in its pristine sharpness the complex of the observed reality and the emotion it had kindled in me. I see now that my ambition wasn't so humble after all.

But these little pictures were made for my own private pleasure, and sometimes they were successful, at any rate as aids to memory. In a way, they were no more than snapshots, and from time to time, after the same end, I would lug my camera into the country with me, tripod, black cloth and all; but it was never so satisfying. Part of the fun lay in the attempt, bound as it was to fail, to pin down the incommunicable.

Horace was merely civil about my attempts at painting. He had small sympathy with it, for he himself was so proud that he would try nothing at which he could not excel. He thought I was wasting my time in a foolish way producing my amateurish daubs; and besides, I was wasting his time too, for while I painted he must wait. George, on the other hand, approved heartily of my painting, as he did of all my activities, even though he would shake his head and tell me I was an incorrigible dabbler. I admired him so much that it was a constant shock to realise he admired me in turn; and I could not see why he did. Yet he did, and there were moments when I understood why. It wasn't that he exaggerated my talents. When I had a spell of dreaming that it might be possible for me to become a professional fiddler, however humble, he gave a decisive no. 'Billy, you're kidding yourself. You're not good enough.' What he appreciated was my wide-ranging curiosity, my childish eagerness to have a go, as they say now. I was behaving, I think he felt, as a free man should. In a sense, he saw me, perhaps, as a prototype of the worker of the future, when the revolution had been won. He often laughed at my enthusiasms, but they were disinterested, and in a way my very existence was a reassurance to him. When he took Mr Glover at his word and became active in the union and in public affairs he dropped everything else. He gained much: you might say he found himself, for, a man in whom power resided, he revelled in the manipulation of power. But only I know how much he lost as well. What he gave up he sacrificed deliberately.

And only I know how thankless the task he had set himself often seemed. He had a large vision to steer by: the men he worked for had for the most part nothing like it. Foundry-workers in those days were generally a hard-drinking, hard-living lot. Their aspirations were limited to a little more money, a slightly shorter working day, and George had no illusions about what they would do with them when they got them. They had no notion at all of using their corporate strength for political ends. Intrinsically, for what they wanted George could have small sympathy. But he had his vision, his guiding conception of a better, fuller life, and I sometimes think that for George my function was to be the touchstone in reality of that vision.

All the same, as George became more and more immersed in politics, so, tagging behind him, did I. As soon as it was realised he could sway the foundry-workers the Liberals wooed him, and for a time we were Lib-Labs. Not that George was deceived. Liberals were no better employers of labour than Tories. 'So far as we're concerned, Billy,' he'd say, 'there's not a ha'porth of difference between them.' Or rather, there was this difference: the Liberals could be used as the Tories could not: they made it possible for a few working men to be returned to Parliament. They were more susceptible to pressure from Labour than the Tories. 'Their consciences are guiltier,' George used to say.

When the Independent Labour Party was founded we naturally joined, and formed a branch in the St Barnabas Ward. We were laughed at, of course. I remember I had to go to the police station to apply for a street speaker's pitch in St Barnabas High Street. 'What's the name of your organisation?' the police inspector asked. 'The I.L.P.,' I answered. 'What does that mean?' 'Independent Labour Party.' 'Oh, cranks!' He couldn't have been less interested. We were cranks. The *Journal* made fun of us: we were impractical anarchists carrying old-fashioned bombs that wouldn't go off, harmless maniacs, as became obvious when, after a year's existence, we put up a candidate for the municipal elections and polled twenty-three votes. 'The British working man,' the *Journal* said in a leading article, 'who is as shrewd and sensible as any man in the world, knows that two parties are enough to choose from. He knows, too, that whether he chooses Liberal or Conservative, he will have gallant gentlemen and sound business men to lead him, not hare-brained crackpots.' I might have been dismayed, but not George. Whole streets of foundry-workers lived in the St Barnabas Ward; it included some of the nastiest slums in the town. We fought the ward at every municipal election, always with George as the candidate. Within six years he was elected, and the significance was that St Barnabas was in the heart of the parliamentary constituency that returned the Liberal Unionist leader himself, with a thumping majority election after election.

I loathed street-corner speaking myself; it was my Friday evening nightmare. I had often passed and pitied soap-box orators, kerbside evangelists and temperance reformers whom *I* had thought of as cranks, hating the knot of tipsy men who jeered at them, and respecting them for their courage in testifying to unpopular convictions. Now I was one of them. In fact, no one jeered very much, and in a sense that was the more disheartening. I was a very poor speaker, I had no fluency of language, and my voice was a feeble tenor which could scarcely be heard against the raucous cries of the hawkers and street-vendors, the brisk chaff of the shopkeepers and the traffic noises, the horses' hooves and the iron cart wheels on the cobbled roadway. I suffered, I could almost say, in silence. My job was the humblest imaginable: to carry the little platform we spoke from, with the letters I.L.P. painted upon it—I had painted them myself—set it up, mount it, and go through the motions of addressing an audience until George arrived. I felt such a fool, for I would stand there above the street shouting away in my weak voice, gesticulating, a parody of political passion, and for minutes on end no one took the slightest notice. It was as though I was invisible. And then two or three children would come and gawp at me; an old woman with a shawl over her head would pause to see what the children were looking at; one or two idle men would drift over out of that curiosity which is the reflex of boredom. When the crowd numbered seven or eight a policeman would materialise, and inevitably, it seemed, I'd then catch out of the corner of my eye the figure of George approaching, and hastily, with enormous relief, I'd stop in mid-sentence and shout as loudly as I could, 'But here, Comrades, is Comrade George Thompson himself!' I'd turn towards him, clap my hands like mad, and jump down. George would mount the platform like a champion, monarch of all he surveyed.

George became a Friday-evening institution in St Barnabas High Street. Soon there was a small crowd waiting for him regularly, waiting for me even, whose rôle was now merely to herald his coming. He was a splendid speaker and as a local union leader in that district he had a ready-made audience. I don't think he ever won the foundrymen's love; his austerity and a touch of arrogance he never quite managed to conceal, prevented that; but they held him in an awed respect. He was too far removed from them to be exactly popular but they knew there was no one like him, and they cheered even when they did not understand. At first the Liberals and Tories ignored our meetings, out of contempt, I suppose; but when we began to poll a hundred or so votes at elections they changed their tactics and began to send their hecklers to interrupt and argue. They were no match for George. I see him now, smiling down on them as he noticed them in the crowd, and beginning the meeting by attacking them before he was attacked himself. 'Well, comrades, I see we have with us again our friends from the Tories and the Liberals, ganging up against working people—as they always do!'

My own career as a street-corner orator was brief: I saved my energies for door-to-door canvassing, at which I was more at home. It is difficult for me now to recapture the feel of those years of my life which were dominated by the idea of Socialism. The police inspector had called us cranks, and so in a way we were, but that is much more plain to me now than it was then. I think that what I should now consider crankiness appeared to me in those days rather as an irksome discipline one accepted for the sake of what we called the Movement. George, who was not a crank at all, accepted it much more easily than I did, perhaps because he took it less seriously and could regard it as a necessary part of the tactics of Socialist politics. The truth is, dissent—and we were far gone in dissent, with all the fervour of an extreme Nonconformist sect—simply because it is dissent and therefore off-centre, can easily lead its more silly and uncritical adherents to behaviour that appears to the rest of the world lunatic or outrageous. I didn't understand this, then. Nothing made us more indignant than the accusations of our opponents that Socialism meant free love or, as it became later, the nationalisation of women. They seemed to us malicious and unscrupulous lies, and so very often they were. We were almost fanatically respectable, and it wasn't until years later that I realised how inconsistent we were in this. When I read the novels of Wells and the works of Bernard Shaw, mainly because Phil was interested in them and urged me to do so, I was at first horrified at what I found there, and I saw that our enemies had known more of the implications of some sides of the early Socialist movement than I ever had.

Most of the crankiness that I experienced was just silly. Much as I loved William Morris and his works, I could not understand why belief in Socialism necessarily involved the wearing of sandals and participation in Morris dancing, which for years I believed had been invented by the great craftsman and poet. Fanny and George spent their holidays at a Morris community in the Cotswolds, but they could not persuade Rose and me to join them. On the face of it, it was exactly the kind of idiocy that George despised, but he endured it stoically, partly I think because he accepted it as an at least temporary aspect of the movement that had to be used, partly out of loyalty to Fanny, who took to such things like a duck to water, adding, indeed, for a time vegetarianism to them. And perhaps it was I who was the inconsistent one here. My Socialism stemmed in part from my dislike of industrialism; misguided though I think the Morrisites were, they were at any rate thorough: they were demonstrating that it was possible to live outside a machine-dominated society; but I still can't think Morris dancing as good as football.

Fanny took to the attendant lunacies of the movement like a duck to water. She identified herself with them completely; she was possessed with a lust for advanced causes. When I think of her now an image of her comes to mind. She is standing, short, thin, erect, in the congregation of the Labour Church singing with passionate, heart-felt indignation our Socialist hymn 'When wilt thou save the people, O God of Mercies, when? The People, Lord, the People! Not kings nor lords, but Men!' Her harsh, high-pitched voice soars beyond those of the rest of us; she is at least a bar ahead. Her eyes flash with fury behind her pince-nez, and her scraggy neck vibrates angrily. She is a very fierce woman. That is the first image; but there is another. She is marching at the head of a procession demanding votes for women, carrying one of the poles on which a banner is hung. She is going into battle seeking martyrdom. And how she gloried in it when she got it! For though she never achieved the distinction of going on hunger strike and suffering feeding by force, she did at least spend a night in the cells, for poking a hat-pin at a policeman. It was a great vexation to George. Of course we were in favour of votes for women, but most of George's foundry workers were against it. Still, he endured Fanny's behaviour nobly.

The truth is, I never liked Fanny and privately thought she was a powerful argument against granting women the suffrage. She lived in an excessively simple universe and was strident and domineering, quivering always, it seems to me as I remember her, with indignation. With her, indignation was the form that love took. I found it difficult to be patient with her and remember the fury I discovered in myself when I found her teaching Will, a child who could say little more than 'Mama' and 'Papa', the words 'Votes for women.' It seemed to me monstrous, treating my child as though he were a parrot. And when I remonstrated with her she floored me by telling me, those pale blue eyes flashing behind the pince-nez, 'How can you say such a thing, Billy? No child is too young to be taught these great truths.'

I am afraid Fanny and the silly side of those years exist in my mind together. That Labour church! I can't think of it now without feelings of embarrassment—but am I merely being superior at the expense of my former self? Certainly I never attended the Labour Church without experiencing a sense of dismay, though I was a member from the beginning and remained one theoretically for many years after I had ceased going. It was not the physical environment: we met in the assembly hall—three classrooms with the shutters between them removed—of the Menai Street Infants School: dark-brown pitch-pine and dark-green walls, with narrow ecclesiastical windows and desks into which we cramped our adult bottoms. Uncomfortable and dingy enough; but it is exactly in such surroundings that dissent has always thrived. Indeed, brother Horace, for whom holiness went hand in hand with corrugated iron, might have scorned it as luxuriously soft. Nor was it the bareness of it, the austerity, for all that was part of our tradition, as it was of the Quakers and Primitive Methodists who were in a sense our close kin. No; it was simply that I couldn't help wondering what the devil we thought we were doing there. There was an awful complacency about it, and as I looked about me at the faces shining with moral earnestness it sometimes seemed to me that, unwittingly and with the best will in the world, we were taking part in a blasphemous parody, unwittingly because we had no inkling of the meaning of what we parodied.

Socialism we thought of as what in these days is called a way of life. As Socialists we had, so to speak, withdrawn, divorced ourselves, from the society in which we lived. We were making our own society; and since the society we had rejected had its religions and churches so we deemed it necessary to have a religion and church likewise. But of course we had no religion at all in any true sense. We had noble aspirations and much indignation, but these are different things. It goes without saying that our services didn't lack for references to Him Whom we called the Carpenter of Nazareth, but in so far as He existed for us at all it was as a very shadowy early trade union agitator who had been done to death by Jewish capitalists and Roman imperialists. God meant nothing to us; some of us were atheists and most agnostics. I suppose we might have said, if challenged, that we worshipped humanity. One of our favourite scriptures, which was constantly being recited to us, was 'Abou Ben Adhem,' and I am sure we all felt Ben Adhem's name rightly led all the rest for loving his fellow-men and not the Lord. Well, this emptiness of belief was reflected in the poverty of our services, if that is what they are called. We had no prayers, for we had no one to pray to. If it was humanity we worshipped, how could we pray to ourselves? We had our hymns; there was even a little book called *Socialist Hymns*; but they were very few in number: 'The Red Flag,' 'When Wilt Thou Save the People,' 'The Land for the People,' and one or two others; and since we were accustomed to sing them at our public meetings as well they scarcely sounded a religious note. The bulk of our proceedings consisted of some kind of entertainment and an address. Sometimes the entertainment and the address were one and the same thing. Just about this time, little Socialist groups of one kind and another were proliferating on all sides. There was the Clarion Choir, which sang for us; there was the Clarion Players, which gave us a play-reading, an early play of Bernard Shaw's, as I remember. I was myself much in demand for fiddle solos. The addresses proper were supplied either by our own members or by speakers associated with other dissenting groups not so very different from us. The local branch of the National Secular Society could always provide us with a fierce young man who talked about Haeckel and a white-bearded old gentleman who lectured to us on Shelley's 'Queen Mab,' though Phil has since told me that if the old gentleman attached so much importance to 'Queen Mab' he must have had a singular notion of Shelley. The Theosophists also sent speakers; and how we lapped up their message! It was as though we combined ardent scepticism with extreme credulity; and the fact is, I think, that many of us were prepared to believe anything, no matter how nonsensical, rather than what the churches and chapels of our youth had taught us. That we repudiated, and we did so because the churches and chapels seemed to us irredeemably tainted by capitalism. To us they were the respectable façade of exploitation. The churches, and the chapels too, with one or two exceptions like the splinter-groups from Methodism, were the mouthpieces of the bosses. I would not say I believe this now; and yet how often have I found—and left because of it—a Nonconformist chapel, a Quaker meeting-house, dominated by a wealthy business man who treated it as his own property.

Of course I over-simplify. In a sense, we were an assembly of the lost; and I see now that for many of us it was possible to hold at one and the same time mutually contradictory creeds, or beliefs that had no necessary connection one with another. Some of us could switch over from the National Secular Society to theosophy overnight with no apparent realisation of inconsistency. Indeed, Mrs Besant, who was a great heroine of ours, had done precisely that. In a similar fashion, being a fanatical suffragist seemed to make it easier to be a fanatical vegetarian. What was important was not the belief so much as the rejection of conventional values it implied; and women like Fanny felt themselves enhanced by the very gestures of rejection. And we were at least like every other church in one respect: the women outnumbered the men by three to one.

I have no doubt I was as inconsistent as everyone else. Our meetings consisted of a mixture of propaganda for the converted and a vaguely uplifting concert: harmless enough and not even silly. They were the expression of a confused realisation that agreement on politics was not enough to bind us together, the symbol of a craving for closer bonds, for a more organic unity. What I could not stomach was the complacent impertinence with which we arrogated to ourselves the name of church. Now, my position here is a peculiar one, and one I have never been able to resolve, it may be because of a defect of my own character. I am not a religious man, though I have often tried to be, and since I do not find it difficult to be moved by the beauty of the Christian story as myth, I have in my time taken the wish to be religious for the substance of religion. But I am now tired of this modern habit of dignifying aspiration, however noble, with the name of religion, of finding religious men in earnest atheists and high-minded agnostics; it is a sloppy dishonesty; and so I disclaim being religious altogether. From time to time I have caught glimpses of what seemed transcendence in music, mountains and the ocean at night. I value these glimpses enormously, but I cannot pretend they revealed to me a loving and adorable God. I believe I have read all the arguments for and against the existence of God, and all I can say is that He has never spoken to me. This proves nothing, I know, but it matters to me. I have waited, and nothing has happened. Perhaps it has been my own fault: I sometimes think I must have spent my life in the state that is called invincible ignorance. I don't know, and those who I am ready to believe do know have not been able to help me. I remember trying once to explain this to Father Andrews, a good man if ever there was one, a Christian priest whose Christianity was plain in everything he did. He was very impatient. 'You make mountains out of molehills, Ashted,' he said. 'All you need is faith.' But how get faith, or what indeed faith is, he could not tell me. What was self-evident to him was incomprehensible to me, and he obviously thought me perverse and self-willed. Maybe it is as simple as that. All I know is that though I have often longed, and prayed desperately, to be able to subject myself to the discipline of faith, to become as a child, as they say, I have never succeeded in achieving it.

The paradox is that simply because I have always been conscious of being without God, of being somehow cut off from God, I have valued the idea of Him all the more. I have never found any satisfaction in my lack of belief; rather, I am aware of deprivation. I have read somewhere that if Christian doctrine is not true then life is a tragedy, and that is what I think. Life is a tragic mystery, and much of its tragedy, it seems to me, comes from the fact that man has been able to conceive the idea of God. That, really, was why I was uncomfortable at the Labour Church and why I rebelled against it. There was no room in it either for the conception of life as tragedy or for the grandeur of the idea of God. The mystery was explained away in terms that were relatively mean. We were there simply to admire ourselves, and it was not good enough.

It was my dear wife who brought this home to me. I was awakened from sleep one Sunday night to the knowledge that Rose was awake beside me and weeping to herself. As you may guess, I was very worried. What was the matter? Rose was an inarticulate woman; the world she dwelt in was not one of words; she lived by values much more simple than mine, and held unreflectingly. I was never sure what she was thinking or feeling at any time, and it took me years to understand that the very act of my making a rational translation, as it were, of what I guessed she was feeling or thinking was in itself to distort the purity and simplicity of her emotion. When at last I managed to get out of her what it was that was troubling her it seemed to me very small indeed, certainly not worth tears and a sleepless night. 'Of course we won't, my dear,' I assured her; 'we won't go any more if you don't wish to.'

It was the Labour Church she was weeping about. At first she did not want to tell me. It was nothing, nothing at all. Then why these tears? I demanded, for to me, as to nearly all men, tears are very serious things. In the end it came out, and still I did not understand. 'I hate it, Billy,' she said; 'I hate it.' 'But why?' I wanted to know. Was it the other members? No. I plied her with questions, for I was bewildered at the intensity of her feelings, the cause seeming so trivial. At last she said, in a small voice: 'It isn't like a church at all.' And then: 'Billy, need we go any more? I hate it so.' 'Of course we won't, my dear,' I cried in mighty relief; 'we won't go any more if you don't wish to.'

I lay awake after Rose returned to sleep. I felt chastened and humble. 'It isn't like a church at all.' Rose's words had gone to the heart of the matter. Of course, that was it! They illuminated wonderfully the growing dismay and distaste I felt myself on Sunday evenings there. It wasn't like a church at all because it lacked the essential thing that makes the greatest cathedral and the tiniest tin-tabernacle of a kind: the sense of devotion, the adoration of the mysterious presence that might or might not exist but at any rate was real to its worshippers. It was, literally, unhallowed.

Rose did not go again, and I only on rare occasions, in order not too much to offend the comrades, or to play my fiddle when asked. For a time, but not for more than a few months, we went to All Saints, in Bromford Bottom, the old part of the town and in those days as filthy a slum as ever I saw. We went there because of Father Andrews. He was a Christian Socialist who often spoke on I.L.P. platforms, and he had asked me to help him in a boys' club he had started in his parish. I admired him as a man of power and I suppose for three years, long after I had ceased going to the church, I assisted him at the All Saints Club. It was tough going. Those boys were very poor, to the point, many of them, of being without boots to their feet; they were, indeed, what were called in those days street arabs, lawless, untrained, without any notion of discipline. Admittedly a ridiculous specimen of manhood, I would not have survived an evening with them had I not taken their measure at the start. Father Andrews was not there that first evening. Him they held in some fear. He was a man of fine physique, an imperial figure in his vestments, and besides, he was not to be offended: he represented a source of boots, even at times a source of food; and behind him, both naturally from his very presence and as brute fact, stood all authority. No one forgot, meeting Father Andrews, that he was standing before the Church of England as by law established and all those institutions that go with it, the monarchy, the House of Lords, the police, and so on. But when they saw me, what instantly flashed through all their two score minds was that here was the golden chance to wreck the clubroom, smash the furniture and break the windows.

They ringed me round mockingly, nudging one another, giggling, whispering to one another 'Four-eyes!', this in contemptuous recognition of the fact that I wore spectacles, which were then regarded among the poor as evidence of physical weakness and even of effeminacy. I felt anything but comfortable. 'Well, boys,' I said mildly, 'let's begin with a boxing match. You,' I said, picking out the biggest and oldest of the lot, a shambling lout of seventeen, half a head taller than I, and obviously the leader of the gang, 'you, what do you say to three rounds with me?' They laughed derisively, the lout rubbing his hands with glee and swinging his fists in clumsy sparring gestures. I remained mild, asking them if they knew the rules of boxing, ordering one of them to fetch the gloves, another to chalk out a ring, and so on. I took off my spectacles, placed them in the pocket of my jacket, which, when I had removed it, I handed to a boy to hold; having taken good care before I arrived, on Father Andrew's advice, not to have anything on my person worth stealing. Then I put on the boxing gloves and waited for my opponent, who was enacting in vigorous pantomime what he intended to do to me. I could not help smiling; every motion the boy made betrayed his utter ignorance of boxing. On that, of course, I was gambling, safely enough, as I knew from previous experience; in those days the number of working men with the slightest inkling of what boxing as opposed to rough-housing meant was small indeed, and anyone with a rudimentary knowledge of the art can always hold the rough-houser at arm's length, even if he can do no more.

He swaggered towards me, as cocky a lout as ever I saw, and lunged wildly at me without even waiting for the time-keeper to tell us to begin. I parried easily and rapped him sharply on the chest, and then said: 'And now, if you please, we'll start properly and wait for the time-keeper to give us the word Go.' It was child's play, pitiable really. He was, as they say, a chopping-block, or would have been had I let him. As it was, I made no attempt to hit him; I merely wished to make him appear foolish in the eyes of his mates by proving to him and to them that, try as he might, he couldn't hit me. His motions became wilder and wilder. At the end of three rounds I asked him if he had had enough. He was very angry indeed and cursed viciously, so we went on. Still he could not hit me, but at the end of the sixth round I tapped him fair and square on the nose and fell back in a fluster of apologies, like one who does not know his own strength.

That was the finish of it, and from then on I had no trouble with those lads. Indeed, though they went on calling me 'Old Four-eyes' behind my back, they treated me with great respect. Exaggerated notions about me grew up, for example that I had been fly-weight boxing champion of the Midlands in my time; and in that vile slum district, which the police patrolled in pairs, I was never once molested. I think I even did some good. The boys were wild but responsive. After my bout with Cloggy Martin, they all wanted to learn to box, and I taught them, and one or two became very handy. Then, Father Andrews providing some instruments, I started a fiddle class; and we had a drawing class as well. Once, but only once, I took them for a ramble in the country; for while I could control them when I had them in a confined space it was hopeless in the open, and I had to put my hand pretty deeply in my own pocket in order to placate an angry farmer one of whose gates they had dismantled. In the country, they were savages: their immediate impulse on seeing any living thing, whether a cow or a perching bird, was to slug it.

Father Andrews's boys' club became well known; and though I hated the practice myself, Father Andrews delighted in bringing social workers in to see what could be done with what would now be called delinquent boys. I sometimes believe I must have had a gift for teaching; certainly I handled those poor boys more successfully than I ever did my own children. The magistrates and police approved of our activities; from time to time I found myself appearing in the witness-box on a boy's behalf—they were always in trouble, for non-attendance at school, pilfering or damaging property—and membership of the Club always stood them in good stead. Indeed, joining the Club was often a condition of probation.

Though I could ill afford the loss of time from my other interests, I looked forward to my evenings at Father Andrews's boys' club. Why did I give it up? The truth is, Father Andrews and I never hit it off. He was hurt when Rose and I stopped going to All Saints. Yet what could I do? Rose was almost as unhappy there as she had been at the Labour Church, though in a very different way. Christian Socialism and High Anglicanism seem to go together, and All Saints was very high. Father Andrews made it higher. Incense, the ritual celebration of the Mass, bowing to the altar, even the vestments of the priests, all these were utterly alien to Rose: I know she would never begin to understand them. For her it was all 'Roman,' and she held it not merely in suspicion, she was afraid of it. Then, because she had been brought up in dissent and not confirmed in the Church of England, she was barred from full participation in the worship. For her, the service really was a mumbo-jumbo show that she watched uncomprehendingly. It was I, seeing how she suffered, who said, 'We won't go any more.' I admit that I, too, found it unsympathetic. I had been brought up in the Church, but in the Low Church, and I found the ritual theatrical and therefore offensive; and foreign as well: I might, it seemed to me, have been worshipping in a church in Italy, so strong was the sense I had of exclusion. Involuntarily, I was a more violent dissenter than ever, and I was dissenting, I suppose, from the notion of the priest as the man with a special vocation. I took the good old Nonconformist view of every man his own priest.

Rose, who was devout as I was not, and simple in her faith, was unhappy in any church much removed from the chapels she had known in her childhood. She wanted what she had always known, the old hymns, the old ways of prayer, the Nonconformist sermons. She didn't want cathedral magnificence, the anthems that soared with the soaring arches; they made her uneasy for she wasn't at ease with them. She wanted the homely holiness of the bare chapel and the harmonium and the preacher in good plain broadcloth who, when he stepped down from the pulpit, might be Mr Grits the grocer round the corner or Mr Chip the master carpenter who might one day employ her brother or her son. Rose's religion was purest homespun, as it were, and after we had tried All Saints I did my best through the years to subordinate my own inclinations to Rose's and endured, with what patience I could, the illiteracy and arrogance, the moral and intellectual narrowness, which are so often characteristic of the chapel; though I have to confess that I sometimes flew off the handle, generally in the most irrational way. I recall, for instance, persuading her we must leave one Baptist chapel we attended after some months of a new pastor. This man roused me to such a pitch of fury Sunday evening after Sunday evening that I feared truly I might so lose control of myself as to chuck a hymn-book at him during the sermon. I would, I suppose, have resented his appearance and manner in any case, he was so glib and unctuous, so shining with soap and holiness, but it was the matter of his discourse that drove me to the last outpost of endurance. For the fellow had reduced, or rather compressed, all the sins of man, all the evils of the world, into one enormous wickedness that blotted everything else out of his sight. This was gambling. He inveighed against it Sunday after Sunday; and I, who have never betted in my life or taken part in a sweepstake or football pools, was, as I say, driven to fury by this monstrous disproportion in his vision that made him see in a man's putting a shilling on a horse mortal sin and cause for damnation.

On another occasion—it was just after the General Strike, I remember, during the miners' lock-out—I refused to attend yet another chapel. At that time it was a common practice for chapels and churches to have on a notice board outside the building what was called 'The Wayside Pulpit,' a text or slogan that was changed each week. I always found them distasteful and had got into the habit of averting my eyes when passing them, in order to prevent myself from losing my temper. But one I could not ignore, because Phil, who was an undergraduate at the time, with an equally hot-headed friend tore it down in anger. It read: 'A drop in a man's wages is bad enough, but a drop too much is worse.' The minister and the deacons were very cross with the boys and threatened to suspend them from church membership, whereupon I felt compelled to write to the minister in support of them, saying that I hoped that, had I been their age, I would have had the pluck to treat so mean a message as they had done.

But I am racing ahead of myself. I did my best to explain Rose's feelings to Father Andrews; with no success. He was quite simply incapable of understanding and he was brusque and unsympathetic. I really believe that the only Christian church whose existence he recognised, apart from his own, was the Roman. For him, dissent was an expression of the sin of spiritual pride; and I could not make him see that for poor Rose the kind of Christianity in which she had been raised was the right and natural one for her. I don't think he made any effort to see. He was an aristocrat by birth, an Honourable and Reverend, the younger son of a well-known Warwick-shire peer, and by background and training an ingrained authoritarian. His attitude was feudal, and his Christian Socialism was bound up with a dream of the Middle Ages dominated by an all-powerful church. His birth and upbringing made him an ideal priest for a slum parish, for no one could have been less contaminated by association with the bosses; he had an aristocratic disdain of them as being middle-class tradesmen. To this extent, he was on the side of the workers. But he also saw himself as their natural superior. So I was always ill at ease with him. It sounds melodramatic no doubt, but I felt he wanted me body and soul. He would upbraid me for not taking communion, or going to Mass, as he called it; and when I tried to explain that I could not, because I did not believe, he plainly thought I was straining at gnats. His attitude towards me was that of the army officer to an N.C.O. I resented this, and when I told him that I was not concerned with his church but with the social work connected with it, he told me I must go. And go I did.

These middle years of my life seem further away from me now than the days of my childhood and adolescence. Great events were taking place, in which I played my small part and to which I responded passionately, but when I recall them at this moment I find it hard to distinguish between my own experiences of them and what I have read later about them in books. All that remains is the personal, and I find this saddening, for the light it seems to throw on human behaviour.

It is as though the world the ordinary man inhabits must be small, no wider than he can reach with his two outstretched arms. Everything outside that compass, no matter how terrifying, how epoch-making, how much fraught with consequence for the whole human race, is abstract and academic. Man seems hamstrung by the narrowness of his own affections. A year or so ago, Phil went to some international conference in Paris, UNESCO I think it was, and there he met an old friend, a Czech scientist, whom he had not seen since the war days, the Czech having gone back to Prague in 1945. They saw each other every day for five days, but: 'We were only able to talk, that is communicate, for ten minutes,' Phil said; 'at an official cocktail party, where the noise was so great that no one could possibly eavesdrop. Jiry's no more a Communist than I am, and he'd get out if he could. He made that plain enough; but he's got a young family and aged parents. He's caught.' 'And what's he doing now?' I asked. Phil shrugged his shoulders. 'You don't ask that sort of thing,' he said; 'but knowing his line of work, I don't doubt it was something directed towards the ultimate destruction of the human race, our part of it, anyway.'

Compared with the personal, everything dwindles into insignificance, and except when one is young, even those things one has experienced oneself become unreal in memory if too far removed from the normal routine of one's life. Men go through wars, and afterwards it is as though nothing had happened, nothing, that is, worse than a nightmare from which one wakes. What do I have in my mind now about the Boer War but a generalised series of pictures made up of *Illustrated London News* drawings of the relief of Mafeking and the scenes in London when the news of it came through, stereotyped battle scenes, and cliché-images of Baden-Powell in his boy scout hat and Churchill escaping from prison. Many of the names that were so familiar to us at the time, Buller, de Wet, Cronje, are now almost meaningless even to me, who lived through the time. Yet at the time, George and I felt ourselves passionately involved in it all. We hated that war, in direct proportion, it seems to me now, to the general enthusiasm it commanded. I thought, as I think now, it was unjust and unnecessary, a case of plain capitalist bullying. And this I did not find an easy view to take, for I have never been a man who supported every country but his own. I believe, indeed, there may come a point when a man must say 'My country, right or wrong,' but I am sure we never reached that point in 1899. How unpopular we, Horace, who followed Lloyd George, and George and I were. The taunt 'pro-Boer' carried almost as much emotion and hatred as 'pro-German' did in the later war. I remember that at the workshop Mr Darnley would not speak to me for months except in the way of business. I saw George refused a hearing and pelted with eggs by his own foundrymen at a meeting we held jointly with the Lloyd George Radicals. I think the country has never been so divided, feeling never so partisan, as it was in those years. And ours was a Unionist city.

What dismayed George and me about that war was the revelation it gave of the sheer effortless power, as it were, of emotionalism. It was something that had not entered into our calculations before. Without precisely believing that human beings were always reasonable, we had taken it for granted that men of goodwill—and we assumed that most men were that—would respond to the appeal to reason, especially where their own interests were involved. But in that war, not at all. It was such a silly war, and such a mean one; there was nothing dignified about it, nothing tragic. It was just a war of exploitation between a great power and a very small one; and ordinary human decency alone must have made the impartial observer support the small nation. Yet for millions of Englishmen there was never a war more popular, and it is impossible to deny that the vast majority of them were men of goodwill. And thousands of ardent young men dashed off to join the colours it seemed in relief that a century of peace had at last come to an end.

I don't mean that I learned the lesson immediately. Perhaps I didn't realise that I had learnt it at all until August, 1914. We of the I.L.P. and the Labour Movement went on maintaining that war between Britain and Germany was impossible because the workers of both countries would rise against their governments to prevent it. I remember that in 1913 we had a German comrade, a chemical worker from Düsseldorf, stay with us for a week. He was a Social Democrat, a rigidly orthodox Marxist who lectured me at great length in English that was grammatically perfect but vilely mispronounced. One thing we were absolutely sure of: all wars were capitalist in origin; therefore the workers would never again fight in them. A year later, the German Social Democratic party was supporting the Kaiser in his war almost to a man; and the only thing that surprised me in this was that I was not a bit surprised. Unconsciously, I had come to realise there were emotions more powerful than simple economic interests.

But the immediate effect of the war in South Africa and the unpopularity it plunged us into was to bring George and me even closer together than before, if that was possible. Its secondary effect was a partial disruption between us that lasted for several years. It was the unpopularity we found ourselves in that finally moved us to take a step we had discussed for years. We joined together and rented a house in which our two families could live as one. There seemed everything to recommend it. We saw it as a form of practical Socialism, and we had plans of enlarging our community if and when we found a congenial family to come in with us. Materially, there could be no question of the advantages it offered. For much less than our old rents combined we took a house that seemed to us a mansion, away from the road in half an acre of ground. We admired the proportions of the rooms, the space, the elegance of it all. And from the beginning everything went wrong: all the old maxims about no two women being able to share one kitchen came up to meet us and were proved true. We had intended to have our meals in common. Think of the saving: in time on the part of our wives, in money in the buying of provisions. Meals in common lasted precisely one week. After that we were two separate families inhabiting a single house with a common sitting-room between them which, in practice, each used less and less.

What happened? Nothing that I ought not to have been able to foresee. Of us all, none had been more enthusiastic for our living communally than Fanny. I know that I find it difficult to be fair to Fanny. I see her as a silly woman; but this is not the whole truth. She was a woman of energy and imagination, though I do not think her imagination often chimed with reality. She had grand notions beforehand of what our living together could mean, and these alone should have been enough to make me think twice. She saw our communal house as a centre of light in a benighted town. She saw it in anticipation as a combination of the Cotswold Morris colonies she delighted to stay at and of something like a great lady's salon. I recall her crying, as we made our final plans, her pince-nez flashing with fervour, 'We shall be free! Free!' Free from what, free to do what, was not clear: she was rapt in a dream. In practice, of course, the trouble was that she had too little to do; there wasn't enough scope for her energies, with the result that they were immediately misdirected. They were, in fact, directed at Rose. Fanny was a born boss, an implacable, nagging boss, and to make it worse, she considered herself a superior person. Before she married George she had been a schoolteacher. In a sense, she had married beneath her. She regarded her former status with some complacence and never allowed us to forget it. Rose was frightened of her and Rose had to endure her all day long. Fanny was the sort of woman who made a great point of frankness, of speaking her mind, always, of course, for other people's good. In the event, this meant, as it always does, plain bullying. And Rose was no match for her, for, in addition to her airs of superiority, which she wore with the self-consciousness of a saint in his newly-acquired halo, she was capable of a degree of sarcasm that I myself found barely tolerable. She nagged Rose about the housekeeping, the way she dressed, the way she brought up the children, and finally she patronised her on her failure, as she said, to be an 'intellectual companion'— God save us all—to me. This last, of course, wounded Rose more than anything else. I was as angry as I have ever been in my life when I heard of it. I had the greatest difficulty in preventing myself from striking Fanny. I marched into the common room we shared with George and Fanny and declared that this bullying, this nagging, this patronage, this interference, must stop, that I would not put up with it. When Fanny turned to me in all her smug armour of self-righteousness I shouted her down as I have never before or since shouted at anyone. 'Shut up!' I cried. 'I am talking to George, not to you!'

It was all very undignified and embarrassing. I was sorry

for George, for I knew how devoted he was to Rose. I knew, too, that he had to be loyal to Fanny and I would have respected him less if he had not been. But I was sorry for him for another reason: I suddenly realised, from his unwontedly shamefaced attitude, that for a long time he had been acquiescing in Fanny's behaviour for the sake of a quiet life.

Well, we decided to start again, but of course the breach could not be healed. I found I could scarcely bear to be in the same room as Fanny; and the day before the quarter-day George said to me quietly: 'I'm going in to see the land-lord tomorrow to give a quarter's notice,' and I nodded in agreement.

So it was with enormous relief that at the end of the next three months Rose and I and the children moved into a house in Harland Street, slightly bigger than the one we had occu-pied before, with an extra bedroom in which I had the landlord install a bath. That first night in the new house I was suddenly conscious of a lightness of mood, an absence of oppressive tension, and I realised that I had been angry for months, angry with myself for having put Rose in a position in which she could be hurt. And I was aware of something else during the next few weeks, as I watched a revived Rose making and rejoicing in a home of her own again. Men, by which I mean the male of the species, are, it seems to me, born campers-out; I can myself live anywhere and anyhow, oblivious of my surroundings. But most women are not like that. Certainly Rose was not. She *needed* a place of her own, a home, some-where she had made herself. If we had been doomed to live in a corner of one room, as used to happen in Russia, I am sure that as soon as she had realised the situation, she would have busied herself in making that corner a special and individual niche personal to ourselves. It seemed as instinctive a process with her as that by which birds begin building nests in spring. I used to smile at this instinctive activity, in a lordly masculine way, and smile, perhaps, to hide my own discomfiture; for, to tell the truth, I think this home-making instinct on the part of women a great trapper of men. But I smile no longer. Now, I find it awful, in the strict sense, for I see it not merely as truly creative but, as it were, the fundamental in human creativity. All order, I begin to think, stems in the first place from the female impulse to make a home for her mate and her offspring, to draw a circle round them that shall be theirs and no one else's and differentiated from all other such circles. That is why I now believe it is true to say that women are the great civilisers and the founders of civilisation.

It was several years before we were again on visiting terms with George and Fanny. George, it is true, came to see us, and we men went on meeting weekly in Boswell's Pie Shop. But it couldn't quite be as it was before; there were reservations, sensitive areas in each of us the other was at pains not to touch. I think it was the sense of this almost deliberate restriction upon our intimacy that caused us to seize with such avidity upon Jimmy Sillitoe, whom we met about this time and who began to join us at Boswell's. I had as a matter of fact known him casually for years in the jewellers' quarter of the city; like Horace and myself, he was a designer, die-sinker and engraver, though with little of our feeling for the craft. He already had his own small business. But George and I really came to know him when he joined the I.L.P. The curious thing is, though now I see that it was not so curious, if, as I think today, we were in a way using him for obscure ends of our own, he was a man we had no respect for; I partly because of the kind of work he chose to do, which was the cheapest and vulgarest possible. He blamed this on the existence of the capitalist system, which discouraged excellence and rewarded the shoddy. In fact, I am pretty sure he was incapable of excellence and loved the shoddy. He took himself deadly seriously; he had read *The Communist Manifesto*, and he had always at the tip of his tongue the clap-trap and clichés of the movement. He delighted in bringing out such phrases as 'the expropriation of the expropriators': you could positively see him listening to himself admiringly as he used them; and since he used them with great assurance he was not without effect as a public speaker. His speciality, as George said, was what we called 'blinding them with science,' but he was quite unaware that he was doing so. George was fascinated by him and was constantly prodding him to see what he would say next. He became, as it were, a private jester for us.

'Sillitoe, you're incorrigible,' George would say, and Jimmy would grin with delight, in a naïve self-satisfaction, believing that he was being praised. He fawned upon us and was zealous to agree. George found him useful, for there was no job for the movement, however boring, that Jimmy would not gladly do. He was a great addresser of envelopes and a great canvasser at election-times; except that he never completed his stint of houses. He was an ingratiating, humourless man who would spend hours in conversation on people's doorsteps, not converting or convincing them but, according to George, stunning them with his polysyllabic loquacity. In appearance, he was very tall and very thin. He had an extremely long nose, surmounted by gold-rimmed eye-glasses, and his nose seemed to be disproportionately wide at the nostrils, which he had a nervous habit of twitching at the same time as he blinked his eyes; so that it seemed, as he peered forward, that he was calling in his sense of smell to make up for the deficiencies of his sight.

His great function for George and myself, as I realise now, was to bring us together at a time when in some ways we were asunder. George in particular was fascinated by him and would drop fragments of Marxist jargon into the conversation specially for the pleasure of hearing Jimmy mouth them the next time we met. It seemed at times as though George was obsessed by him as an unfailing source of entertainment. When we left him after our evenings at Boswell's George and I would walk home together roaring with laughter at him, reciting his absurdities and inventing new ones for George to induce him to adopt. It was characteristic of neither of us so to laugh at and mock another man; but somehow, in the laughter, we obtained release from the inhibitions which just then restrained our intercourse. Jimmy Sillitoe was, as it were, neutral territory between us that we occupied with joy.

George, however, was wiser than I. 'All the same, Billy,' I remember him saying one night as we walked back from Boswell's, 'we mustn't kid ourselves. Sillitoe is more formidable than we think.' This seemed absurd to me, assessing the man in terms of his work and his illiterate parroting of political catchphrases; and I said so. 'No, Billy, you're wrong,' George said. 'I'll tell you the clue to Sillitoe: it's his nose.' And straightway as he thought of that nose he collapsed into laughter. 'Oh dear, oh dear, oh dear,' he sighed, 'the way he twitches and sniffs! Still, that nose is the clue. He's sniffing round. He's on the scent of something. He doesn't know what it is yet; but mark my words, Billy, it isn't us. That nose of his will lead him on and take him somewhere else, a long way from the likes of us.' This appeared to me fantasy, but George was right, of course. In the meantime, though, Jimmy served his purpose.

13

SOMEONE, I have been told, has described the years in England between the end of the South African War and 1914 as a long summer afternoon. He was thinking of the England of the very rich, yet when I look back, the words seem apt even for my own life. My existence in that Edwardian period seems to me now idyllic—and unreal. That is an illusion, of course; but I think only partly an illusion. We were excited or made anxious by the events of the day; we rejoiced in the great Liberal victory of 1906 and the great increase in the number of our own Labour M.P.s; we cheered Lloyd George's Limehouse speech and his budgets, even though they did not go far enough for us; we demanded as fiercely as anyone the reform of the House of Lords; we reviled Carson and F. E. Smith; we were disturbed by Agadir. We were passionately partisan over a hundred things. Yet today, it is only by an effort of memory that I can recall what those things were, and I am amazed that we could ever have thought them important. They seem not to have touched the centre of things at all.

The centre of things was the life I lived in my family, my hobbies and my work. It was a narrow life, but an intense one, and what happened in the world outside, cataclysmic as it might appear at the time, was not in fact big enough to disrupt it. At the time, it sometimes seemed to me a selfish life: I had moments of guilt because, though my beliefs had not changed at all, apart from canvassing, addressing envelopes, going to meetings and voting, I had dropped out of politics altogether. It was as though George had taken over all my political zeal, as I had taken over his cultural aspirations. George—by 1906 we had composed our differences, and our two families were as close as ever they had been—was now very active indeed, a man of affairs, whose union duties took him to London regularly and who was in demand as a speaker on Labour platforms throughout the country. Though not at the heart of things, he knew what went on there. George, as it were, was doing my political living for me, and on the whole I was content with that, getting enormous vicarious satisfaction from his activities.

So, when I look back on those years, I have a generalised picture of myself; practising the fiddle like mad (three hours daily, to be precise) in a mingled frenzy of disgust at my incompetence and of optimism that one day I should play as well as I prayed to do; going to the workshop five and a half days a week, secure in the knowledge that whatever reputation Darnley's had in the trade rested on my shoulders; attending W.E.A. classes two evenings a week; walking in the country, sketching, taking photographs at week-ends; and somehow, with it all, reading. I read, I thought, to find truth, expecting each famous book as I took it up to give me final revelation. But I read, in fact, to little purpose: I was like a small child that has been given the freedom of a toy-shop; there was altogether too much that was glittering and exciting and novel all about me for me to be able to settle down to any one thing, and no sooner had I tasted Plato than William James became irresistible, not because I was tired of Plato but because life was too short to pack in all the books I must read. Simply, I was undisciplined. But I don't complain.

And of course there were the children. Harry was born in 1898, Will in 1901, Phil in 1907, Tom in 1911. I recapture as I watch Will's behaviour to his children my own attitude of forty and thirty years ago as he and his brothers were growing up. I see in him the same awful realisation that one's children are indeed hostages to fortune and the same awful love, compounded of a sense of the ideal, of fear that it will never be realised, and of the sheer impossibility of communication, that so often expressed itself in anger when anger is the last emotion one wishes to feel. And I want to cry out to Will, 'No, don't. It doesn't matter. Leave the child alone. It will be all the same twenty years on. You don't know best. It's his life. He's not you but a different person, a unique being.' But of course I don't say it, for what would be the use? These are the things one learns too late. Children catch us in our deepest anxieties, and when we upbraid them we are upbraiding our own unworthiness, our disappointment in what we have made of ourselves. And I was as bad as any other father, ambitious for my children in a way and to a degree that I would have recognised as absurd for myself. It seemed that, given my guidance, all the promises I had made and not kept could easily be fulfilled in them. And so every step through childhood became for me, the father-observer, a personal agony or a personal triumph. Trifles were magnified by me into major achievements or the sign of major sins: I reacted accordingly, in exaggerated delight or exaggerated despondency. But children are both tough and pliable; they can be bent, but when the pressure is released they spring back into their natural stance, like saplings. I suppose I was no worse than other fathers. We all, in every generation, have to forgive our fathers, even as we have to learn to forgive ourselves, and that's the hardest thing of all. But I sometimes think our race would be happier if we were taught to say 'Our Mother, which art in heaven' and not 'Our Father.'

All that is what I forget when I see those Edwardian years as idyllic, though they are certainly idyllic by comparison with those that followed. In July, 1914, reality broke in again; and more and more reality has come to mean whatever disrupts and makes precarious the centre of things. We were on holiday at Scarborough in July, 1914, all of us except Harry, who was in camp near Evesham with the boy scouts. I think all people whose minds were not in blinkers had seen this war with Germany coming for years; indeed, for us Socialists the clash that was to come was axiomatic; it was to be the Armageddon of the capitalist system. But no one really *believed* in the war we knew was coming; the imagination could not conceive it, it was so long since we had had any experience of large-scale war. So, before the event, it was easy to be rational about it. It would be a war of capitalists, in which Socialist workers would refuse to fight. We even tried to have it both ways, for Norman Angell had proved that even to the victors modern war would be unprofitable, and surely the capitalists would recognise their own best interests. We made much of this factor of the cost of modern war: it was so great, we argued before the event, that any major war must be brief, a matter of months. So the war, when it was at last undisguisedly imminent and could not be argued away, came as a shock. That is too mild a word. For my part, because there was nothing in my experience against which I could measure it, it seemed like the end of the world.

I did what everybody else did who was away on holiday that last week of July: packed my family into the first train we could catch and went home, as though there safety lay. We expected I know not what, but certainly complete upheaval. The train was full; I stood in the corridor all the way from the Yorkshire coast. Years later I heard Tom, who had been only three at the time, describe this journey on the eve of war to another boy. 'And all the fields we passed,' he said, 'were full of soldiers.' And, though I know it is absurd, that is how I, too, remember that journey: every field full of bell tents and cavalry horses and soldiers drilling.

When we reached the house who should we find in the kitchen waiting for us but Harry. The scouts, too, had broken camp. I see him now, standing on the hearth with his kit-bag and haversack and scout's pole on the floor at his side. He looks very young and slight in his scout's jersey with its patrol-leader's chevrons on his breast and the proficiency badges on his arm and the clasp-knife dangling from his belt. He stands very erect with his head thrown back and his lips parted as though in anticipation. Very young and vulnerable; and as I see him in memory I feel again the sudden stab at the heart: he was sixteen, and I realised as I saw him standing there that there was no guarantee in the nature of things that the war would be short.

I do not often think of Harry now; he has become detached from me as my other sons have not, I suppose because for so long he has been outside any influence I could have on him or any anxiety I could feel for him. Yet at that time, in 1914, he was much the closest to me of all my children, no doubt because he was the eldest. I was proud of him and—the word may seem odd—respected him, he was such an honest and honourable boy. In a sense, it seems to me that his personality was already complete. I had no misgivings about him and had reconciled myself to the disappointments, which in a way were the consequence of his solid worth. He had been a grave little boy, with the, as it were, natural elderliness, the anxiety to assume responsibility for others, that so often characterises the eldest of a family. In this respect I could see Lizzie in him. He was not brilliant in anything, or even very clever. He was at this time still at the grammar school, the school I had gone to myself, though since then long settled in a building of its own. In a form of thirty boys he was generally placed between thirteenth and seventeenth, which seemed to me a just estimate of his ability: the one thing he shone at was drawing. He did not take as much interest in school affairs as I could have wished; his energies went into the scout troop and the Sunday school; it was in the scout troop, not at school, that he found his friends, and they seemed always boys like himself, serious, responsible, elderly, and dedicated, I can't help but think now, to a concept of honour which perhaps in its early days the scout movement, much as we Socialists suspected it, gave to its members.

He stands there, in that last week of July, 1914, on the hearth in the kitchen in his scout uniform, pole, kit-bag and haversack on the floor beside him; and so in my memory he will always stand. And as soon as I saw him there I knew what would follow. His one fear was that the war would be over before he was old enough to get there; and it was such a boy scout war as he imagined it, something out of Baden-Powell's *Scouting for Boys*, a feeling that was intensified by the events of the war as it began and the propaganda that accompanied them; the 'contemptible little army,' 'brave little Belgium,' the boy scout Jack Cornwell dying at his gun, game to the end.

All I could do was make him promise that he would do nothing until he was eighteen. But nothing would satisfy him but that he left school straightaway. Unwillingly I agreed. I had hoped that he would become a schoolteacher, but it seemed that the war, young as it was, had made long-term plans and policies utterly academic; and I allowed him to go to work with brother Horace, knowing that at any rate there he would be taught a craft.

The war changed my life. It split the ranks of us Socialists. George, Jimmy Sillitoe and I all resigned from the I.L.P. when it took its pacifist line. No doubt it was we who were inconsistent. I believed that the war was still a capitalist war but

I also believed it was something else besides. In any case, I found our former glib talk of the workers' refusing to fight now rang hollow indeed. I decided that I would rather be wrong with the mass of my fellow-countrymen than right, if to be right separated me from them. I don't think this was cowardice on my part, though that was what our former comrades in the I.L.P. accused us of. I found that I profoundly distrusted a rightness that isolated one from one's fellows. I respected the comrades who followed Ramsay MacDonald, but if I had done so myself I would have considered myself guilty of moral high-falutin. And I believe that even if I had been persuaded that theoretically MacDonald was right I would still have done as I did. I could not set myself apart for a theory. I knew that Harry was living largely in a world of illusions but I still had to applaud the sense of chivalry that impelled him, and I wanted to be at one with Harry, not sundered from him. Whatever my fate might be, I did not want it to be different from his and from that of the millions like him.

I behaved quixotically. Everyone told me so, and I knew it very well at the time. I was also told I was behaving irresponsibly. Jimmy Sillitoe said so, and talked about the war effort and how men like himself—he had just got his first government contract—could do more for the country at the bench, as he put it, though his days at the bench were now over and the days of motor cars and whiskies-and-sodas in hotel lounges in sight, than firing a rifle in the trenches. Jimmy had discovered he was indispensable. I had no such illusion. I thought as I do now that there are times when the man with the rifle is the only man that matters. In short, I did my best to join up. Not very successfully at first. It was the days of the Derby Scheme: you volunteered and if you were not needed at once you were given a khaki armlet with a crown upon it to wear on your sleeve. I went to the recruiting office and presented myself to a recruiting sergeant who was disgusted at the sight of me. I was aware that my appearance was not impressive; I was five feet two inches in height, had poor eyesight and was over forty. The sergeant's professional pride was outraged at the spectacle I made. He would have given anything rather than take my name, but I insisted. 'Things has come to a pretty pass, mate,' he said to me; and when it came to recording my physical peculiarities he ordered the clerk to write down, 'Duck's Disease'; turning to me and saying, 'You know what Duck's Disease is, mate?' I didn't. 'Having your arse too near the ground,' he said. And then, when the proceedings were ended and he had had to accept me, he chucked the khaki band at me and said, 'Take your bloody armlet and go 'ome.'

I went home in a fine state of humiliation: I had set out in a fine state of patriotism. I took the band off my arm and hid it in a drawer, never to wear it again. Yet within a few hours I was able to laugh at myself and at the recruiting sergeant. He was fighting the wrong war, a war that had already been fought: as for me, well, didn't the whole episode show the irreconcilable difference between one's own vision of oneself and the world's?

That was in 1915. Within twelve months I was in the Army. I was there before Harry. Why did I volunteer? Many things were involved. There was the wish to do my bit, and I could not see that the kind of war work we were doing at Darnley's served any very useful purpose. There was also the wish to assert and demonstrate my solidarity with my fellows—I had advocated conscription from the first, as the only fair thing. Always the passionate egalitarian, I now demanded equality in suffering. Both these sentiments were genuine, I am sure; but I have to admit that other men who felt them just as strongly made no effort to volunteer. Indeed, of my friends and brothers and brothers-in-law, of all the men I knew fairly well of roughly the same age as myself, I was the only one who became a soldier. And when I volunteered—and to me it was an act of tremendous daring—I was surprised to find that no one else was surprised. It's just what you'd expect of Billy, they said. So it must have been in character. I can only think, therefore, that my response to the war was different from theirs. I compare myself with Harry. To him, with his boy scout chivalry, his uncomplicated sense of honour, it was inconceivable that he should not go to the war. He saw it as his duty: it was as simple as that. But I had no such moral imperative. For me, I feel now, the war came as a test, which I could either refuse to accept or voluntarily undergo. Self-respect was at stake, for it was a test of manhood: one was putting oneself to the completely unknown, and it was necessary to discover whether one could endure or not. I had to prove I was as good as other men, as good as Harry, perhaps. But it was bound up, of course, with something else, which I realise now as I did not then. My friends, who were very alarmed at the irrationality of my behaviour, urged upon me the duty I owed to my wife and children. I wasn't, they argued, a free agent. It would be time enough to go when the Government made me, they maintained. Then the decision would be out of my hands; until then my duty was to stay at home. Rose needed me, the boys needed me.

I did not know how to answer this. I could only fall back on such argument as 'I could not love thee, Dear, so much Loved I not Honour more'; but I did not, for even to me it seemed unconvincing. No; I was caught up in the terrible attraction of war, which is not the promise of glory (though I think it was for Harry) but the promise of the unknown, the promise of release from rut and routine into a condition of being the whole essence of which is that anything may happen. For many men, war is a promise of freedom or at least of a life utterly other than that which they normally lead. Some men submit poorly to domesticity. In peace-time, they are indistinguishable from their fellows, but war finds them out. It found me out. It gave me the chance, backed with the approval of church and state and all right-thinking people, to slough off the responsibilities and obligations that I believed I had willingly accepted. If I had known the quotation then, and had been honest with myself, I would have exclaimed joyously, 'To the destructive element submit yourself!'

And now I have to confess that in all my three years of soldiering I did not hear a gun fired in anger and, indeed, after my short, very sketchy initial training, never even saw a gun. No soldier could have had a cushier war than I. Conscious of the irony, I made the best of it I could. I found myself an orderly in the R.A.M.C. stationed, of all places, in the University building, which had been converted into a military hospital for officers, so that throughout my war service I was never more than four miles away from home. I saw almost as much of my family as I did in normal times. And I truly believe it was a case of the War Office being thoughtful on our behalf. We were an entirely local unit and, except for patients and nursing sisters—and they were very warlike indeed, 'Shrapnel Kates' we called them—as unwarlike a body of men as you could meet. Our officers, the surgeons and doctors, were local specialists who looked and behaved for the most part as though they had put on their uniforms in a fit of absent-mindedness. My mates, the other orderlies, were mainly men of my own age and class; they were, if I may use the word, superior working men with jobs of some responsibility which they had left voluntarily, knowing, as I had done, that their chances of being called up for service in the normal course of things were very slight indeed. We were very respectable, incurably civilian. I made no close friends among them. I think we were on our guard with one another, I suspect now because we were aware of the ironical situation into which our romantic notions had brought us. The atmosphere was so unmilitary that we could never seriously believe we were soldiers. I don't believe I ever heard on their lips the four-letter Anglo-Saxon monosyllable that commonly interlards the soldier's speech, though I heard it often enough from the patients. We were so little soldiers that off-duty we addressed one another as Mister, as working men commonly did in those days.

Nevertheless, and perhaps partly because of this, it was a time of bizarre horror. For whole hours at a stretch, once one had accustomed oneself to wearing the rough khaki clothes, one could forget one was a soldier. One was rarely conscious of military discipline in the ordinary sense; as I have hinted, it was only certain hard-faced moustachio'd ward-sisters who bore heavily upon us. And there were always the odd hours that could be snatched at home; in retrospect I seem to have spent whole days of my life travelling on the trams between the hospital and Harland Street, with my unmilitary fiddle-case under my arm. I came to know everyone on the route, the conductresses, the regular passengers, the military police who patrolled the centre of the city: I was treated by all, even the redcaps, with a respectful familiarity, as a not entirely comic figure. All this was an approximation to normality. The contrast lay with the horrors within the hospital, and it was the horror that became the reality, so that, when on an evening off I found myself with Rose at George's or Horace's or Hugh's or, much more occasionally now, at Jimmy Sillitoe's, suddenly among the decorous conversation, the small talk of everyday, I would realise what was happening at the hospital. The ambulance train in the siding was being unloaded, the stretcher-bearers were carrying in their burdens to us, who awaited God knows what twisted wrecks of young men. I knew that if I spoke of these things round that sober supper table, to which we had taken our own tea and sugar and margarine, they would not be understood; and I knew that it was there, among those torn bodies, those blasted faces, that I most truly wanted to be.

I mustn't pretend I didn't loathe it. I loathed every minute of it; and all the time I was there I was terrified that when at last the war was over I should be haunted by the sights I had seen, that in nightmare I should hear the screams, the filthy delirium, the whimpering of the shell-shocked, it was my duty night after night to preside over. In fact, I did not dream of these things; in that respect, I came through the horrors unscathed. I never showed my loathing; and what made it bearable was the pity and indignation I felt for those poor brave young men. In their presence, the only thing possible was self-abnegation. One could only minister. And this feeling became all the stronger when Harry was called up late in 1916. I reached the point where every young man whom I tended seemed to be Harry.

These young men, though I must remember that some of them, professional soldiers, were in fact not so much younger than myself, were all officers. They had to be treated as such; that is to say, between them and us orderlies the rigid punctilio of military discipline was still supposed to be observed. It was easier for me to conform because they were all profoundly sick men; even so, I acquired a sixth sense which told me when punctilio could be ignored. The relations between a medical orderly and his patient are, after all, necessarily intimate, and with most of the men I tended I soon reached a genuine intimacy that had to be forgotten as soon as they were convalescent. I became, it sometimes seemed to me, a nurse in a much fuller sense than the normal. Without any wish on my part, I became their confidant. I was called on by some to write letters for them, even love letters. To others I had to talk by the hour. Yet others I read to, and I played endless games of draughts and chess and simple card games. I had even to reassure men in their religious beliefs, which I did not myself accept.

All this I believe I did successfully, yet in an impersonal way, for I kept myself, as it were, withdrawn. I had moments of reward. A lot of these young men called me Dad, and though in the beginning it was nothing more than the nickname that any old sweat earns by virtue of his grey hairs I sensed that often it meant more than that. Once, too, a red-faced major, a regular officer whose life on the surface was dedicated entirely to point-to-point meetings and champagne suppers, suggested to me that when the war was over I should become his valet. I respectfully declined. 'Why the hell not, man?' he wanted to know. I explained that my principles would not permit it, that I was a Socialist and believed in the equality of man and man. 'A Socialist! Good God!' was his first response. Next night, though, he greeted me with the words: 'You know, I've never met a Socialist before. But you're a good chap, or I'd not have suggested what I did; so I expect my ideas of Socialists are all wrong. Tell me all about them.'

So in a curious way we made contact, this man and I. He was a gentleman, born of a family of soldiers and brought up from his earliest days to be a soldier. 'Soldiers don't have to think, you know,' he said; 'bad for them.' What I had construed as his frivolous life I found was the obverse of his unreflecting dedication to duty and his simple piety. Of course we couldn't agree, we had nothing in common, and my notions, as he called them, bewildered him. Every man should know his place; all in some sense had to serve and to obey, and service and obedience were honourable things. Automatically I had taken his suggestion that I should be his valet as an insult; but after our talks I knew it was a compliment; it was the index of the respect he bore me as a man and proof of the efficiency with which I was doing my job. I thought our arguments had made no dent on him at all, but before he went off to the convalescent hospital, he said: 'I can't agree but I think I see what you mean; and if I wasn't me, if I'd been born in a slum in this filthy town, damned if I wouldn't be a Socialist myself! Though of course when your revolution comes I'll be on the other side and shoot you cheerfully, but with no hard feelings, in the way of duty!'

This man was a great prop to me when I needed a prop as I had not done in my life before. On March 31, 1918, we had the telegram from the War Office telling us that Harry was reported missing, believed killed in action. My instinct was to keep the news to myself and tell no one. I felt numb and beyond feeling; it was as though there was a complete blank in front of me. I remember that my face felt wooden, as though its place had been taken by a rigid, expressionless mask. It carried me through the day, but I could not hide the truth from my major. We were silent for a time as I busied myself about his bed. Then, very quietly, 'There's something wrong, isn't there?' I found I couldn't speak, and nodded. 'Your son?' I nodded again. He put his hand on mine. 'I'm sorry,' he said; 'I shall pray for you both'; and I felt the great simplicity and certainty of the man like a rock to lean on. This man had included the fact of death in his philosophy as I had been unable to do, and I seemed to take strength from his strength.

I went on working in silence. He said: 'If you tell the C.O. he'll give you compassionate leave straightaway, you know.' I answered: 'I don't want leave. I'd rather be here.' He nodded approvingly. 'That's why you're here,' he said; 'isn't it? Because you feared this for Harry? All the same,' he went on, 'you should take that leave. Your place is with your wife now, man.'

He had recalled me to what was my true duty at that moment. Very gently he said: 'Go along to the C.O. now'; and as I was leaving the room he added, 'You mustn't be afraid to weep, you know.'

I was braced to meet Rose's grief, which I had been dreading. But Rose, as I should have known, was stronger than I. She had always been quiet; there was what I can only describe as a gentle stillness at the heart of her, a stillness that was all-consenting. I think, after Harry's death, she was quieter than before, if that was possible, and graver. She mourned bitterly and yet submitted to the fact of his death without reproaches or recrimination, if you understand me. It was as though the weakness of her human nature made her mourn but at the same time she made allowances for it. She saw it as weakness;

it implied no questioning or anything less than acceptance of God's will. I write stumblingly and falter in my explanation, for I confess I did not and do not understand her attitude; it had a beauty of acceptance beyond anything I was capable of. I mourned bitterly and hopelessly, I am tempted to say personally and vindictively. My heart was filled with rage against the scheme of things, and if I had believed in a god I would have cursed him.

It seems to me now that my work as an orderly, tending the wounded, became a saving passion. Every boy as he was brought in on his stretcher I felt was Harry; for as long as he was officially only missing there was still the possibility, however remote, that he was alive. There were times, indeed, when I was wrought up almost to the point of hallucination and actually believed, at least momentarily, that the young man I was ministering to was Harry and found myself calling him Harry. Yet, if an agnostic can use the expression, that work was a godsend to me, and in the depth of my grief at the time it took on almost a religious significance. I do not profess to understand this. I do not think my major was right when he said that I had undertaken the work in the first place out of my fears of what might happen to Harry; but if it had called for justification before it needed none after Harry's death. It became an act of expiation; and again I do not know what I mean.

I was haunted by Harry. And then I lost him. I found I could feel no longer; and then my lack of grief, the death of my grief, became itself the source of grief, but grief for sensibilities that seemed to have become calloused and unresponsive. I know now that this was a necessary stage in my making peace with the dead. But when, as we have to, we make our peace with the dead, we often lose them; as I lost Harry. Rose did not; for her, the body alone died, and, as I know, Harry was near to her till the end.

The war finished and I was demobbed. I had not thought of myself as a soldier and, physically at any rate, I had scarcely been away from home. Yet I returned to a world utterly different from the one I had left three years before. It was as though I had been so immersed in the life of the hospital that I had failed to notice what was going on outside. The realisation came as a shock. I discovered, for instance, that some of my friends and relations now had motor cars. They had made money during the war and were employers of labour. Jimmy Sillitoe had done so well that he had moved away from the city altogether and bought a house in the country with a croquet lawn, a rose garden and a vegetable garden. Rose and I went there and were received by a maid in a white cap and apron. We were acutely uncomfortable. We had tea on the lawn, with tea from a silver teapot and little thin sandwiches of cucumber and tomato, 'from our own garden,' as Millie Sillitoe told us. Jimmy was as garrulous as ever, but he was no longer ridiculous. Indeed, I thought him formidable and realised how just had been George's prediction about him. It seemed to me his nostrils twitched no more, because it was no longer necessary that they should. He didn't have to feel about for the scent, he had found it and was following it wherever it might take him. He had dropped his Marxist jargon and his conversation was now studded with equally high-sounding abstractions such as one finds in the financial columns of the press and leading articles in the *Daily Telegraph*. He exuded an innocent pleasure in his new surroundings and the new associates he could not help mentioning, prominent local industrialists and so on, that I found utterly disarming. He took it for granted that I would rejoice with him in his success, and indeed I was very willing to do so. He told me he still believed in the ideals of Socialism but knew now that we had been on the wrong tack: all those things we wanted to get through Socialism could be more easily achieved through enlightened capitalism and mass-production. He had discovered mass-production: the new chain stores which sold nothing over sixpence had given him a huge market for his wares. I was not impressed by his arguments; I thought he was merely rationalising his own behaviour. No doubt in part he was, but all the same I was under-estimating him, as I found out when I reported our conversation to George. To my surprise, George took it very seriously. 'Yes,' he said, 'it's going to be the new line: enlightened capitalism, the partnership of capital and labour, mass-production. Jimmy's one of the first in the field; and though it isn't true it's very plausible.' Three or four years later, George tossed a book at me. It was Henry

Ford's autobiography. 'There you are. But Jimmy Sillitoe said it before Ford.'

Jimmy, indeed, earned a certain reputation for saying it. He was much in demand as a speaker at Rotary Clubs, Chamber of Commerce dinners and the banquets of employers' associations not simply in his own right as a successful if minor business man but also as a convert from Socialism to Capitalism. He was always very brave about it and loud in his respect for the ideals Socialism was working for; it was simply that they could be achieved more quickly and efficiently through capitalism; and besides, he said, Socialists were impractical dreamers. When he said that I was pretty certain he meant me.

But that was after Rose and I went over to tea with him and Millie at his new house. Then he was aware of the troubles he had come into with his new status, and he confided in me. He had led me solemnly after tea into the house, into the room he called his study, where he went through the motions of offering me whisky. I refused, since I did not drink. I remembered that he used not to drink either, but now it seemed whisky was something he had acquired with his position and the house. He assured me the doctors recommended it, 'taken in moderation, of course.' 'But it isn't all jam, believe me, Billy. You come up against things you never thought of before. Voices, for instance. I never thought there was anything wrong with my voice; seemed to me I talked just the same as everybody else. Now I know I don't. I know my voice sticks out like a sore finger. When I'm sitting in the Beaconsfield Club in London talking with business colleagues, men from the ministries, that sort of thing, I feel myself going hot all over as soon as I hear the sound of my own voice. "Black country chap," it says: I might just as well have it branded on my forehead. I know I'm as good as any of them; I reckon there are one or two of them I could buy up already; and they're glad enough to take my advice. But when I hear the noise my mouth makes I don't *feel* as good as them, see? Think I ought to have elocution lessons, Billy?'

I was amused, of course, but it suddenly struck me he wasn't just blowing his own trumpet; very likely his friends at the Beaconsfield Club were glad to take his advice. After all, the house we were sitting in and its appointments were evidence of his success, and I had never believed success was easy. Then

I had noticed that though he smiled as readily as ever his absurd, self-deprecating, almost perpetual grin had become like a mask: there was no smile in the eyes that peered out through it; they were cold, intent, watching. Oh, he was formidable enough. I could not persuade him not to drive us home in his motor car. I rode back full of thought. It was not merely the spectacle of Jimmy's success; though he had done better than anyone else I knew, it seemed that all who were close to me had gone ahead as well and that I was left behind. From the material point of view I had made the wrong choice and, by doing so, had missed an opportunity. I did not regret the choice I had made, but one always wants to have one's cake and eat it, and I was envious of Jimmy and my brothers. I caught myself falling into self-pity and thinking that their success, or my lack of it, was unfair. What galled me most of all was that all my life I had longed to be my own master. Had I let the chance to be so slip by unawares?

That night I discussed it with Rose. Should I take the plunge, leave my safe job at Darnley's and set up for myself? She, dear soul, was agreeable to whatever I wished and was sure that I could do just as well, if not better, than Jimmy and the others. I have to confess I wasn't, but I would not admit it even to myself. It was a sign of my misgivings, as I realise now, that I did not even consult George. Had he been at home I could not have dodged this, but he was in London. I was, of course, repeating the impetuosity that had marked my going to America years before. Next morning I saw Mr Darnley and gave him my notice. I told him my intentions. He did his best to dissuade me, I am sure quite disinterestedly; he even offered to increase my wages. He pleaded with me. 'I know things are booming now, Billy, but mark my words, it won't last. You've left it too late.' But I was firm. Generously he said he would put work in my way if he could and suggested that it would be in the interests of us both if, instead of working my week's notice, I continued with him for a month on a part-time basis. It would help me to find a workshop to rent and to get a connection in the trade. I was glad to agree. I found my workshop, two rooms round the corner from Darnley's, and got promises of work from all sides. Everyone agreed to help me and everyone was sanguine on my behalf, all, that is, except

Jimmy Sillitoe. 'I'll put what work in your way I can, Billy,' he said; 'but if you take my advice you'll think twice about it. The times are too good to last, and it's the newcomers who'll be the first hit.' God forgive me, I put this down to jealousy and said huffily, 'I've got something up my sleeve that'll surprise you.' 'I hope to God you have, Billy,' he answered. 'And when it's ready you bring it along to me.'

If only I'd talked to George! But by the time he was back from London I had thoroughly committed myself. Honour itself was at stake. He made no bones about the risks I was taking; to my surprise he agreed with Darnley and Jimmy Sillitoe: things were too good to last: a slump was on the way.

I was shaken but would not admit it. I still trusted in what I had up my sleeve, my secret weapon, as it were. During my last months in the Army, especially while waiting for demobilisation when the hospital was rapidly emptying and I was able to be often at home, I had been working on a new enamelling process, whereby I sought to obtain by chemical means the sheen and iridescence of mother-of-pearl. I was successful, and the trial runs were pleasing: I had made a number of round brooches bearing the countenance of the Virgin Mary shining through the opalescent surface I was able to obtain. They were something new, and they were much admired by the handful of people who had seen them, all men whose judgment, in this respect at least, was valuable. I had taken out provisional patents and I foresaw a large market for the goods, and others in which the same process could be used, among Roman Catholics. It would depend, of course, on whether it was possible to produce the wares in sizeable batches cheaply. I thought I saw how it could be done—it was ultimately a matter of furnace control—but I knew it would need some time and that till the method was perfected I should have to rely for my living on die-sinking and engraving.

Well, Mr Darnley, Jimmy Sillitoe and George were right: before I had been in business on my own account for a year the slump had hit us. In a slump the silversmith's and jeweller's trades are always among the first to be affected. It lasted another fifteen months before the stark facts of my bank account forced me to shut up shop. We always maintained the polite fiction at home that it was the depression that had finished me, and I am sure dear Rose accepted it without question. It was not as simple as that, as I knew only too well. Had there been no slump I think I would have survived, for I solved the problem of producing my chemical film in continuous batches of even quality, and then, realising that the marketing of my products was a matter I was temperamentally unfitted to deal with, I went to Jimmy Sillitoe. He was interested in what I had to show him and impressed, but he shook his head. 'Two years ago, Billy,' he said, 'this would have been a winner. And it may be, perhaps, in two years' time. But now, it's hopeless, Billy. I'd have backed it to the hilt two years ago, but today, I don't mind admitting between ourselves, I scarcely know how I'm going to meet next week's wages' bill. I tell you straight, I'm up against it, and I could kick myself. I saw this coming and still I didn't take sufficient precautions. I've been a fool like everybody else. In two years' time, perhaps, if I'm still in business . . .'

Jimmy weathered the storm, but in two years' time he was interested in other things and I knew that I must be a journeyman for the rest of my life. I'd had my fling and I'd learnt once again that I was the last man in the world to make a living as his own boss. Freedom to me was like strong drink to an alcoholic: irresistible and fatal. In it, I forgot everything else, responsibilities, obligations. For what had I done? Neglected almost entirely the work I could have earned money by, or did it grudgingly in last-minute desperation. Instead, between the bouts of anxiety and guilt that affected me, for I knew how foolishly I was behaving even though I seemed incapable of doing otherwise, I indulged myself. I worked long and hard hours to solve the problems the chemical film set me and enjoyed doing so; but I ought to have been doing other things and knew it. And in between, for hours at a stretch, I played my fiddle. I had an orgy of fiddling such as I never had before or since.

And when I emerged, when the bank manager brought me to my senses, I knew I had been fortunate it had not been worse. I was out of work, our savings were gone; but at any rate I was not in debt. I was unemployed for two months and then found a job at the bench doing the kind of work Jimmy Sillitoe had kindly put in my way when I was on my own and

I had scorned almost in physical revulsion. I stayed in that job for the rest of my working life. I had learnt my lesson. I would kick against the pricks no more. I have never been a man to get much consolation by counting my blessings, but I realised I was lucky. I looked at my children and it struck me that over the years I had worried about them needlessly. Will was already a man, safe, reliable, earnest, putting in night after night at the Technical College with a doggedness I could only admire, working for his professional qualifications as an engineer and combining with them the external degree of London University. Phil had passed his matric with distinctions in maths and physics and English and was in the Sixth Form; university scholarships seemed, and in fact were, a certainty. And Tom, a bright, happy boy, popular wherever he went, with children and grown-ups alike, had won a free place at the Grammar School. I had at times fretted about the others: they had done so well, there seemed no reason at all to fret about Tom.

14

AT the General Election of 1924, George won the Central Division of the city for Labour. It was unbelievable, fabulous. We had been confident that we should poll more votes than ever before, but none of us had dared hope for victory. I was with George in the Town Hall while the count was taking place, the Town Hall strangely different from its usual appearance; emptied of chairs, the floor-space occupied by trestle-tables each of which was islanded, as it were, in a sea of intense activity and concentration, for each represented one of the dozen Parliamentary constituencies into which the city was divided. We stood, George, his agent, the Party officials and workers and myself, on one side of our table, a little withdrawn from it; on the other side were our opposite numbers among the Tories. But they were nearer to the table; it was as though we felt diffident about coming too close, almost as though we hadn't the right to. And George and I stood a little apart from our own group. George, I could see, was bored and irritated by the procedure. 'We'd have done better to go to Boswell's, Billy,' he said. 'This is a waste of time; as for the atmosphere——' The atmosphere was choking: you could scarcely see as far as the other end of the hall for tobacco smoke; it caught at the throat and stung the eyes. But I did not want to be anywhere except where I was. Not that I was interested in the business of counting: the result was a foregone conclusion; after all, Central had been a safe Tory seat for thirty years, ever since the Liberal Unionists had split away from the Liberals. I was absorbed in the simple fascination of being behind the scenes. For me it had a dramatic quality, not the least part of which came from the realisation that, after a hard-fought campaign which had left us all feverish with tiredness, we were now willy nilly in a state of neutrality. There were our enemies, the Tories, on the other side of the table. I couldn't keep my eyes off them. It seemed to me like the interval between the rounds in a boxing match; the neutrality wasn't real; the relaxation of both sides was just a pose; beneath our appearance of casualness we were all waiting for the bell.

In particular, I couldn't keep my eyes off Sir Willis Edgar, the Tory candidate and former member. He reinforced this fantasy I had of being present at a prize-fight. He stood at the centre of his group, very much the happy warrior, joking with the sycophantic supporters who swarmed about him. He looked a jolly old sporting gentleman, with his port-wine face and his flourish of white moustache. He had changed into evening clothes for the occasion, which for some reason I construed as calculated insolence, and gleamed and flashed with white linen and diamond studs. Between his fingers he held an enormous cigar; he was, as I recall him now, almost a parody of a Tory M.P., a left-wing caricature of the wicked capitalist; and every so often he would glance in our direction and wave his cigar cheerily at George, a gesture I interpreted as a jovial 'You wait and see!' as from an amused and well-fed Giant to Jack. His every movement, his very look, proclaimed a man so sure of his own strength that he could afford to bear no malice, for all George had harried him hard during the campaign. George had been merciless, and now, as Sir Willis waved his cigar at him in expansive *bonhomie*, he nodded curtly.

I think it was I who first noticed the change in Sir Willis. Idly I remarked the Tory agent speaking to him urgently, and then I saw Sir Willis wheel round, all concern, to scan the table and the mounting piles of votes upon it. I saw him, as he bent forward, stick his cigar into his mouth, and had a sudden absurd impression of a very large pink baby having a comforter jammed between its gums. And then I realised what it was all about and I seized George's arm and said, 'George!' George stared and, 'My God!' he said, and then we were all alert, on both sides of the table, watching intently, for now the pile of Labour votes, which at the beginning had been so much smaller than the Tories', was steadily mounting. I glanced at George: he was very pale. 'My God, Billy,' he said, 'it's going to be close.' And still our pile mounted. We were catching up: there were now two Labour votes to every one of the Tories'.

'It doesn't mean anything,' George muttered; 'it's probably just St Barnabas Ward.' But though the ratio of votes shifted and sometimes, it seemed for ten minutes at a time, it was two Tory to one Labour, still there was the evidence before our eyes: our pile was growing more rapidly than theirs; and now, on both sides, we watched with all the concentration we could command, all, that is, except me. We were back in the ring, the bell had rung, the fight was on again; but involved as I was, I was still a spectator and fascinated though I was by the rising mounds of votes I was even more fascinated by Sir Willis. I saw that his cigar had gone out. I saw the inch and a half of ash at its tip slowly fall and settle like grey dust in the folds of his white waistcoat, and I saw that he did not even notice it. He was a jolly old sporting gentleman, a very large pink baby, no longer; he was as concerned as he'd ever been in his life, and his concern, I could have sworn, had fined him down, so that he did not even look the same man. He looked infinitely more dangerous, powerful and purposeful. There was no *bonhomie* in him now; and almost before the returning officer's assistant had stated the number of votes each candidate had polled he was shouting, 'A recount! I demand a recount!' He was very imperious indeed.

There were no less than three recounts, and in the end George was declared elected with a majority of 167 votes. We ought to have gone mad, and indeed in its report next morning the *Journal* suggested that we did, contrasting our unbridled hysteria with the decorum and grace with which the Tories accepted defeat. We, it alleged, howled Sir Willis down when he stepped forward to congratulate the victor. Well, we had no cause to love Sir Willis or his party, and it is true that one of our members did shout, 'Put that in your pipe and smoke it, Sir Willis!' But as I recall it, we were really very quiet indeed; we were so unprepared for what had happened that we did not know what to do about it. Afterwards, we enumerated all the things we ought to have done. We ought to have carried George shoulder-high from the Town Hall; we ought to have had a band to play 'See, the Conquering Hero Comes!'; we ought to have had a torchlight procession through the streets. But we had never anticipated the need for a band, and we simply hadn't the material for making torches, even if we had thought of doing so in time. We were, for the most part, dumb with surprise, and as far as we were capable of feeling at all what we felt was the solemnity of the occasion. It wasn't until the official proceedings were almost over that someone began to sing 'The Red Flag.' The *Journal's* reporter was very shocked by this and wrote that it 'heralded a black day for the city and for Britain.' He noted with pleasure that the Tories immediately countered with 'God Save the King' and succeeded in drowning us. And there I think he was right, for the truth is, a lot of us, myself certainly, were sometimes a bit embarrassed by the words of 'The Red Flag.' I noticed we often tended to sing the part about the martyrs' blood having dyed its every fold rather self-consciously, playing it down as it were, though we always let ourselves go when it came to the last lines:

> *Though cowards flinch and traitors sneer*
> *We'll keep the Red Flag flying here.*

We could sing that defiantly enough.

As a matter of fact, we were taken so much by surprise and were so unprepared—I don't speak for George, of course—that we had the feeling that something had gone wrong. We had no code of behaviour for the occasion; and I have felt that herein we reflected in little the Labour movement as a whole. We never thought we would get in and in a sense had luxuriated in being a minority. We knew exactly how to behave in opposition. If Sir Willis had won that election only by the majority that George did he would have done very badly and we would have had a moral victory. We were used to moral victories, which in some ways are nicer than real ones; at any rate they can set up an equally satisfying glow. If Sir Willis had won, we wouldn't have been nearly as embarrassed by that bit about the martyrs, for we'd have felt slightly martyrized ourselves, and our rendering of 'The Red Flag' would certainly have drowned the Tories' 'God Save the King'; and we'd have gone away from the Town Hall happy in the knowledge that the Day was coming nearer but had not yet come.

As I say, I do not speak for George. He would have dismissed our regrets for bands and torchlight processions as so much sentimental nonsense. He was perfectly in control of himself and the situation; and as I looked up at him standing at the

Lord Mayor's right hand on the balcony of the Town Hall I had the feeling that already he was removed from us, raised above us, become apart from us, in a more than merely physical sense. And even if we suspected something had gone wrong for us there was no doubt at all that something had gone wrong for Sir Willis. Our surprise was nothing compared to his. He made no pretence of taking defeat well. The result was a personal affront, and though we murmured in the crowd about his lack of magnanimity I must admit that I warmed towards him, seeing him for the first time as a human being. I felt I could suffer with him. He stood on the Lord Mayor's left, but a little apart and slightly turned away, as though wanting to have nothing to do with the whole affair. He held himself rigid, as though forcibly holding himself back from running away. A new cigar was stuck in his mouth: it no longer seemed to me like a baby's comforter but a bung tightly pressed down to bottle up the explosive fumes within. Remove it, I felt, and there would be immediate disintegration. In the end, of course, discipline and good breeding prevailed. He managed to remove his cigar from his mouth without disintegrating, managed to smile and second the vote of thanks to the returning officer, congratulate George and shake him by the hand. But I heard someone say in the crowd, 'Some poor bugger'll be having the sack in the morning,' and I must say I was glad not to be in Sir Willis's employ just then.

George's victory made him a national figure. He was more than ever in demand as a speaker on Labour platforms throughout the country. I saw him less and less. He still had his union job, but while Parliament was sitting he spent most of his time in London, where he shared a small flat with two other Labour M.P.s. It was only during the recesses that I saw much of him, and though I am sure he was unaware of any change in himself I could feel it. Curiously, it was not unlike the change that had taken place in Jimmy Sillitoe. George had gone into a world entirely different from any I had ever known, a story-book world. He did not think he had left me behind; indeed, he seemed to assume that he had taken me with him. There was no loss of intimacy or frankness between us; it was simply that a whole area of experience which daily he took more and more for granted was outside my ken. And curiously, his growing familiarity with it seemed to make it only the more remote for me. He talked of Jimmy and Ramsay and John and Arthur and Philip and Maggie and Davie and Harold, not with any ostentation, but as one of themselves, for so he was; but this did not make them any more real to me, and it made George less real. I discovered there was a gulf between the George I had known all my life and the George Thompson, M.P., that he had become. He was being shaped into a man I did not always recognise. At times I think he was conscious of this; and what he was becoming one half of him enjoyed enormously while the other half regarded with acute suspicion. He said to me, years later, 'The British ruling class never try to bribe one or buy one: they're simply terribly nice. They make a point of treating you as one of themselves, and it's a form of flattery almost impossible to resist.'

For one thing, he fell in love with the House of Commons. It would be accurate to say that it seduced him, for he had brought himself up partly on Carlyle and quite sincerely believed, till he got there, that its forms and traditions were so much flummery. In a sense, he believed this until the end: I remember—it was some years later, when he was no longer in the House—a young Labour M.P., maddened by the apparent futility of what we used to call the 'Talking Shop,' picked up the mace and ran out with it; George shook his head and said, 'It won't get him anywhere, but how I wish I'd had the guts to do it.' As it was, he found the forms and traditions, the atmosphere and history of the House, irresistible. I am sure the most thrilling moment of his life was when, after his maiden speech, he was stopped in the lobby and congratulated by L.G. and then by Winston; and the second most thrilling the first time the policeman on duty in Parliament Square recognised him and stopped the traffic so that he could cross the road.

Knowing George, I can understand all this. He was a man born to rule. He knew it as well as anyone; and when he went into the House of Commons it was as though he was at home at last. He was an immediate success, and I am sure he felt like a prince who comes into his own after long exile. For a few weeks, until the greater *débâcle* of 1931 obliterated the memory of it, he was the most hated man in the Labour movement and he had to give up everything he had lived for; but he was never corrupted or bribed or bought, as his enemies said. It wasn't like that at all. George did not budge from his ideas and principles an inch. He was a Socialist to the end.

But that is anticipating. Though he was at home straight away in the House of Commons he was dismayed by it. For one thing, he had not bargained for the fact that the House of Commons is a club. 'They're right, Billy,' he once told me, 'when they say it's the best club in Europe. And it's damned insidious, let me tell you.' He found that a man's political label was considerably less important in the Palace of Westminster than it was in the chamber; and he found that he liked some of his political opponents considerably more as human beings than he did many of his colleagues. He was very much on his guard in the House of Commons as a club. Yet, as I say, he was affected by it. He began to appreciate what are called the good things of life; he found he liked cigars and wine and whisky; he found he liked being waited on and the appurtenances of comfortable living. He'd not known these things before, and he treated them with caution. He felt rather guilty about them: he had always been austere almost to the point of puritanism. I admit it came as a shock to me when I first discovered this change, small as it was, in him. I had gone up to London on a day excursion and called on him at his flat. There was a bottle of whisky and a syphon in the living-room. It need not have been his at all; in fact I took it for granted it belonged to one of the other M.P.s who lived there. But George, tapping the top of the bottle, said, 'I've acquired a vice, Billy. I suppose I can't tempt you? . . . Then I won't have one, either.' He smiled rather ruefully. 'The bad habits one learns in the House of Commons,' he said. I have to admit that my mind immediately went back to the afternoon Rose and I had visited Jimmy Sillitoe in his new house, and I found the breach between George and myself, which neither of us had made, a little wider because of my knowledge that that bottle of whisky was his. Years afterwards, it seemed to me that in a curious way he was trying to confess to me; but I had been as impercipient as ever and behaved as though the whisky did not exist. I did notice, though, that when he was with Fanny at home there was no sign of whisky then. It was as though he had split into separate parts and was living two lives, that he was very carefully not allowing his right hand to know what his left was doing. And now, as I write this, I am more than ever convinced that that noon in the flat in Wilton Road, Pimlico, he was trying to confess or was pleading for understanding.

I suppose my censoriousness was obvious enough. I find it hateful to remember now. But though I said nothing I thought the more and whenever we met watched the more and, of course, as one does, found, or thought I found, what I watched for. I found, or thought I found, evidence not of self-indulgence exactly but of excessive tolerance of it. I remember his telling me, on one occasion, details of the private lives of two very famous trade union leaders who were also members of the Parliamentary Labour Party at the time. The details were of an almost classic conventionality; champagne suppers with actresses, week-ends at Brighton, that sort of thing. If they had been related to me about Sir Willis Edgar I would not have turned a hair. I wouldn't have been shocked even; it would have seemed to me just the behaviour to be expected of a member of the ruling class, the behaviour indulged in, as I knew, by many of the officers I had nursed during the war, officers I also knew from my own observation to be gentlemen not merely in a nominal sense. And George was not telling these stories maliciously or as idle gossip, but, rather, in wonder, as important facts about human behaviour that he had just discovered and that we must take into account. They horrified me; their conduct seemed to my conventional mind a black betrayal of the class they came from and represented; and George's attitude, which I took to be one almost of acquiescence, so little was there of moral disapproval in it, shocked me nearly as much. I was pretty sure that, only a very few years earlier, George would have been as outraged as I. I was hot and loud in my indignation against these men. 'And yet, Billy,' George said mildly, 'you must admit that it doesn't in the least affect the work they've done for the movement. Between ourselves, they're both coarse brutes; but that makes no difference to the fact that the dockers have every reason to be thankful they existed. Or does it?' I had to admit it did not; and for some reason felt saddened by the admission. And George, I feel now, was saddened by my stiff-necked righteousness. He said very quietly: 'You know, Billy, you and I have lived in a very small world.'

This conversation came back to my mind when we were talking a day or two before he died. He knew death was near. He said: 'I suppose if I had my time over again, as they say, I'd do exactly the same as I did. But you know, Billy, I sometimes think we may have been wrong, concentrating so much on the future instead of enjoying the present. There are so many good things, and sometimes I think enjoyment is one of those we missed. But you're a puritan: you won't agree.' I didn't then; but now I myself have only a few months more to live, I find I do. I recognise the smallness of the world I've lived in.

George's recognition of it, of course, was one of the changes the House of Commons wrought in him. Lagging behind him as I did, I feel now that I failed him. My stock responses, my black-and-white judgements, were no use to him. He had to find his own way; and if he was dismayed by the personal habits of men whom he had respected and admired for years he was also, I think, dismayed by the Parliamentary Labour Party itself and by its leaders. He was loyal and kept silent, even to me, as long as he could; when at last he burst out I felt behind his outpouring a pressure of disillusionment that could no longer be restrained.

It was the day the General Strike ended. I was eating my evening meal. We were all at home, and silent. What had we hoped for? Now, it is difficult even to remember; but then, it seemed as though everything was finished, the movement we had spent our lives in, shattered. The door-bell rang. I remember that Phil went to answer it, and I heard the gruff peremptory voice: 'Hallo, boy. Your father in?' And without waiting for an answer George walked in. He stood in the doorway, without speaking, his hands spread out in a gesture of hopelessness. Both Rose and I jumped up in alarm: his body seemed to sag, so that I expected him to topple over. He looked twenty years older than when I had last seen him, and his clothes were crumpled and creased, as though he had not taken them off for days; which was almost literally true, for he had lived throughout the strike at the local strike committee's headquarters, snatching his sleep and food as he could between meetings there and meetings in outlying towns. His eyes were red with weariness, and I noticed how tight the skin was over his high cheekbones. Fearing for him, I stepped forward to support his swaying body. But he waved me away. 'I'm all right, Billy. Don't worry'; and he slowly propelled himself into an armchair. 'Take no notice of me,' he said; 'your supper'll be getting cold, Billy. I'll be all right in a minute.'

I signed to the boys to leave the room, and Rose brought out the miniature bottle of brandy she kept in the house for emergencies. George ignored the glass she offered him and drained the brandy from the bottle. He shook his head, blinked, and looked round as though he had only that moment realised where he was. He smiled wanly. 'I was all in,' he said. Then he closed his eyes and I thought he was falling asleep. I pushed my plate aside, the meal half-finished; I could eat no more. I couldn't take my eyes off George. That's what a fugitive must look like, I thought; and the spectacle of George, of all people, defeated seemed finally to set the seal on my own apprehension of the defeat we had suffered.

But he wasn't asleep. He suddenly shook himself and opened his eyes with a start. 'Give me your pouch, Billy,' he said; 'I'm out of the stuff.' I passed him my tobacco pouch and he filled his pipe. He'd pulled himself together; he was master of himself again. 'No, Rose,' he said, anticipating her, 'I won't have anything to eat. But I'd love some tea when Billy has his. I'm all right now.'

I was still fearful for him. I thought he was like a man newly come round from a terrible beating. He drank his tea in huge gulps as though his thirst was unassuageable. And we were silent. I dreaded what he might say. But at last he heaved himself out of his chair and started to pace the room. He began to talk, at first as though thinking aloud and then more and more directly to me, but with many pauses between what he had to say.

'Baldwin will be generous. He knows he can afford to be.' He gave a short, bitter laugh. 'He's not a Churchill or a Birkenhead. But there'll never be a general strike again. He'll see to that. They'll bring in legislation right away. . . . Ah, well . . .' He swung round to me, and his voice was low. 'It's hell, Billy; and it's been hell from the very beginning. And do you know what the worst hell of all has been? *Knowing* that this would happen. Talking to the poor devils out there day after day, rallying them, keeping their spirits up, urging them on, assuring them of victory if only they'd stand firm; and *knowing* all the time they'd be let down. I don't see at this moment how I'll ever be able to look them in the face again. Because I knew, Billy; I knew from the start, and there was nothing I could do except keep my knowledge to myself and hope to God I might be wrong. . . .

'We're beaten, Billy, hopelessly, ignominiously beaten. We've caved in and we're crawling back, and we've left the miners to fight alone, to be finished off in the coal owners' own good time. But we weren't beaten by the Government; it wasn't Baldwin who stopped us, or Churchill with his *British Gazette*. I'll tell you who it was beat us, Billy. It was our own men, our leaders. Jimmy Thomas and Clynes and MacDonald. They were scared from the start. They never wanted the strike; they were terrified of the consequences before it began, terrified of the forces they were unleashing; and if they'd had the chance they'd have given in before this. They never wanted to win; and if we had won they wouldn't have known what next to do. But how could we win, with that lily-livered lot leading us? If it weren't tragic it would be ludicrous, Billy, it's been a farce from the word go, and God help me, I guessed it. I knew they hadn't got the guts to go through with it, and I had to pretend . . .'

He flung himself in the chair. 'What we do now, Billy, where we go from here, I cannot even begin to think. I feel we're bankrupt, that *I'm* bankrupt, morally, spiritually. It looks to me as though the sum total of all our endeavours has been to keep the Royal Enclosure at Ascot safe for Jimmy Thomas.'

We sat there together in a raw misery, I full of a deep pity for George, for the measure of his disillusionment had come home to me. We were silent mostly but sometimes he spoke. I remember he said: 'I suppose we'll go back to the House and it will be as though nothing had happened. We'll take up the play-acting at the point where we left off ten days ago, and nothing will be said on either side except by Baldwin, who will say there must be no bitterness . . .'

At half-past ten, Rose came in from the kitchen and said

timidly, 'George, don't you think Fanny will be wondering where you are and wondering about you?' And George got up slowly and said, 'Yes, I must go home, I suppose. Billy, be a good fellow and come part of the way with me.'

So we went out together and wandered the streets. We passed a fish-and-chip shop. The smell of frying fish and the tang of vinegar assailed the nostrils, and George stopped. 'What's the matter, George?' I asked. 'I've suddenly discovered how hungry I am,' he said. I was about to say that Fanny would soon have a meal ready for him when I realised that he didn't want to see Fanny, that he didn't want to go home. I did not pause then to wonder why. 'Why don't you have some fish and chips?' I said. 'Yes, I think I will,' he answered, but still he hesitated. 'It's pretty full, isn't it?' I saw what he meant. He couldn't bear the prospect of showing himself where he might be known: the defeat of the strike was a bitter personal shame to him, a humiliation. 'It won't take long to get them,' I said, and I went into the shop and bought two fours of fish and two fours of chips; and we strolled the streets eating them from the grease-stained paper bags.

I don't know how far we walked that night. Nowhere in particular and always in the direction of George's but always veering off, taking another road, as we approached his house, without either of us saying a word to the other about why we were doing so. We spoke scarcely at all, but I felt very close to him. I heard a church clock strike, and it was half-past eleven. I said: 'George, I think you ought to go in now'; and he replied: 'I don't want to, Billy; but you're right. I must go in now.' I asked him if he'd like me to come in with him but he shook his head. 'Just walk with me as far as the front door,' he said; and then, as he put his key into the lock he said, 'Bless you, Billy.'

I told Rose nothing of this. I thought I had better not, for when I got home I found her angry with her brother, who normally could do no wrong in her eyes, and disturbed by his behaviour. 'It was very wrong of George,' she said; 'wrong and thoughtless. What did he come here for? He ought to have gone straight home to Fanny.' And when I tried to defend him she said: 'He's a married man. He should have gone to his wife first. That's what a wife's for.' Even then, I did not draw the obvious conclusions; I was blind to the nature of Rose's anxiety for her brother and privately thought she was making a lot of fuss about nothing. It did not strike me that George's behaviour indicated alienation from Fanny. I am afraid it seemed to me the most natural thing in the world, we had been so close to each other for so many years. Besides, I had never had much regard for Fanny; she had always seemed to me a silly and unserious person; but in this there may well have been an element of the unadmitted jealousy that I think men often feel towards the wives of their old friends.

Well, normality of a kind returned. It was almost as though the General Strike had not taken place. George was right: bygones were to be bygones; that was the official line on both sides. The Labour leaders lapsed happily into their old routine. It was said there was a new spirit abroad in industry, a spirit of co-operation between capital and labour. I remember that Lord Melchett and Ben Turner were prime movers in this; and it was at this time that Jimmy Sillitoe came into his own as the evangelist of industrial co-operation, the converted Socialist who had retained all his old ideals but discovered they could be better realised under capitalism. It was the Baldwin age, and very nice too so long as one did not remember the miners who had been left to rot. The trouble was, one could not fail to remember them, and the shame of it bit deep into us.

George had no illusions. 'A new spirit in industry my arse,' he said; 'nothing in that a small slump won't cure.' After that night, he had not referred to the Strike again. He too had gone back to his routine. He had made his mark in the House; at the election of 1929 he increased his majority—and that time, forewarned, we'd ordered the band well in advance; and when MacDonald formed his Government George was made a junior Minister. This meant that he had to be almost continually in London and on his increase in salary as a junior Minister he was able to move out of the rooms in Wilton Road he had shared with two other Members and take tiny quarters for himself in a block of flats that had just been built near Russell Square in Bloomsbury.

Innocence such as mine seems to me a discreditable quality in its possessor, for it consists largely of the faculty of being blind to what one does not wish to see. One Saturday in

February, 1930, I took the morning off from work and went to London on the football special; the City was playing Arsenal. Not that I was especially interested in that; my destination was elsewhere. I had suddenly awakened to an interest in paintings. It was not new, but it had taken a new turn. Up to this time, the only paintings I had looked at with real pleasure were those of the English water-colour school; partly because I was constantly trying to paint water-colours myself, much after the manner of David Cox, who for years had been my ideal, and partly because I had had practically no opportunity of seeing anything else, except the work of Victorian academicians, of which the local gallery contained numerous examples. I had thought for years that the great Italian art of the Renaissance meant nothing to me. The most accurate way I can express this feeling will sound silly: I had a sneaking belief that it wasn't for the likes of me, and so I had shied away from it, always ready, of course, to raise my hat in respect to it but honestly believing that what had been painted four or five centuries ago for princes and popes and doges could not have anything to say to me. In a way, I think I kept it deliberately at arm's length, out of a perverse pride.

I was shaken out of this timidity and inertia, for both were involved, by Phil. This was happening more and more. Phil was now a research student at Cambridge. For some years, he had been talking to me as though he were the father and I the son, or at least as though he were the master and I the pupil. He delighted and amazed me. I felt that I had done less with my life than I might have done because I had dissipated my energies and interests over too scattered a field, and I feared for a time that Phil might repeat my failing. I was wrong: he had known from the beginning what he wanted to do and gone straight for it, and yet at the same time he had kept a questing mind. Physics was his base, but from it he made, as it were, darting sallies of exploration, forays into other and one would have thought alien territories; and he would return full of joy in the trophies he had secured. And he wanted to share them with me. 'Look, you must read this,' he'd say, pushing a book that had excited him into my hand; 'it's good. You mustn't miss it.' And when I feebly protested that I hadn't the background, the equipment, to appreciate his new poet, that

I didn't know enough, he would brush my protests aside impatiently and say, 'Look, it's simple. You're making difficulties where none exist. It's like this'; and there'd follow a lecture on the elements of prosody, perhaps, or simply on what I was not to look for in the writer he was urging me to read. Generally I resisted his enthusiasms, for more than half the time I was right: I did lack the background and the equipment to understand them; and besides, I had my own interests and not enough time to follow them. All the same, I was over-joyed by his eagerness to make me a partner in his discoveries and was influenced by him more than I realised. In his own way he had become in my late middle age what George had been to me in my youth.

For many of my pursuits he had a good-natured scorn. He had come back from Italy mad about what he had seen there and turned the full blast of his enthusiasm on to me. He told me I had never seen painting, real painting, and when I ventured mildly to say something about Girtin and Cotman and Cox he broke in with, 'Look, dad'—as with George, almost every sentence he uttered seemed to begin with 'Look' —'the English water-colour school is all right. I say nothing against it. But don't you see, it's just an eddy in a backwater. It's miles from the main stream, it's parish pump stuff. It just doesn't exist by comparison with the real thing. Don't be such a stick-in-the-mud. You talk of Girtin: go and have a look at Titian for a change. Go and look!' And, as often, I retired ruffled. Did he think he was telling me anything I didn't know? But then, when he was safely back in Cambridge, it began to dawn on me that I was a stick-in-the-mud and that my ignorance was wilful ignorance. Why didn't I go and look at Titian?

The next time the City played in London I went, too. Of course I did not tell Phil: I was going to surprise him later, with a casual remark about Titian or Botticelli dropped into the conversation. When the train reached Watford I ate my luncheon sandwiches and from Euston I went straight to the National Gallery, stayed there until it closed, and was as enthusiastic as Phil could have wished. Then, outside, at a loose end among the pigeons and postcard sellers in Trafalgar Square, it came into my mind to call on George in his new flat. I had not, in fact, any great hopes of finding him in, for at week-ends he was in great demand as a speaker at Party meetings in the country. But that did not matter: I was killing time, for my train did not leave Euston until half-past eleven. So, even if I had belonged to the generation that uses the telephone as a matter of course (and I am of an age and class that uses it as little as possible, thinking it a dangerous instrument to be reserved only for the gravest emergencies), I would not have done so. Though I naturally hoped to see George it did not in any real sense matter whether I did or not. I strolled along the Charing Cross Road with the whole evening before me, and when I reached Oxford Street, greatly daring I went into the Corner House and had egg-and-chips and a pot of tea. So at my leisure I found my way to Russell Square.

When I saw the block of flats in which George lived, with its several entrances and swing-doors at the head of flights of steps, I very nearly turned away. All my old reflexes at the sight of what I assumed to be wealth and luxury asserted themselves. My first impulse was to think it much too grand for me. But what nonsense that was, I reflected. If a Labour M.P. lived there a constituent could visit him, and how much more so when that Labour M.P. was George. So in I went, to be abashed by the red carpet, by the aquarium of tropical fish set in the wall, above all by the flunkey reading a newspaper behind a counter in his cubby-hole. He did not bother to look up as I entered. I had never been in a block of flats like this before and was in two minds what to do. I felt I had to declare myself to the flunkey, so I went to the counter and said, 'Is Mr George Thompson, M.P., in?' Without lifting his eyes from his paper he said, 'No. 189, fifth floor. Lift straight ahead.' But I did not trust myself to that lift; I saw that it was automatic and I was not sure I'd know how to work it and I certainly did not intend making an exhibition of myself before that flunkey. So I climbed the five red-carpeted flights of stairs.

It was all new to me, and I walked along the corridor in some surprise. There were cooking smells and the sounds of wireless sets, but somehow these seemed irrelevant. Those wireless sets seemed scarcely to disturb the silence. I couldn't hear the fall of my feet; it was as though the radios played on in an empty, lifeless world; and what principally struck me as

I passed blank door confronting blank door was the faceless anonymity of it all. I might, I thought, have been wandering through the corridors of a deserted liner, but a liner infinitely more modern than those I had sailed on. I could not associate George, or anything connected with my life, with it at all.

I came to No. 189 and pressed the bell. As I waited, I caught the smell of cooking behind the door; and then it was opened by a young woman wearing a small apron over a dress that even I could see was elegant. We backed away from each other in mutual astonishment. I looked wildly at the number on the door; I couldn't understand it. 'I think I must have come to the wrong flat,' I said; 'I'm looking for Mr George Thompson's.' 'This is Mr Thompson's,' the young woman answered. 'He's out at the moment, but he won't be long. I thought you were he. Won't you come in?' She smiled down at me, and I realised she was beautiful and a lady.

I smiled foolishly back at her. 'It doesn't matter,' I said. 'If George isn't in . . .' To tell the truth, I scarcely knew what I was saying.

'Oh, but you must,' she said. 'You're one of his constituents, aren't you?' I nodded: my accent had told her that. 'Then you certainly can't go away without seeing George. He'd be very cross with me if I let you.' And she smiled again, so sweetly, that willy nilly I had to enter.

George's flat was tiny; a miracle of compactness, it seemed to me. It consisted of a single room, mainly taken up by a divan, a desk, bookshelves, an armchair and an office chair at the desk; together with a very small bathroom and an equally small kitchen. I noticed the fur coat thrown on the divan. I noticed, too, the half-typed sheet of paper in the typewriter on the desk, the pile of typescript sheets beside it, and the open books that lay about on all sides.

'Do sit down. George won't be long. He's just gone round the corner to do some last-minute shopping.'

I was sure in my bones that I ought to go, but I seemed powerless to move. I had lost my bearings completely. It was as though a spell had been cast upon me, and all I could do was to wait for George to return and restore me to sanity by the very fact of his being there. It was not just the suddenness and unexpectedness of the circumstances I found myself in: it was partly to do with the physical presence of the young woman. I realised that I was staring at her fascinatedly and, as I turned my eyes away in embarrassed consciousness of my rudeness, I felt my cheeks burning. I knew with complete certainty that she was the most beautiful woman I had ever seen and I felt with just as much certainty that her beauty of face and body reflected a beauty of mind no less great. In that moment of apprehension, as I sat in George's armchair feeling foolish, I was a Platonist without reservation.

I said: 'I've spent the afternoon in the National Gallery.'

'Have you?' she said, very seriously. Equally seriously, I said, 'Yes.' I have often blushed for shame to think how silly she must have thought me and my halting conversation; it must have seemed to her exactly like a small child's who doesn't know what to say and says the first thing that comes into its head. In fact, I was acknowledging a miracle. But how was she to know? What I meant by my pompous remark was that, having steeped myself that afternoon in Titian and Botticelli, I had stepped into the abandoned hulk of a luxury liner and discovered in the flesh a beauty that seemed to sum up and symbolise all the beauty that had exploded on my astonished eyes in the National Gallery. No wonder I was lost and spellbound, and I think it was because her beauty was such, or perhaps merely because my sensibility, after its exposure to great art that afternoon, transmuted her beauty into something, as it were, ideal and abstract, that I failed to draw the conclusion from her presence in George's flat which would have been plain to anyone else.

I said: 'I've not been to this flat before.'

She said: 'It's very cramped, isn't it? There really isn't room to swing a cat, even if one wanted to.'

I said: 'You must meet everybody, being George's secretary.'

She nodded. 'And very boring some of them are, too.' And then, indicating the typewriter and the pile of typing beside it, 'That's George's speech for Burnley tomorrow night.'

'Ah, Burnley.' I knew about Burnley. There was to be a great meeting, with Oswald Mosley and George as the principal speakers.

The bell rang. 'That will be George.' She jumped up quickly. 'I'll tell him you're here.'

She ran out of the room and I waited. There was a mutter of talk behind the door, and then George came in, the young woman following him. 'Good God, it's you, Billy! What are you doing here?'

'The City's playing Arsenal. I came up on the football special,' I said.

'And went to the National Gallery instead of Highbury,' the young woman added.

'That reminds me,' George said. 'Have you introduced yourselves? Sally, this is Billy Ashted, my oldest friend. Billy, this is Mrs Strode.' We shook hands. Mrs Strode—the name conveyed nothing to me—picked up her fur from the divan. 'It's too bad, Mr Ashted,' she said; 'but I'm afraid it must be good-bye as well. George took so long over his shopping I'm a bit late.'

George took her to the door of the flat. There was again a mutter of talk. Then he returned. 'Have something to eat with me, Billy. Sally was kind enough to cook me a meal, and I dare say there's enough for two.' So I had a second meal that evening, and very good it was even if I didn't quite know what I was eating, for it was cooking of a kind I had not met since I had visited the little Italian and Greek restaurants in New York.

I do not recall what George said that evening. He was vigorous and decisive as ever but, I felt, preoccupied with something outside our conversation. I taxed him with this, and he said that tomorrow's meeting at Burnley was very much on his mind, and explained why. He had to speak before Mosley, who was in the Cabinet, and introduce him, but he did not see eye to eye with him. 'He's the best speaker we've got; as an orator he's first rate. And he's ambitious. He wants to be P.M. and one of these days he probably will be. But more and more, Billy, I trust him less and less, and the nature of his appeal. He's an aristocrat, and the fact is, Billy, the Movement will eat out of the hand of any aristocrat who comes along, especially if he's as brilliant as Mosley. But somehow, *I* think he's out of place among us. God knows I've admired him as much as anyone; and in a way I still do. All the same, I'm going to be damn careful what I say in my speech. I'm still not happy about parts of it.'

So I left early, walked to Euston and sat in the train for an hour before it departed. The City had beaten Arsenal; the train was crowded and noisy and drunken. The man sitting opposite to me pressed his open bottle of beer on me, and though I hate the stuff, for the sake of peace I took a swig of it. I was very happy. It had been a rich day. I had spent the greater part of the evening with George, and that had become a rare thing. I had seen the Botticellis and Titians in the National Gallery and I had met Mrs Strode, who was part of their beauty and glory. And soon I dozed, and I slept until the train came into the station.

I have thought since that it is significant I never mentioned Mrs Strode to Rose. Rose was full of sisterly concern for George; it seemed to her terrible that he had to live by himself in a flat, and despite all my assurances, she held to the working-class belief that flats were not really proper places to live in. How could he eat regularly, with no one to look after him? She was convinced that he must live entirely on sandwiches. And his socks were bound to be in holes! She fretted about George and was indignant with Fanny because she spent so little time in London with him. But I knew knowledge of the existence of Mrs Strode would not console her. On the contrary, she would have been very alarmed indeed. She would have been scandalised by the situation: a married woman, young and beautiful into the bargain, visiting a married man in his flat and cooking meals for him. She would not, since it was George, have read more into it, but in itself it would have been sufficiently horrifying. She would have believed George in danger from his thoughtlessness. I have never, in fact, let on to anyone that I've met Mrs Strode; and there was another reason for my not mentioning her to Rose. Rose would have felt bound to censure her; and I wanted to keep Mrs Strode unspotted, as it were, by the world's calumny, even Rose's. For I am afraid my own first impulse was to take what I knew would be Rose's view of the situation. It had shocked me, until I had second thoughts and persuaded myself that George was now living in a larger world governed by different and more liberal conventions than those that ruled in ours. But I knew very well what the enormous majority of his constituents would think. That I repudiated utterly, but to do so I had to fashion

Mrs Strode in my mind into an angel of beauty and light. I was helped in this because I have never been able to equate beauty with wickedness or even ordinary human failings; irrational as it is, I have always felt that physical beauty was a promise of moral goodness. And when I have found this not so I have felt that beauty conferred upon its possessor rights denied to the rest of us; which I see is not a very moral attitude.

But though I no more forgot Mrs Strode than the Botticellis and Titians of the National Gallery, I was able to put any misgivings I might have about her and George out of my mind. There were no further developments that I was aware of, and besides, surprising things were happening in the Labour Movement. Mosley broke away from the Party, and a handful of Labour M.P.s followed him. George, needless to say, was not among them. He was just as much disheartened by the Labour Government's failure to cope with the depression and mounting unemployment as Mosley and his followers, but, as he said to me, 'Mosley has no policy either.' Indeed, George saw and denounced the Fascism implicit in the New Party, as Mosley's organisation was at first called, long before Mosley's deluded but honest supporters realised it. But of them George said: 'In politics, intellectuals are nearly always innocents.' George was one of Mosley's most vigorous opponents. I remember a meeting of the New Party we went to in the Town Hall, a meeting that George took charge of. That meeting terrified me; not physically but for what it foreshadowed. I think it disturbed even George. It was the first meeting at which Mosley appeared as the Fascist leader, even if only tentatively. Of course I am being wise after the event. At that time, Fascism was still something foreign, almost funny. We were scarcely aware of Hitler, and there had been no Abyssinian War. Even so, we were consternated by the number and array of stewards. I had been to a great many political meetings in my life and this was the first at which I had sensed physical violence as a possibility, at least since Boer War days. Mosley had very few sympathisers there that evening, apart from the stewards, and there were not nearly enough of them to intimidate us. We sat in the middle of the hall, a solid block of Labour men from the Central Division, probably three hundred of us; and there were a dozen other solid blocks of Labour men from other constituencies on the floor and in the galleries. Mosley was greeted from the beginning as someone who had deserted the Movement; and superb orator as he was, he could scarcely be heard for the first fifteen minutes. It was then the stewards began to get ugly. I was frightened not of them but for them; I thought that if they did translate their menaces into action they might very well be seriously hurt. I foresaw some unpleasant rough stuff. Mosley stood on the platform, with the microphone in front of him. There were cries of 'Sit down!' and people began to sing 'Tell me the old old story!' The audience was still fairly good-tempered, but I felt that it needed only a blow, perhaps only a word, for the mood to change entirely.

Then without warning, George, who was sitting next to me, rose and climbed on his seat. He held his hands high above his head for silence. For a moment there was indeed silence; and then cheering broke out from all parts of the hall and cries of 'Good old George!' and 'Speech!' and 'You go on the platform, George!' George went on holding his hands high above his head, and there was silence again. 'Comrades,' George said, 'I've come to hear Mosley. You've come to hear Mosley. We've all come to hear Mosley. He's going to tell us what his policy is; he's going to tell us how he'll cure unemployment. That's something that interests me very much, and it'll interest you very much. Comrades, let's keep the questions till afterwards; Mosley will answer them if he can. But first, let's hear what he's got to say.' More cheering; and George, waving a hand to Sir Oswald as though inviting him to continue, jumped down.

After that, Mosley was listened to with attention; but no sooner was his speech ended than there were cries for George again; and once more he climbed on his seat and spoke, but this time at length. And when the meeting was over, and Mosley's supporters escorted him back to his hotel, we gathered round George outside the Town Hall, and then he spoke for Socialism and the principles of the Party with a passion I had not heard him equal before.

It was George's greatest triumph. He was acclaimed that night as few men have ever been in the Town Hall. He had emerged as the champion of the Labour Party. I am sure that by his action he had prevented an ugly situation which would have involved bloodshed. But it did him no good and perhaps even harm; for he had at a single blow made two sets of enemies who from then on were out to get him: the Fascists because he had exposed them as Fascists, and the Communists, because he had thwarted them in their deliberate intention of provoking Mosley. Thereafter, the Communists talked and wrote of George as though he were a black traitor to the Labour Movement.

It was also George's last triumph. A week later, it was in all the papers: George had been named as co-respondent in a divorce action for adultery brought by Francis Strode, M.P., against his wife, the Hon. Sarah Strode. The case is forgotten now, as Strode and George are; but at the time it seemed part and parcel almost of the break-up of the Labour Party itself, symptomatic of a general disruption. George's position was such that all sides could make him the target of their hate. The case aroused strong class feelings. Francis Strode was a Tory member, Sarah the daughter of a Tory peer: I am sure that for thousands of the upper-class the case made George a symbolic figure of social revolution at its most calamitous. All their fear of the lower orders, the mob as they called it, was projected on to George. It was a fear akin to that felt by the white rulers of coloured communities: George had dared to sleep with Sarah; it was a warning that in future none of their wives and daughters could be regarded as safe. George was emblematic of unnatural presumption, like the Negroes who were lynched in the southern United States for being disrespectful to white women.

Working-class attitudes to George's behaviour would at any time have been divided. Intense disapproval from the respectable and the religious could be safely predicted, and amused tolerance from the rest. But the latter, I think, were not often in those days supporters of Labour. In any case, working-class attitudes were complicated by the feelings aroused by the split in the Labour Party. MacDonald, Snowden and Thomas had joined Baldwin and the Tories to form the National Government. Good Socialists considered them renegades. George, of course, had remained in the Labour Party, but Fascists and Communists joined together to make their mischief. If it proved nothing else, and whether he was guilty or not, the

Strode divorce action revealed that George had been intimate with the enemy, with the upper class. It was a time of great suspicion, when faithful Labour supporters were bewildered by the fact that many whom they had most intensely admired seemed traitors in the end; so that, at that period of divided loyalties and passionate partisanship, it was difficult even for the thoughtful not to see George as somehow guilty by association; while for the thoughtless, led astray by the smear campaign against him organised by the Fascists and Communists, George was just another old Labour stalwart who had ratted to the Tories or been bought by them. And the curious thing was, not even the most detailed record of George's service to the Movement, not even the simple demonstrable fact that he was still a Labour member accepting Lansbury's leadership, could dissuade them from their insane conviction, as it appeared to me.

All the same, I think it possible to make too much of the special circumstances of the time. Twenty years ago, an M.P. who figured in a divorce case placed himself in a very vulnerable position; it would have been incredible then that we should ever have a prime minister who had been the guilty party in a divorce action. And a Labour M.P. in a divorce case was even more vulnerable than a Tory. Then the very facts of the case were against George. 'Dirty old man' was the phrase commonly applied to him, and I suppose it was inevitable. It came out in court that when he first met Sarah he was just twice her age: for some reason, the elderly lover always appears simultaneously a vicious seducer and a figure of fun. And all along there was this question of loyalties to bedevil public opinion. It often seemed to me that in the eyes of the world George's real crime was not that he had committed adultery but that he, a Labour M.P., had committed adultery with the wife of a Tory M.P. If Sarah had been a Labour member's wife, I got the impression that it would not have seemed so bad. Sarah herself unwittingly reinforced this impression. She was in love with George and gloried in it; she was defiant and unrepentant; and she not only declared herself a Socialist but claimed that she had been a Socialist before she met George, that it was through her Socialism, indeed, that she had first met him. This, I don't know why, nobody believed;

so George was guilty of two crimes, of seducing another man's wife and, further, of seducing her from her true allegiance, which, Tories and Socialists alike seemed to agree, ought to be to her husband's beliefs.

George was as dignified as any man could be in the position in which he found himself. He bore the ordeal of the scandal and the trial stoically. Where he acted wrongly was to insist on fighting the Central Division at the 1931 election. He had failed to get the Labour nomination for the seat and he had been forced by public opinion to resign from his trade union office. These were injustices he could not accept, and he insisted, against everyone's advice, on fighting Central as Labour Independent. One knows now that George could not have held the seat even if he had been the official candidate and with his reputation unblemished. It was not possible in 1931. As it was, the only issue he could fight the election on was the personal injustice he had suffered, for he made it plain that, if elected, he would support Lansbury's party and vote for its policies. He never realised, I think because he was himself so much a rationalist, the strength of feeling against him. He could not understand how it was that the foundry-workers of the St Barnabas Ward, for instance, had turned against him. Indeed, he would not believe that they had until the night of the poll, when he came at the bottom, with less than six hundred votes, and forfeited his deposit.

I was with him when the poll was declared: I had acted as his election agent because there was no one else to do so. I remember how ashen his face was, and how for a moment he flinched when the announcement of his total of votes was greeted with laughter and jeers and boos. But the drawing back was momentary, and the rest of the proceedings, the speeches, the congratulations, the vote of thanks to the returning officer, he endured in calm dignity.

That night we paced the streets again, as we had done after the failure of the General Strike. We walked in silence. What was there to say? That night, too, I realised a general truth about human nature: that the least secure of all men is he who is the cynosure of all eyes or the crowd's darling. Let him once but slip and the crowd that has applauded him will push him down, almost as if in glee. The greater his distinction, the loftier his eminence, the greater the rejoicing with which it will greet his fall. It is as though the crowd, the mass of men, 'the public,' hates eminence and turns on it in vindictive fury as soon as it betrays the slightest sign of weakness, as soon as circumstances compromise its commanding position.

George bore the whole wretched sequence of events with what seemed to me an iron self-discipline. He had lost the job he had held for a lifetime; he had been expelled from the Party. He was forced, through sheer economic necessity, to accept a job as adviser on labour relations to the employers' organisation; and then he did in fact seem a traitor. His former enemies proved more generous to him than his friends. But what hurt him the most, what for him was the final and most tragic irony of all, was the fact that, in spite of Sarah's divorce, he was still not free to marry her. And here I must recount Fanny's extraordinary behaviour. He begged her to divorce him, but she refused, telling him, as she delighted in telling the whole world, that there was no need, that she had already forgiven him so far as forgiveness was called for, but that mere physical fidelity in a marriage such as theirs was a minor matter. She was perfectly willing, she added, to share him with Sarah. What especial virtue was there in the possession of a wedding ring? A man's sexual relations were a private matter. So George found himself imprisoned in the bonds of his wife's emancipation. Fanny was a deeply sadistic woman.

I see George's fall as truly tragic. I watched it with a kind of terror. It shook my life as nothing had done before. I couldn't pass judgment. I quarrelled with brother Horace about it. Horace had never liked George, and in what happened to him saw the hand of a just and chastening God. Horace was not naturally a mean-minded man, but in George's fate he observed a wonderful example for the wicked times. I had to tell him I did not care a straw for his God or for moral examples but that if he wished to live in peace and harmony with me he must never speak of George in such terms again. I lived during those weeks of the trial and the general election in a grim anger; I was ready to cut out of my life anyone who in my hearing spoke of George disrespectfully. Rose was hurt and saddened by his behaviour. She knew he had done very wrongly. She forgave him because he was her brother and she loved him. But she could not understand how he had come to act as he did, and I am afraid that all her life afterwards Sarah Strode was the Scarlet Woman. She never dared utter her name: but when she mentioned 'that woman' I knew whom she meant.

And did I understand the inner nature of George's behaviour? I don't know. I suppose if it had not been George who was involved in what came to be known as the Strode case but any other Labour Member, I would probably have felt about him as the rest of the world did. I was uncomfortably conscious of this at the time; and ever since I have been on guard against feelings of moral indignation in myself. I almost think now that moral indignation is the most suspect and most worthless of all emotions. But George's conduct certainly cut right across the notions of the moral life both of us had inherited from our particular section of the working-class, which was that section which had been influenced by evangelical or dissenting religion. I say 'our notions of the moral life': the passionate condemnation accorded to George's behaviour by members of his class showed me, as I had not realised before, that we had equated our notions of the moral life almost exclusively with sexual morality. I am sure that when we recited the Lord's Prayer and said 'Lead us not into temptation,' we should all of us, if challenged, have construed temptation automatically in sexual terms. For late Victorians like myself, sin meant sex. George had violated the great tabu, and it was more powerful in our class than in any other.

And now I scarcely know what I feel about the subject. In this I remain inescapably of my generation: I cannot help myself. I am not aware that I was ever tempted as George was. I have been to W.E.A. courses in psychology and dipped into the works of Professor Freud: I have not been able to recognise myself, my own nature, in his pages. I know what the Freudians will say to this and I am not denying they may be right. I have not been conscious of repression as a fact in my own life; or it may be that I have a natural talent for sublimation; I can see that the way Mrs Strode became transformed in my imagination, became a work of art, as it were, which was characteristic of how my mind worked, may have been sexual in origin. As I say, I scarcely know what I feel about the subject, except—and here the Freudians will pounce—that contemplation of it has always made me uncomfortable. It was something not to be thought about, or to be put as much out of mind as possible. It does seem to me strange now to recollect that in all our years of intimacy George and I never discussed sex, at any rate never discussed it as something we ourselves possessed and were involved in.

I suppose we should have said we took it for granted. What we took for granted was the silence enshrouding it. This silence seemed right to us. Thus, I could never have brought myself to speculate on the precise nature of George's life with Fanny, though I see now it is fundamental to any assessment of his relation with Mrs Strode. It would have seemed improper to me, indecent, and lacking in respect to George. The hell that must have been his life with Fanny is now glaringly plain to me, and it must have been to all of us; but we suppressed our awareness of it and pretended it did not exist. My guess is that George, until he met Mrs Strode, did the same. For these were things that were not admitted; we did not permit ourselves to make comparisons in the realm of sexual emotion and behaviour. We allowed ourselves to remain in ignorance, in ignorance about ourselves and others.

I am tempted to say that we were conditioned by our ignorance. But of course, we were not ignorant in any real sense. There was just as much sexual licence in the world then as there is now, and we were aware of it, very painfully. We were not ignorant; we were respectable, a very different thing. The sexual licence did not occur among the respectable. That was almost a definition of the respectable. The lives of the respectable, some might say, were governed by negatives: the respectable did not drink, they did not fornicate or commit adultery, they did not break the Sabbath. And so on. Now I have too much regard for the motives that prompted us to respectability to sneer at it; but respectability is always on the verge of becoming Podsnappery. Its besetting sin is hypocrisy, the pretence that one is other and better than one is. And it strikes me at this moment of writing that one reason for the indignation felt at George's behaviour, indignation on the part of those who, one might think, had not the right to feel indignant, the majority of George's foundry-workers, for example, who were certainly not respectable in our sense of the word, was disgust at what seemed to them hypocrisy unmasked. When hypocrisy is uncovered we can all be glad. George was exposed as no better than they, who had never pretended to be better than they were.

We assumed an ignorance of sex we did not in truth possess because of our extreme fear of its power. It was as though we had all joined in a conspiracy to believe that some things, some modes of behaviour, were unthinkable. And I still think that for us respectable people this did provide a safeguard—up to a point. It worked so long as the *status quo* remained unchanged. I believe if George had not been elected to Parliament but had stayed all his life at home, he would have remained faithful to Fanny; partly, of course, because it would have been much less easy to be unfaithful. In fact, I believe the notion of infidelity would not have entered his head. I say I was never tempted as George was. My married life was immeasurably more happy than his; but apart from this, the course of my life was such that I was never placed in circumstances in which that kind of temptation could easily occur. Opportunity, as the proverb says, is a fine thing. I say that not cynically but as a statement of simple fact. Thinking of George's fall, if that is the word, I have often contemplated the old phrase about the straight and narrow path and thought how fortunate a man is whose life has been cast in such an easy course. Once off the beaten track, what may not a man have to negotiate in the way of sloughs and thickets and blank walls? If he comes through unscathed he is lucky indeed. Yet the implications of such a view are horrifying; they exalt the blinkered man and make routine and rut the paths to virtue; and that I cannot accept.

Between ourselves, I now believe we set too much store on a rigid sexual morality. And there is a paradox, too. The price George had to pay for breaking the conventions was altogether too great. It was absurdly high, and I mean 'absurdly' literally, for though one cannot say the rest of his life was wasted yet his great capacities were certainly not used to the full. He enjoyed his work as a magistrate and committee man, but it was an anticlimax all the same. At times he must have resented it. Yet in the last days of his life, when he was lying in his bed waiting for death and casting, I suppose, the account of his life, as now I am doing mine, it was to Mrs Strode that his mind returned all the time. At the end, he regretted nothing. 'If it had to be as it was, Billy,' he said; 'if those were the conditions of the whole thing, then I wouldn't have had them otherwise. It was the most wonderful thing that ever happened to me. Nothing that happened before it had half its reality. With Sally I lived on an entirely different plane of being; and I have existed on the memory of it ever since.'

I record what George told me as I remember it. It was something right outside my own experience, as much so as if it had been a mystical experience. I realise that, compared with George's, my emotional life had been placid and tranquil, not passionate and intense. George believed that he had been changed by his. I accept the fact of the experience for him as I do that of the mystics.

George told me how he had met Mrs Strode. She had spoken to him after a lecture he had given at the Fabian Society. He didn't know who she was; she was Miss Hemingway—her maiden name—to him until they had discovered they were in love with each other. It was only then she told him her real identity, that she was Francis Strode's wife. 'It was at that point that I suppose I behaved wrongly. I ought—but you see, Billy, there were things that outweighed that "ought." I was frightened, I don't mind admitting it; but when I analysed my fear I found it wasn't consideration of right or wrong that held me back but only a superstitious regard for the conventions, the fear of scandal, in other words. I didn't act lightly. Both of us knew that, in the public gaze, we would seem, I especially, to have behaved shabbily: but we did not admit that our behaviour was any concern of the public's; the shabbiness, we believed, was not in us. And perhaps I believed this the more easily because I knew Strode. He was not a man I had any use for, and his own morals were not, I'd have thought, such as to have allowed him to cast stones at anyone else. But I'll say nothing of that. I don't defend my behaviour. These affairs always appear indefensible anyway, because we assume, falsely, that the public aspects of them are more important than the private. I very well understand what a cad I must have appeared in the court. In the court, I could scarcely realise it was me counsel and judge were talking about. I could have assured them it was nothing like that at all.

'But what's the use of brooding on that side of it? Even if it were truly as they claimed it was, even if I were convinced that I was a sinner, I should still have to set against all that my memories of Sally. She was the brave one, I the prudential; and she made me ashamed of my lack of courage. For years, Billy, I've been going over the whole business in my mind and I've often wondered just how much vanity played in it all, vanity on my part, of course. It's very flattering to a man in his middle age to have a girl half his years in love with him, especially a girl as beautiful as Sally. And of course I wasn't insensible to what Sally represented. After all, the Hemingways have done the State some service for many generations; there aren't many families like them; and I'd known her father, though only slightly, and admired him, for all we didn't exactly see eye to eye politically. Sally represented a whole world, a way of life and history and tradition, that I admit I found more and more glamorous. I envied the older parties their possession of it, for it gave them a native strength and stability we lacked. Yet when I've gone to the limit in self-accusation, when I've assessed as scrupulously as I know how the effects of vanity upon me, I still honestly believe they were outweighed by the real thing, by pure and disinterested love. And what convinces me of the truth of this is the character of Sally herself. I used to ask her what every lover asks his girl: What on earth can you find to see in me, in *me* of all men? Love makes one humble, it is always, one feels, so undeserved, so disproportionate to one's merit. And she'd return the question; and my answer to that was easy. She was so splendidly free; she had her father's true-blue aristocratic damn-you disdain for everything that was common, mean or middle-class. She was so much more of a free spirit than I. I found it impossible to believe that any man *she* loved could be worthless. It may sound silly, but I felt that though I wasn't noble before I met her, her love had made me noble. And I'm bound to say that I never worked harder, more effectively or to such good purpose as I did during those years with her. She pitched her expectations high. She was a revelation to me. She made me realise that women, some women at any rate, are better than men. She was, as it were, naturally in love with excellence; she hungered and thirsted after it. She was looking for a destiny. Life to her was a continual promise, and she responded to it with an ardour and generosity that frightened me. She was bigger than I, Billy; and she was unlike us in her reckless-ness. She was like a gambler who is willing to throw all he has, including his life, on his bet. She was magnificent, and the wonder is it was me she chose to raise to her level.'

George was silent for a moment, and then said: 'But all this is words, Billy. I can only stumble on the edge of what she meant to me. I despair of being able to express it. But you know, Billy, this last year or so I've been reading the great novels, Tolstoy and George Eliot and Meredith and Henry James, and I think what I've been looking for in them is an adequate image of Sally. It's in them that I come nearest to recapturing the sense of her, in Tolstoy's Natasha and Anna Karenina, at any rate as she is at first, and Dorothea Brooke and Clara Middleton and Isobel Archer. You'll find her there, Billy. Once upon a time, I used to despise novels.'

That was what George told me two days before he died. He told me, too, that in his relation with her he had experienced what human living could be and should be. He accepted it as a revelation of truth. It was what he wanted for all men. He died, you might say, a thorough-going romantic.

George had what is called a fine funeral. When the news of his death was announced it was as though the city suddenly woke up to the realisation that a great man had been in its midst. There were long obituary notices, in which the Strode case was scarcely mentioned; a stranger might have got the impression that George had given up politics in order to take up less controversial forms of public service. His funeral was the biggest I have ever been to. There were representatives there of this organisation and that, of the bodies that had disowned and expelled him as well as of those he had become associated with afterwards. It was very impressive. And yet for me it was all irrelevant. It was a beautiful May morning as we stood at the graveside. Earlier, it had rained, and trees, grass and flowers still sparkled with a pristine freshness. The sky was a most exquisite pale blue, with scarcely a cloud. The earth, the open grave itself, smelled of spring. And suddenly, as the parson began to read over the coffin the solemn words of the burial service, I was aware of the carolling of the larks. There seemed a hundred of them, and they fairly flung themselves into the sky in an ecstasy of song, as though literally intent on taking heaven by storm. I could not take my mind off their song. I delighted in it and was absorbed by it; somehow it reduced the pomp of the funeral service to its true proportions. The soaring noise of the birds quite drowned the priest's professional voice and what at that moment, for all their beauty, seemed to me his professional words; and I felt that George's ironical spirit, which over the years had grown more and more sceptical of ceremony and organisation, would have been pleased.

I was chief mourner with George's younger brother, Hugh—Morgan had died years before. I knew scarcely anyone at the graveside, and if I noticed a woman who stood alone and apart, an observer rather than a participant, it was merely because there were so very few women present and because she wore no mourning. If I had thought of her at all I expect I would have put her down as one of those morbid females who haunt cemeteries. The service over, we walked back to the waiting motor cars, I by myself, leaving it to Hugh to make conversation with the parson, and as I approached the gate and the line of cars the woman stepped forward, from nowhere it seemed, towards me. She held her hand out to me, 'Mr Ashted,' she said.

'Mrs Strode.'

We shook hands and walked away together. 'I've tucked my motor away round the corner,' she said, and I forgot all about Hugh and the hired cars waiting and the funeral baked meats Fanny and Rose had ready at the house for the mourners, and climbed in beside her. We watched the black cavalcade drive sleekly away.

'I had to come,' she said. 'And when I saw Fanny wasn't there I didn't see how I could do harm if I came to the graveside.'

I nodded. She looked much older than she did when I had first seen her nine years earlier, but she was still beautiful.

'I didn't know he was dead till I read it in the papers,' she said. 'These last years we have been able to see so little of each other; and when he became ill it was impossible for me to see him at all. . . . You were his best and truest friend, Mr Ashted. You were very dear to him. He talked about you a great deal.'

I said: 'Two days before he died, he talked to me about you'; and I told her what he had said. She listened in wonder. 'Did he really say that?' she asked when I had finished; 'about feeling that though he wasn't noble before I met him, my love made him noble?'

'Yes,' I said, 'he said exactly that.'

'You see, that is just how I felt about him: that though I wasn't noble before I met him, his love made me noble.'

We sat in silence. Almost unnoticed, another funeral caval-cade drew up, another coffin was lifted out of a hearse. 'Will you tell me about his illness?' she asked. 'Did he suffer?'

I told her. At the end she said: 'I used to think I had ruined his life.'

'He didn't think that,' I said.

'No, he didn't.' She switched on the ignition. 'He was a wonderful man, Mr Ashted.' We drove off. 'Can I drop you anywhere?' she asked. 'If you can take me to the bus terminus in the city,' I said.

She drove in silence; and then, as we turned into Council Street, she said: 'You know, Mr Ashted, all those things you told me he said about me: he might have been describing himself. That's the wonderful thing.'

I got out of the car at the bus terminus. We shook hands without a word. I caught the bus to George's. I did not tell anyone why I had been delayed. I never saw Mrs Strode again.

15

I AM almost at the end of my story, Lizzie, and to tell the truth, I am very tired; I don't need to look at my birth certificate to know I am all of seventy-six. I have gone deaf, Lizzie. I have not told Will and Beryl because if I did they would be concerned and immediately start telling me how wonderful hearing-aids are these days, bless their hearts. I don't want a hearing-aid; but if I told them so they would think me pigheaded and inconsiderate. The fact is, I do not know whether I am deaf because my sense of hearing is really failing or because I no longer want to hear. At times it seems to me I can hear perfectly well; but half the time I just don't want to hear at all. I don't want to be bothered. It is a form of selfishness: I have an obstinate conviction that no one is going to tell me anything that will interest me very much or that I don't already know. I only wish I didn't, for politeness' sake, have to go through the motions of showing interest. I do, because it would be unforgivable not to; but the truth is, I no longer care. In this house, there is a whole set of lives clashing about me, passionate, self-absorbed, dramatic; to those who live them, it is as though empires fall daily, every moment is big with fate. I am expected to be struck with fond amazement because Timmy has been measured for his first evening dress suit and to be angry because, the other night, he was seen in a cinema with a girl no one knows when he had said he was spending the evening playing billiards at a friend's house. Or Susan falls off a pony and, who knows, may have concussion. It is very serious, and all we can do is wait and hold our breath. If I am to be honest, to me it all seems a lot of fuss about nothing. I do my best to hide it, but the fact is, I have no part in the life of this house and want none. The old, Lizzie, are very selfish. I am sorry, but there it is. The old are parasites, taking but not giving.

It is evening, and down below they are having a cocktail party. I have only just begun to write. I have sat in the sun all day in a deck-chair, dozing and half-dozing, seeing myself, as from a height, an old man shrunken, dozing in the sun; seeing, too, Beryl peep at me from time to time, happy and relieved because I am behaving as an old man should. That I should come to this! So far as I have had any thought today that has been all, and even that I have registered only faintly and with no genuine indignation. The noises of the cocktail party rise up to me: I am reminded of the evening chatter of the starlings as they restlessly fly hither and thither round the Town Hall preparatory to sleep. Beryl has already been up with my supper-tray, apologising because I have had to be relegated to my room, where I would much rather be, anyway, and because, she says, it is such a scratch meal, though there is more than I shall be able to eat. She is flushed with excitement, and I see she is looking very pretty: she has lost twenty years and is again the delightful girl, at once shy and eager and sparkling without knowing it, that she was when Will first brought her home to Sunday tea. It is a very important cocktail party: Beryl has thought about nothing else for days. Its importance has been explained to me many times, usually in the form of apologies for implied neglect of me that I have not, in fact, been aware of. Will has been laughing it off for days, pretending to consider it a great bore but taking it just as seriously as Beryl. 'You won't mind, will you, dad, if we give you supper in your room? It will be so much more convenient for Beryl. It's a lot of nonsense really, and these things cost a packet of money; but it's the sort of thing one has to do from time to time, and between ourselves, it may be important.' Why it may be important I have forgotten; but the road outside is lined with very fine motor cars and the ladies, as they climb out and come up the drive to the house, screech and flash in their gay dresses like parrots.

Between ourselves, Lizzie, until this evening I had not written a word for more than a fortnight. In my lucid moments, I have been ashamed of my laziness and not the more pleased because of the approving nods and smiles of Will and Beryl. 'That's right, dad. Take it easy. You've earned a rest. Enjoy the sun while it lasts.' Have they actually said those things, or have I merely imagined them? I don't know. I have lain in the sun in a death-haunted doze. It has taken the form of complete captivity to the memory of a story I was once told, which, whether true or not, has always seemed to me the most horrible I have ever heard.

Once upon a time there was a great American millionaire, the richest man in the world and perhaps the most powerful in terms of real power. He was very old and he did not want to die. All his enormous wealth was put to work to keep death away from him. For years he was kept alive on a diet of human milk, and the country was scoured for healthy young wet-nurses, who were cherished and guarded, tended as zealously and scientifically, as a prize dairy herd. They had one function: to feed the millionaire. Even so, he died.

I used to think that millionaire's fear of death must be the consequence of the wickedness of his life; that he was frightened of judgment. I now know, God help me, this was very naïve of me. I see, in the manner the old millionaire preserved his life, a terrible symbolism. The instinct to live and to keep on living is as blind, imperious and unceasingly demanding as the baby's craving for its mother's breast. It does not diminish with age. Indeed, as everything goes but life itself, it becomes the more urgent and unappeasable. I could be that millionaire.

In the room below they are chattering like starlings and screeching like parrots, and I sit here alone, an old superannuated man. Objectively, I have outlived my time and am just a nuisance. I know it, and ought to be glad to go. And yet, the smaller one's demands on life become, the more fierce and intense they are, so that now, at this moment, they seem to have become concentrated in the one overwhelming cry, *I do not want to die*. Death is how far away from me? A matter of days, of months at the most. And I cannot conceive it. It is essentially incomprehensible, the one thing one can never grasp. For more than ten years I have lived in constant consciousness of death. I have watched the three people who were closest to me die; and I have seen young men die in hospital. I saw George die, and he died easily, it seemed, without pain. I saw Horace die; and his death was a drawn-out agony of suffering and humiliation, as though the appalling God he worshipped so faithfully was bent on sparing him nothing in the way of ignominy. Rose died easily, as though even while alive she had been a freeman of death's kingdom, as in a sense I think she was, for I truly believe that during her last months she felt Harry as near to her, and as clear, as she did me. I ought to be schooled in death, but it is a subject the study of which one permanently postpones.

It is the ultimate statement about the human condition that one can envisage the extinction of those dearest to one but never one's own. To imagine oneself dead is impossible. Not to exist, to be no longer *me*—how can one conceive it? And now that I am so close to the inconceivable I understand better the twists and turns and squirmings of the ego that lead to belief in immortality. I know there are good philosophical arguments for it, but beneath them all, wrapped up in ingenious rationalisations, is the simple human inability to believe that *I*, *I* of all people, can cease to be *I*, can be put out as a candle flame is put out. The most one can bear to admit is that one may be changed by death, changed and yet in some mysterious way remain in essence the same, as though one were to sleep and wake to find oneself in another room.

The last motor cars are driving away. The party is over. I am suddenly aware of silence below, and then of the wireless turned up loud, as though after the noise, the starling-chatter, the screeching of parrots, silence were unbearable. I hear Will's footsteps on the stairs, he knocks at my door, I bid him come in. 'Just to make sure you're all right, dad,' he says, rather vaguely it seems to me. He stands in the doorway, swaying ever so slightly; he is very big and his face very red. He is smiling a little sillily—and it is unkind of me to think that, for I see it is really a private smile, that though the party is ended it is not yet over for him. I remember my manners. 'And was it a success, son?' I ask. He ponders the question seriously and for a moment frowns, then smiles happily again. 'I think so, dad. Yes it was,' he adds decisively; 'it was a very good party indeed, though it's myself that says so. And I think it's served its purpose.' He adds, 'The trouble is, people never know when to go.' But that is perfunctory, a concession to the ritual the occasion demands. Then he is suddenly awake, awake to me. He is concerned. 'But you haven't had your supper, dad.' I look at the tray on the small table and see that

I haven't. 'I'll have it very soon now,' I say. 'I didn't feel hungry, and I got immersed in what I was writing.' He nods in understanding. 'You won't overdo it, will you, dad?' he asks. 'I won't, my boy.' He turns to go. 'Just put the tray outside, if you don't feel like coming downstairs, dad.' And then—a sudden prick of unnecessary compunction—'I do hope we didn't disturb you too much. It must have seemed a fearful din up here.' 'You didn't disturb me at all, son.' He is relieved. We bid each other good night. Will is a good son.

I am pulled in opposite directions. Anything rather than extinction. Anything to be alive, even in the feeblest, the faintest sense. There are moments when it seems it would be enough if consciousness were no more than to be aware of the sun's rays as a warmth on the skin; this and no more. Yet my mind revolts against this ignominy of clinging to life, this abject parasitism. It is the passiveness I loathe. I would be brave if I could. Death is bearable only when it is taken as a calculated risk or is made the instrument of a man's will; when it is chosen. Only then does a man triumph over death and bend it to him. So we are right to praise martyrs and those who die rather than renounce an idea, just as the old Norsemen and the Red Indians were right to set warriors who died in battle above cowards who died in bed. I know where the argument takes me. I wish I could believe I had courage enough.

When Rose went blind I prayed that I should be allowed to keep life and health for as long as she lived; so that I could look after her. Given that, I thought I would not care what happened afterwards. I was sincere in my prayer, but even the most disinterested sincerity is embedded in a mass of selfishness. And now I find myself praying, crying out to the void, Let me first see Tom again!

I wrote that four days ago. It did me good to put down on paper my fear of death, because it brought me up against myself. Having written it, I woke up next morning with the clear conviction that this being haunted by fear of death was intolerable. It was nothing less than death in life; and I said to myself, if I haven't got the guts to end it, and the fact that I can pray to Nothingness, Please let me first see Tom again! seems to prove that I haven't, I can at least make myself as comfortable as I can with the equivalent of a fine blaze and glorious din. And I got out of bed and looked to see how much money I still had left in my Post Office savings book. While Rose was alive it was a matter of the greatest importance to me, for I wanted very fiercely not to be beholden to anyone, but do as I might, by degrees it dwindled. Since Rose died, however, I have had no occasion to touch my savings, and indeed my capital has been increased by the sale of our furniture and household possessions, little though they brought in. I have had no reason to touch it, for my wants have been small. I draw my old age pension every week and hand it over to Beryl, keeping back ten shillings for tobacco and small change. At first Will and Beryl were unwilling to take the money. But I explained that I had always paid my whack and it was a habit I was too old to break, and if they could not accept it I would have to go elsewhere. And of course Will saw my point. I know as well as anyone that my small contribution makes no difference to him. I do not even know whether it covers the cost of my keep. I have not bothered to try and find out. The gesture is what matters. It allows me to maintain the illusion of independence, and it is an illusion we are all the happier for not disturbing. And I say nothing, for to do so would only embarrass everyone, when, as often happens, I discover a new two-ounce tin of tobacco or a half-pound bag of old-fashioned humbugs, my favourite sweets, on the table in my room.

So I was not astonished when I saw I had £126 and some odd shillings still untouched in the Post Office. I was so anxious not to lose time that I pulled on my shirt and trousers and ran downstairs. Will and Beryl and the children were still at the breakfast table and very surprised to see me, for I do not normally appear until after Will has left for the factory and the children for school. I could see Will was somewhat alarmed, so, without preamble, I said: 'Will, I wanted to catch you before you go. Could you spare me a moment?'

'But of course, dad. Let's go into the study.' And he picked up his cup and saucer and led the way, Beryl following hastily with a freshly poured cup for me.

I still had my Post Office bank-book in my hand, and I waved it in front of him. 'I don't wish to delay you, son, but there's a favour I'd very much like you to do for me; and if you could do it right away, or get Miss Tipton to do so, I'd be obliged.' Miss Tipton is Will's secretary. 'Will you bear with me?' I asked anxiously.

'Of course, dad. Anything I can do.'

'Well, then,' I said, 'I've got £126 13s. 6d. in the Post Office, and I want to buy a gramophone and some records. I'd like them just as soon as it's possible. If I can have them today, so much the better. So could you telephone from the office and ask a shop to send them straightaway?'

Will answered, as I expected he would: 'But there's the gramophone in the drawing-room, father. It's never used, except by the children. Wouldn't that do for you?'

I had thought of that solid piece of furniture, like a sideboard. I had to be firm. 'It is kind of you, son, but I need a long-playing one, and I want it in my room. I could go into the town myself, but it would save me much trouble if you would act for me.'

'Yes, of course, dad. I only thought I could save you money, perhaps.'

'You tell me how much it all comes to,' I said, 'and I'll write to the Post Office and withdraw the money. But I'm paying for it myself, you understand,' I added, suddenly suspicious.

'I'll get Miss Tipton to deal with it right away, as soon as I get to the factory. Now, what about records?'

I told him, and he wrote them down. I knew exactly what I wanted: the Brahms violin concerto, the Mozart, the Beethoven, the sonatas, one or two others.

'But what recordings do you want?' Do you know, this had not entered my head, and for a moment I was nonplussed, seeing my plans suddenly held up. 'Campoli, Loveday, Szigeti? People like that?'

'Yes, yes,' I said; 'so long as they are long-playing.'

'Then I think we can leave it to Miss Tipton's discretion. She's not entirely stupid, and she'll find out what the shop has.'

'Thank you, son, thank you,' I cried.

'It's as good as done, father.'

Then I was anxious again. 'You'll explain to Beryl?' I asked; 'and you won't mind the din for a few days?'

'Of course not, father.'

'You see, son,' I said, 'I'm going to have a last glorious orgy. I'm going down with all the bands playing, full musical honours.'

I knew immediately that I had said the wrong thing. 'Whatever do you mean, dad? You mustn't say things like that. You're good for years yet.'

'Take no notice of me, son,' I said. 'I don't mean anything at all.' And truth to tell, I had scarcely known what I was saying; when I heard it I was shocked myself. I had been carried away by my own excitement. However, the incident passed off without further commotion; and Will was as good as his word. Before midday there was the gramophone delivered and installed in my room. As soon as it arrived I sat down and wrote a letter to the Post Office, giving notice that I wished to withdraw the necessary sum from my account. This gave me enormous pleasure, of a kind I had never experienced before. I felt as I suppose a truly civilised millionaire must feel: for the first time in my life I understood the value of money, which is to enable a man to obtain those things he needs in order to realise himself. This is a pleasure the ordinary man, keeping himself and a family on the wage he earns, can scarcely ever know, for the things I refer to are not necessities in the basic sense and have no material use. The indulgence in them is entirely disinterested, and to be able to indulge them a condition of real freedom.

Then, having posted my letter, I played my gramophone. I played all the records I had bought one after another, right through; and when I had come to the end of them I began again. And so I have filled up the time until I began to write this morning. I have soaked myself, I could almost say pickled myself, in the greatest fiddle music ever written. The gramophone is silent now, but I feel that I have only to close my eyes to hear in my mind whatever I choose to, the last movement of the Brahms concerto, the Beethoven, whatever I like, in all its detail. It is as though the gramophone is now within my skull and I am independent of the instrument itself. And to take up the metaphor of pickling, I have found this complete submission to my records—and except for the unavoidable time off for sleeping, eating, etc., it has been complete—a most wonderful and potent preservative of the spirit. I have taken strength from these great men and their music, for I have been in the closest communion with that which death cannot touch. Music of all the arts, it seems to me, is the furthest outside death's sovereignty. Paintings flake and fade; in the end the strongest building falls; statuary corrodes or is eroded; but the sounds that music makes cannot die. And I have heard in the music my gramophone has played for me a sublime defiance of death. But defiance is the wrong word: rather, the pure and untroubled assertion of life itself. This four days' submission to Bach and Mozart and Beethoven and Brahms has somehow changed my feelings about both life and death. I see now that one can be as much the slave of life as of death and that the greater one's fear of death the more slavish must be one's relation to life. This has not been plain to me before. Even in the blackest moments of my fears of extinction, what most horrified me, to the point of utter self-contempt, was that I could conceive of myself as willingly putting myself in the place of that American millionaire who was kept alive by the milk of wet-nurses. This was a depth of degradation in myself I could not understand and could scarcely bear to contemplate. Who would want life on such terms? And yet I did.

I see now that I had mistaken mere existing for life. The greater part of what we call living is purely mechanical. Most of the time we are automata, machines of flesh and blood that must take in oxygen and give out carbon dioxide in order to work, and be stoked up with food and drink three times a day. Most of what we do is done in order to provide the fuel that will enable us to function. If this were all, once it was seen as all, who would bother to go on? And life lived in time, life lived in terms of the body, can never be much more than this, even though we raise the preparation of the fuel we consume to the art of cookery and idealise our biological impulses as love. Not that I scorn cookery or the concept of love. On the contrary. They are pointers towards the discovery I have made. The mere routine of existing, the mechanical round of inhalation and exhalation, of eating, drinking and defecation, the merely biological level of life, is intolerable to man. You may say the merely natural is intolerable to man; so that even to the process of taking in the fuel necessary to maintain him he must give the dignity of ceremony and art. By so doing, to that extent he lifts himself above the flux of mere nature and compels life to conform to a pattern of his own devising, a pattern that is beautiful and significant in proportion to the loftiness of his conception of man, which means his conception of himself. The most beautiful and significant of these patterns are those we call systems of thought and works of art, and though they are the products of life, since they are the creations of men who have lived, they seem to have been lifted outside life altogether. They exist in a different order of being; and because they are outside life, they are outside death too, and untouchable by it.

So my fiddle music assures me. To that, death is irrelevant, and so, except inasmuch as it gives heart to men who must live, is life. And yet man still exists in the realm of the natural. It remains the basis of his being, and he cannot escape from it. Therein is his tragedy. And the longer he lives the more he is subject to the tyranny of the natural, whose law is decay and death. The process may be stayed; it cannot be put off for ever; and fear of it, fear of extinction itself, means only that a man becomes life's slave and grovels under the dominance of nature, which he himself has made omnipotent. For nature is omnipotent only if man allows it to be. That millionaire was the inventor of his own self-torture; by clinging to life he reduced himself to the lowest form of life. Even so, death trod him under its foot.

At any rate, I am fortified to continue the rounding off of my story, if only, as Will would say, 'for the record.' George and Horace died within six months of each other, and their deaths diminished me. My life became narrower. But the process of diminishment had begun earlier, with the failure of my little business. That had cured me of any serious ambition. It meant that for the rest of my working life I had to earn my livelihood at work that would have been distasteful if I had let it be. For some years I still dallied with the notion of playing the fiddle for a living. The coming of talking pictures killed any idea of that, for what I had thought of was playing in a cinema or a café orchestra. I realise now that to have had to play continually the kind of tea-time music such orchestras performed day in, day out, would have soon been even more disgusting to me than my work as a journeyman engraver. I am glad now that that ambition, modest though it was, came to nothing. But increasingly my working life lay outside what I thought of as my real life.

The other notable change the failure of my business brought about was that we had to leave the house we had dwelt in for so long. I could no longer afford the rent. We took, instead, a smaller house, with three bedrooms and an attic. It was a come-down, which I resented for Rose's sake; for once again we were without bathroom, indoor lavatory and front garden.

Yet, as I knew even at the time, I had been lucky, and for the most part the luck held. What with my fiddle and my classes, my leisure was full to bursting: there was not time enough for all the things I wanted to do. And where Will and Phil were concerned there was no need for worry; their progress made me very proud and happy. We could have wished to see more of Phil, but we knew his absences were unavoidable: he had gone from Cambridge to the United States, to a research studentship at the Massachusetts Institute of Technology, and when he returned it was to go back to Cambridge as a fellow of his college. But Will was still near at hand. It wasn't until he was close on thirty that he left home and shared a flat with two other young engineers. But he always came home for tea and supper on Sunday and when he was courting Beryl, brought her, too.

Rose and I were very happy for him when we met Beryl. She was so pretty and unspoiled, and they were very much in love with each other. She seemed to me so young that I could scarcely believe that she was a university graduate and an English mistress at the Girls' High School. What surprised me, though I don't think it did Rose, was how immediately she seemed to change when she married Will. It seemed as though her university degree, her career as a schoolmistress, her intellectual interests, had all been so much play-acting she put aside as soon as life became serious. There was never any question of what in life Beryl thought serious: it was to be a wife and mother. And a splendid one she has been. She has remained as sweet and kind as ever she was, and, as I saw the other evening at that cocktail party, she can still be pretty, almost as though she can summon prettiness at will. Yet I regret the loss in her of those early qualities she laid aside so readily, even though I am sure the loss, assuming she is aware of it, means nothing to her.

It was Tom who was my only source of worry in those years. I refused to admit that there was anything wrong with him long after it was apparent to everyone else. Often I was made cross by what I thought Will's censoriousness, which seemed to me to argue a lack of sympathy and affection for his younger brother; and I noticed that Phil appeared to regard him as someone for whom especial allowance must be made. I felt this was slighting to the boy, whom I still saw, I suppose, as the delightful child he had been. I have already told of the shock it was to me when he was expelled from the teachers' training college. It upset me very much, but even then I still managed to persuade myself that the cynicism he had displayed on that occasion was merely the surface bravado of a sensitive youth too proud to confess his shame. I fought as long and as hard as I could against the realisation that he was without conscience and without the ability to distinguish between right and wrong. Or rather, though he knew the difference between them, he did so, as it were, only in terms of social convenience; it was expedient not to be found out in wrong-doing; otherwise, everything was permitted.

How blind one can be! Among other things, I worried about his future: having been expelled from the college, what was there open to him? He was already almost twenty. So I was very relieved when he got a job on one of the local weekly papers as a junior reporter; or so he said. It was plausible enough, for he had been at school with the editor's son. The fact is, we saw very little of him; he slept at home, and that was about all. Whatever he may have been up to, a reporter's job was the perfect cover for him. He had, or said he had, meetings to report most evenings, and on his free evenings, according to himself, he was attending evening classes at the Commercial College in order to learn shorthand. I am the more convinced that he was for a time on the local weekly because he has described himself as a journalist ever since, and though, as he once told me, 'Chaps who live by their wits commonly call themselves journalists, just as tarts call themselves actresses,' when to my knowledge he has earned money honestly it has been by writing for newspapers. But there came the day when he told me he was no longer working on the *Herald*. He had been fired, most unjustly as he claimed, for a reason I have now forgotten, but he didn't regret it, for the job had given him the entrée into the newspapers of the city, and he now proposed to free-lance. And I believe he did, in part at any rate; being a free-lance journalist gave him the kind of prestige in his own eyes that he craved for. Later, Will told me that Tom's knowledge of what was going on in the city at this time and of the lives, public and private, of its leading citizens, was really remarkable, and I have no doubt he turned it to good use.

Was I more naïve than most fathers in my walk of life would have been? I doubt it. I was, to tell the truth, rather impressed by the amount of money he seemed to be earning, but then, I was completely ignorant of the world of newspapers and journalism; and that he had some talent I firmly believed, and still do. The blindness fell from my eyes when, one evening, a plain-clothes policeman came to the house. Did Thomas Edwin Ashted live here? Then it came out. Tom had been arrested for stealing books from one of the bookshops of the city and next morning he appeared in the magistrate's court. George was sitting on the bench that morning but left it as soon as he discovered who was coming up before him. Tom was charged with stealing a book, to wit, one copy of Gray's *Anatomy*, value three guineas. It was impossible for me to dodge the truth any more. Though this was the first time Tom had been caught it was clear that he was an extremely expert book-thief, knowing exactly how to steal and what. He had been suspected for months, and had been caught because he had gone back to the bookshop too soon after a successful haul. His guilt was as plain as a pike-staff to the magistrates, and to me also. He was sentenced to twenty-eight days.

I was allowed to see him after he was sentenced. I told him I was convinced of his guilt. He replied by telling me that he had learned a lesson: he had been stupid to plead not guilty; he would have got off more lightly if he had admitted his guilt. 'They've sent me down for twenty-eight days,' he said, 'not for stealing a book but for wasting the Court's time. I'll know better in future.' I did not find that promising but I told him I would always stand by him and that I would be there whenever he needed my help. He smiled gaily, as though amused by my concern for him. 'Don't you fret about me, dad,' he said. 'I'll be all right. I know how to look after myself.'

That evening I took my grief to George. He had discussed the case with his fellow-magistrates and with the police. 'What can I do for the boy?' I asked him. 'You can do nothing, Billy,' he answered; 'in the last analysis, only Tom can help Tom. It's up to the boy himself.' 'Then how have I failed him?' I wanted to know. 'Billy, you haven't failed him.' He went on to tell me about what are now called psychopaths, though I do not think he used the word. 'You mean,' I said, 'that Tom is a sort of moral cripple, that there's a deficiency in him analogous perhaps to a vitamin or glandular deficiency?' 'I'm afraid it looks like that, Billy. There's a chance, of course, that the dose of prison he's getting may pull him up sharp and make him more careful in future.' 'You don't put it higher than that?' 'If I'm to believe the experts, Billy, I can't. But in these matters, even the experts know very little at present. They're as baffled almost as much as we are, for all their jargon; and perhaps there's hope in that.' I told George I had assured Tom I would always stand by him and be there if he needed me. 'Of course you will, Billy,' George said, 'but I am afraid you must accept him as a cross to be borne.'

For all its irrationality, I have never been able to throw off the conviction that somehow I have failed the boy; though I don't see how. He had a good home; from his earliest days he was surrounded by love and care; he had excellent examples all about him in his brothers. And all this, as I see, is pathetically beside the point. When he came out of prison he disappeared for several months, and then turned up with a very fast motor car. He told me he was on to big things and vanished as suddenly as he had appeared. When we saw him again he was without his motor car and in need of money, but was still on to big things. So it has gone on. Sometimes he has seemed extremely prosperous, more often he has been unashamedly broke; but always radiating self-confidence, though that, Will has maintained from the beginning, is just part of his stock-in-trade, and I am afraid Will is right. There have been times when I have tried to reason with him. 'Look,' I have said, when he has come to me in dire want, 'look, son. This course of life you have been following all these years, where is it getting you? Up to a point, I could understand it if it brought you in good money, but it obviously doesn't. Even at the most sordidly material level, it's a failure.'

Then he'd smile in the way he does and say, 'I'd be better off if I were honest?' And I'd agree, and he'd say, 'You may be right, too,' and smile the brilliant smile that has always defeated me, defeated me because it suggests an amused, even sympathetic pity springing from depths of knowledge from which I am by nature barred, from a profound and private realisation of *something*. But what that something is I shall never know. Tom makes me feel a bewildered innocent, and I think he has had this power over me from his childhood. He has only to smile for me to realise anew the futility of talking. In a curious way, he has always been open with me, almost as though inviting my complicity. He has horrified me with stories of his experiences, of nights spent in the most squalid doss-houses when he has been without money, and so on. 'But why, son, why?' I have cried out, 'why go on with this way of life, if that is where it leads you?' And in answer he has smiled his tolerant, compassionate, secret smile, and has revealed himself, it has seemed to me, as somehow dedicated to a way of life utterly outside my comprehension. There have been moments when he has seemed to me a sort of perverted saint, even. His very quality of disinterestedness makes him inexplicable to me. Difficult though I find it to write the word, he is a crook; yet his dishonesty bears no relation to any obvious material end. He is not moved by the desire for easy money, or anything as simple as that.

When he plagues Will, mocking him by long-distance telephone calls in which he announces his imminent arrival in the town, it cannot be just the need for £20 that is prompting him. He could get it more easily and more quickly merely by writing and asking for it. But that would not satisfy him. Where Will is concerned, he enjoys making mischief. It is a sort of fun he indulges in; if the phrase made sense, I should be tempted to call it unmalicious malice: he enjoys seeing Will jump. His persecution of Phil is by comparison half-hearted. He goes to Cambridge first, and Phil pays up and tells him to go to hell. Then he goes to Will, but with a full belly, and plays with him as a cat with a mouse, drawing out the agony until in the end it is almost as though he were conferring a favour on Will by taking his cheque. And Will, the silly fellow, reacts to the goads, the pin-pricks and the insolence as Tom intends he should.

And the tricks that land him in jail seem often no more serious and suggest, indeed, that half the time he is playing a complicated private game. He seems to be able to convince anyone he wishes that he is other than he is, and to do so is obviously in some way I do not understand a necessity to him. I think how typical of him his war career was. He joined up as soon as war broke out and almost immediately was back on leave, a swaggering, battle-scarred warrior: it took quite an effort, meeting him, to recall that neither side had yet fired a shot at each other. He was never, in fact, out of England and within eighteen months he was discharged from the Army; why I never learnt, though I think Will's explanation as good as any, that not even the Army at its most stupid would be silly enough to have Tom around once it had rumbled him. But it was after his discharge that he really blossomed out as a soldier. He was in the rearguard of the Dunkirk evacuation as a major of Royal Engineers; he was a tank-commander at El Alamein; he was one of the first officers ashore on the Normandy beaches. As a fighter-pilot he shot down German bombers over London during the Battle of Britain, and later he helped to bomb Peenemunde. It happened time and again, and every time the counsel prosecuting said how plausible he was, for he took in not merely gullible women but hotel-keepers, professional men and once, even, a retired admiral. I am sure that on each occasion, for a brief space at least, he was as much the victim of his fantasies as those who lost their money by them. I am sure, too, that if any one of those taken in by him had replied to his first advances with, 'Don't be a bloody fool,' he would have roared with laughter. When once I taxed him with this he grinned and said, 'You may have got something there, dad!' He remains to me essentially mysterious, and what makes him mysterious is the lack of any obvious motive for his behaviour, which at times seems none other than that of a compulsive practical joker.

Still, what George said was true: Tom has been a cross I have had to bear. It was either that or cutting him out of my life altogether, and though there have been periods when I have considered doing so, when it came to the point I could not bring myself to do it; and in recent years I have found it unthinkable. The cross was heaviest in the early days of his career, when I could still persuade myself he might reform. Now, if I have not heard of him for six months, I worry about him, worry, I am afraid, much more than about my other sons, who have never given me any trouble at all.

Tom was my only worry until 1939. Then, with the deaths of George and Horace, I had suddenly to face it that I too was mortal. I had already heard strangers refer to me as 'that little old gentleman,' but had been merely amused, for I did not feel old. But in the summer of 1939 it became clear that Rose was going blind and that nothing could be done for her; and then my survival became terribly urgent to me. Whatever happened, I must outlive her, for I wanted to look after her to the end. Will did his best to make us go and live with him and Beryl, but we were determined to keep our independence to the last. I did not, in fact, foresee a long term of life for either of us. I took it for granted that we would not survive the war, envisaging, like everybody else, death from the air. I was reconciled to this, so long as we could die together.

But the war was less important than my own private affairs. It was not that I was unpatriotic, just that I was too old to be of any use in it. There was nothing I could do to help, whereas I was the only person who could help Rose. I gave up my job in order to be with her all the time, and we moved into a tiny house on the outskirts of the city. Rose's disposition became even gentler, if that was possible, with her blindness. She did as much in the house as she could, and I did the rest. Our wants were small; we had our old-age pensions and our savings, and Will and Phil were generous; it was hard to get them to believe that we did not need help all the time. Often, I did a little out-work, and we added the wages from that to our savings. As in the past, Rose had charge of the money; I think her black handbag, which contained our Post Office bank-book, identity cards, birth certificates, insurance policies and ration books as well as cash for current expenses, was always at her side. If I had wanted to, I could have taken on more out-work than I did, but I had become impatient of it. As I say, I had no expectation of long-continued life for either of us, and I had achieved a very satisfactory *modus vivendi* for myself. In the morning, I did my chores: the housework, which was not as sketchy as you might suppose, since dear Rose followed me round, testing the furniture for dust with her finger, and the shopping, such as it was, for the shop at the corner supplied most of our wants. To Rose's dictation I did the cooking. Then, in what was left of the morning and throughout the afternoon, I ground my lenses, breaking off periodically to take up my fiddle. In the evening, we listened to the wireless, and I put up with a multitude of funny men whom I could cheerfully have seen strangled. Then, I'd play my fiddle again for an hour or so, and the evening ended with my reading aloud to Rose. We got through a lot of Dickens and Arnold Bennett's *The Old Wives' Tale* as well. I read, too, a very learned paper by Phil, that I suppose was comprehensible to only a few hundred people throughout the world. It was mainly in mathematical symbols, and some of them I had never seen before; but I read it to the best of my ability, and Rose and I derived great pleasure from it.

I found that I was what is called a character in the neighbourhood. This was partly because of our circumstances. We were frequently sentimentalised over, and the consequences were then embarrassing. It is unpleasant to know one is an object of pity, and galling when, as with us, there is no call for pity. But this suddenly becoming a character was also an attribute of age. When we moved from the old house to the new we moved into what was tantamount to another world. We had always lived in the old parts of the city, in streets of terrace houses within a mile or so of the centre; and we had to get away from them to realise how high the average age of their inhabitants was. Life in a new housing estate was entirely novel to me; when I had last seen the district it had been open country, farmland. Now, though one still felt the country near—the air was fresher and cleaner—it had become, or so it seemed at first, an ordered wilderness of trim, small houses in which I feared privacy would be impossible. The houses were semi-detached, each pair set in its patch of garden. Compared with what we had known before, it was all surprisingly open and public; one looked from one's windows not on to a street and the façades of houses in a continuous strip, but on the activities of neighbours on all sides, behind, before, and on one's flanks. And wherever one looked, there were children; they were everywhere; I don't think I ever saw so many in my life in one place. But we were surrounded by the young even apart from the children. I had only to go out of the house to be struck by the fact that Rose and I were thirty years older than the next oldest couple for a quarter of a mile in any direction.

We certainly could not complain of any lack of the respect due to age. We were enthusiastically adopted by our neighbours, who were pleasant young people. The husbands worked for the most part at the Spitfire factory a mile away. I found them very different from the men I had worked with all my life. It was not only that they were a younger generation: they were much more independent and self-confident. I do not think they were more ambitious but they seemed to have a greater pride in themselves, perhaps because they were skilled men whose crafts were in demand. They seemed to me less class-conscious than we had been; or rather, their expectations from life were pitched higher. They took it for granted that their children would receive secondary education and they themselves possess motor cars. Though their childhoods must have been passed in the shadow of their parents' fears of unemployment, they were very prosperous. They behaved, it seemed to me, with an ease that came from the awareness that they belonged to a class that was taking over.

We were objects of curiosity and I think our neighbours took a pride in us just because we were different. As I say, they adopted us. And then, in addition to being a character, I found I had been elevated to the status of wise old man. The children were responsible for that. When I began my lens-grinding, I set up my work-table in the bow window of the front room, in order to get the benefit of the light; and naturally the children were intrigued and peered over the privet hedge to see what I was up to. So I invited two or three boys in to show them what I was doing and explained the nature of lenses to them. Next thing I knew, I was giving them telescopes as soon as I had made them. I gave them only to boys I thought would value them and soon I found I had started a wave of interest in astronomy in those boys. The fathers of some of them also took it up. One thing led to another. On Saturday mornings and during school holidays the house seemed full of boys, without any prompting from me, and before I quite realised what was happening I had a little class to whom I taught the fiddle. Their parents wanted to pay me, but I wouldn't let them. Then one evening, one of my star-watching fiddlers knocked at the door begging for help with his homework. He had just started at the grammar school and was bewildered by the mysteries of Latin and French. I helped him as best I could and was rewarded by the pleasure I myself got from the exercises he had to do. My own Latin and French had never amounted to much in any event and I had forgotten almost all I had ever known, so in effect young Bryan and I learnt the languages together. He got a very good school certificate. Then I was asked by a neighbour whether I would coach her child for the grammar school entrance examination, and again before I quite knew what had happened I had a small coaching class. I must admit I was gentler with these children than I had ever been with my own, I suppose precisely because they were not my own. But they were nice intelligent boys.

Although I refused payment for any of this, for it gave me pleasure to do it, I was more than adequately recompensed by their parents. The women practically took over my shopping and were constantly making me presents in kind, which was a great help when the range of food obtainable became narrow and to get it meant standing for hours in queues. Their husbands as good as kept me in tobacco and were kind in other ways as well. During the air raids they looked after us most zealously, coming in at regular intervals during the course of the bombing to assure themselves we were safe and not over-frightened, for we refused to go to the shelters. When fire-watching was introduced they watched our house as well as their own, and they insisted on making me chairman of the street fire-watching committee, as a strictly non-playing member, as they put it; telling me they knew I would be impartial and they could not trust any among themselves to be. So it fell to me to draw up the rota for the street, and I do not think my allocation of duties was ever once challenged. When they had the street party on VE-Day they made Rose and me sit at the head of the table.

Thus, in those years of anxiety and war, I found myself, unwittingly and for the first time in my life, a member of a community, with a recognised place in it. I enjoyed it and am grateful for it. It was most warming. It made life at a reasonable level of comfort possible, and though we were left alone when we wanted to be, we never had to feel lonely.

It was when Rose took to her bed for good that the strain for me began. 'You can't really cope, you know, Mr Ashted,' the doctor said; 'Mrs Ashted ought really to go to hospital, for both your sakes.' Rose wept bitterly: both of us knew that if she did we should never be together in this life again; and Rose had all the old working-class horror of the infirmary wards in which the aged poor used to die. The doctor, a sympathetic woman, understood. 'Well, we'll see how we get on,' she said; and with the help of the kind district nurse, we did not get on too badly. All the same, the strain at times was great, and my temper and patience were often frayed by the endless chores of nursing. It was very tiring, and when I was tired I found it all too easy to frighten myself wondering what would happen to Rose if I cracked up. I was beginning to feel old. What put me on my mettle, I believe, was the discovery that it was me and not Rose the doctor was thinking of when she said Rose should be in hospital. At first, I was indignant; and then it was as though honour was at stake. I had to go on.

Rose and I knew she would not get up again, and during those months she lay in bed she was consciously preparing herself for death. Indeed, her serenity was such that I felt she was already half outside life; and the nearer she came to the end the greater her serenity was. I still read to her in the evenings, but now it was her favourite passages from the New Testament and the Psalms that I read, and her favourite hymns. She was in no pain, and death came gently to her.

If I had had my way, I would have stayed on in the house alone. It was what I wanted to do, but I see now that it would have been wrong. Routine might have carried me along for a bit, but very soon I know I would have lapsed into an apathy in which everything that had to be done would have been too much trouble. I was very tired and morose; and nothing mattered. Left to myself, I would have degenerated into one of those wretched old men who are found dead among their dirt days after their demise.

Yet it is neither nice nor easy to have to relinquish your independence, and I went to Will and Beryl's with an ill grace. As I look back on those early days with Will and Beryl, it seems to me I was slightly crazed. I was sullen and obstinate, and full of self-pity, bitterly ashamed, for no reason at all as I see now, of being a superannuated man. I felt that, with Rose gone, I was necessary to no one and that I was an object of charity. I wanted no one's charity. I had been alone only a month when Will and Beryl descended on me while at my lens-grinding and bore me off, but already I had lapsed and hardened into a querulous egocentricity. I did not realise that the new relation of dependence in which I found myself with Will and Beryl was as difficult for them as for me. I had ceased in that short time to be a social being, and I had painfully to submit to a process of what I can only think of as learning to be house-trained again. Will and Beryl were very long-suffering and gentle with me, but that was not how I saw it then. I looked for slights and found them everywhere. I found them in their style of living, which was naturally and properly different from what I had been used to. For a long time I could not make the necessary adjustment to it. I did not want to. I rebelled passionately against the new relation with Will; all my old hatred of authority, of bosses, came to the surface again, but now in a twisted form. I loathed the whole state of being a superannuated man. I felt myself the victim of monstrous injustice. I found myself obsessed, as though it had been burnt on my brain, by Goneril's cruel question to Lear, 'What need you five and twenty, ten, or five?'

And so, Lizzie, I ran away. It was the smallest trifle that set me off. I had behaved badly, perversely, for several days, with a deliberate lack of consideration. I was like a small child in a tantrum, who goes further in his naughtiness than he has intended and finds he cannot withdraw because of pride and so must plunge deeper into naughtiness. To be quite honest, I had suddenly become very foul-mouthed and kept no curb on my tongue at all. Will rebuked me, as good-humouredly as he knew how. He could not do otherwise; I must have been making life unbearable for him and Beryl. But I could not accept the rebuke, and early next morning I crept out of the house before anyone was awake, vowing never to return.

That, at least, was as it was on the surface, and small credit to me. But the deeper reason for my running away was that I was sick for the loss of my independence. I had to recover the sense of my own manhood, and it seemed I could do it only by running away. It was as though I had lost awareness of my identity. I had to get back to my roots to rediscover it.

Well, by running away I learnt much that otherwise I might not have done. I was enabled to see myself through the eyes of others. What I saw shocked me. I caught a slow train which took almost four hours to travel the hundred miles from Will's. It was full of workmen who boarded and got down at inter-mediate stations. They called me 'dad' or even 'grandad' and were solicitous for my welfare. They seemed amazed that I should be travelling alone so early, and I could not under-stand their concern. Where was I going? Was I being met? Who was meeting me? Their questions made me angry, and frightened as well; and first I was sullen and then I refused to answer. I turned away from them in my corner and closed my eyes against them. They had been sent to spy on me, I thought. I fell asleep and had to be wakened as we were coming in. Again the questions. Would I be all right by myself? Did I know how to get to where I was going? Almost before the train stopped I jumped out of the carriage and ran along the plat-form, hoping to shake off my persecutors in the crowds. But I could not run for long. When I had climbed the steps into the hall of the station I saw coming towards me a little bent old man, shabbily dressed, dragging a fibre suitcase that was obviously too heavy for him. He looked broken and forlorn. Why isn't there someone to look after him? I demanded of myself, and I stopped, the better to scrutinise him. And he stopped too; and I realised it was myself reflected in the plate-glass of a show-case.

We stared at each other defiantly, my image and I. I

repudiated it altogether. So that was how I looked, was it? Well, it wasn't true. I refused to accept it. It wasn't me, and if it appeared to be, then be damned to it, and to them, too. And I braced myself, picked up my suitcase and walked as jauntily as I knew how out of the station into Council Street. Now, I had no definite plans at all; I had fled back home like a sick animal, believing that as soon as I set foot in the place where I was born everything would be resolved. I really thought that, which shows how childish I had become. But when I was actually in Council Street I was mazed. I scarcely knew where I was, because though everything was as it had always been, yet everything was different, as though I was looking at its reflection in a distorting mirror. It seemed that the proportions of things had been radically changed. I stared across the street at the Cathedral that I had loved all my life: it had dwindled into a tiny, unimpressive toy dwarfed by the buildings round it and by the towering, swaying yellow buses that threw between it and me a barrier of movement I did not dare to penetrate. I saw those buses and thought of plunging untamed stallions whose rearing hoofs would dash me to the ground. I was terrified by the traffic and the din, and felt lost and very small, so small that I was afraid I might not be noticed among the crowds but be brushed aside and perhaps trodden on and even killed in my insignificance. I was caught in a living nightmare, and as in a nightmare I knew that even if I shouted for help no sound would come from my lips.

Then I remembered that Boswell's used to be just round the corner. Surely Boswell's, if it was still there, would not let me down; and I forced myself to walk against the crowds to the corner. I crossed the street very cunningly by placing a woman with a pram between myself and the oncoming traffic, skipping along at her side like a child. For a brief space I was safe again: as I entered I saw that Boswell's had hardly changed. I sat down at what I fancied was the table in the far corner that George and I had always occupied and sniffed with delight at the good old smell of meat pies and gravy and tobacco fumes and coffee and wet macintoshes. The steam and smoke swirled about me—and that must have been an illusion, for Boswell's was deserted except for me. I ordered bacon and eggs and tea, because I had had no breakfast and I thought the meal would

240

do me for midday lunch as well. It was wonderful to be there, and very peaceful. I was suddenly intensely happy with the relief of it. George came in and sat down opposite me; and it was the most natural thing in the world. I told him very earnestly that I had run away and explained why; and he wholeheartedly approved. It was good to see him; I was excited as I had not been for years.

And then it began afresh, the suspicion and the questioning. When I asked for my reckoning, instead of coming over to me the waitress fetched a man who I suppose was the manager, and he asked me whether I was all right and where I lived and if anyone was meeting me. I was frightened again and lost my temper, and I swore at him and told him to mind his own f—— business. I saw him look at the waitress and shrug his shoulders. I flung the money down and walked out. I felt more lost than ever. I suddenly knew that George had not been there at all and that I had been talking aloud to myself. I was frightened then in a different way, frightened lest I was going out of my mind.

I went and sat in the sun on a bench in the Cathedral gardens, with the confused intention of thinking everything out. But I did not seem capable of consecutive thought and after a while I fell asleep. Rain woke me; I must have slept for a long time for it was the middle of the afternoon. At first I did not know where I was, and when I did I could not understand why I was there. I must have lost my memory, for though I knew who I was everything else was a blank. It was like being a child again, and lost, so overpowering was the sense of helplessness and hopelessness that possessed me. I sat on the bench and the rain poured down on me. Why was I where I was, and where had I come from? I remembered nothing. And then, Lizzie, I thought of you. It was as though you were the one person I knew in the whole world, and I had to find you. Straightaway I got up in a panic of excitement, not thinking at all where I was going but suddenly discovering myself in John Street, outside the house you lived in when you first married Paul and had the coal-yard. Outside the house: but when I looked at it I realised it wasn't there. Instead, there was a space carved out of the terrace: it was a bomb-site. That was something else I couldn't understand. I knocked at the doors of the houses on either side to find out whether the people there knew where you had gone. But they had never heard of you; and when they asked how long ago it was you lived there and I said '1894,' they looked at me very oddly, and the questions began again.

I walked away without answering, and as soon as I was round the corner in James Street, I began to run. It was still pouring with rain, and I was wet through; but all I knew was that somehow I had to reach you. Well, I did, but how I don't know. I can remember nothing between running down James Street and banging, hours later and five miles away, on your front door, blarting like a baby. The door opened, and miraculously you were there. And then I cried with relief. You took me in and made me drink a cup of hot Oxo and we had bubble-and-squeak and sausages and then brandy and hot water. You were there, Lizzie, the one constant factor in a changing world. You clouted me and then you wiped my snotty nose; and when Johnny came off the late shift you sent him out to telephone Will.

Everything is told now. I have come full circle. When I started this letter I thought by the time I had finished I would have surprised and pinned down the secret that would explain everything. I was sure some great generalisation about life would have emerged. I have not found the secret and I cannot make any generalisations.

But it doesn't matter, Lizzie. Last night, I dreamt that I saw Tom. He was standing at the end of a very long tunnel-like corridor, caught in a beam of white light, standing slackly, with head bent as though deep in thought. He was very far away, as remote, it seemed, as the end of time itself. But I cried, 'Tom! Tom!' and he heard; and looked up and saw me, and his face lit up with joy, and he began to run towards me. I woke then, but I didn't mind. I was happy. And I am happy still, for I know he will come soon and that it is not too late. I shall be ready to go then, and Bach and Mozart, Beethoven and Brahms, will play me out.

THE HOGARTH PRESS

This is a paperback list for today's readers – but it holds to a tradition of adventurous and original publishing set by Leonard and Virginia Woolf when they founded The Hogarth Press in 1917 and started their first paperback series in 1924.

Some of the books are light-hearted, some serious, and include Fiction, Lives and Letters, Travel, Critics, Poetry, History and Hogarth Crime and Gaslight Crime.

A list of our books already published, together with some of our forthcoming titles, follows. If you would like more information about Hogarth Press books, write to us for a catalogue:

40 William IV Street, London WC2N 4DF

Please send a large stamped addressed envelope

HOGARTH FICTION

Walter Allen

Tradition and Dream

The English and American Novel from the Twenties to
Our Time

New Afterword by the Author

This new edition of Walter Allen's invaluable critical
survey of British and American fiction throughout the
twentieth century continues where his classic study *The
English Novel* left off. As well as discussing the most
famous novelists of this century, it is notable for its early
recognition of authors – such as Willa Cather and Patrick
Hamilton – whose works are generally praised, and of
those who have yet to achieve the fame they deserve.
Entertaining and comprehensive, *Tradition and Dream*
will long remain indispensable both to the student and to
the general reader.

John Hampson
Saturday Night at the Greyhound

New Introduction by Christopher Hawtree

'A book I greatly admire' – *Graham Greene*

As twilight draws in, the staff at the Greyhound – Tom, homosexual, devoted to his sister Ivy; Ivy's wastrel husband; Mrs Tapin and the sluttish Clara – look forward to another night's drinking with mixed feelings, and back over years of hopes and regrets. Rich in drama, never sentimental, this hypnotically simple and ominous book is long overdue its just recognition.

Raymond Williams

The Volunteers

A worker is killed in the striking coalfields of Wales.
Some months later a government minister, connected
with the death, is also shot. So begins this timely and
provocative thriller. Lewis Redfern, once a radical, now
an international political analyst and journalist, follows
up the case; a lonely and absorbing hunt that leads him
through an imbroglio of Civil Service leaks and international wheelings and dealings to a secret organization: a
source of insurrection far more powerful than anyone
could have suspected – the world of the Volunteers.

Frederic Manning
Her Privates We

New Introduction by Lyn Macdonald

'It is the finest and noblest book of men in war I have ever read' – *Ernest Hemingway*

On July 1st, 1916, the Somme offensive began. This is the battle from behind the lines, of those sardonic, humorous troops honoured from *Henry V* to *The Virgin Soldiers*. No grand heroics here, but as they try out their French on village beauties and wangle a cosy billet, dodging shells and sergeant-majors, Privates Bourne Shem and little Martlow build up a friendship which supports them through terror and pain to the edge of the grave.

Edmund Wilson
Europe Without Baedeker

New Introduction by Jonathan Raban

When Edmund Wilson came to Europe he had no need of his *Baedeker*, for the Second World War had just ended and ancient ruins were replaced by a heap of new ones.

He arrived in Europe as an ally, but his contentious reports from the shabby and squalid continent – the United Kingdom, Italy, Greece all teeming with demobilised British officers – made an embittered Establishment pour scorn upon him, for he was, and remains, 'the most formidable Anglophobe on record' (Jonathan Raban). These hugely enjoyable despatches, a mixture of reportage and fiction, will continue to delight and chastise all who read them today.

J.L. Carr

A Day in Summer

New Introduction by D.J. Taylor

This, J. L. Carr's first novel, displays the same rare gifts as later works such as *The Harpole Report* and the Booker-shortlisted *A Month in the Country* and *The Battle of Pollocks Crossing*.

It is a festive summer's day when Peplow, a quiet bank clerk, arrives in Great Minden to shoot the killer of his son. But his task is complicated when he meets a couple of old wartime colleagues – only two of the townsfolk with problems of their own. Written with a wry understanding of the tragedy and folly of everyday lives, this is a blackly comic thriller, moving towards an ominous climax – for little can the folk of Great Minden suspect how their day will end.